SUNSET

DOUGLAS REEMAN joined the navy in 1941. He did convoy duty in the Atlantic, the Arctic, and the North Sea, and later served in motor torpedo boats. As he says, 'I am always asked to account for the perennial appeal of the sea story, and its enduring interest for people of so many nationalities and cultures. It would seem that the eternal and sometimes elusive triangle of man, ship and ocean, particularly under the stress of war, produces the best qualities of courage and compassion, irrespective of the rights and wrongs of the conflict... The sea has no understanding of righteous or unjust causes. It is the common enemy, respected by all who serve on it, ignored at their peril.'

Sunset is Douglas Reeman's thirtieth novel under his own name and he has also written twenty-one historical novels featuring Richard Bolitho, under the pseudonym of Alexander Kent.

SUNSET

Douglas Reeman

PAN BOOKS
IN ASSOCIATION WITH HEINEMANN

First published 1994 by William Heinemann Ltd

This edition published 1995 by Pan Books
an imprint of Macmillan General Books
Cavaye Place London SW10 9PG
and Basingstoke

in association with William Heinemann Ltd
Associated companies throughout the world

ISBN 0 330 34024 7

3 5 7 9 8 6 4 2

A CIP catalogue record for this book is available from
the British Library

Phototypeset by Intype, London
Printed and bound in Great Britain by Cox & Wyman Ltd,
Reading, Berkshire

We are all islands in a bitter sea.
Chinese Proverb

Acknowledgements

The author wishes to thank his friend Robert Cheung,
and the Royal Navy at H.M.S. *Tamar*, Hong Kong,
for their ready assistance.

Contents

1

Colours

The khaki staff car rolled to a halt, and after some hesitation the Royal Marine driver offered, 'No boat there yet, sir.'

'That's all right, I'll send for one. Take my gear down to the hut on the jetty. Then you can go back to H.Q.'

The marine shrugged. He was used to the ways of regular naval officers; at least he thought he was. His passenger had spoken no more than a few words on this early morning drive from Kirkwall, but had looked directly ahead along the deserted road as if he was preparing for something.

Lieutenant-Commander Esmond Brooke climbed from the big Humber car and stamped his feet on the stone paving. He was stiff, weary from the long journey from the south, and was surprised that he had been unable to sleep in the small, spartan cabin they had found for him in Kirkwall. It was early morning, and he saw some gulls bobbing on the undulating water. Even they were not ready to start their search around the many anchored warships for scraps flung over the side.

It was just that he could not bring himself to wait any longer, go through the business of having breakfast

1

with other officers on transit whom he would not know and might never see again.

He shivered and watched the great expanse of gently moving water. Quiet, deceptively so for this place so well known to sailors in two world wars: Scapa Flow, a safe anchorage for big ships and the many other smaller vessels needed to protect their every move. The sky was colourless and only the sea's horizon, resting between the islands of the Flow like the water in some huge dam, showed any life. Like an unending silver thread, he thought.

This was the first week of April, 1941. Southern England, which he had left three days ago, was already responding to the hope of spring, if nothing else. Here in Scapa only the weather changed. The islands that crouched around this protected place were bleak and weathered, and the sea's face could alter here within an hour, with currents that could make even the most experienced commander grit his teeth when his ship suddenly seemed to be under a greater control, and rain, sleet and murderous winds that chilled a man to the bone.

This was Scapa's rarer face. But to Brooke this was not just another day.

The marine clicked his heels and saluted. 'All done, sir.' He hesitated, still unsure. 'If you're certain, that is?'

Brooke nodded. 'Thank you, yes.' He turned as the man strode away and crashed the car's gears to show what he thought about it.

Esmond Brooke was twenty-nine years old, but felt ten years older. He examined his feelings again. It was easier without the watching eyes, the curiosity of the H.Q. staff who regarded newcomers as a link with all they had left behind. Scapa was a refuge and a retreat, while the war which had raged in other parts of the

2

world for some eighteen months had seemed like another existence.

He looked at the water below Scapa Bay. Sheltered, yes, but the war had intruded even here. In the second month of hostilities a German submarine had risked everything to breach the booms and defences, and had torpedoed the battleship *Royal Oak* while she rested at her moorings, with the appalling loss of over eight hundred lives. Like many others, Brooke had been stunned in those early days by the apparent ease with which the attack had been executed. But that had been then, when the whole nation had still believed in the invincible might of the Royal Navy. Peace or war, it had seemed the one sure shield they could rely upon.

Brooke thought of the ship he had just left: H.M.S. *Murray*, one of the fleet's big flotilla leaders, built in the mid-thirties, a new ship when compared with all the veterans that had been flung into the front line of war when the Germans had marched into Poland.

The *Murray* had been taken out of commission at Portsmouth while she underwent a complete and much needed overhaul, with new weapons to be fitted, and men who were trained to use them in what had become a very different sort of war. He had left behind, too, a different Portsmouth. Acres of bombed and blackened buildings, whale-like barrage balloons on the hills and beyond the city to snare any hit-and-run bombers, while in the dockyard men worked all hours to repair the damaged ships, turn them round and get them to sea again without delay.

Brooke's mouth lifted in a wry smile. When they were not on strike, he thought bitterly.

Murray's people would be scattered to the demands of the fleet. To fight through the hard-pressed convoys which were somehow keeping Britain from starvation, to cover the troops as they fell back from one military disaster after another. Holland, France, Norway and now Greece and Crete; the list seemed endless. *Murray* had taken part in most of it. Brooke had been first lieutenant to the flotilla leader, the Captain (D), a four-ringed skipper of the old school, who had feared nothing but had been totally unprepared for what had been expected of him and his handful of destroyers.

Somewhere in the far distance Brooke heard a bugle call. From one of the battleships most likely, where the hands would be already turned-to, washing down decks, spit-and-polish, war or no war.

Then breakfast, Jack's favourite: bacon and eggs, except that after a year and a half of war spam had replaced bacon and the eggs came out of a tin. The thought made his stomach contract. He could barely recall when he had had a proper meal. No wonder the Royal Marine had given him such a strange glance. Another one going round the bend, he had probably thought.

And now he was here. The moment which had denied him sleep was a reality. He walked to the edge of the jetty and watched the water rising and falling against the weathered stone, as if some great sea creature was about to break surface.

He thought about his captain, the last handshake before Brooke had quit the ship to make way for the dockyard maties and their murderous cutters and welders. It seemed unlikely that the captain, old for his rank, would face the fury of a full gale again. To a new training establishment, perhaps? One of the many which overnight had acquired war-paint, with a White Ensign to make the transformation official, and where, equally, schoolboys were transformed into temporary officers in three months, and clerks and fishmongers into gunners,

4

torpedo men and stokers. Even in *Murray* there had been a couple of hostilities-only officers called '*Wavy Navy*' because of their stripes, and accepted with affection or otherwise as their efficiency dictated. Within another year there would be more reservists than regulars. Brooke bit his lip. *If we survive that long.*

He heard another car coming down the narrow road and knew that his isolation was over.

It was a small van, and an equally small Wren slid from behind the wheel and gave him a brief but searching glance.

Brooke wore a plain raincoat, and his cap was the same as that of any other naval officer below commander. She would not know who he was. He turned and looked back towards the town and saw a touch of pale sunshine light up the weather vane on the top of St Magnus's Cathedral steeple.

He was wrong. The girl saluted, something quite rare up here except for senior officers. The Wrens could be choosy. After all, there were some six hundred sailors to every one of them.

She said, 'Commander Brooke, sir?' She looked concerned. 'You shouldn't have been kept waiting like this!' She sounded indignant for one so small and young. 'I'll ring H.Q., sir.'

Brooke smiled. 'It's quite all right. I needed to think.' He guessed she was from naval headquarters. They seemed to know everything even before you did.

She nodded. 'You're *Serpent*'s new commanding officer.'

He looked at the Flow again. 'Yes.'

She kicked a stone into the water. 'I'm waiting for the NAAFI manager's boat.' In the pale light she might have blushed. 'He's trying to get me some stockings. Silk ones.'

Brooke smiled again. The truly important things against the dull panorama of war.

She persisted, 'They're not expecting you at this hour, sir.'

The girl watched him curiously. At H.Q. you soon got used to sailors, especially the officers, *more* especially the married ones, and the Wrens had a quarters officer who had been a teacher in a very smart school for young ladies at Harrogate. A real battleaxe, and she made sure that her 'chaps', as she called them, were kept out of harm's way. Most of the time.

This one was different, a bit like some of the other young officers from the battered escort vessels that came and went as frequently as the tides. Young, grave faces; strain in their eyes and around their mouths that spoke of a war she could only imagine, despite the maps and charts in the H.Q. plotting rooms. Crosses to mark slaughtered convoys, or familiar names which had been wiped away like chalk from a blackboard.

When he removed his cap and ran his fingers through his hair as he was doing now, she saw that same look. Inner control, wariness, the inability to relax. He had unruly hair, untidy even for a regular, and she saw small flecks of grey on his sideburns. He was not yet thirty: as a regular he would have been given a more important command otherwise. She saw him start as the sound of a chugging harbour launch broke the silence.

Brooke said, 'Your NAAFI manager, I believe?'

The lower deck had its own translation of *NAAFI*, he thought. *No Ambition And Fuck-all Interest*. The girl was looking at him with a little smile, as if she guessed what he was thinking.

'I think I'll cadge a lift.' It was better than waiting and wondering. He moved along the jetty and did not notice her surprise.

She stared past him as the launch puffed into view, followed by morning gulls and surrounded by diesel fumes.

But not before she had seen his eyes. Tawny and very steady. It might provide the old battleaxe with a real challenge, she thought. And me.

The NAAFI manager sent his mechanic to fetch Brooke's luggage from the hut and passed a small parcel to the waiting Wren. 'Best I can do, love.'

She walked towards the little grey-painted van, then turned and saluted him again.

'Good luck, sir. I – I don't know how you all do it!'

He looked at her for several seconds. Afterwards she thought he had been trying to remember something, or somebody.

He said, 'We do it for you, and those like you.' Then he swung himself aboard the launch, which was immediately cast off.

He did not look back, but knew she was staring after the boat.

He said, 'I hope this isn't taking you out of your way too much.'

The manager grinned. 'No, sir. I've got a few "rabbits" for the old *Resolution*'s wardroom on board.' He darted a glance at his unexpected passenger while the harbour launch lifted and dipped across the endless swell. It was the closest he would ever get to going to sea, if he could manage it. A destroyer type, he thought. Rather him than me.

They moved on in silence while other small craft appeared from the moored grey shapes of capital ships or the dazzle-painted escorts. A harbour coming to life. Another day.

Brooke removed his cap and shaded his eyes while he stared at the neat lines of small buoys that supported

7

the webs of anti-torpedo netting protecting the anchorage. Beyond that there were green wreck marker buoys to show where a huge net had been spread over the sunken shadow of the *Royal Oak* and her sleeping company.

Brooke tested his injured leg on the gratings and thought of the Wren and her black-market stockings.

He could feel his inner excitement rising, as well as the bitterness he had carried for so long. What would the NAAFI manager say if he knew that the destroyer which had been given him to command was his first? At this stage of the war any regular was worth his weight in gold.

He doubted if many cared or even remembered the reasons for the Spanish Civil War, especially now that their own country and survival were at risk. Brooke had been in destroyers then too, a young lieutenant with his life and career stretching out like an adventure. Like his father and grandfather before him: it was something he accepted, took for granted. After a small boarding school in West Sussex, an establishment long approved for the sons of serving officers, he had joined the Royal Naval College as a cadet. He had been twelve years old.

Even Spain had been an adventure, the closest thing to all that training and preparation he could have imagined.

Then one day it had become very real to the men and ships of several nations who had been trying to protect their own people as Franco's fascist army crushed all government resistance except in the areas of Valencia and Barcelona. Refugees, Britons working at the consulate or for the Red Cross, men and women in all walks of life were ordered to leave. The Royal Navy's ships were given a task they had come to know so well since Dunkirk; but they were amateurs at evacuation in 1937.

While dive-bombers had screamed overhead, piloted, it was alleged, by Hitler's own *Luftwaffe*, the Royal Navy had made up for its other deficiencies with a bluff mixture of courage and patient good humour.

It was said to have been a small mine that had blown Brooke's whaler out of the water, killing all but two male civilians, a woman who had lost her legs, three seamen, and Brooke himself.

Four years ago, and Brooke was not certain which hurt him more: the throbbing pain in his scarred leg and foot, which at one time had almost been removed by a surgeon in Malta, or the despair of being told he was no longer needed for active duty. In a war where he had seen men die in every sort of terrible circumstance at sea it was sometimes hard to believe he had considered killing himself. *Was I the same man?*

'There she is, sir!'

He nodded, holding on to the moment, not wanting to share it.

The NAAFI manager took his silence for uncertainty.

'H.M.S. *Serpent*, sir. Don't build 'em like her no more!'

Brooke barely heard him. As the launch began to turn in a wide sweep he watched the moored destroyer, his mouth suddenly quite dry. She was exactly the way she looked in her peacetime photograph, and much the same as the day she had first tasted salt water in that other war in 1916. *When I was four years old*. It was easy to imagine her in this very mooring when Jellicoe's Grand Fleet had been here. Small when compared with the flotilla leader *Murray*, and a good sixty feet shorter, but *Serpent* retained a rakishness which even her old-fashioned straight stem could not fault. Apart from one

9

remaining sister-ship she was the only three-funnelled destroyer left in service.

Newly painted in pale grey, she seemed to stand out from the dull, shadowy shapes beyond her. Her pendant number, H-50, was also sharp and clear after her recent overhaul.

Brooke saw two figures by the short accommodation ladder, one of whom had his cap tilted sloppily on the back of his head.

'I believe they're expecting a new skipper today, sir?'

Brooke watched one of the figures hurry to the ladder as if to wave them away. Then he reached for his cap and jammed it on to his tousled hair.

He smiled, but it did not reach his tawny eyes. 'Yes. Me,' he said.

Perhaps for the first time, he knew how his father had felt.

On this particular April morning the destroyer's wardroom seemed quite spacious when compared with *Serpent*'s cramped and slender hull. As is the way of destroyers, new or old, personal comfort took a poor second place to machinery and fuel, magazines and stores. The wardroom, which was situated well aft of the engine and boiler room and separated from the rest of the ship by heavy watertight bulkheads, was a separate world from the overcrowded messdecks in the forecastle, and the nerve centres of bridge and weapon spaces. It ran the whole breadth of the hull: one side was used mainly for the officers' meals or for snatching a hot mug of something during those precious hours off watch; the other was where they relaxed when, like now, the ship swung gently to her cable. There were comfortable, if worn, red leather chairs and bench seats, magazine and letter racks, a locked glass case of revolvers, and the inevitable portraits of the King, in naval uniform, and Her Majesty on the opposite side of the outdated wardroom stove with its club fender.

In the centre of the bulkhead was the ship's crest, a serpent that looked more like some fairy-tale dragon, with the motto beneath it: *Hostibus Nocens, Innocens Amicus* – Deadly to Foes, Harmless to Friends. Near the small hatch that acted as a bar was the builder's plate: John Brown & Co, Clydebank 1916.

Lieutenant Richard Kerr toyed with a half-empty cup of coffee and considered the silence. As if the ship were still asleep, he thought. It was hardly surprising, with three-quarters of the ship's company of ninety souls on leave of one sort or another. Long leave for many of them while the refit had been completed, local leave for 'natives' and compassionate leave for two sailors who had been sent home to face the pain of bombed homes and dead families. The small duty part of the watch would be falling in again soon, knowing that by the end of the week every man would be back on board. Kerr was the first lieutenant and had a thousand things to remember. With a new commanding officer expected aboard today it was bad enough, but in addition the ship had lost two lieutenants, Rowley the gunnery officer, and the pilot, Lieutenant Johns, key members of their little team. A new navigator was supposed to be joining within the next couple of days, but their one and only sub-lieutenant was to have the gunnery department put on to *his* shoulders.

Kerr glanced along the table. It was strange to see the place so deserted. The familiar faces, the nervous jokes after some particularly hairy convoy or air attack, the flare-ups of temper like those within most close-knit families. In the same breath he admitted that within a month or so the two missing faces would be forgotten. He felt envy too. The two lieutenants had been snatched away, one for promotion, another to a brand-new destroyer still being completed.

He dropped his eyes to his cup. Even the captain, Lieutenant-Commander Greenwood, had been promoted to full commander of a powerful fleet destroyer just off the stocks. A dream for any destroyer man.

He looked up as one of the other two occupants cleared his throat and closed yet another gardening catalogue. Ian Cusack had a home in Newcastle but spoke with a Londonderry accent you could cut with a saw. He was *Serpent*'s engineering officer, the Chief. It was unusual to see him decked out in his best uniform, presumably because the new commanding officer would need to know the state of the engines as well as the man who controlled them. Cusack had a seamed, polished face, and when he was in his working rig he wore a faded woolly hat with a bobble on top, so that he took on the appearance of a small, darting gnome. Apart from the purple cloth below his single gold ring which marked him as an engineer, he wore the same rank as the sub-lieutenant. But the subbie and the Chief were separated by more than many years of service. Their worlds were completely different. The former was only eighteen months out of training; the latter had begun as a boy and then gone on from one engine room to another in almost every sort of ship until, as a senior commissioned warrant officer, he had become the head of his own department. Good with his own people, the stokers, mechanics and artificers who kept the screws turning and watched like hawks over the ship's greedy intake of fuel, but he was quick to react to criticism from all others.

Kerr had heard him snap at the gunnery officer on

12

one occasion, 'If you lot were wiped out on the bridge I reckon I could take over at a pinch! Fat lot of use any of you would be in the engine room – couldn't fit a new battery in a torch, most of you!'

Cusack said now, 'What d'you think, Number One? About the new skipper, I mean?'

Kerr shrugged. 'Probably hot stuff. He was first lieutenant in a flotilla leader. And this will be his first command, I'm told.'

Cusack pricked up his ears. Like his engines, he could sense a change of beat or rhythm without even thinking about them. He had detected the hint of bitterness in the first lieutenant's reply. Kerr was a good officer, cool in a tight corner, and never one to let things get slack. With the war spreading in every direction even junior officers were having their promotions advanced for the duration, although how anyone could gauge that must be a magician. He had thought the departing skipper might have persuaded someone to use some influence for Kerr. Cusack's bright eyes sharpened. It was suddenly as plain as a pikestaff: Kerr had been expecting to get this ship for himself. It might seem the obvious solution. Losing the captain and two inexperienced lieutenants, Kerr would have held the team together until his own promotion took him to greener pastures.

Cusack sighed. 'I'll not be sorry to get back to sea. I'm sick of the stench of all this new paint.'

Kerr forced a smile. 'I wouldn't have thought a plumber would even notice it!'

The other officer, who was watching the solitary messman pour the last of the coffee into his cup, remarked, 'I bet they'll take some of our key ratings too when we next attract the attention of some admiral.'

Kerr watched him thoughtfully. Vivian Barlow, who wore the single thin stripe of a warrant officer, was the

13

gunner (T), torpedo expert, and an old dog for this kind of work. *Serpent* was Barlow's first ship as an officer. He, like Cusack, had come up the hard way, and for much of his service he had been more used to a chief petty officers' and P.O.s' mess than a wardroom.

If it had seemed difficult for himself, Kerr knew how much worse it must have been for a man like Barlow to change everything he had taken for granted since he had joined the navy at the tender age of twelve.

They had been invited to the destroyer depot ship at Rosyth for some celebration or anniversary dinner, and Kerr had had to force himself not to watch while Barlow had hung back to observe the uses of various knives and forks as practised by other officers.

A year in *Serpent* had given him confidence, and his rugged seamanlike comments about almost everything had made even the hard men chuckle.

Kerr said, 'We'll have to accept it. With the way this war is going we must hope we get time to train the new entries.'

Cusack looked across. 'At least you've kept your torpedoes, Podger. Most of our old sister-ships have been turned into minelayers and patrol vessels.' He glared around the wardroom with something like defiance. '*Serpent*'s a destroyer, not a bloody relic!'

The curtain across the door swirled back and Sub-Lieutenant Nigel Barrington-Purvis swept into the wardroom. He was tall and fair-skinned, with perfectly cut hair, the very picture of a naval officer.

Kerr watched him calmly. He was the first lieutenant and could not allow himself to have favourites in so small a company. Or the opposite, he thought. But try as he might, he had never been able to like Barrington-Purvis. What made it more irritating was that he was good, and more than competent for one so junior.

14

Usually, as now, he wore an expression of keen dis-approval, and nothing anyone ever did seemed to come up to his own standards. The son of an admiral, he would make life hell for his men when eventually pro-motion came his way. As it certainly would.

Barrington-Purvis said, 'Just checked the iron-deck, Number One. It'll need another going-over before stand-easy.' He glared at the messman. 'Fresh coffee, Kellock.' He never said *please*.

Kerr said, 'It's all finished. Time to get things moving anyway. The new commanding officer will want to see everyone, I expect.'

The sub-lieutenant scowled. 'I certainly want to see *him*!'

Cusack stood up and groped for his cap. 'I'm sure that'll put the shits up the poor fellow!' He went out, grinning.

Barrington-Purvis sniffed. 'What can you expect?' He followed Kerr to the door. 'I mean, Number One, I didn't *want* to get lumbered with the gunnery depart-ment when Rowley left the ship.'

Kerr regarded him evenly. 'Not too difficult, I'd have thought? Three four-inch guns and a few short-range weapons. It's not exactly the *Warspite*.'

Barrington-Purvis clenched his fists but saw the danger just in time. 'It's not that, Number One. I have to think of my career, my future. I don't want to get stuck in an old ship and sent out to some station where the war's just a rumour.'

Kerr's mind clicked into place. The subbie's father was an admiral. Maybe he had told his son what lay in store for them. The dockyard had put in new fans and the old Atlantic dazzle paint had been covered by a coat of pale grey. Maybe it meant the Gulf, or some backwater like Ceylon. Barrington-Purvis would certainly care about that. He seemed to think more of advanced promotion and appointments where he would be noticed than anything else. Perhaps that was why he had shown no emotion during the air and sea attacks while he had been aboard *Serpent*. The war was to be *used*, not feared. That was for lesser people.

'Well, let's get the bloody war over first, eh?'

The duty quartermaster thrust his face around the curtain. He ignored Barrington-Purvis, who was officer-of-the-day, and looked at Kerr instead. 'Beg pardon, sir, but the NAAFI boat is headin' our way.' He grimaced. 'Won't do the new paint-job much good if he barges alongside.'

Kerr sighed. 'Deal with it, Sub. The NAAFI boat isn't due today anyway.'

Barrington-Purvis pushed past the quartermaster and ran up the ladder to the quarterdeck lobby.

Kerr nodded to the messman. 'You can clear away, Kellock.' He was angry with himself for being so curt with the subbie, that he had shown his irritation so openly, although he knew he had felt the same way about the last captain's promotion and appointment.

The tannoy squeaked and the quartermaster's voice filtered through the ship.

'D'you hear there! Out pipes, duty part of the watch fall in!'

Kerr glanced around the freshly painted wardroom. Without effort he could see it after that last convoy from St John's, covered with used dressings and every space filled with injured men, merchant sailors from some of the vessels they had lost on that terrible convoy. Forty ships had set out from the harsh coastline of Newfoundland. Less than twenty had reached Liverpool. Some of the men who had lain here had already

16

been rescued from other ships, only to have their rescuers blasted from beneath them.

You shouldn't have joined if you can't take a joke. The navy's way of overcoming even the most horrific disaster. But the old black humour didn't seem to work any more.

He frowned as he heard Barrington-Purvis's aristocratic tones from the upper deck.

'Stand away, there! We don't need you here!'

Kerr swore silently and jammed on his cap. If they stayed in Scapa much longer they would certainly need the NAAFI boat.

He reached the quarterdeck and the hard sunshine even as the boat came expertly alongside the accommodation ladder, while Barrington-Purvis screamed, 'Not *here*, damn you!'

Kerr strode to the guard-rail. In one glance he saw the luggage in the cockpit, the officer in the plain raincoat, and the way the boatmen were watching with unconcealed delight.

He snapped to the startled quartermaster, '*Pipe!*'

He strode in front of the sub-lieutenant and raised his hand to his cap. The newcomer ran lightly up the ladder and returned his salute, while a solitary boatswain's call made every face peer aft.

'Welcome aboard, sir.'

Brooke looked at him gravely, sensing the tension. 'My fault. Couldn't wait any longer.' He glanced at the sub-lieutenant and added in the same calm tone, 'Barrington-Purvis, I presume?'

It was the first time Kerr had seen the subbie wilt, as if the new captain had shouted some terrible obscenity at him.

Brooke walked a few paces and saw the duty part of the watch falling into two ranks. His mind was

17

crammed with details about this ship, her state of readiness and her immediate past record, like a history of the war itself. Narvik, Dunkirk, the Atlantic, one disaster after another. The men he would have to discover for himself. If he was to know them, they too must know him.

One square figure was facing aft, his hand to his cap in salute. It was the coxswain, next to the first lieutenant the most vital man in the ship. This one was shorter than he appeared but built like a tank. The familiar crossed torpedoes on his lapels, the chief petty officer's cap badge: he was someone you would not forget. The coxswain was the man who took the helm for all the difficult tasks, entering and leaving harbour, anchoring or picking up a mooring-buoy in a force eight gale. Above all, in action, he was the core of the ship. He was also father-confessor, guardian of the company's welfare, policeman at the defaulters' table, feared if necessary, but above all respected.

Kerr saw the exchange of glances, and was surprised. George Pike, the coxswain, rarely showed emotion. He always seemed to be above it.

He said, 'This is the cox'n, sir.'

Pike shambled towards them. 'I'm sorry about this, sir.' A deep throaty voice, once from London, Brooke thought, but not for many years. 'I wasn't sure till you come aboard, sir, otherwise I'd have bin there.'

Kerr watched them. The sudden resolution on Pike's reddened features, the wariness on the new captain's face.

'You know me, then?'

Pike said, 'This was my first ship, sir. I was a rookie torpedoman when she first commissioned.' His eyes clouded. 'When your father took command. I saw him just now when you come over the side.'

Brooke smiled. It was hard to regard himself as the image of the man he had last seen a few days ago. Broken in health . . . He tried to accept it. *Dying*.

Kerr said awkwardly, 'I – I didn't realize, sir.'

Brooke turned and gave a casual wave to the NAAFI boat as it moved astern, pouring out even more diesel fumes.

Kerr said, 'I'll show you your quarters, and lay on some breakfast, if you like.' He watched his profile. Good, even features but deep lines at the mouth, and shadows beneath the steady, tawny eyes. A man with a past. And only George Pike had known and understood.

Brooke said, 'I'd like that.' He followed Kerr through the quartermaster's lobby with its little desk and the officers' name board with its slides labelled *Ashore* or *Aboard*. He turned to glance at a rack of cutlasses and a stand of rifles. Last resort, perhaps.

Kerr was saying, 'I'm afraid Petty Officer Kingsmill, our wardroom steward, is still ashore, sir. But I'll . . .' He broke off and did not know if the other man had heard him or not. He watched him throw his raincoat and cap on to the neat bunk and saw the DSC on his left breast and another darker ribbon on the right side, which he guessed had been awarded by the Humane Society. Brooke was looking up at a small skylight in the centre of the deckhead, the glass reflecting the water and the gulls, the steel shutters raised like a sign of peace or welcome.

A voice whispered at the door and Kerr explained, 'Time for Colours, sir.'

Brooke heard him hurry away up the ladder again, no doubt wondering what sort of a nut he had been lumbered with. An experienced officer, a man who might resent that he was being kept aboard to hold the new captain's hand. But he knew there was more to

Kerr's uneasiness than that. He moved about the cabin and saw the other one through an adjoining door. The day cabin. He smiled, and some of the tension seemed to drain away. What luxury!

There was another crest here too, the ship's battle honours displayed underneath. A part of history, another war. His father's.

Dover Patrol. Belgian Coast. Zeebrugge.

Feet shuffled overhead and the tannoy squeaked again. 'Attention on the upper deck! Face aft and salute!'

Then another voice, almost directly overhead it seemed. '*Colours, sir!*'

And Kerr's acknowledgement, crisp and formal. '*Make it so!*'

The calls trilled, as they would aboard every ship in the Flow. Brooke could picture the Ensign rising to the staff. Routine, even necessary perhaps, despite the war, despite everything.

'Carry *on!*'

As the call died away the ship seemed to come alive again. He imagined the men discussing him, wondering how the new captain might affect their lives. In battle, or across the defaulters' table. Men he would come to know: the good, the bad, the brave and those who would crack if badly led.

He tried to think of his father standing in this cabin, not as the broken man he had last seen in hospital.

Tell me how she looks, eh?

Brooke opened his small case and took out the framed photograph which his father had insisted he should take to the ship. He must have known they would not meet again.

Aloud he said, 'She looks fine, Dad. She'll do me.'

It was a new beginning.

*

The officer in the crumpled naval raincoat sitting by a window in the first-class compartment stirred, and was immediately still again. Tensed and listening like an awakening animal. He groaned and peered at his luminous watch. Dawn soon. It could be anything beyond the covered window with its glued protective netting, which was supposed to shield you against flying glass. He grimaced. Not much fear of an air attack up here, he thought.

He seemed to have been on one train or another for ever. Dank R.T.O.'s offices at various stations, crowded compartments, and noise, always noise.

He stretched his legs and remembered just in time that there was a young woman seated opposite him, who had boarded the train at Edinburgh.

He gathered his wits. The other two passengers, army artillery officers, were asleep, one with his mouth open. They could have been dead.

It was so dark in the compartment, with only tiny screened lights above each of the seats, that he could not tell if the woman was awake or not. He had felt her watching him, no doubt curious about his destination.

He must have slept without making any noise. Calling out. Fighting the madness which was always with him.

Perhaps when he joined his next appointment, the destroyer H.M.S. *Serpent*, he could lose himself again. Forget . . . He had looked up the ship several times. Small and old. Very old. He felt his stomach contract violently. She would seem tiny after a carrier.

He felt the woman's shoe touch his leg and heard her instant apology.

'I – I'm so sorry. I must have fallen asleep after all!' She peered at the window uncertainly. 'Where are we, do you know?'

'Inverness in an hour at this rate.' He did not want to talk. He was not ready.

She said, 'It's been a long ride, ah . . .'

'Toby Calvert, Lieutenant.'

She seemed to gain confidence now that he had acquired personality. 'I'm hoping to meet . . .' She hesitated again. 'My husband quite soon.'

Calvert had already seen the diamond brooch on her coat, like a miniature cap badge. Naval officers often bought them for their girlfriends or their wives. He had also noticed the self-conscious way she had twisted the wedding ring around her finger. That was new, too.

'Shore job?' He sensed her sudden caution and added, 'Sorry, careless talk costs lives. I know all about that.'

He saw her teeth in the gloom as she smiled. 'I'm not used to it yet.' She lifted her chin with obvious pride and said, 'He's serving in the *Hood*.'

He said, 'I'm joining a destroyer. The *Serpent*. I'm a navigator – now.'

Boots stirred and scraped in the corridor as the train shook itself awake. Calvert had forced his way through that same corridor during the night to reach the toilet. Men and women of all three services had crouched on their kit or suitcases; some were even propped against one another in search of comfort. Cattle travelled better, he thought.

She asked him, 'Do you know the *Hood*?'

He found that he was smiling and wanted to record it somewhere. 'Of course. I thought everyone did. Biggest warship in the world, or was once. I've seen her a few times.' What was *Hood* doing here? The great battle-cruiser had been at Gibraltar when he had last heard.

He said, 'Lucky chap.' He did not realize he had spoken aloud.

She studied him and found herself speculating. Late twenties but looked older because of his fair beard. She had seen him touch it several times as if he were not used to it yet. Her husband had told her young officers grew them to make themselves look more like old sea-dogs. But not this one, she decided. In profile when he tried to look through the window he had an air of hardened experience, the cause of which she could only guess at. Watchful: not a man capable of relaxing much.

'I wonder what it will be like,' she said.

He looked at her. 'Much like Edinburgh, I expect. Raining and cold. As you go further north only two things happen. It gets more dismal, and there are fewer trees.'

They both laughed and one of the army officers almost choked in the middle of a long snore.

He added, 'I've a bit further to go yet.' He allowed his mind to examine it. *Scapa.* He had last been there when his ship was leaving for the ill-fated Norwegian campaign. He thought of all the missing faces. Maybe they would blur in time; he would accept that they were dead. No more landings on the big carrier's deck in all kinds of weather. No more wild parties and then more take-offs on patrol above those incredibly beautiful coasts and fjords. He shivered. Beautiful, and so bloody cruel.

He touched his beard, his eyes in shadow. He might be able to shave it off soon, but some scars would remain. People would stare at him. Ask questions. On and on . . .

He closed his eyes and listened to the gentle regularity of the wheels. *Clack-clack, clack-clack.* There was a faint hissing sound too, probably sleet, quite common in April up here. He wondered about his new ship and the men he would share her with. No room to hide

23

your feelings from others. But a ship: a different sort of life.

The navigation course and the intricacies of ship-handling and pilotage had seemed unexpectedly simple after being a flier.

He would never fly again. Once he had believed he would rather die than accept such a verdict. Now he knew he *could* not fly. Ever.

The train slowed even more and he heard a hoarse voice calling along the corridor, '*Inverness! Inverness!*'

There was the usual tension amongst some of the servicemen who did not have the right travel documents or tickets, who were stealing some leave to see a loved one, who were 'on the run'. Out there the enemy would be waiting, the military police in their red caps, the R.A.F., and the naval patrols in white belts and gaiters. There would be some on board the train who were simply too afraid to go back.

He said abruptly, 'I'll get you a porter – '

She stood up and held on to the luggage rack as the train jerked to a violent halt. Doors were already banging open, people were running and shouting; the bitter air filled the compartment like an icy wind.

He heard her say, 'Thank you, but no.' She watched him pull her case down. 'I've someone meeting me.'

Whatever was happening on the platform it had become quiet. The corridors were deserted, the sprawling gunners were gone as if they had been imaginary.

She was staring at him. In the grey light she looked uncertain, troubled. Wanting to go and yet unwilling to leave.

'Thank you for talking to me.' She held out one hand and waited for him to take it. 'And good luck, Lieutenant Calvert.' She said it so seriously that it made her seem suddenly vulnerable.

Calvert reached for his cap. Good luck? That had run out on that terrible day off Narvik. Ten months ago. Was that really all it was?

He said, 'I shall try and . . .' But the compartment was empty.

He smiled and reached for his cases. She had not even told him her name.

Then he stepped down on to the wet platform, very aware of the cold in his bones. He seemed to feel it more than ever now.

A petty officer in a white webbing belt sauntered out of the gloom and offered what might have been a salute.

'Mr Calvert, sir?' As he turned over a docket in his hands he added, 'The rail transport officer has fixed up breakfast for you. I'll take you across.' He squinted at the printed travel warrant. 'Then on the next train to Thurso, right?'

Calvert nodded. 'Scapa.'

The P.O.'s weathered face split into a grin. 'Says it all, dunnit, sir?'

Calvert gripped the man's arm without knowing it. The sudden companionship had reached out to him like a forgotten friend.

He was back.

2

Scars

Richard Kerr, *Serpent*'s first lieutenant, watched curiously while the new commanding officer struggled out of the suit of white overalls he had borrowed for his engine room tour.

It was a Sunday, just over a week since Brooke had made his unorthodox arrival in the NAAFI boat, and during that time he seemed to have explored more parts of the ship, weapons and equipment, as well as going through all the books and watch bills, than the previous captain had ever done. To Kerr it appeared to be more than a sense of duty or an attempt to impress. It was like a need which drove Brooke forward without respite.

Brooke reached for his jacket and grinned. 'Bit chilly after the Chief's engine and boiler rooms.' He shook his head admiringly. 'He keeps his department on top line. You could almost eat off the cat-walk!'

Like a boy again, Kerr thought, the tension suddenly gone from his face. He was curious about the captain's limp, which became obvious whenever Brooke was thinking about something else and made no effort to conceal it. But he was still no closer to him as a man; and he wondered if it was because Brooke was aware of his disappointment at not being offered a command. Many others had been given ships of their own, ranging from old destroyers to armed yachts; even reservists were being put on their own bridges. Disappointment? Or was it a resentment which the previous captain's sudden departure had sharpened into something worse?

Brooke could feel the intensity of the other man's scrutiny, but was still thinking of the Chief's pride in his engines and what they could do.

In his harsh voice he had patted a shining safety rail and exclaimed, 'Twenty-seven thousand horsepower, sir! Old lady mebbe, but I can still give you thirty-six knots at a swing of the throttles!' He was right to be proud. Few new ships could match that.

He glanced at the first lieutenant. Kerr was good at his job and obviously respected by all the senior rates he had met so far. Not a Number One to take any flannel from anybody. Tall, gravely good-looking with dark hair that never seemed out of place: the ship was lucky to have him. For a while longer anyway. He gave a half smile. *I'm lucky to have him.*

How different the ship felt. With almost a full complement again, *Serpent* was alive. The new navigator was expected at any time now and only a single rating was absent, one of those sent on compassionate leave. The other had returned, watched in silence by his messmates, who knew that after the bombing of his home he had nowhere else to go. Brooke could smell the heady odour of rum pervading the ship, an all-important event, especially on a Sunday in harbour with a lazy make-and-mend for everyone but the watch-keepers.

Brooke sat down. 'Gin, Number One?'

Kerr smiled. 'I'd like that.'

Brooke pressed a bell. It was a good sign. Kerr was loosening up a little bit. Before, he had made excuses. Maybe he had thought the new skipper was testing him, waiting to see if he drank too much or was trying to be too friendly.

Bert Kingsmill, the petty officer steward, a lugubrious, even dour-looking man, slid through the door and opened the drinks cabinet. He looked after the wardroom but his first loyalty was to his commanding officer.

Brooke returned his attention to Kerr. Greenwood, the previous skipper, had made the usual report about him, but there had been nothing special. Two words, *impulsive and stubborn*, stood out, but without any further explanation. In destroyers it was sometimes necessary to be one or the other. Kerr was still distant, but he would find out the reason for the comment eventually.

A small but fairly typical wardroom, Brooke thought. He had even discovered why Barlow, the gunner (T), had given himself the nickname Podger. For some reason he had decided his real name, Vivian, was too effeminate for an active-service torpedoman. The sub-lieutenant, Barrington-Purvis, seemed good at his work, and Kerr had confirmed this, but he was obviously blessed with a monumental conceit which could make him heartily disliked. The fact that his father was an admiral did not lend him humility.

Kerr asked suddenly, 'The new navigating officer is ex-Fleet Air Arm. A bit unusual, isn't it?'

Brooke picked up his glass and realized that it had been smoothly refilled. Petty Officer Kingsmill must have glided in soundlessly as if he moved on wheels. *I shall have to watch out.* But it was good Scotch. One of the perks of command to help settle the scales.

He replied, 'He should be joining today. He'll tell you all about it, I imagine.'

Calmly said, but Brooke saw the shadow fall like a

28

curtain. Kerr asked, 'What about sailing orders, sir?' The first lieutenant again. *On duty.*

'Tomorrow, I expect.' He saw Kerr's eyes shift to the silver-framed picture of the ship which now adorned the cabin desk. No doubt he was still blaming himself for not knowing or bothering to discover that his captain's father had been *Serpent*'s first C.O. The coxswain had known. It probably irked Kerr that he himself had not.

Brooke said, 'Warn the gangway staff that the new officer will be arriving just as soon as you get the signal.' He gave a wry smile. 'Our shore telephone has been disconnected – for some more important newcomer, I have no doubt.'

Kerr hesitated. 'Will you care to drop into the wardroom this evening, sir? A bit less formal.'

'Thank you, Number One.' He looked at the nearest polished scuttle, the sudden bars of heavy rain against the thick glass: Scapa showing its other face.

He added, 'Probably the last time for a while.'

Kerr watched him, suddenly alert. Rumours were rife throughout the ship. Leave was over: the ship was as ready for sea as she would ever be, so where to? The pale grey paint suggested a warm climate, as did the new fans. Ceylon was the favourite amongst the messdeck bookmakers. Some said it was the Med, where, after losing so many destroyers in the Greek disaster and enemy attacks showing no sign of lessening, even a small replacement would be welcome.

But not the bloody Atlantic again. Not yet. Slow, overloaded convoys which reduced the speed of all to only a few knots made the escorts' work even more uncomfortable. *Serpent* had been built for speed, one of the Grand Fleet's greyhounds, not to be flung about through forty-five degrees with the sea flooding over the open bridge like a mill-race. On one such convoy the seas had been so rough that the captain and the officer-of-the-watch had been unable to leave the bridge, while the other officers had been marooned aft until the weather had abated.

It was good to be getting away from the brutal power of the Western Ocean, if only to be spared the losses and the new strategy of Hitler's U-boat command. With the fall of Scandinavia, the Low Countries and France, the enemy now held a coastline that stretched from Norway's North Cape to the Bay of Biscay: nearly five thousand miles, each one of which afforded a threat to those desperately needed convoys and their tightly stretched defenders.

As George Pike, the burly coxswain, had remarked, 'Let some other bugger take the strain! Palm trees an' dancin' girls'll do me!'

Some hopes, Kerr thought.

The tannoy squeaked and then muttered through the ship like someone speaking underwater.

'D'you hear there! Hands to dinner!'

Kerr saw the captain smile, thinking probably of the unspoken part of the pipe. *Officers to lunch!*

Kerr left the captain's quarters and made his way to the wardroom. His companions sat by the fire on the club fender, or in the well-worn chairs.

Kerr relaxed slightly. Perhaps they all needed a change, a new horizon. He signalled to the messman. 'Pink gin, please!' He thought of the man he had just left, alone in his cabin. Maybe Brooke needed it too.

Kerr took the glass and signed a mess-chit, then glanced through the streaming scuttle.

Anything would be better than Scapa.

*

It was dark very early on this particular Sunday, and although the rain had eased the Flow was choppy with serried ranks of white horses, and the ship's upperworks shone like glass.

In the wardroom Petty Officer Kingsmill watched gloomily while his assistants put finishing touches to the array of glasses, and the selection of small snacks which they had produced for the occasion. Some officers were coming over from another destroyer to help make it more of a party for the new captain. Kingsmill was proud of his various skills, but never showed it. As always, his frowning features suggested he was paying for all the food and drink personally.

Kerr glanced at the bulkhead clock and wondered what Brooke would make of his small wardroom when he saw them *en masse* instead of on duty.

A face appeared in the doorway. 'Beg pardon, sir! *Leicester*'s boat is coming alongside!'

Kerr said, 'Off you trot, Sub, and greet our guests. You *are* the duty boy, I believe?'

'Why is it always me?' Barrington-Purvis put down his glass and strode out of the wardroom.

Kerr said to the two warrant officers, 'I'll wait until our guests get settled, then I'll call the captain . . .' He broke off as he saw a youth with a telegraphist's badge on his sleeve peering into the cheerful-looking wardroom, and doubtless making comparisons with his own tightly packed messdeck.

'Signal, Evans?'

'Aye, sir. From H.Q., sir. The new officer is waiting at the pontoons to be picked up.'

Kerr grinned. 'Tell Mr Barrington-Purvis. It will make his day!' The others laughed. It had started raining again.

Moments later they heard the next pipe. 'D'you hear there! Away motor-boat's crew!'

It would be a lively crossing in *Serpent*'s little motor-boat, the 'skimming-dish' as it was called.

The other officers came in to the wardroom and immediately relaxed. They all knew each other, and had worked many of the same convoys on some of the really bad runs.

Barrington-Purvis burst in, his shirt-front patterned with rain.

He was fuming. 'H.Q. won't send a boat, Number One. It's up to us again!'

'Take it off your back, Sub.' Kerr saw the *Leicester*'s first lieutenant grinning at him. If you didn't carry a midshipman to chase up, a subbie was the next best creature.

'Signal to him to catch the NAAFI boat like the Old Man!' That was Podger Barlow. The Old Man indeed, Kerr thought. Was Greenwood already forgotten?

He found the captain standing by his desk, an empty glass by his side.

'Ready, sir?' He waited, trying to gauge his mood. Nervous, unsure of the meeting.

Brooke straightened his jacket. 'I'm glad you invited *Leicester*'s lot, Number One.'

Kerr saw his tawny eyes staring into the distance. Another memory, and obviously not a good one.

'I've sent a boat for the new lieutenant, sir.'

Brooke entered the wardroom and caught the petty officer steward's mournful glance as he held out a tray with a glass of Scotch in dead-centre.

Kerr watched as his captain seemed to merge into the throng. Just the right number. He nodded his approval to the petty officer, but Kingsmill seemed to look through him.

There were whispers at the door and Kerr turned irritably as he saw someone holding a signal pad.

He hissed, 'What the hell's wrong now? Has our motor-boat got lost?'

But it was not a telegraphist this time; it was the petty officer who headed that department, Alan Brock. He had obviously been called from his mess and his gilt buttons were incorrectly fastened. He had probably been sleeping off his tot. But something in the man's face made Kerr contain his irritation.

'What is it?'

The man shifted his feet and peered past Kerr's shoulder.

'For the captain, sir. Personal.'

'Can't it wait? He's just . . .'

Brock said quietly, 'His dad's just died, sir.' He handed Kerr the signal flimsy as if it was too delicate to hold.

Kerr glanced at it. Must have happened this morning, when Brooke had been going round the ship. His father's ship. 'Oh, God.' He saw Brooke looking straight at him. Later he thought it was as if he had known.

Kerr handed him the piece of paper and said, 'I'm very sorry, sir. At a time like this . . .'

'Yes.' Brooke's eyes passed over his face without any expression. 'Keep things going, will you. I have to get something from my quarters.' Then he was gone.

Leicester's first lieutenant, who had overheard, asked, 'Shall we all push off, Dick?'

Kerr shook his head. 'No, Bill, I don't think it's what he wants.'

The other man sighed. 'Nobody else seems to have noticed, anyway.'

Kerr touched a messman's arm as he bustled past.

'Pass the word for the cox'n, will you? Tell him to come straight to me.'

Someone was laughing wildly as if he could not control it, and several glasses had already been broken. Kerr looked at their faces. After what they had been through on the last few convoys it was a wonder that anything mattered. He thought of the captain's youthful smile when he had been talking about the Chief and his engine room. *But it did matter.*

On the deck above the wardroom Sub-Lieutentant Barrington-Purvis swore under his breath as rain ran off his cap and touched his neck like ice. He had heard the same wild laughter and in his imagination saw them all standing around, armed with drinks which the ship's wardroom would pay for, and which he would miss unless the motor-boat's crew got a move on. After taking the newcomer to the accommodation ladder they had had to move the little boat out to the ship's boom and then clamber up themselves. The fact that they too would be soaked gave him no satisfaction at all.

He heard the quartermaster speaking with the new officer and swung away from the guard-rails, his voice sharp. 'Hold on – I'm the O.O.D.! You don't just barge in!'

Lieutenant Toby Calvert watched his gear being carried into the lobby, away from the streaming superstructure. God, she's small, he thought. You could lose her on a carrier's hangar deck.

'Now, whoever you are . . .'

He fell silent as the newcomer turned towards him. 'Calvert, Lieutenant, come aboard to join. As the O.O.D. you should have been told, I'd have thought?'

It was quietly said, but to Barrington-Purvis it was like a slap in the face.

'Of course I knew!'

'Well, then.' Calvert stepped over the high coaming of the lobby and waited for the sub-lieutenant to follow, his wet uniform shining in the deckhead lights like black silk. He remarked with some amusement, 'You're rather wet, old chap.'

'Here, I'll show you the way!' Barrington-Purvis tried to reassert his dignity, and did not see the quartermaster and gangway sentry exchanging grins at the lieutenant's comment. 'And the captain wants to see you without delay!'

It was hopeless. This insolent newcomer, trying to play the old salt with his crumpled raincoat and jaunty beard, was unimpressed.

Calvert heard the noise from the wardroom. 'Oh, having a party? Looks like I got here just in time.' He spoke casually, calmly, if only to contain the sudden fury which had exploded through him like fire. Another moment, witnesses or not, and he would have laid the subbie on his back.

Barrington-Purvis saw a steward in the tiny galley, sucking gratefully on a cigarette.

'Ogle! Take this officer's coat!' To Calvert he added severely, 'Not worn in the wardroom. Cost you a round of drinks!'

Calvert slipped out of his coat and handed his cap to the steward. 'Thanks.'

Then, with the subbie close on his heels, he stepped into the wardroom.

A tall lieutenant came towards him. 'I'm Kerr, Number One. Most of the others here are visitors from our chummy-ship *Leicester*.' Calvert saw his glance drop to the pilot's wings above the curl on his left sleeve. Or maybe he was looking at the two wavy stripes, wondering what was happening to his navy.

In those few seconds Barrington-Purvis had managed

35

to down a neat gin, and it seemed to work almost immediately. He was possibly the only member of the wardroom who had never realized that he could not hold his drink.

He said loudly, 'Our first reservist, Number One!' There was a sudden silence as he added, 'And he has a medal too!'

Kerr was about to intervene when he saw the captain framed in the doorway. His hair was tousled, his eyes red, as if he had been sick.

Brooke walked past them and gripped Calvert's hand, recognising his barely controlled anger.

'Welcome aboard, Pilot.' He smiled, with great effort. 'I really *can* call you that.' He half-turned towards Barrington-Purvis, and the smile was gone. 'Take a closer look, Sub.' He watched the young officer's confusion and then snapped, 'You don't see the Victoria Cross too often!'

Calvert said, 'I'm sorry about all this, sir.'

'So am I.' He looked at Kerr. 'Get him settled in. I'll speak to all of you tomorrow.'

He turned to Calvert again. The man who had tried to warn his parent aircraft carrier that he had sighted two German battle-cruisers off the Norwegian coast; who had seen his ship blasted by their great guns, her thin armour no protection from their shells. His ship, his home, his friends, dying and burning. The tiny useless aircraft toppling into the sea as she had started to capsize.

The man who had turned back towards the enemy in his slow, outdated Swordfish torpedo-bomber, and had attacked those ships until it too had been blasted out of the sky. His crew had died that day, and Brooke knew that he was thinking of them whenever anyone remarked on that little piece of crimson ribbon with its miniature cross. *For Valour.* It probably aroused many bitter memories, and pain for the men he had taken to their deaths.

A messman slipped away and Brooke knew it would be all over the ship in seconds. He thought of the coxswain, who had come to his cabin only minutes before this scene in the wardroom. George Pike, who had served under his father and seen him reappear in his new commanding officer.

He had stood by the desk and had taken a glass of Scotch without hesitation.

'Just 'eard, sir. There's no words for this kind of thing.'

Brooke had heard himself reply, 'He'd been ill for years. Never took care of himself. We both knew. I just wish I could have told him about the ship before . . .'

The coxswain had put down his glass. '*Our* ship, sir.' Then he had gone.

Barrington-Purvis's voice intruded like an irritating hornet. 'I only meant, sir . . .'

Brooke looked at him, his eyes cold. 'If the time comes for me to write your report, Sub, please tell me if you can think of anything worthy to mention. So far I can discover nothing in that direction.'

As the curtain fell across the doorway, Podger Barlow tweaked the sub-lieutenant's sleeve, still wet from the upper deck.

'You'll have to learn to take a bottle as well as hand them out, Sub. You've had that coming for a long time, and I couldn't have put it better myself.' He grinned. 'So come and make it up. Can't afford enemies in this ship, see?'

Petty Officer Kingsmill produced more drinks for the new arrival in what he considered to be *his* wardroom, and for the first lieutenant. He had overheard Podger

Barlow's gentle warning. What a laugh, he thought. The day those two made it up would be *the* bloody day.

He glanced over at the new officer and realized with a start that Calvert was looking directly at him. He thought for an awful moment that he had spoken out loud.

One thing was certain. Whatever this Calvert had got the V.C. for, Kingsmill could well believe him capable of it.

In his cabin by the light of the solitary desk lamp Lieutenant Commander Esmond Brooke sat, alone with his innermost thoughts. Long after the visitors had departed for their own ship and the hands had been piped down for the night, he considered the fate or coincidence which had brought him and his father's ship together.

He listened to the occasional thump of feet on deck as quartermaster or sentry did their rounds. He could sometimes hear the sluice of the current along *Serpent*'s flank so that she seemed to stir as if reawakening. *Our ship*, the grim-faced coxswain had called her.

He hoped his father had not suffered or been humiliated at the end. Brooke had seen so many die, always without the dignity they deserved when death had marked them down.

He reached out for the whisky bottle and stared at it with some surprise. It was empty, and yet he felt nothing.

With great care he took out his wallet and removed a small photograph: Sarah, who had promised to marry him. Instead she had married his brother. Together they would deal with all the necessary arrangements. Without fuss. He replaced the picture in his wallet and got to his feet. Without much feeling, either, he thought.

He staggered slightly and knew it was not the fault of the ship.

He sat down heavily on the bunk in the adjoining cabin without remembering how he got there, but he could not stop the other memories: when he had last seen him at the hospital. His illness had made him older, but he could still give a wink to the nurses and pull their legs with a doubtful story. Smoked too much, drank too much, but always good company. The ex-naval officer who had once commanded this ship.

His head hit the pillow and he felt like death.

Serpent's first captain, and now perhaps her last.

With one arm outflung, he was instantly asleep.

'Lieutenant-Commander Brooke, sir.' The small Wren held the door open and glanced at the visitor before closing it again.

The long room was warm and strangely safe and quiet after the lively crossing in the ship's motor-boat. Great windows looked across part of the fleet anchorage, covered with salt which had drifted up in the wind, so that sea and ships looked like a gigantic panorama on stained glass. The chief-of-staff was stabbing tobacco into a large briar pipe with powerful, capable fingers, and had a match going even as Brooke sat down.

A plain-faced Wren petty officer writer sat at another littered desk, hemmed in by telephones, signal folders and tea-cups awaiting collection.

'Good to have you, Brooke.' *Puff-puff.* 'Sorry to hear about your father.' *Puff-puff.* 'I'd have given you leave, but you know how it is.'

Brooke found he could relax with this tall, square-jawed captain. He had dispensed the sympathy. Now he could get on with the rest. 'How is the ship?' He did not wait for an answer. 'Good, good.' He was now wreathed in smoke, and Brooke wished he had brought his own pipe with him.

The chief-of-staff added, 'Wish we had more time, but there's never enough of that around here.' He glanced at the patient-looking Wren. 'Bloody Scapa, eh, Brenda?'

Brooke said, 'I'm lucky to have so many trained hands. I know it can't last, but . . .'

'Don't be too sure.' He regarded him through the smoke. 'There's talk of a big push about to begin. The Germans are reported to be ready to get some of their big ships out into the North Atlantic. More powerful than anything we've got, so the C-in-C is forced to keep battleships and battle-cruisers tied up here, just in case.'

'I didn't realize we were that hard-pressed, sir.'

'You've been too busy to notice, I expect.' He tapped his pipestem in time with his words. 'In eighteen months or thereabouts we've lost fifty-three destroyers, thirty submarines and over a hundred sweepers and auxiliary vessels. We can barely keep pace.'

The Wren said, 'Maintenance Commander on the phone, sir.'

'Tell him to wait.' His eyes crinkled. '*Ask* him to wait!' He continued. 'There is always a risk of invasion too, although after what the high-fly boys of the R.A.F. achieved last year I doubt it. At sea will be the real test, the final decisive battle.'

Brooke could sense the man's energy and his impatience. 'When do I get my orders, sir?'

The eyes scoured him thoroughly. 'Keen, eh? Thought you might be a bit dissatisfied with such a small command.' It was not a question.

He looked at a large wall-map and said, 'Convoys from all over the world, food, weapons, fuel and . . .'

He looked at the younger officer and added quietly, 'And men.'

Brooke prepared himself. Another hopeless campaign? Surely not now? Pictures flashed through his mind. Burning coastlines, gasping half-drowned soldiers staggering down to the waiting boats while jubilant, screaming Stukas dived over them like hawks, churning the land into bloody craters.

The Wren said carefully, 'Message, sir. The admiral's on his way.' Her voice was hushed.

'Humph – in that case . . .' The chief-of-staff stood up and brushed off his reefer jacket. 'You'll get your orders this afternoon. Local leave only and no loose talk.' He dropped his voice. 'I'm sending you to Gib.'

Brooke felt vaguely surprised, disappointed. The Med, then.

There were doors slamming, shoes clicking in one of the corridors. God was coming.

'With talk of a German breakout I can't afford to delay.' He held out his hand. 'Top secret.' The interview was over. Then he added, 'Really sorry to hear about your father . . .' But his eyes were on the door.

Brooke stood aside as the procession tramped past him. He had a brief impression of the cap with a double row of oak leaves around the peak, a large rectangle of medal ribbons, a severe face and thin mouth.

Suddenly the admiral came to a halt and one gold-embellished sleeve shot out.

'Who are you?'

'Brooke, sir.'

There was almost a smile. Almost. '*Serpent*, right? Good lad!' The procession surged on.

The motor-boat was bobbing about on the choppy water with several others waiting nearby for their respective lords and masters. Brooke returned a couple of salutes and then realized that the small Wren who had opened the chief-of-staff's door for him had been the same one who had met him when he had first arrived. The boat's bowman was on the jetty loosening the painter, and the coxswain, a red-faced whale of a man in his shining oilskin, stood up and saluted.

Macaskie was his name, and Geary was the bowman, a frail-looking youth who nevertheless had been punished by the last captain for fighting ashore. Face by face, Brooke concentrated on them, and came to the third crew member, the stoker. But the man's name was still lost with most of the others. He had heard, only too often, officers who commenced some order or other by saying, '*Here, you!*' If you expected them to respect you, you should always show respect for them.

He thought suddenly of the new navigator, Calvert. How could you ever get to know the ship's company of a carrier? His ship must have carried some thirteen hundred officers and men. He recalled Calvert's eyes when he had turned to respond to the subbie's offensive remark. Calvert had obviously known enough of them to mourn them, and to try to avenge them.

The motor-boat curved away from the jetty, flinging spray high over the cockpit.

Brooke remained on his feet, both hands gripping the safety rail, the stinging spray helping to drive off the remnants of his headache.

Moored ships flashed past, a cruiser, two oilers, and in the far distance some battleships. Waiting for the Germans to sneak out of their fjords in Norway and smash through the Denmark Strait into the Atlantic as their raiders had done in that other war.

There was that lingering stench again, churned up as the boat dashed over it. Oil seeping up from the great hulk of the *Royal Oak*. Local people maintained that it was the foul odour of decay from the corpses trapped inside.

He found Kerr waiting with the side-party as he clambered up the ladder, conscious of the familiar pain in his injured leg.

All eyes were on his face as he said, 'Orders arriving today, Number One.' They fell into step and walked away from the others. 'First to Gib.' He saw Calvert watching some seamen who were splicing wire with a skill that made it look easy.

Brooke repeated for the other man's benefit, 'Gib, Pilot.' He smiled. 'I'm still not used to it.'

'Nor me, sir.' Calvert made no other comment, as if he no longer cared where they were going.

Then he pointed to the far-off, hazy shapes of the great capital ships. 'Is *Hood* one of those, sir?'

Brooke shrugged. 'Could be. There's quite a show of strength building up here. Why? Heard something?'

Calvert touched his beard and thought of the young woman with her new wedding ring. 'Just a rumour, sir.'

Brooke looked away. I'll bet, he thought.

'Local liberty tonight, Number One. No overnight leave, not even for the P.O.s. Right?'

He hesitated and glanced up at the small turret-like bridge. Where he would spend his days and nights once they were at sea.

He said, 'I'll have some mail to be sent over, Number One.'

He felt the same private anguish. He should telephone from the shore. Express sympathy. Explain. But Sarah would most likely take the call. He still could not bear to hear her voice or imagine her being held as he had once held her.

Abruptly he said, 'Bring the orders to me as soon as they arrive.

43

Cusack, the Chief, clumped past, then paused to rest his gloved hands on the guard-rails when, right on time, the guard-boat sped towards the ship, the bowman rigid with his boat-hook as if it were a Fleet Review.

Cusack watched the satchel being signed for. *Orders.*

Very quietly he said, 'Here we go again, old girl. Back to bloody war!'

Kerr had the satchel in his hands, and said, 'Pilot, after I've given this little lot to the Skipper I'll help you sort out your charts, if you like.'

There was no reply, and when he turned he saw that Calvert was staring fixedly into the distance, his blue-grey eyes the colour of the Flow itself in the weak sunlight.

Kerr shaded his own to see what it was that held the other lieutenant as if he were mesmerized.

Then he saw it: a tiny black speck which seemed to be flying very slowly above the water. He had heard there was a carrier at Scapa, so it was probably one of hers.

A chill ran through him. Of course. It was probably an old Swordfish torpedo-bomber, a *Stringbag*, as they were affectionately called by the men who flew them.

Kerr glanced back at his companion and then walked away quietly into the quartermaster's lobby. Not for anything could he watch the emotion on Calvert's face, nor share the anguish he had seen there.

As he ran down the wardroom ladder he thought of the new captain. He had been the only one amongst them who had understood.

He was both moved and humbled by this discovery.

3

Of One Company

The *Serpent*'s chief and petty officers' mess, like its members, stood somewhere between the overcrowded forecastle's upper and lower decks, and the aloof distance of the wardroom down aft.

The fourteen members of the mess, as in any warship, represented the backbone of the whole company, and their skills ranged from seamanship to gunnery, engine room to the W/T and signals departments and much more beside. The good-conduct stripes worn by the petty officers to display their years of service, or *years of undiscovered crime* as the sceptics would have it, in this one small mess added up to almost a hundred years of naval experience. It was a comfortable, welcoming place, decorated with framed photographs of past events, darts matches, a whalers' race at Malta in happier times, and a small bar displayed souvenirs from various ports of call, lifted during some lively run ashore.

Presided over by George Pike, the coxswain, and assisted by McVie, the P.O. supply assistant, the mess was run with a discipline which was as rigid as any wardroom.

It was evening now, the deadlights sealed across the scuttles, the ship blacked out, a shadow on the uneasy

Flow. A game of darts was in progress and two other men were writing letters, the last chance before they got under way. One, Roy Onslow, the yeoman of signals, was the only member of the mess who still wore a rating's square rig but had the crossed anchors of a full petty officer. He had been due to be up-rated when the last captain had quit the ship so suddenly for a grander appointment. Lean and tanned although he had not served in a warm climate for over a year, Onslow was typical of his trade. He ran the signals department on the bridge in all weathers – and an open bridge at that, which had no respect for a man's skin or complexion – and guided his young signalmen, one of whom was only just out of training. He could be relied on to read a lamp or a hoist of bunting before anyone else. A yeoman of signals was also privileged more than most to study and observe his officers on watch or at action stations. Their doubts and their uncertainties he would keep to himself. Onslow was proud of the trust.

The petty officer sick berth attendant, named Twiss and known behind his back as 'Sister' Twiss, was watching the darts match without much interest.

He asked, 'Where are we going to, Swain?'

Pike put down his book and regarded him impassively. 'Gib.'

'Then what?'

Pike sighed. 'Well, you of all people should know that. All them vaccination checks we've had, an' *real* doctors to watch over 'em too.'

Sister Twiss scowled. *Serpent* carried no doctor and he ran the sick-bay without difficulty, even when the ship had been crammed with survivors choking on oil fuel after being torpedoed, or burned almost beyond recognition.

He said, 'Some of those doctors! No better than

46

medical students, most likely! The blunter the bloody needle the more they enjoy it, seems to me.'

Vicary, the torpedo gunner's mate, said, 'Ceylon, that's my bet. Fast convoy. Make a change to get cracking instead of rolling about the ocean like a tart in a trance!'

They looked at one another as the deck gave a tiny quiver. The gnome-like Chief was down there doing something. A generator or a pump, or some last-minute job on his work-bench. A sign of departure.

The coxswain took out his private bottle of rum and stared at it gravely. Supper had been cleared away, the duty part of the watch had been mustered. It would soon be time for Rounds. So why had he done it?

Jimmy the One would be doing Rounds this evening. He admired Kerr for several reasons; he was firm but fair when it came to the defaulters' table or to the men who wanted leave for one crazy reason or other. As coxswain, Pike was the first lieutenant's right arm, but he needed an officer who would back him to the hilt. He had expected Kerr to be relieved and sent to another ship. He was good and would be an asset to any sort of vessel. Pike was glad he was staying in *Serpent*: they were a small team, a family, and to have a new Jimmy the One as well as a fresh skipper – he shook his head.

Aloud he said, 'I remember when the Skipper's father was in command, and when *Serpent* commissioned for the first time . . .'

There were several groans and Andy Laird, the chief stoker, shouted, 'Swing the bloody lamp, somebody!'

Pike grinned. He had asked for that.

A messenger peeped into the mess. It was rare to see all these chief and petty officers together.

Pike asked, 'Well, what is it, my son?'

The youth stammered, 'First Lieutenant wants the yeoman of signals down aft.'

Somebody said, 'Off you trot, Yeo – maybe it's a signal for you to send! Tell us where we are all going to end up!'

Onslow laid his pen very carefully on his uncompleted letter and reached for his cap. 'Some hopes of that, John.'

The tannoy droned, 'Men under punishment and stoppage of leave to muster! Night boat's crew to report to the quartermaster's lobby!'

Fox, the chief boatswain's mate, stood up and bared his teeth. He would be doing Rounds with the first lieutenant and there would be a nice nip of something strong from the wardroom bar if he played his cards right.

Pike glanced at him. When he grinned he did look exactly like a fox, he thought.

They all stared at the door as Onslow re-entered the mess. Even the darts players froze and watched in silence as the yeoman of signals moved to the table and seemed to collapse against it.

Nobody spoke or moved until Pike asked quietly, 'What is it, Yeo?'

Onslow seemed to see his unfinished letter for the first time. He exclaimed, 'Can't be! Must be a mistake!' He lowered his face and added brokenly, 'Cathy and the kid, they said.'

Pike was a heavy man but could move like a cat if need be. He had uncorked the bottle of hoarded rum and poured a full glass for the stricken yeoman. Not once did he take his eyes from him, nor did he spill a drop.

'Get this down you, Yeo.' Onslow's home was in London. He could guess the rest. The kid had been what – two years old? The skipper had allowed her to be christened on board, with the old ship's bell used as a font.

Onslow looked at the letter with his pen still resting across it. 'Must finish it . . .' He broke off and lowered his face across his arm. 'It was the whole street. They couldn't have felt anything, could they?'

Laird the chief stoker gripped his shoulder. ''Course not!' But a glance at Pike said everything. The wartime myth that nobody suffered when they were torn apart. Especially kids.

The tannoy said sharply, 'Will the chief bosun's mate lay aft immediately.'

Fox groped for his cap. He had forgotten all about Rounds. The face of war had once again invaded their private world.

Pike asked quietly, 'Did you see the Old Man?'

Discipline and routine were taking over again. It was just as well, he thought. Being a Portsmouth ship, many of *Serpent*'s company came from London and the south. It was grim when you considered it. Pike had moved from Bethnal Green, where he had been born, to a little house in Portsmouth so that his wife would be spared the bombing. His big fists tightened on the table. Last year and as recently as four months ago, Old Portsmouth had been laid in ruins after continuous and relentless air raids. The old *George Inn* where Nelson had stayed, the fine Guildhall and many other landmarks were destroyed, and only the desperate courage of the fire-fighters had managed to save the cathedral, which, with its plaques and memorials, was a history of the Royal Navy itself. Nowhere was safe any more. But his wife had come through it, his 'old girl' as he called her. Hundreds and hundreds of others had not, and many still lay in the ruins of some three thousand devastated houses.

'Yes.' Onslow's voice was faraway. 'He was very nice to me. So was Jimmy the One. I bloody near broke down, Swain.'

'Stand by for Rounds!'

Petty Officer Fox pulled back the curtain while Kerr hung back in the lobby. To the mess at large he said, 'Carry on!' but his eyes were on the yeoman of signals. Then he said compassionately, 'The captain will try and get you some leave, Yeo. It's not impossible.'

Onslow raised his chin and afterwards Pike thought it was an act of pure courage. Onslow said, 'They're all I've got, sir. *Had.*' He shook his head. 'I'll stay with my mates.'

They heard the Rounds moving away to the main messdeck, and Pike said, 'If there's anything . . .'

Onslow stood up. 'Thanks, Swain, but no.' He looked past the untouched rum without seeing it. 'I'll go and check the signals.'

Then he picked up the letter and folded it with great care. As he left the mess the others watched without speaking. Some of them had shared the misery he was enduring, but there were no words: there never had been. At least up there on the deserted bridge amongst his flags and signal lamps he would be safe. For a while.

Pike sat down heavily. 'Another casualty.'

Andy Laird, the chief stoker, glanced meaningly at the rum. 'What about us, then?'

Pike forced a grin and poured another glass. '*Sod it!*'

A dart hit the board and somebody had switched on the wireless speaker: some dreary girl crooner doing her bit for the war effort.

But it worked. The face of war had departed.

*

Lieutenant Richard Kerr tapped on the door marked *Captain* and waited for a steward to open it.

With the deadlights clipped shut and the fans turned down the cabin seemed almost humid, and Kerr was surprised to see Calvert, the new navigator, sitting at the same table as the captain, both without their jackets.

Brooke was smoking his pipe while Calvert was leafing through some of the intelligence pack the guardboat had brought out to the ship.

Kerr said, 'Rounds completed, sir.' He was surprised and rather angry with himself for feeling a spark of resentment – or was it plain jealousy that Calvert should be here and not him? He thought of the yeoman's face when Brooke had broken the news about the signal. Simply said, with no ponderous offerings of hope or promises he could not keep.

Kerr could not imagine the previous captain, James Greenwood, showing the same sincerity. He knew it was Brooke's manner that had prevented the yeoman from breaking down completely.

Brooke glanced up at him and Kerr realized he was coming to know those quick, searching appraisals.

He asked, 'All settled down?'

Kerr smiled. 'A few comedians as usual, sir. Ideas of where we are bound this time. Most think the Med.'

Brooke waved him to a chair and pushed a bottle of gin and some bitters across to him. 'Help yourself.'

Kerr poured a measure and watched the pink bitters tinge the glass like a stain. He noticed that the navigator was drinking what looked like barley-water. Something to do with his past and the experience which had marked him for life. It was common enough for some officers to prepare themselves for a bad convoy or the prospect of action with several large drinks. Usually

51

they did not live very long, and neither did the men who were relying on their judgment under fire.

Kerr swallowed the pink gin and said, 'All libertymen are aboard, sir – not even Eggy Bacon's adrift.' He saw Brooke's quick puzzled frown. 'Sorry, sir. Leading Seaman Bacon, the chief quartermaster.'

Brooke smiled and again the lines of strain seemed to smooth away. 'Don't apologize, Number One. It takes a while, but I'll get to know every man-jack, given time.' He became serious just as quickly. 'We should get plenty of *that*.' He glanced at the pile of papers and instructions, the signatures and the Top Secret stickers. 'Fact is, we're eventually meeting a fast convoy when we've left Gibraltar.' He thought of the chief-of-staff's emphasis on convoys and the ships needed to carry the most precious cargo of all: *men*. 'To Singapore, then on to Hong Kong.' He saw Kerr's sudden interest and added, 'Fast troopers apparently, but Intelligence will fill in the gaps at Gib.'

'Are they expecting trouble, sir?'

Brooke shrugged. 'They say it's unlikely. But there are some valuable and experienced troops out there who would be better employed at home or in the Western Desert. These will be a holding force, a show of strength rather than anything more definite.' He reached out and turned over one of the papers. 'The Admiralty seem to believe that the Germans are going to try and break out into the Atlantic with some of their big chaps, ships like the *Bismarck*, the floating fortress as they call her. It might explain the urgency – getting us and the convoy safely clear of the usual convoy routes.'

'If a battleship did break out . . .' Kerr hesitated as the captain's eyes settled on his.

Brooke answered quietly, 'It would be a massacre.'

'Why us, sir?'

'*Serpent*'s fast, and will have no difficulty in keeping up with converted liners or whatever they are. There will be others with us.' He held a match to his pipe and was surprised that his hand was so steady. Perhaps he should have told Kerr the truth about the choice. Somehow the word *expendable* seemed to linger at the back of his mind.

He looked around the quiet cabin with sudden resentment. When he had been taken back into the navy in spite of his earlier discharge for ill-health and personal injury, one thing had haunted him: that in the two and a half years since he had been put on the beach, he would have been left behind both in experience and strategy. He need not have worried. The greatest navy in the world had still been controlled by minds obsessed with the line of battle, and most senior officers had been originally in the gunnery branch. As his father had scornfully commented when they had discussed it, 'All mouth and gaiters!'

Battleships and cruisers had taken precedence over carriers while the aircraft and the torpedo were considered something not quite decent. Little destroyers like this one had been well built, and had they been properly maintained, held in reserve even when the first rumbles of aggression had come from Germany, the navy would never have been so desperate for convoy escorts when they were most needed.

Instead they had taken over fifty lease-lend destroyers from the U.S. Navy, elderly vessels which were totally unsuitable for anything but calm seas. Because of their four funnels they were nicknamed 'Uncle Sam's four-pipers', and were notorious for rolling so much they could do it on wet grass. The fleet was certainly paying for it now, and with U-boat sinkings outstripping every

53

shipbuilding programme, Brooke had sometimes wondered how they had managed to survive so long.

Calvert looked up from his pile of papers and the list of new charts he would be needing.

'I think the Japs will attack Singapore, sir. They have nothing to lose and they're hell-bent on controlling the whole of the Far East while we're occupied everywhere else.'

Kerr said incredulously, 'They were our allies in the last war!'

Calvert went back to his work. 'So were the Italians.'

Brooke smiled. 'At least it would bring the Yanks in . . . maybe.'

He glanced at the framed photograph his father had given him. *Tell me how she looks, eh?* Almost the last words he had spoken to him, and he could still hear them clearly.

Brooke had always been close to his father, especially when they had kicked him out of the service. His father had shared a similar fate in the twenties when lieutenant-commanders had been two-a-penny, and discharged officers, lost without their naval environment, had wandered from one job to another, becoming secretaries of golf clubs, publicans, chicken farmers – the list had been endless. Brooke could barely remember his mother: she had died immediately after the Great War in one of the sweeping 'flu epidemics. But unlike many service wives she had always had money, quite a lot of it. Brooke's father had held on to the old house on the Thames and had turned it into a country hotel for the sort of people who wanted to fish and shoot, and, remarkably, in a time of recession and unemployment with discharged soldiers and sailors filling the dole and soup queues, it had worked. Soon after the outbreak of war the buildings and grounds had been taken over by the army, and an anti-aircraft battery and other personnel had transformed the place into a military camp. It had broken the old man. No more boats to offer river trips for fishing and sightseeing; no petrol either. The world had turned its back on leisure and hope.

Clogged lungs and a bad heart had done what the Zeebrugge raid in 1918 could not.

Brooke glanced around again, seeing it as it must have been, imagining how his father, as the captain Pike the coxswain could still remember, must have looked and behaved.

He stood up and faced his two lieutenants, the one so hungry for his own command, and the other haunted by those who had died for his V.C.

He said, 'Oh-eight-thirty tomorrow. You know the drill, Number One. A day we'll all remember.'

For a few seconds they were lost in their own thoughts, Kerr no doubt recalling the convoys *Serpent* had tried to defend, burning ships and drowning seamen, while Calvert's mind obviously still lingered on the image of his carrier, capsizing under fire from the German battle-cruisers, and the recollection of the madness which had driven him into an attack, David and Goliath. Brooke felt the gentle quiver of machinery and wondered if the ship, *our ship*, as Pike had put it, was feeling it too. Like the yeoman of signals and the young rating who had lost everything, and even his own father, who had loved this ship more than any other.

Kerr seemed to sum it up for all of them.

'I'm not sorry to go. It can't be any worse than this.' He downed his drink and added, 'I'll tell the others, sir.'

Calvert, too, was leaving. He said, 'It's all so *quiet*, sir.' It sounded like an apology. 'After a carrier, I mean.'

Brooke thought he could feel the man's anguish, and

said gently, 'I'm glad you're here, Pilot. What we are doing *is* important. It has to be, otherwise there's no point in going on.'

When the door closed Brooke turned and looked at the ship's crest again.

He gave a wry smile and asked aloud, 'How's the new captain, Dad?'

It was only some of the Chief's machinery, of course, but he could have sworn he heard him chuckle.

'*Starboard watch to defence stations! Special sea-duty-men close up!*'

Brooke glanced around his compact sleeping-cabin, ensuring that nothing was left lying about that might be broken if the sea got up.

He caught sight of himself in the mirror, observing himself as though he were a stranger. He was wearing the old sea-going reefer jacket, with the lace on the sleeves more brown than gold after so many months of watchkeeping. He had lost some weight so that the jacket was too large for him, but that enabled him to wear even the thickest sweater underneath. Grey flannel trousers and his scuffed leather sea-boots: they were older than the jacket, he realized.

'*Close all watertight doors and scuttles! Down all deadlights!*'

A ship reawakening, preparing to return to the life she understood. Back to the ocean where only vigilance marked the margin between survival and death.

Brooke could feel the insistent vibration of machinery, the Chief waiting for the telegraphs to ring out the first orders from the bridge.

Kerr had already been down to report that the ship was to all intents ready for sea. The postman was back on board, the galley secured: everything about which a good first lieutenant should be informed. To question any such item would be resented. He smiled, recalling how he himself had once felt when his own commanding officer had wanted to query some small detail.

In his mind, he could see it all and guess the rest. The cable had been unshackled from the buoy and replaced by a powerful slipwire, the only thing that was holding the ship captive. He had heard the thud of feet as the lower deck had been cleared to man the falls and run the dripping motor-boat up to her davits; the rating who had been the luckless buoy-jumper was probably soaked through by lively wavecrests.

'*All the Port watch! First part forrard, second part aft! Hands to stations for leaving harbour!*' The tannoy had not stopped since breakfast had been cleared away.

Brooke felt in his pockets although he knew the drill by heart. Pipe and tobacco, two or three handkerchiefs and a dry towel to wrap round his neck if it got wet in the open bridge. He slung the heavy binoculars across his chest, tossed his stained duffle coat over one arm and took a last look around, then he walked out into the passageway where he saw the petty officer steward fastening up a cabinet with a padlock. He was wearing a deflated lifebelt over his uniform. The old hand, he thought. It was not unknown for a ship to be torpedoed or to hit a mine immediately on leaving harbour. Then up the ladder to the lobby and out into the open. It was surprisingly cold, but he walked slowly and deliberately along the deck and saw the bridge framed against a grey sky. The Flow looked bleak, the islands and heavier warships almost hidden in what appeared to be mist. Brooke knew it was drizzle, which had been coming and going since dawn. The three funnels with their low tails of smoke, like the oilskinned seamen and the narrow decks, were shining with it.

He could almost guess what the leading hands were saying as he walked by.

'There's the Old Man. What d'you reckon to him?'

He glanced in passing at the two pairs of torpedo tubes, a small broadside when compared with the new fleet destroyers.

The gunner (T) saluted, and Brooke said, 'It'll be lively outside!'

Podger Barlow grinned. 'She can 'andle it, sir.'

There it was. *Pride*, the one quality that was never shown on any list.

Past the funnels, feeling their steady warmth, and then up the first ladder to the Oerlikon gun mountings. Some seamen glanced at him uncertainly – the usual collection, he thought. The hard men and the youngsters, new recruits and old stripeys who knew it all.

The open bridge was crowded. The team. The ones he would get to know. Or else.

Sub-Lieutenant Barrington-Purvis saluted, his face totally blank. He had been keeping a very low profile since the incident with Calvert in the wardroom. The latter was bending over the ready-use chart table, the hood of which hid everything but his buttocks and a pair of lambswool-lined flying boots. A glimpse of his past.

Onslow, the yeoman of signals, was at the rear of the bridge, his powerful binoculars trained towards the land. Brooke had made a signal about his promotion, which should be granted without any more delay. It was the least he could do. A boatswain's mate, two look-outs and another signalman completed the visible part of the team. Below in the wheelhouse Pike the coxswain would be at the wheel, the quartermasters on either side of him manning the telegraphs for engine and revolution orders. The plot table and the navigator's yeoman completed the complement.

'From Flag, sir.' Onslow was speaking to Barrington-Purvis, but was looking at his captain. '*The boom will be opened in twenty minutes. Proceed in company with Mohican.*'

Brooke stood on the scrubbed gratings beside the tall chair; he would spend much of his time here. He had seen the other ship already, one of the big *Tribal* class destroyers, like Vian's famous *Cossack* which had swept alongside a German supply ship, the notorious *Altmark*, to rescue the many merchant seamen imprisoned in her after their ships had been sunk by the raider *Graf Spee*. A rousing moment in a war plagued by defeats and failures. '*The Navy's here!*' had been the cry of the *Cossack*'s boarding officer. It could have been intended for the whole country.

Brooke stood in the forepart of the bridge and looked down at the glistening forecastle deck. The slipwire was running through one fairlead, down to the buoy and back to the opposite side where Kerr's party stood in their oilskins, with their chin-stays down to keep their caps in place and so avoid any criticism from some watching senior officer, and wearing their stout leather gloves. There were often broken strands which slipped the attention of the handling party, and without gloves a wire could lay open a man's palm like a carving-knife. A shivering signalman stood right in the eyes of the ship, ready to lower the Jack once the wire was slipped.

Brooke controlled his breathing. He had taken the big flotilla leader *Murray* to sea many times. But this was different. It was like being someone else. He saw Kerr peering up at him, his face shining with rain. Perhaps he was seeing himself on the bridge as he might have been. *Stubborn. Impulsive.* What had really happened?

'Stand by, sir!'

'Warn the Chief.'

Calvert said, 'Done, sir.'

Onslow called, 'Carry on, sir.'

Brooke chopped the air with his hand and heard Kerr yell, '*Slip!*'

'Slow ahead together!'

Brooke heard the glass screen begin to rattle and saw the big mooring buoy slide away as if under its own power.

'Port ten! Steady! Midships!' He heard Pike's throaty voice echo up the brass voicepipe as he put the helm over. Men were dashing about below the bridge, tackling the treacherous slipwire and subduing it into one shining coil. Then, as Kerr shouted an order, the forecastle party fell into two swaying lines while the signalman scuttled from sight with the Jack in his arms.

Onslow said angrily, 'From *Mohican*, sir. *Please proceed. Age before beauty!*'

One of the look-outs muttered, 'Cheeky sod!'

Brooke picked up the red handset and waited for Cusack to answer.

'Captain here, Chief. Our ability is being challenged. Can you give me full revs when I call for it?'

Cusack must have known what was happening, or maybe it often occurred. He sounded almost cheerful. 'Too right, sir.'

'Signal from boom-gate, sir! *Proceed when ready!*'

They did not have long to make their exit. Since *Royal Oak* had been torpedoed right here in the Flow it was always feared that another U-boat would slip through the boom when it opened for an outgoing vessel.

There was no point in using unnecessary helm orders. Brooke spoke directly into the wheelhouse voicepipe.

'Steer straight for the boom-gate, Cox'n.' He could picture Pike down there with his beefy hands on the wheel, his head turned as if he had guessed there was more to come. Brooke said, 'Now ring down for full speed!'

It was as if *Serpent* was sharing it. She seemed to pounce forward, a huge bow-wave slicing from the stem like an axe through ice.

'Attention on the upper deck!'

Brooke raised his glasses and watched as his ship tore abeam and then past the other, more powerful destroyer. He could see the gold oak leaves on her captain's cap, even his astonishment as the *Serpent* overtook the big *Tribal* and swept on towards the open boom.

'Half-speed ahead together.' He watched the wash boiling astern like a waterfall so that the other ship's bows were momentarily drenched with falling spray.

Onslow said quietly, 'That showed him, sir.'

Brooke felt it again: pride, and he knew he was sharing it.

'Not quite, Yeo. Make to *Mohican*. *Do you require a tow?*'

'No reply, sir.'

And so *Serpent* and the ninety souls in her company went back to war.

4

Rumours

Lieutenant Toby Calvert climbed the last few steps of the bridge ladder and hauled himself through the gate. For a few moments he leaned backwards, taking his weight on his arms while he let the early sunshine explore his skin. It was not very warm, but the air was fresh and alive, and the open bridge was no longer a place of mystery. He belonged.

The morning watchkeepers were still in their various attitudes of tired stiffness, waiting to be relieved, to snatch some rest before returning to their defence stations in another four hours. Watch on, watch off, for this was the Atlantic, and although the ocean stretched away on either beam in glistening emptiness it was never a time to relax.

Calvert saw the first lieutenant on the forward gratings, his binoculars training from bow to bow. Leading Signalman Railton was splicing a broken halliard, while the look-outs on either side swept their arcs of vigilance with slow care, probably very aware that their captain was on his tall chair on the port side, his head cradled on his arms below the screen, his tousled hair rippling in the breeze.

Kerr turned and said, 'Nice and early, Pilot! That's how I like it. What's for breakfast?'

Calvert grimaced. 'Bangers.'

Kerr watched some gulls swooping after the ship. Where did they nest, he wondered?

Throughout the ship gun-crews were exchanging places, and down in the wheelhouse a new helmsman had just reported that he was taking over the helm.

Together they opened the weatherproof screen over the chart table, and bent to examine the pencilled courses and positions of the previous watch.

Kerr said in his usual business-like fashion, 'Course to steer is two-one-zero, one-one-oh revolutions.' He glanced over the screen and Calvert saw the dark stubble on his chin. When he next appeared the first lieutenant would be freshly shaved, smart as paint.

He said, 'Cape Finisterre is about two hundred miles to port. Weather report good.' He frowned and Calvert saw the returning strain, but it was quickly past. 'There were some signals around dawn. Convoy in trouble to the south of us. But nothing else yet.'

A boatswain's mate, a silver call dangling from a chain around his sweater, called, 'Port watch closed up at defence stations, sir. Able Seaman Monk at the wheel.'

Kerr turned away from the voicepipes. 'Better watch that one. Dozes off if you don't chase him.'

Calvert waited, knowing there was more. A criticism, perhaps? Instead, Kerr said, 'What do you make of it, Pilot? Fifteen hundred miles, from Scapa to the sun. You've really settled in, right?'

Calvert climbed onto the compass platform and checked the magnetic compass. The casual enquiry was not the real reason why Kerr was hanging around.

He replied cautiously, 'I'm still finding out where everything is.'

Kerr glanced towards the captain. One of Brooke's

arms had slipped from its perch and was swinging slowly in time to the ship's easy roll.

'When did you take up flying?'

Calvert made himself relax, muscle by muscle. It was not the question he had been expecting.

'A long time ago. It was all I ever wanted to do.' He found himself measuring every word before he released it. 'Eventually I became an instructor at a flying club and organized trips over the Channel during the summer holidays.' He sighed. 'Hard to believe now, isn't it?' He realized that Kerr was waiting and went on, 'I joined the local R.N.V.R. unit and persuaded them to attach me to the Fleet Air Arm. I was a civvy instructor, so it was like learning from scratch, a part-time Richthofen!' Kerr saw the smile, the cost of talking so freely. 'So when the balloon went up, I was one of the first to be called. Just as well – I couldn't *do* anything else.'

Kerr said, 'We all think like that sometimes.'

'Yes, I expect so. The regulars I meet . . .'

'People like me, you mean?'

Calvert searched for sarcasm but there was none. 'Yes, if you like. Everything mapped out, from the training college to a brass-hat if you're lucky. I've known several like that, bent on personal advancement and totally unprepared for the untimely interruption of war in their ordered world. I've often found that the hostilities-only chaps are better able to take it. They joined up to fight, not to make a career of it.'

'You're not married?'

Calvert smiled. 'Nearly. I was too young. Now I'm too bloody old, or feel like it!'

Kerr thought of what he had heard about the captain. How his girl had married his brother instead.

Calvert raised his face again to the sunshine and Kerr thought he could see a cluster of scars through his beard; then he slipped out of his duffle coat. Beneath it he wore a blue battledress blouse, what the navy called 'working rig'. His pilot's wings were above the left pocket, but as it was working dress no decorations were ever worn with it. Was that why he clung to this old uniform? So that the V.C. would remain something private?

Since Calvert's arrival at Scapa, Kerr had made a point of checking up on the award and the act of valour for which he had received it in the records at naval H.Q., and when he considered his findings he understood the expression he had seen on Calvert's face when the solitary Swordfish had flown slowly across the swirling currents of the Flow. The two battle-cruisers *Scharnhorst* and *Gneisenau* had already made a name for themselves throughout the Norwegian and North Atlantic campaigns. Fast and powerful, they had been the cream of the *Kriegs-Flotten*.

Kerr had wondered what it must have been like for Calvert and his two-man crew, first sighting the two great ships and then being able to communicate their discovery to their carrier only with an Aldis lamp. But it had already been too late, and the carrier along with the *Courageous* and the *Royal Oak* had become the first heavy casualties of the war.

'If you two can't stop nattering I might as well go down to my hutch and grab a wash!' Brooke slid off the chair and stretched.

The bridge messenger bent over a voicepipe and then said, 'From W/T, sir. *Mayday* from one of the ships in that eastbound convoy.'

Calvert flung himself across the chart table, seizing his brass dividers and parallel rulers, a pad already to hand.

Kerr peered over his arm. 'The convoy must have scattered. We might be able to help if we crack on speed.'

They both turned as Brooke said, 'Disregard. Carry on with the sweep. You know our orders. It is not my intention to disobey them.'

He saw Kerr's eyes spark with something like anger. He added quietly, 'A gesture, Number One? That's not what it's all about, you know.'

Then he was gone, and they heard the stammer of Morse as he paused by the W/T office on his way to the sea-cabin, the hutch, as he called it.

Kerr said harshly, 'There may be men out there, waiting for their ship to go down under them, or already treading water without hope of rescue. Is that of no importance?'

Calvert watched him. *So that was why he fell out with the previous captain.*

He said, 'U-boats hang about near stragglers, don't they? Just in case some ship comes looking for survivors.'

Kerr did not seem to hear him. He exclaimed, 'Anyway, what's wrong with making a gesture? *You* bloody well did!'

Calvert gave a brief smile. 'I have the watch, Number One.'

Kerr opened his mouth but closed it again. *What would I have done?* He saw Pike the coxswain waiting by the forward funnel with a clipboard in his hand, waiting to waylay him, but all he could think about was the finality in Brooke's voice and Calvert's incisive little comments. *The untimely interruption of war ...* He reached the iron-deck and asked crisply, 'Something for me, Swain?'

He was the first lieutenant again.

Number Seven mess was situated on the starboard side of the lower deck. There were three other messes in this cramped space, each consisting of a scrubbed table with bench seats on the inboard side. Other members of a mess would sit on the lockers that lined the forecastle's curving side. Shelves were crammed with ditty boxes in which the older men kept their treasures, metal hat-boxes, and inflatable life-jackets, which were either worn or kept very close to hand. In the centre forepart of the mess were the nettings where sailors stored their hammocks. These were not supposed to be slung at sea in case they jammed a door or an escape-hatch if the worst happened, and unless one watch was ashore as libertymen there was never enough space to sling all the hammocks anyway. But although the men moaned about the discomfort and overcrowding it was unlikely that any true destroyer-hand would exchange it for a battleship or cruiser, where the bugle and spit-and-polish ruled as in a barracks.

Seven Mess was no different. The rolled oilcloth was unfolded on the table, and mess-traps were handed around while the cook of the mess clambered down from the galley with trays of greasy bangers and pans of steaming baked beans. A fanny of tea, some last remaining stocks of stale bread which had survived all the way from Scapa Flow, and maybe a biscuit or two: it was not much of a banquet, but it lined the stomach and drove the ache of watchkeeping away until the next time.

The leading hand of the mess was the captain of the forecastle, Bill Doggett. He was a great block of a man, with wrists as thick as most men's arms. A true seaman, his waist was hung about with handmade leather holsters in which he carried the tools of his trade, a wicked-looking knife as well as the regulation one or 'pusser's dirk', a marlin-spike for splicing wire, even a pouch of lead pellets for the buoy-jumper to hammer into the big mooring shackle so that it did not unscrew itself as the ship tugged on the cable.

Doggett was a formidable character who could be foul-mouthed, even violent when required, and he ruled his mess with a rod of iron. Ashore he was often fighting mad and appeared regularly as a defaulter for some misdemeanour or other. That was why he had never moved up to the petty officers' mess: not that Bill Doggett cared, but he ran the forecastle deck with all its complications of anchors and cables, slips and stoppers, wires and fenders like a magician.

As he had been heard to remark, 'Even Mister toffee-nose Barrington-Purvis can't find nothin' to drip about!'

He was rolling a cigarette now, his thick fingers like sausages but the movements deft and supple. His features were set in concentration.

One seaman, called 'Ticky' Singleton because of a nervous twitch in one eye, said, 'After Gib, Hookey? What d'you think?'

'Far East. Obvious, innit?' Doggett gave him a pitying glance. 'I done a commission out there once. Hong Kong – now there's a place. Suit me, it would. All them little girls at Wanchai . . . make yer 'air curl, they do!'

The table was cleared, the oilcloth rerolled. It would soon be time to muster for work.

Singleton persisted, 'The new skipper don't say much, do he?'

'To *you*? Got more mouse than that!' Doggett gave a huge grin. 'The old *Serpent*'s in good 'ands. One officer short, a bomb 'appy navigator, a pisshead of a subbie, and now a Skipper who's probably a real death-or-glory bloke. *Our* death, '*is* sodding glory!'

'There's always Jimmy the One.'

Another voice called, 'Hookey only sees him across the table!'

Doggett was rolling another cigarette from his duty-free tin. It would be ready in time for stand-easy.

'He an' I 'ave an understandin' . . .' The cigarette stayed motionless in his hand as the tannoy rasped, '*Away* sea-boat's crew! Lowering party to muster!'

Doggett punched a man who had fallen asleep at the table.

'Shift yerself, Bobby! One 'and for the King, remember?'

Only one narrow ladder to the deck above, and yet in seconds the lower messdeck was empty, leaving sea-boot stockings drying on a deckhead pipe, a half-finished letter, somebody's local newspaper, sent perhaps to remind him of that which he could scarcely remember. For *this* was their home, and for all their banter it was what really mattered to them. That, and survival.

Up on the open bridge, the voicepipes and telephones muttered like hidden spectators while Brooke, his wash and shave forgotten, levelled his powerful glasses above the spray-dappled glass screen.

'Cox'n on the wheel, sir!'

'All short-range weapons closed up, sir!'

Brooke heard but ignored them. He was watching the vast span of unbroken ocean ahead of the bows, undulating in a regular, steady swell as if the sea were breathing. Glistening and endless, with the horizon too bright and blinding to look at.

Kerr was beside him, his eyes keen and questioning.

Brooke said, 'Probably nothing, Number One, but I'm putting down the sea-boat. See to it, will you?'

Kerr hesitated and then raised his own binoculars before he slid down the ladder again.

Someone unused to the ocean and its ways would see nothing to begin with. And then . . . He turned back to the ladder and caught one of Onslow's young signalmen staring at him, biting his lip nervously. From bow to bow there were a million tiny fragments, lifting and falling on the swell, black in the blinding light.

Brooke crossed to the port side and leaned against the screen.

'Tell the Chief. Dead slow.' Dead was right. He leaned over the side of the bridge and saw Kerr already down there by the whaler's davits, the boat's crew sitting on their thwarts in oilskins and life-jackets. The boat-handlers were loosening the falls around the gleaming staghorn bollards, crouching like athletes, waiting for the order. Kerr was speaking with Fox, the chief boat-swain's mate, his right arm when it came to seamanship.

Brooke raised his glasses again. He said, 'Who is the senior Asdic operator?'

Calvert would not know. Yet. But Onslow called, 'Raingold, sir.'

'Get him for me.'

A boatswain's mate handed him a handset and Brooke said shortly, 'Captain. Sweep from bow to bow. We are approaching wreckage. More than one ship by the look of it.'

'Aye, sir. I'll begin now.'

Calvert asked, 'U-boat, sir?'

'Unlikely, Pilot.' He sounded completely absorbed. 'That bastard'll be off after the rest of the convoy. If there's any left.' He looked at Calvert's tense face. Of course, he would have little experience of this; his would have been the bird's-eye view.

'When a ship goes down after being tin-fished she'll sometimes capsize, and if the bulkheads and hatches hold she can assume neutral buoyancy – like a submarine, right?'

He turned and waved down to Kerr and saw the flurry of hands around the boat's falls.

'Even at this speed, a wreck like that could take out our keel like the string from an orange.'

Calvert watched him. So calmly said. Not to impress; there was no bravado.

'Turns for lowering!' Kerr's voice was quite clear even up here. There was not a breath of wind, unusual out here on this empty ocean.

'*Lower away!*'

Calvert dragged his eyes from the sea of drifting fragments and concentrated instead on the boat jerking down the ship's side towards the small, frothing bow-wave.

'Avast lowering! *Out pins!*'

The whaler's coxswain and bowman held up the retaining pins to prove they were removed from the falls. In times of terrible emergency it was not unknown for one man to overlook this, so that when the boat was dropped into the water only one end would be freed. The crew and passengers, if there were any, would be flung into the water and probably sucked into the screws.

'*Slip!*'

Kerr had timed it perfectly. The boat made barely a splash as it dropped on to the small bow-wave and then veered away on its rope, the oarsmen already thrusting out their blades. Brooke found time to wonder how many times he had lowered the sea-boat like this.

Calvert asked, 'How long since it happened, sir?'

'A few days, no more. No leaking fuel about, but the flotsam is still too close together for it to have been much longer.'

Calvert stood and watched as *Serpent*'s straight stem pushed slowly through the scattered remains. A mile or so of tightly lashed bales, cotton or wool, perhaps for uniforms in England. Broken life-rafts which had never

71

been lowered, an upturned boat towards which the whaler was pulling strongly. To get the vessel's name and registry: to ignore the rest. Several corpses rolling over in their life-jackets, faces destroyed, blackened and bruised by the explosion, and by the sea birds if any other flesh remained. Splintered hatch-covers, a couple of life-buoys: it stretched in either direction. More human remains bobbed along the side, trailing their scarlet weed. Perhaps the ship had been carrying explosives too.

'Boat's calling us up, sir!' Onslow's face was like stone. The whaler's coxswain was standing in the stern-sheets using only his hands to semaphore across the water. How good *Serpent* must look to him at this moment, Brooke thought. 'She was the *Mary Livingstone*, registered in Sydney.'

Brooke felt for his pipe, but it was down in the hatch.

'Log it, Pilot.' *Why can I never get used to it?*

The whaler was right amongst the bigger fragments but was still clinging to the useless life-boat.

The hands were waving again and Onslow exclaimed, 'There's a woman and kid under the boat, sir.'

Their eyes met across the crowded bridge. Like a cry for help, or an unspoken bond.

A bridge messenger asked, 'Are they dead, Yeo?'

Onslow swung on him, his eyes blazing with fury.

'Of course they're fucking dead, you stupid little bugger!' The rage faded as quickly as it had arisen, and Onslow said, 'They want to know what to do, sir.'

Calvert stood very still, deeply aware of the importance of this moment. Two men looking at each other, held together by circumstances.

The captain said in the same level voice, 'Tell them to fetch them aboard, Yeo. It's the least we can do.'

Calvert said, 'That was a fine thing to do, sir.' He waited, half expecting Brooke to turn on him.

Brooke was watching the whaler returning slowly towards the ship, the oars rising and falling like tired wings.

'It's important to him, Pilot. They're not just victims. To him they're what he's lost.'

'*Clear lower deck! Up whaler!*'

Routine was taking over again.

When Calvert looked again the whaler was snug against the davits, the seamen going about their business.

Brooke said, 'Bring her back on course, Pilot, one-one-zero revolutions. Tell Number One we shall exercise damage-control before *Up spirits*.'

That night, with Lisbon somewhere far abeam, the destroyer *Serpent* stopped her engines once more.

In one canvas bundle the unknown woman and her child were buried at sea, as they had died, together.

The staff operations officer, roundly built and wearing an open-necked white shirt which was far too tight, was reaching up with a walking-stick to jab at one of the old-fashioned revolving fans. Except that it was not revolving.

In between pokes he gasped, 'Like a bloody oven in here when the generators pack up!'

Brooke sat without speaking, still tired from the final approach and entry into Gibraltar's broad anchorage. Every kind of ship, he thought, from cruisers to landing-craft, hospital ships to troopers, the latter with every inch of rigging spread with khaki washing.

He was always impressed by Gibraltar: the Rock. Towering and somehow reassuring, the fortress at the

73

Mediterranean's gateway. From one window he could see the sunshine glittering on ten thousand windows: Algeciras. No doubt eyes had watched *Serpent*'s arrival, Spanish and German. What Churchill would denounce as one-sided neutrality in a country from which the enemy could and did spy on their comings and goings. Brooke half-smiled. The Germans were hardly likely to be interested in one small survivor from the Kaiser's war. Their reports would focus more on the hospital ships and empty supply vessels, evidence, if any was still needed, of the closing stages of the campaign in Crete.

The staff operations officer, a commander in rank who had obviously been brought back from retirement, gave a satisfied grunt as the fan began to revolve again.

'The F.O.I.C. would normally want to see you, old chap, but you know how it is. Big flap on just now.'

Brooke felt his jacket sticking to the chair. *Isn't there always?*

'Fact is, orders have been changed. My secretary is fixing 'em right now. You're to go alongside an oiler without delay. I've arranged for you to have anything you need from the dockyard. Then you'll be off again. It's all in the orders.'

Brooke remained calm. 'Can I be told, sir? Or is that a secret too?'

The commander eyed him doubtfully. 'On to Simonstown and the Cape. You'll pick up the other ships there. Wish I was going with you!' He grinned and covertly glanced at his watch. 'How are things in England?'

Brooke thought that if he had said that the King had signed a surrender with the Germans, not a word of it would be heard.

'A bit bloody at times, sir.'

'Good, good, that's the ticket!'

Brooke sighed inwardly. 'I'll get things cracking, sir.'

The Ops officer looked relieved. 'One thing. You've another subbie joining you. Be there by now, I shouldn't wonder.'

'Oh? I haven't read anything about him.'

'No? An oversight, I expect.' He glared at a lieutenant in the doorway. 'Coming, James. Can't do every bloody thing.'

The lieutenant glanced at Brooke and winked.

Outside it was dusty and humid, and there were oil-slicked patches in the anchorage. Brooke shaded his eyes to stare at Spain. His leg and foot seemed to ache in response as if they, too, sensed where they were.

All those watching eyes, he thought again. Watching as they always had, even in Nelson's time when his ships entered and left this enclosed sea. Fast horsemen to carry the word. He grimaced. Now all it took was a phone call.

Kerr strode along the iron-deck and felt the heat through his shoes. The air rang with drills and hammers and the screech of saws, whilst above the dockyard the cranes and derricks dipped and rose like hungry monsters at a feast.

'I don't want any dockyard maties on board without my knowing,' he said sharply.

Fox, the chief boatswain's mate, stood with his cap tilted over his eyes and nodded. 'I know Gib, sir. If you don't screw everything down, it goes!'

Kerr looked around. Beneath the towering Rock and

75

hemmed in by every sort of vessel, he felt trapped. After the passage from Scapa this was a nightmare, and some of the sights were uncomfortable, demoralising, to say the least. The huge piles of cheaply made coffins on one landing-craft. The shell-damage and buckled plating which was evident everywhere. Where would they stop? When could they hold them back?

He thought of Brooke when he had ordered the whaler away to examine the wreckage. He had imagined him callous, even uncaring when he had brushed aside the idea of searching for the convoy straggler. Now he knew better, or hoped he did.

Fox coughed politely. 'Beg pardon, sir, but I think Sub-Lieutenant Barrington-Purvis is gettin' embarked on some bother.'

Kerr frowned and strode towards the gangway.

Barrington-Purvis stood, hands on hips, lower lip protruding like a spoiled boy's, and glared at the new-comer who was strolling up the brow.

He was dressed in khaki shirt and slacks like a soldier, with a white cap cover and a tarnished badge to prove that he was not. The cap cover was none too clean. Barrington-Purvis's angry stare settled on the officer's shoulder straps, even more tarnished: the single, wavy stripe of an R.N.V.R. sub-lieutenant. A thin figure, untidy and sloppy.

He snapped, 'Who the hell are you?'

The other man raised one foot and placed it very carefully on the ship's deck nameplate as he stepped on to the quarterdeck; then with equal care he touched his cap with his fingers.

He smiled. 'Sub-Lieutenant Kipling, no relation I'm afraid. Come aboard to join.'

Barrington-Purvis was almost beside himself. 'First I've heard of it!'

'Well, now.' Kipling regarded him with quiet amusement. 'What do you do around here, exactly?'

Barrington-Purvis flushed. This so-called officer had some kind of accent. He could not place it, but it sounded rather common.

He replied stiffly, 'Gunnery officer.'

Kerr stepped between them. 'I've just heard on the shore phone. You *are* expected.' He held out his hand. 'Dick Kerr, I'm the first lieutenant *around here*.'

With Kerr present Barrington-Purvis had recovered slightly. He asked haughtily, 'What's your line?'

The sub-lieutenant in the crumpled khaki looked along the narrow deck. 'Nice little ship.' He seemed to recall the question and gave that same gentle smile. 'Line?' He shrugged. 'I blow up things. People too sometimes.'

Kerr hid a grin. 'Come down with me. You'll have to share a cabin, I'm afraid.'

They paused beside the accommodation ladder and Kipling said, 'Not with *him*, I hope.'

The P.O. steward was waiting watchfully, and Kerr wondered what Kingsmill would make of the new member of the wardroom.

Kerr himself knew only a little about him. Kipling was from the navy's Special Force in the Eastern Med, one of the cloak-and-dagger crowd who fought the war their own way and without rules. The Glory Boys, motor gunboats and schooners, anything that could carry the war into enemy-occupied territory.

He studied Kipling's gaunt features. He could sense it even in the slight, untidy figure. *Danger.*

'This way . . .' He shook himself. What the hell would they need an officer like Kipling for, where they were going?

He felt something like an icy hand on his spine.

It was madness even to consider the possibilities, and he told himself not to be stupid. But when the captain returned on board the dread was still with him.

5

A Night to Remember

To most of the *Serpent*'s company the two weeks that followed their departure from Gibraltar seemed unreal, an unexpected reward for their endurance in the real war, which they had left astern. Some of the old sweats like the coxswain and the gunner (T) had served in the Gulf and even in the Far East, but for the most part the company was a young one, with a large percentage of junior rates who had been flung into the brutal realities of the Atlantic and the Mediterranean with little experience of the kinder face of war.

Southward along the coast of Africa with land only occasionally in sight, pausing at Freetown so that the Chief could top up his fuel bunkers before steering south-east towards the Cape of Good Hope.

At Freetown they had joined company with another destroyer named *Islip*. A much larger ship than *Serpent* and built in the late thirties, she was to be the senior escort of the troop convoy supposedly awaiting their arrival at Cape Town. In the meantime every day brought places, sights and experiences that made the younger sailors round-eyed with wonder. No screaming alarm bells in the middle of some freezing storm with wretched merchantmen burning and dying under torpedo attacks; no sense of helplessness and defeat when they saw the drifting remains of another slaughtered convoy, the corpses parting across the bows to offer their own sense of shame.

The *Islip*'s captain, Commander Ralph Tufnell, whom Brooke had met over drinks at Freetown, had been content to leave them to their own devices. A great bear of a man with a thick black beard, he had suggested, 'Give 'em a break. If they're like my lads they deserve it!'

A man you could work with, Brooke thought, one who would be easy to respect.

Tufnell had revealed something that had taken him completely by surprise.

'Be a bit strange for you, I suppose. Probably the last place you'd expect to be running into your own brother.'

Seeing Brooke's expression, he hastened to add, 'Sorry, old chap – I thought you knew. Pretty hush-hush these days.'

That was not the only thing he had learned from Tufnell. His brother Jeremy, two years his junior but already advanced to commander, was attached to the staff in Hong Kong with other responsibilities to the admiral at Singapore. A staff job: and yet he had never mentioned it, not even to their father. He wondered if Sarah had known, if she was with him. They must have left England immediately after the funeral.

It should not matter any more. Brooke turned as Kerr, accompanied by the new subbie, Paul Kipling, came on to the bridge and Barrington-Purvis handed over the watch.

The two sub-lieutenants made an odd pair, Brooke thought: Barrington-Purvis, the admiral's son, every inch the naval officer, and Kipling who looked anything but. The former still sported the remains of a black eye, which he had gained at a rousing Crossing the Line ceremony when *Serpent* had crossed the equator off the Gulf of Guinea. Pike, the coxswain, had been King Neptune, with Sister Twiss his lovely queen, and had put all the uninitiated hands through their paces. Foam beards and rough barbers had given everyone a rumbustious crossing, and it was only later that Barrington-Purvis's shiner had been revealed.

In all fairness to him he had not complained, although it had obviously been something very personal.

When Kerr had asked Kipling if he had ever crossed the line, he had admitted cheerfully that he had never been south of Ramsgate before he joined up.

It was difficult to know when Kipling was being serious, or even if he was capable of it. He seemed to have no secrets or guile, no 'side' as the Chief had described it.

He came from a large family in London. His father had been a regular soldier, a sapper in the Royal Engineers, and that he had remained until he had been reported missing, presumed killed, in France.

Kerr recalled with amusement Barrington-Purvis's expression of shocked horror when Kipling had remarked one night in the mess, 'All the Old Man ever did was knock out another kid when he came on leave!' It was obvious that he had found Barrington-Purvis's weaknesses and thoroughly enjoyed getting under the skin of his supercilious opposite number.

Kipling had found his way into the navy by a roundabout route – as he seemed to have done with almost everything. He had left school at fourteen and talked himself into a job in a busy garage on London's North Circular Road: he made a point of calling it a *garridge* just to make Barrington-Purvis wince. He must have learned his trade well, and when he joined the navy (*I didn't much care for the idea of square-bashing in the army*) someone had seen his possibilities and selected him for the torpedo branch, where his knowledge of engineering and wiring soon made themselves apparent. When volunteers had been desperately needed for the bomb-disposal and render-mines-safe section, Kipling had put down his name without even a blink.

He had been put to work with a lieutenant, a man he was reluctant to speak about and probably the only officer he had ever really trusted, Brooke thought, and together they had made safe a large collection of mines during the first devastating raids on London and the south coast.

One night on the middle watch he had stood beside Brooke's tall chair on the open bridge, his lean profile framed against a ceiling of a million stars. Kerr had been checking something or other, and they were alone.

'His luck ran out. I suppose we got a bit cocky, full of ourselves. It was just another mine.'

Brooke had been filling his pipe but had stopped to listen.

'He came to the door of this house where the mine was through the roof. He couldn't get through, but he could have run off an' saved himself.'

Brooke guessed he had gone over it many times. Like Calvert, like Onslow and some of the others.

'He yelled, "The bloody thing's live! Run for it!" I never even heard it explode. I was dug out three days later.'

'And he was killed?'

'Never even found a bloody button!' He flinched. 'Sorry, sir.'

'I can understand how you felt.'

'Feel, sir. Feel.'

Brooke had learned quite a lot that night while the ship had run south towards Sierra Leone. Kipling had been offered a temporary commission and in a few months had been crammed with the basic rudiments of navigation, gunnery and seamanship. He said in his matter-of-fact, detached manner, 'O.L.Q.s, officer-like qualities as they called them at *King Alfred* – well, I never did get the hang of them.'

He had served in the Levant and amongst the Greek islands, in armed launches and schooners, preying on the enemy's coastal convoys, which chose the sea rather than face the merciless attacks by partisans on land. Kipling and his companions had soon become an even greater danger.

In just days he had settled down on board, even in the wardroom. A balance, like now with Kerr. Chalk and cheese.

Kipling's orders stated that he was to remain in *Serpent* and perform normal watchkeeping and divisional duties until instructions came to the contrary. He had brought some of his 'toys' aboard with him, watched over anxiously by Barlow the gunner (T) until they had been safely stowed to his own satisfaction. Kipling had admitted, 'I don't know *why*, sir. If Hong Kong is attacked I might be ordered to blow up harbour installations.'

Brooke had not commented. It was possible but unlikely, according to those who knew best. The Japanese were busy fighting the Chinese Nationalists, as they had been for years. Their lines of communications were far too stretched to risk a war. And what would be the point? The C-in-C in the Far East would be better informed and better prepared than anyone.

Kerr said, 'The troopers we're to escort, sir. Do we know how many?'

'Not yet, Number One. Even *Islip*'s skipper's in the dark.'

83

A voice echoed up the wheelhouse voicepipe and Brooke saw Kipling lean over to acknowledge it. Old for his junior rank, but he had been a rating longer than most hopefuls. A thin, interesting face, lined before its time. Twenty-four years old; but he had seen more than most men experienced in a lifetime.

Kipling said, 'Able Seaman March on the wheel, sir.'

'Very good.' Strange how close he felt now to his little team.

Each was different from the other and the way each man behaved showed too the character of the individual, despite the order and discipline which controlled every aspect of their daily life.

Each watch, except the dog watches, lasted for four hours. No helmsman was supposed to spend more than two of those hours at his trick on the wheel. It was a strain on the man, especially on the great expanses of ocean: the same course and engine revolutions mile after mile soon dulled the mind. Brooke had noticed that Kerr never insisted that any helmsman did more than an hour at a time. He had learned that what was best for the watchkeepers was usually the best for the ship. Barrington-Purvis, who shared his watches with the gunner (T), was the very opposite. He went by the book. Two hours it said; two hours it would be, and God help the man who dozed off at the wheel.

Calvert was different again. Brooke had observed his obsession with pin-point accuracy, and the exactness of his navigation was remarkable.

Perhaps as a flier Calvert had become very aware of the need for perfection. A fraction of a degree out when he was flying back to his carrier and he might have missed her and flown on and on until his fuel had run out and there was no alternative but to ditch into the sea.

Kerr said, 'We shall be sighting land within the hour if the visibility holds, sir.' He smiled. 'Cape Town. No black-out, no rationing – I'll have the chef get some provisions brought on board. Fresh fruit, eh? Think of it!'

They both looked round as Kipling said thoughtfully, 'I wonder what would become of *us*, sir?' He waved vaguely towards where the land must lie. 'I – I mean, suppose England is invaded while we're out here somewhere?'

Kerr tried to laugh it off but Brooke took it seriously. 'If we're beaten, you mean? Surrender?'

Kipling thrust his hands into his pockets. 'It's happened everywhere else, sir. Holland, France, Norway and the poor old Danes – now the Greeks and the Yugoslavs. Nobody seems able to stop 'em.'

Brooke climbed into his chair. 'Then we'll have to make sure we *don't* surrender. Right?'

Kipling seemed satisfied. 'I mean, sir, I wouldn't care to end my life in a bamboo hut an' eating nothing but rice.'

Kerr grinned and clapped him on the arm. 'You'd miss the old fish and chips, is that it?'

Onslow the yeoman said, 'I'd settle for a plate of jellied eels right now, sir.'

They all laughed. So even Onslow was being drawn out of the grief and despair that had burst out of him when they found the dead woman and child in the sea.

Brooke tilted his cap over his eyes and separated himself from the men around him.

All in all, he could have asked for no better company. He smiled and touched the protective steel plate beside him. And no better ship.

That afternoon with the sun changing Table Mountain to the colour of pink salmon, *Serpent* glided to her

85

anchorage. The men off watch and not required for immediate duty lined the guard-rails and stared at the great slab of mountain, which was breath-taking to even the most unimaginative. They were away from the Western Ocean and the fought-over Mediterranean, and even the news from those theatres of war seemed remote and of no immediate concern.

Brooke leaned out and looked down at the deck. Skins showing signs of tanning, or in some cases angry-looking burns. Sun and speed together had no respect for the unwary.

He studied some big ships at the far end of the anchorage. One had been a cruise-liner, the other a cargo and passenger vessel probably on the Australia and New Zealand run. Troopers. *Our* troopers now, he thought.

He watched their companion, the destroyer *Islip*, frothing round in a wide arc before going astern and dropping her own anchor. The gin pennant would soon be hoisted, and old friends would meet. A part of the family where the war could be held at bay, if only temporarily.

Onslow lowered his glasses. 'From *Islip*, sir. *R.P.C. at twenty-hundred hours!*'

'Reply, Yeoman. *Our pleasure.*'

There was much to do before Brooke and his officers could go across to *Islip* for the party. Refuelling to be arranged, the Operations people to be seen, leave to be sorted out for as many as possible, the latest instructions to be studied. But just for a moment longer he wanted to be here alone, his eyes drinking in the majesty of the land. The telegraphs were rung off, and down in his hole the Chief would greet the *Finished with engines* with well-earned satisfaction. The wheelhouse would be empty for the first time in weeks, and an awning

86

spread to create a peacetime atmosphere and cover the depth-charges and torpedo tubes.

For a long while Brooke stood there and realized that he could not recall feeling such a sense of peace. He had not known that he had needed it so much.

Ship and captain were at rest.

The holiday atmosphere and a sense of escape for *Serpent*'s ship's company continued for the whole of her stay in Cape Town. The hospitality shown by the local community, most of whom had British connections, had its effect even on the hardest men. *Islip*'s Commander Tufnell said it was even better than the welcomes he had experienced on some of his longer-routed convoys beyond Good Hope.

Surprisingly, even the news from home could not dampen the general good spirits. The continuing bombing of towns and harbours and the mounting savagery in the Atlantic seemed to fade into the distance, and lose relevance in the African sun.

Two more destroyers arrived to complete the troopships' escort, and with them came sailing orders. One last night in Cape Town, then back to the boredom of convoy. Even at high speed it would be hard to take after this.

Calvert went to the captain's day-cabin and found Brooke going through a clip of signals.

He glanced up. 'Drink, Pilot?'

Calvert sat down. 'Juice of some sort, sir.'

Brooke pressed a bell. 'Coming ashore tonight? I see you've volunteered for O.O.D. in Number One's place.'

A white-jacketed messman glided in with a glass of orange juice and left again. Calvert's refusal to take alcohol must have made an impression, Brooke thought.

87

Calvert said, 'I'll have a quiet night instead, sir. I'm not much of a one for parties.' His voice implied that it was because of the past.

'What is it? You won't drink, or you can't?'

Calvert shrugged and rubbed his chin. 'Not sure. Afraid to find out maybe.' He was amazed he could speak so easily about it. Had it been anyone else . . .

Brooke pushed the signals across. 'You'd better have these in case W/T hear of a flap while I'm away.' He smiled. 'Not that we'll be involved.'

He watched Calvert's eyes scanning the flimsies, then slowing down as he exclaimed, 'A German raider? Converted merchantman, they say?'

'They *say*. Reported in the Indian Ocean – fired on a Dutch freighter but her skipper slipped away in the dark. Probably after supplies, otherwise . . .'

'Living off what they can catch.' Calvert guessed that the raider would not last very long. There were too many warships operating from Ceylon for that, some cruisers among them.

Kerr peered in the door. 'Boat alongside, sir.' He touched Calvert's arm. 'Thanks for standing in, Pilot. I'll do the same for you sometime.'

Brooke glanced between them. No longer strangers, if not yet friends.

Calvert wandered to the wardroom and slumped down in a chair close to one of the new deckhead fans with a newspaper. He felt the ship moving very slightly, the occasional thud of feet as the quartermaster prowled around the quarterdeck like a terrier. The news was predictable. A strategic withdrawal somewhere in North Africa: it was never a retreat. Fierce fighting in Crete. A fleet minesweeper lost; she had exploded one of the mines she had been seeking. *Next of kin have been informed*. A typical Fougasse cartoon showing a sailor sitting at a table shooting his mouth off to his girl, while beneath the table Field Marshal Hermann Goering crouched with one ear cupped in his hand. *Careless talk costs lives* was the caption.

He sighed and glanced at the little bar by the pantry hatch. On it was the usual leather cup containing the liar dice for would-be gamblers, as well as mess chits and a half-empty soda siphon.

He thought of going to his cabin. He was fortunate to have one all to himself, but only because the space for a second bunk was filled with a chart cabinet. One of the perks. At least the nightmares were less frequent. No less horrific when they burst into his mind; but he felt certain he was improving. He knew he could never forget, and he realized he did not wish to.

On the navigation course he had been shaken awake by other officers one night when he had been in the grip of reliving it. It was almost a relief that in the navy you never got any sympathy. *Why don't you shut up? Remember the poor bloody watchkeepers for a change!*

If we weren't like that we'd all be round the bend by now, he thought. His head lolled against the chair and he was asleep.

How long he slept in the chair he had no way of knowing.

He awoke with a terrible jerk, to the realization that the nearest scuttle was shining like bronze as if a ship were ablaze, and he also became aware that someone had been shaking his arm.

He said hoarsely, 'Sorry, P.O. Time for Rounds, right?' He should have remembered. The dusk at Cape Town had been preceded by this burnished light each night they had been there.

He stared at the man standing over him. It was not the duty P.O. but Evans, the leading telegraphist.

'Sorry, sir. It's immediate, from Admiralty.'

Calvert's mind cleared. 'German raider? Not round here, I'll bet.' He took the signal and did not see the young sailor's bewildered expression.

His eyes skimmed over the neat pencilled printing and came to rest at the bottom. The words seemed to leap up at him. *H.M.S. HOOD SUNK BY GERMAN BATTLESHIP BISMARCK IN NORTH ATLANTIC. THREE SURVIVORS.*

There was more, but the words seemed to mingle and fade without meaning. When he looked up he saw the young leading signalman wiping his eyes roughly with the back of his hand.

'I saw her once, sir. At the Spithead Review. Knew then I wanted to join the Andrew.' He looked away. 'Sorry, sir.'

Calvert shook his head. 'Don't be. I think every man and woman in Britain has lost something in that ship.'

Three survivors? It did not seem possible. *Hood* had a ship's company of some fourteen hundred officers and men. All gone, just like that? He thought of the girl on the train with her naval brooch and new wedding ring. Three survivors . . .

Calvert pressed the bell and Petty Officer Kingsmill appeared as if by magic. He glanced with disdain at the leading signalman as if he had blundered by mistake into some exclusive club.

'Sir?'

'Give Evans a drink. Have one yourself.'

Kingsmill stared at him as if he could not believe it, but he did what he was told. Calvert saw that the young telegraphist took a glass of port.

Kingsmill watched with interest as Calvert poured himself a large gin. Then he faced them and said quietly, '*Hood*'s gone, P.O. Just heard.'

Kingsmill fiddled with some coasters on the bar as if he did not know what to do.

Then he said, 'God bless the old girl.'

Calvert said, 'I'll call the captain. He left a number. He'll want to know.' But the wardroom was empty. It might have been part of a nightmare but for the empty glasses.

He poured himself another drink and swallowed it, feeling the fire of the gin but tasting nothing.

It took a long time to get through to the number Brooke had left: the home of a wealthy merchant who wanted to give *Serpent*'s officers a night to remember.

On the telephone Brooke sounded very near, and in his mind Calvert could see the tawny eyes as he said quite gently, 'I know, Pilot. It just came through. Three survivors confirmed, two ratings and a midshipman . . . Are you still there?'

Calvert answered, 'Yes, sir.' So the girl was without hope. 'I was – I was thinking of how it must have been.'

Brooke glanced at his officers and the other guests. Even two of the black servants seemed stunned by the news.

Calvert had been drinking; perhaps he had pictured his own ship blowing up and capsizing in those bitter waters. The chief-of-staff's worst fears had been proved right. But at what cost? The world's two greatest warships had met and the mighty *Bismarck* had broken the line. She was probably heading out into the Atlantic convoy lanes right now. There was not a ship to stand against her. A fleet, yes, but nothing less could do it.

He heard Calvert say, 'It's all right, sir. I've got the weight. No need for you to come off shore, sir. Not yet.'

Brooke replied, 'I never doubted it, Pilot. I'll leave

when I can.' He put down the telephone. It was like losing an emblem and a dear friend all in one.

I hope they catch the bastards!

It was surprising, he thought, that after seeing so much killing and destruction he could still harbour so much hatred.

Islip's captain greeted him with a full glass. 'The whole world will know tomorrow. God, what a mess.'

Brooke heard Kerr's voice, terse and angry. 'Watch it, Sub!'

He turned and saw Sub-Lieutenant Kipling, his feet apart as if the floor was moving, his dark hair falling over his forehead while he waved an empty glass.

'What – do the right, *decent* thing, Number One? Behave as if it doesn't matter? 'Cause it damn well does!'

Barrington-Purvis snapped, 'Oh, for *heaven's* sake, man!'

Kipling tried to focus his eyes. 'Why must you always be such *honourable* chaps? Play by the rules, chant *They shall grow not old* once a year on Armistice Day, and everything will be just OK, is that it?'

He saw Brooke and lowered his head. 'I'm sorry, sir. I'm not often like this.' He looked up again and Brooke was shocked to see the despair on his face. 'But unless we learn to fight like them, we'll never win this war in ten thousand bloody years!'

Podger Barlow took his arm and said gruffly, 'Come outside with me. Bit of fresh air, eh?'

Conversation was slowly returning, and their host was urging his servants to replenish all the glasses.

Commander Tufnell said quietly, 'Trouble is, old chap, your strange subbie is bloody well right.'

Afterwards Brooke thought it had sounded like an epitaph.

The next day the destroyers took station on the two big troopships, the decks of which were crammed with cheering, waving khaki figures.

As *Serpent*'s company fell out from harbour stations and glanced astern at the magnificent bulk of Table Mountain, the mood was very different. Many had their hearts and minds in another ocean, where a great ship and a legend had died.

6

Another World

Lieutenant-Commander Esmond Brooke leaned back from his cabin and finished a second cup of coffee, which Kingsmill had brought to him. It was strange to be sitting here while the sea's bright horizon showed itself as it climbed up one glass scuttle before dipping down again to *Serpent*'s steady roll, and he blamed his uncertainty on the fact that it was the first time he had left the bridge at sea since they had sailed from Scapa Flow.

Now that the long journey was almost over he knew he should feel a sense of achievement. Since leaving the Flow this little ship had steamed almost ten thousand miles, and as the distance had mounted astern he had often thought of Sub-Lieutenant Kipling's unanswered question. What would happen if Britain surrendered while the ship was on the other side of the world?

He looked around the cabin and thought of his hutch, where he had spent most of his time when not actually on the upper bridge, and could not shake off a feeling of unreality which was almost guilt. The knowledge that they were in safe waters could not cure him of the habits and the wariness of one who had lived on the edge of danger for too many months.

Here there were no long-range bombers to seek them

out, no U-boats to strike without warning. Even the alleged commerce raiders had come to nothing. It would be an unforgettable experience for his ship's company, especially the younger hands. After leaving Cape Town they had headed away across the great shimmering desert of the Indian Ocean, north-west to Trincomalee. More strange sights, souvenirs and some tattoos which a few of them would soon regret.

Three days after the terrible news of *Hood*'s total destruction came another signal about her mighty enemy *Bismarck*. She, too, had been sunk after a fierce battle with heavy units of the Home Fleet. It had been a near thing all the same. *Bismarck* had been sighted and attacked by a Swordfish torpedo bomber which had somehow managed to weave through the formidable flak and achieve one hit. It had damaged the battleship's steering and slowed her down. Not much, but enough. It should have pleased Calvert, he thought.

There had been few cheers from the messdecks. *Hood*'s loss seemed to outweigh what was seen by many as a one-sided victory. And while *Serpent* steamed her way into warmer climates, the far-off war thundered on. Crete, which had no hope of holding out against massive airborne and parachute attacks, had surrendered. More ships were lost, many troops were taken prisoner. It became harder to put aside, let alone forget, as the sailors wandered ashore to stare at the sights. In the Atlantic and in the Western Approaches at least there had always been mail, letters from home to draw families and lovers together. It would be a long time now before any mail caught up with *Serpent*, an unfamiliar experience except to the old sweats.

Penang, and into the Strait of Malacca, which separated Malaya from Sumatra; and then into Singapore. *Operation Boomerang*, as some genius at the Admiralty had christened it, was almost over, for *Serpent* in any case. There the newly trained troops would be landed and the more experienced men taken off and transported to theatres of war where they were desperately needed. The smaller of the two troopships, a cargo-liner named *Orinoco*, would continue to Hong Kong with only *Islip* and *Serpent* in company.

Into the South China Sea, a place of fantasy and willow-pattern enchantment. Islands that rose straight out of the sea like sharply-pointed mountains, others that lay wreathed in seemingly permanent low cloud. The flotilla-leader *Islip* stayed in the lead. She was lucky enough to be fitted with the new secret all-seeing eye, radar; it would be no picnic to get lost or fogged in amongst the endless scattered islands. The constant movement of local shipping, which ranged from bat-like junks under sail to old tramp-steamers straight out of *Boys' Own Paper*, was another hazard.

Piracy, smuggling, opium dens; it was easy to imagine all of it.

Kerr tapped at the door and stepped over the coaming.

'You wanted me, sir?'

He had performed well and had kept everybody from wardroom to stokers' mess busy with an equal serving of drills and competitive games so that there was little time to brood over what was happening at home. If he resented being passed over for advanced promotion he had not shown it.

'*Orinoco* will be met by tugs and a pilot, Number One. She will berth at the docks on the Kowloon side. They've had a good passage this time.'

Kerr crossed to a scuttle and watched yet another spiky island passing abeam, its summit thinly covered by little trees like wispy hair.

'Then what, sir?'

Brooke pushed his hands up behind his head. 'We shall be under the direct command of S.N.O. Patrols. According to my lists, none too up-to-date I'm afraid, the F.O.I.C. has plenty of ships and submarines at his disposal. He probably won't know what to do with us and will send us back with the "boomerang"!'

'What about the Japanese, sir?'

'We are not to become involved – that's what it says in my orders. They are fighting the Chinese Nationalists. It has nothing to do with us.'

Kerr gave a wry smile. 'Officially, anyway.'

Brooke thought of the Spanish Civil War. They had not become involved in that either, officially. If they had, Hitler might have had second thoughts about invading Czechoslovakia and Poland. An ineffectual government, complacency and weakness had given Hitler all the encouragement he had needed.

Kerr said, 'I think our lads did very well, sir. Even the Chief was pleased.'

Brooke reached for his pipe. 'So did you, Number One. I'll see what I can do about getting you on the road to promotion.'

Kerr said, to his surprise, 'I'm all right, sir. But thanks.'

'By the way, my brother's out here somewhere. He might know what's going on.'

But Kerr was looking at the ship's picture in the silver frame, and his eyes were lost in thought.

'I'd be sorry to leave her,' he said.

The telephone buzzed noisily and Brooke picked it up. 'Captain.'

It was Calvert. 'Bridge, sir. Signal from *Islip*, increase speed to twenty knots.' Then, almost as an afterthought, 'Lamma Island abeam to port, five cables, sir.'

'I'll come up.' He turned to Kerr. 'Commander Tufnell wants to enter harbour well before dusk. I don't blame him.' He picked up his cap, somehow alien with its white cover. 'Time to alter course in an hour.' He smiled but Kerr sensed that his heart was not in it. 'We'll be alongside for tea, or is it tiffin out here?'

He thought suddenly of England. Mid-summer now, but the beaches would be thick with barbed wire and concrete pillboxes instead of families and their kids. A nation under siege, holding its breath. Grim reminders posted everywhere as if people needed any. *If the invader comes! Take one with you!*

Kerr said suddenly, 'When this lot's over, will you stay in?'

Brooke felt his face relax into a smile. He clapped Kerr on the arm and answered, 'Ask me again, Number One, when we've won the bloody thing!'

Brooke lowered his eyes to the gyro-compass repeater and felt them sting in the strong reflected glare.

'Starboard ten. Midships. Steady.' He waited for the ticking compass to settle. 'Steer zero-five-zero.' He straightened his back and watched the narrow channel opening up on either bow to display the great span of Hong Kong harbour. It was both breathtaking and awesome: Brooke had never seen so much or so varied a mass of shipping in his life. *Islip*, which had reduced speed and was leading by about a cable, appeared to be completely hemmed in by every kind of vessel, some thrusting from side to side between Hong Kong Island and Kowloon on the mainland, others moored and surrounded by lighters loading and unloading cargoes without pause. How *Islip* was managing to avoid a collision was amazing. It looked bad enough from here on the upper bridge; how much worse it would appear to Pike and his men in the wheelhouse.

Brooke raised his glasses for what felt like the thousandth time and studied the island as it loomed over the starboard bow: Victoria Peak, which like Gibraltar appeared to swamp the huddled houses and streets along the waterfront. There were some big houses on the Peak, rich Chinese and senior officers. What a view they must have.

Calvert said quietly, 'Now, sir.'

Brooke called, 'Starboard ten.'

Pike's response was instant. 'Ten of starboard wheel on, sir.'

'Midships. Steady.' Brooke dashed the sweat from his eyes. He could not recall such a lapse of attention ever happening before, no matter what hell had been breaking out around him. But for Calvert's eagle eye they might have carved through a wallowing cluster of sampans.

'Steady on zero-nine-three, sir.'

'Steer zero-nine-zero!'

He said to Calvert, 'What a marvellous place!'

Calvert smiled. 'Only wish I could paint.'

It was late afternoon and everything seemed to glow like gold. The churned and busy waters showed no foam or white spray as the traffic surged, intertwining their wakes. The harbour, like the sky, was pure gold.

'Hands fall in for entering harbour! Stand by wires an' fenders!'

Brooke said, 'We're going alongside *Islip*, starboard side-to, so we don't want to scratch the paint, eh?'

The bustling ferries were the worst. If they had some right-of-way procedure they did not openly show it. Crammed with people who barely glanced at the two warships, the little boats seemed to miss each other only by luck and inches.

They were coming up to the narrows where the distance between Hong Kong Island and Kowloon was about eight hundred yards. The naval base lay just beyond the criss-crossing ferries.

'Dead slow both engines.' Brooke watched *Islip*'s masts angling round as she altered course towards the base. Her forecastle and quarterdeck parties looked very smart in their white tops and shorts, but then *Islip* had been long enough on the South Africa run to be properly kitted out for the occasion. *Serpent*'s men might look all right from a distance, but they were still wearing their working bell-bottom trousers and dark blue caps, and their white tops already showed the marks of the greasy mooring wires that lay by the guard-rails in big shining coils.

'Cruiser on port bow, sir!'

Brooke studied the other ship thoughtfully. Immaculately painted, with awnings so tightly spread that they looked as if they could stand the weight of a loaded whaler. She was the light cruiser *Dumbarton*, built for the same war as *Serpent* but left so much further behind by her newer and more powerful consorts.

'There goes the *Orinoco*, sir!'

Brooke watched the troopship standing away, already in the hands of two capable-looking tugs and watched over by one of the pilot boats with its red and white flag. There were nurses on board, and they had exchanged waves many times with the sailors during the passage here.

Brooke said, '*Dumbarton* is our new boss, Pilot.' He shifted his glasses to the light cruiser's deck where a Royal Marine bugler was raising his instrument in readiness.

'Attention on the upper deck! Face to port and salute!'

Brooke stood beside Calvert and saluted while his ship sounded the *still* with boatswains' calls, and the flagship responded with a lordly acknowledgement.

'*Carry on!*'

Brooke returned his attention to the small naval base, but not before he had seen the listless broad pennant of a Commodore Second Class. He knew nothing of the senior officer, except that, like his flagship, he had been on the China Station for six years.

Calvert whispered, 'What's *that*, for heaven's sake?'

Brooke grinned. 'H.M.S. *Tamar*, Pilot, known locally, I am given to understand, as "The Ark".'

It was certainly what she looked like. She had come originally to Hong Kong as a troopship for the Cape and China. With a wooden hull and square-rigged sails she must have resembled one of Nelson's ships, but now, mastless, with extra structures on deck and covered by awnings, she did indeed deserve her nickname.

'*Islip*'s alongside, sir!'

Onslow missed nothing; he had seen the Jack break out on the big destroyer's stem.

'Starboard fifteen – midships – steady as you go.' Brooke peered at the other ship's bridge while *Serpent* moved slowly towards her. 'Port ten – slow astern port!'

He felt the gentle vibration and could picture the surge of foam from the screw even though his eyes were fixed on the narrowing gap, and the men hurrying along *Islip*'s iron-deck with big rope fenders.

Wires scraped over the forecastle deck and he saw the sacklike shape of Leading Seaman Doggett already poised with a heaving-line. Aft it would be the same, waiting for the first contact, the execution of which

101

was the tell-tale mark of a good destroyer captain. Or otherwise.

Brooke leaned over the side. *Too fast. Too fast.*

'Stop port. Increase to fifteen.'

The arrowhead of choppy water was contained and he found time to notice the garbage and filth penned between them.

He saw the heaving-line fly over the other ship's forecastle to be seized and manhandled through a fair-lead with *Serpent*'s wire already bent on.

'Already fast forrard, sir!'

A rating at a telephone called, 'All fast aft, sir!'

'Stop engines, wheel amidships!'

He peered at the darkening strip of water. *Going, going, gone.* There was a muffled cheer from the other ship and some wag called, 'Give a hand to the poor relations!'

Calvert murmured, 'I couldn't do that in a hundred years.'

Brooke let the tension flow out of him. 'But you will, Pilot. I'll see to that!' He had almost said, *And I couldn't fly a Stringbag.*

'All secure, sir!'

'Ring off main engines.'

Brooke glanced along his command, from the clean new Jack in the bows to an equally fresh ensign right aft. He could feel the heat and dusty humidity closing over him. Without the breeze over the moving ship it made him very aware of all the miles they had steamed.

Kerr clattered on to the bridge, his tanned face unusually relaxed.

'Fall out, sir?'

'Yes, please. No leave until I know what's happening.'

Kerr glanced at the land, the press of small houses

102

and the larger, more important ones further inland. 'Different world, sir.' He hesitated. 'I – I thought there'd be more of our ships on this station. I have a friend out here in submarines, a classmate of mine. I wonder if I'll see him?'

He turned as Onslow triggered his lamp busily.

'From *Dumbarton*, sir. *Captain repair on board*.'

Brooke said, 'That was fast.' He had been thinking pleasantly of a warm bath, and a tall glass of something. 'Acknowledge, Yeo.' He waited as the lamp clattered away, then asked, '*Islip* too?'

Onslow watched critically as one of his youthful bunting-tossers folded up the worn, sea-going ensign. 'No, sir. Only you.'

Brooke glanced at their faces. 'Probably just wants to know if we're winning!'

Kerr was getting to know him, well enough to see through the casual comment and sense the sudden resentment underneath.

Brooke looked around at the bridge party, who were waiting to be dismissed.

'Well done, lads.'

The coxswain had just reached the top of the ladder, searching for the first lieutenant as usual. But he remained on the ladder, not wanting to interrupt. It was like seeing and hearing the skipper's father. As if he'd come back.

Some of the others pulled his leg about it in the mess, but he didn't care. He was loyal enough, but not so loyal that he could not recognize a man's honesty or otherwise. He had watched too many defaulters and requestmen over Jimmy the One's little table to be fooled any more.

Pike thought of the last captain. Greenwood had smiled, but not with his mind or his heart.

He grimaced. Old Greenwood wouldn't recognize honesty if it came up the gangway nailed to a cross!

He watched the captain descend the opposite ladder and raised his clipboard. 'First Lieutenant, *sir!*'

While *Serpent*'s 'skimming-dish' tore across the water towards the light cruiser, Brooke remained standing in the cockpit and gripped the canopy with both hands.

Captain repair on board was a signal open to interpretation. It usually allowed for a commanding officer to change into a clean shirt at the very least, and sometimes the appointment if less pressing could be arranged by hand-lamp or telephone.

This curt brusqueness had irritated him, and he was angry with himself for having allowed it. Perhaps Hong Kong, like other farflung outposts of the Empire, had retained the old ideals of instant, unquestioning obedience. He thought of the Western Ocean and felt a smile on his lips. You were lucky to *own* a clean shirt out there in the Atlantic.

He studied the *Dumbarton* with professional interest. A *Danaë* class cruiser, one of several similar types, she had been born in the same period as *Serpent*. There, any similarity ended. Too late for any useful duty in the Great War, her class of ship had found few roles in the thirties other than showing the flag, and acting as miniature flagships for destroyers and other small groups.

Most of the survivors had already been converted into anti-aircraft cruisers, useful for convoy work or covering military operations where no carriers were available, which to date had been most of them. What his father had scornfully described as *the usual horse and stable door strategy.*

She was certainly in immaculate condition. Gleaming, glossy paint, booms rigged for her boats and one for a green launch which he guessed belonged to the commodore. Commodore Second Class was usually an uncomfortable appointment, a temporary promotion for a senior captain which could quite easily end and send the person concerned out of the service and into oblivion. Some were lucky. Commodore Harwood, who had been in command of the American and West Indian squadron at the outbreak of war, had probably seen no further than that. The war had been only three months old when his tiny force had met up with the *Graf Spee* in the South Atlantic in what was now known as the Battle of the River Plate. Like terriers, his ships had harried the pocket-battleship until in desperation her captain had run into harbour and scuttled his ship. Harwood's position and future had been assured.

Brooke turned and glanced along the motor-boat's frothing wake. It got dark early here. Already the Peak and the town were covered with a million lights, while overhead some early stars seemed close enough to touch.

He looked again at the *Dumbarton*. He had once done a cruise in a sister-ship when he had been a cadet. It would be interesting to see how this one had become accustomed to the war.

Macaskie, the boat's coxswain, swung the lively hull towards the cruiser's gangway, where Brooke could see a white-clad side party waiting for him. In his shabby sea-going uniform he felt somehow unclean.

The bowman hooked on and Brooke reached out for the ladder. As his head rose above the side, calls shrilled and he felt vaguely startled. He was not yet used to being piped aboard.

Quick impressions flashed through his mind. The

marine bugler was as before, but he noticed that he was standing on a small rope mat, presumably so that his boots would not mark or damage the gleaming, beautifully laid deck. Every plank and seam was perfect, a shipbuilder's pride even in that other war. Brooke saw one of the ship's main armaments, which he knew consisted of six six-inch guns, mounted separately along the centre line. Breech-loaded by hand and unprotected but for their shields, they were very like the ones he had first been trained on at Dartmouth.

An officer with the shoulder straps of a commander stepped forward and returned his salute.

'Brooke? I'm Larkin. We've been expecting you.' It sounded like *we've been waiting for you*.

Brooke glanced across the surging water and saw his own ship, small against the *Islip*, her hull surprisingly vulnerable with brightly lit scuttles and other lighting around her quarterdeck. After her, *Dumbarton* seemed vast. Down an accommodation ladder, through a passageway with such smooth paintwork that he could see their reflections as Commander Larkin led the way to the aftermost cabin, with a Royal Marine standing stiffly outside. There was a quick conversation, and then Larkin said, 'Please come in.'

More impressions. The big day cabin: it must have been forty feet across. Good furniture, chintz curtains across each polished scuttle, and, surprisingly, a portrait of the late King, George V. Brooke could feel no movement even in this busy harbour, and shipboard noises like the occasional pipe on the tannoy seemed far away, part of something else.

'Ah, *here* you are, Brooke!'

Commodore Cedric Stallybrass M.B.E. strode into the cabin from an adjoining one.

Tall, heavily built; Brooke guessed he was well overweight but his perfectly fitting white drill uniform disguised it. He had very little hair, and what remained was ginger-coloured and cut short around his head and ears like a victor's laurels. He had the sort of skin which defied even the hottest sun, and his face, like his bald pate, was lobster-coloured, unmarked by any sort of burn.

'Saw you come in, Brooke. Take a seat. I know you've a lot to do, must have. I've not forgotten what it was like.'

A steward appeared and produced some fine malt whisky. Stallybrass beamed at him, and it changed his face yet again. His eyes seemed to vanish into a crisscross of wrinkles, like buttons in a leather chair-back.

'Good to have you under my command.'

Brooke realized that the commander had left.

Stallybrass was saying, 'Smart little ships. Knew how to build 'em then, what? But as I always say it's not the age, it's the *standards* that count. Out here people watch everything like fortune-tellers, merchants of gloom. So standards count all the more with the war and everything.'

Brooke saw a white arm shoot out to refill his glass. Was the commodore testing his ability to hold his drink, or was it always like this *out here*?

Stallybrass became serious. 'Entering harbour, for instance. I like . . .' a quick grin again. 'No, I *insist* that all my ships' companies are properly turned out, entering and leaving harbour, on the streets, everywhere.'

Brooke answered evenly, 'My people have had no time, sir. We came directly from Scapa Flow. Before that . . .'

He held up an admonitory finger. 'I know all that. In war we occasionally relax the normal rules of discipline and behaviour. But not out here. The Royal Navy commands respect. It has to, if only to show the world what we stand for. I've made arrangements with the senior supply officer. Your people can be fitted out tomorrow. One thing about this place, eh – no shortage of native tailors.'

He made it sound like the African bush, Brooke thought.

'Now, any questions, old chap.' He was the genial host again.

Brooke asked, 'My first lieutenant was asking about the Fourth Submarine Flotilla. He has a friend in one of the boats.'

'Has he?' He leaned heavily over some papers on a small table. 'Lieutenant Kerr, yes?'

'Good officer.'

'If you say so.' He sounded off-balance. 'The flotilla left a long time ago. Depot ship too. We used to have some damned fine parties aboard her when the last captain (S) was here.' He seemed to recall the question. 'They all went to the Mediterranean. Done sterling service to all accounts. Quite a few of them gone west, I'm afraid.' He added gravely, 'Tragic, really.'

A bugle blared out overhead and Brooke imagined the marine standing on his little rope mat.

Stallybrass said, 'Most of the bigger ships have moved to Singapore, of course. Better facilities. Entire regrouping. But we have the West River and Yangtze flotillas here, and some other useful vessels.'

Brooke looked at his empty glass. It had to be that, or else he had misheard. The *Tamar* base had once been the most powerful on the China Station. Now the commodore was talking about the old river patrols, flat-bottomed gunboats which had maintained law and order in the sheltered waters of the mainland and had been used to protect British merchant shipping and trade settlements. In the face of Japanese military ambitions their continued presence was almost insane.

'I see doubt in your eyes, old chap!' Stallybrass chuckled throatily. 'No need for it. We old China hands are not just pretty faces, you know. We are prepared, ready for anything.' The smile faded. 'That is why I stress the value of *standards*!'

'I shall bear it in mind.' Brooke thought he had gone too far but Stallybrass seemed well pleased with his assurance.

The commodore said in an almost matter-of-fact tone, 'I had the pleasure of meeting your brother recently. Doing very well. He'll make captain before too long, I shouldn't wonder. He'll be in touch with you himself, I expect.' He sounded less sure of himself. 'Yes, should do well.'

Uncertainty, jealousy too perhaps. The arrival of one of the Admiralty's up-and-coming staff officers might be seen as a threat to his own little kingdom.

There was a tap at the door even as Stallybrass glanced at his watch. An arranged signal perhaps?

A lieutenant, his face so tanned against his white uniform that he looked like a *native*, said, 'The Governor's launch will be arriving in fifteen minutes, sir.' He avoided any eye contact with Brooke.

'Very well.' As the door closed silently Stallybrass winked. 'Good officer. Squash and tennis – he's unbeatable!'

It was time to go. He saw the steward getting ready to fetch his cap. Leaving the headmaster's study after a stern word of advice.

Stallybrass beamed at him. 'You'll be getting your patrol orders in a day or so, but no rush. Just get your people acclimatised, eh?'

'Yes, sir. Standards.'

'That's the idea, old chap!'

On deck it seemed almost cool, and he stood by the quarterdeck rail and watched the sprawling, twinkling panorama of lights. Occasionally a black shadow would blot out some of them as a pilot boat or tall junk went about its business.

The commander reappeared, and the side party was assembled as *Serpent*'s motor-boat splashed round from the boom leaving a trail of phosphorescence in her wake.

Commander Larkin suggested quietly, 'A little different from *your* war, I suppose.'

Brooke tightened his jaw. The empty life-boats and blazing merchantmen. People dying, others not wanting to live after what they had suffered. Onslow, Calvert and all the rest. He tested his leg so as not to limp, and answered tersely, 'Another world, sir.'

'You'll soon settle in. Get to like the place – you'll see.'

Down the ladder and into the boat. Perhaps he was imagining it. So much folly, so many failures: it had left him bitter and without trust.

Kerr was waiting for him on the quarterdeck and listened without comment to the information about the clothing issue.

'I asked about the submarine flotilla, Number One . . .'

'Thank you.' He shrugged. 'But I just found out. My friend's boat was sunk in the Med a few months ago.'

Brooke watched his shadowed face. 'Drink, Number One? Not a very decent malt, I'm afraid.'

Kerr did not understand the allusion, but said, 'Yes – thanks, sir. I'd like that.'

Kingsmill had thoughtfully provided a decanter of Scotch and two glasses.

'Make a bloody fine butler,' Brooke said wearily. He filled the glasses and realized he had not eaten since noon.

'Rough, was it, sir?'

'An insight, more than anything else.' He pushed the mood aside. 'The others all right?'

Kerr thought of the wardroom as he had left it. The Chief and the gunner (T) engrossed in a quiet game of crib, Barrington-Purvis and Kipling exchanging insults, while Calvert appeared to be studying a local guidebook although Kerr had noticed that his eyes had hardly moved.

'Normal, sir.'

Brooke smiled. 'I shall be meeting my brother shortly. I might find out what's going on.'

'What's he like, sir?'

Brooke stared at him. It was a shock to discover that he himself did not really know.

'Good question.' They clinked their glasses together. 'To standards, Number One!'

Kerr nodded. The skipper was getting pissed. He hadn't any idea what he was talking about.

'The higher the better, sir!'

Across the water, the Royal Marine stepped carefully on to his little mat and lifted his bugle.

Another day.

7

Lotus

Esmond Brooke paused gratefully in the shadows of the imposing Hong Kong Club and plucked at the unfamiliar white uniform, his 'ice-cream suit', which he had put on for the first time since the Mediterranean. After the fairly normal routine of the destroyer it was almost unnerving to step ashore. He had crossed the *Islip*'s deck from his own command, and by the time he had reached the dock area his uniform was clinging to his skin.

But it was not simply the heat. It was the noise, the traffic, and chattering, bustling crowds which had taken him off-guard. Swamped him. Like recovering from a fever or hangover, with nothing familiar to bring him back to his senses.

His brother had sent a message as to where to find him, in a smaller club around the side of this impressive Gothic structure, which would not have looked out of place in Brighton or Mayfair.

It was afternoon, and as he reached out to push open the swing doors he was conscious of the cool air which flowed out to greet him. He almost fell in the club's semi-darkness as two young Chinese servants dragged the doors away from him and offered polite little bows.

The hall porter, a scarlet-faced man with a lick of hair across his forehead, watched him suspiciously.

'Can I be of 'elp, sir?'

Brooke felt his cap taken from his hand and spirited away by another servant. No ticket was offered in exchange, and he guessed that they had other means of recognition.

'Commander Brooke, if you please.'

The porter, obviously an ex-soldier or a Royal, pursed his lips. 'An' who shall I say, sir?'

'Another Brooke, I'm afraid.'

The eyes darted to his shoulder straps and he nodded sagely. 'Welcome to Hong Kong, sir.' He raised the flap in his little counter. 'Follow me, sir.'

Revolving fans escorted them along a passageway and Brooke was reminded of the sweating staff officer at Gibraltar with his walking stick. There were several lounges where members lay in cane chairs, legs thrust out, eyes closed. Empty glasses stood near to hand, and there was a faint smell of curry.

Although it was a club for naval and military people, Brooke guessed it had become a haven to the many expatriate Britons in business in the colony.

'In here, sir.' Then he boomed, 'Lieutenant-Commander Brooke, sir!'

Jeremy Brooke was standing beside a window observing the street. He turned lightly, like an athlete: he had always prided himself on his physical prowess and general excellence at sports.

An outsider, had there been one, would have instantly noticed the resemblance between them. Almost the same colour of eyes and hair, although Jeremy Brooke, crisp and alert in a white uniform, seemed cool and relaxed by comparison, his smile gentle and slightly amused while he waited for his brother to limp over to him.

113

They shook hands firmly and without warmth.

Jeremy said, 'You look fine. I thought I'd see some grizzled old veteran from the deep waters! It'll do some people a bit of good in H.K. to be introduced to a real hero, instead of just reading about them at a safe distance.'

Brooke studied him, wondering what was different. The immediate acknowledgement of their separate paths, perhaps? The brutal realities of the Mediterranean and the Atlantic, where ships and men were dying even while they spoke in this remote cog of Empire? Jeremy, as far as he knew, had not served aboard ship since the outbreak of war. There must be a moral in that somewhere.

His brother said, 'How's your V.C. settling down? I heard he was a bit bomb-happy.'

Cool, quick, unfeeling. He had always been that way.

He replied, 'Calvert? He still feels it.' Defensively he heard himself add, 'He'll do me, and the ship.'

Brooke found that he was seated, as was his brother. The latter took a pad from a hovering servant. 'Gin?'

Instead of refusing he said, 'Lots of ice. It's the one thing I envy them out here.'

His brother scribbled on a chit. 'Bloody hopeless here, in the club I mean. I only use it for meeting people.'

'Like me?'

The perfect teeth shone in a smile. 'Like you. Exactly.' He leaned forward and Brooke wondered how it was that his hair was always so neat, never a strand out of place. He had seen himself in one of the club's ornate mirrors. Hair too long, uniform jacket too loose. It should be easy to get another one made to measure out here.

His brother took out a cigarette. 'Won't offer you

one. Smoke your pipe, if you like. Everybody else does. They've almost gone native in this place.'

'Where are you staying?' From a corner of his eyes he saw the servant put down the tray, heard the tempting tinkle of ice.

Jeremy eyed him curiously. 'The Pen, of course.' He smiled gently. 'The Peninsula Hotel, across the water in Kowloon.'

'I've read about it. Pretty expensive, isn't it?'

Again the slight, almost pitying smile. 'They must think I'm worth it.' He picked up his glass and eyed him through the cigarette smoke. 'Good to see you. Sorry about the funeral, but there was nothing you could have done. And sailing orders mean just that in this man's navy.'

'What exactly are you doing out here, Jeremy? It all seems rather cloak-and-dagger.'

His brother nodded, amused. 'Yes, I suppose it would seem like that – to you. I'm on D.N.I.'s staff – have been for months.'

'Director of Naval Intelligence? God, I didn't know that!'

'And you don't now, if anyone mentions it. But I know you, old chap, a clam when you want to be.' He leaned forward and rested one hand on the table. 'You're not like me. Ships, blood and guts, that's your war. One we must win. But mine is the other side of it. I like to think it's no less important in the end.' He did not wait for any comment but continued, 'I hear you saw the commodore?' He looked away, and for once his composure was shaken. 'People like him make me sick!'

'I don't follow.'

Jeremy Brooke picked an invisible hair from his gleaming shoulder strap.

'You don't need to.'

Was it a deliberate gesture? Something to remind him that, brothers or not, he was in charge?

He spoke carefully, keeping the bitterness out of his voice. 'Is Sarah with you?'

For a split second he saw his brother taken off-guard.

'No. I was in a hurry. Came down via Suez, too dicey to have women dragging along. You know how it is.'

'Actually, no, I don't.'

They faced one another, strangers or enemies, it was impossible to tell.

Then Jeremy said very calmly, 'There are some very important people here, the ones who count – will count, if things go wrong.'

'Is that what you expect will happen?' It was so quiet he could hear a clock ticking in the passageway.

Jeremy shrugged; he even did that elegantly. 'Winston Churchill has said it plainly enough. No matter what happens in the Far East, Hong Kong will remain under our flag. We have enough ships and men in Singapore and Malaya if we should need them. The rest is purely hypothetical.' He tapped his silver cigarette case with his fingers. 'We have our guidelines.' He smiled briefly. 'But their lordships are not content to sit at Lord's and watch the cricket. Those days are over, I hope.'

'And these very important people?'

'One in particular: Charles Yeung. A very influential businessman. Even the Governor tips his hat to him, in a manner of speaking.'

The servant came back but Jeremy shook his head. He did not ask his brother if he wanted a second drink.

Instead he said, 'There's to be a party at Charles Yeung's house. It's up on the Peak, quite spectacular.'

Brooke thought of the great houses he had seen from

Serpent's bridge when they had entered harbour. Was that really only yesterday?

His brother was saying, 'There will be all the usual people, of course. Showering praise and secretly sneering at their host.'

Brooke said, 'What's he like?'

'Rich. *Very* rich. Has business connections everywhere – here, the U.S.A., just about anywhere he chooses. He's important to us.' He gently raised one hand. 'Just leave it at that for now. Day after tomorrow. I'll send word. Bring Calvert – a V.C. might make everyone feel less remote and insular.'

Brooke said carefully, 'I don't think he'll come.'

Jeremy was on his feet and like magic a youth darted forward with his fine gold-leaved cap. For a moment longer he glanced at himself in a mirror, while he adjusted his cap at a slight angle and composed his parting shot.

Their eyes met in the mirror and Jeremy's voice was suddenly cold as he said, 'I am not asking. It is an order.' Then he slipped some coins to the porter and strode out into the sunlight. Brooke found, very much to his surprise, that he could smile about it, even as he was handed his own cap.

Aloud he murmured softly, 'I wasn't wrong after all. You really are an arrogant bastard!'

Lieutenant Kerr slipped into the cabin.

'All ready for the party, sir?'

Brooke grimaced and toyed with the idea of having a drink before he left, but decided against it. It might, after all, be fun.

'Sorry about you, Number One, but I need you on board to deal with the dockyard people.'

Kerr shrugged. 'I don't mind, sir. I'm just glad Toby Calvert's going ashore with you. He'll take root if he stays on board much longer.'

If you only knew, he thought, recalling his brother's blunt comment. Calvert had had no choice in the matter.

He walked to an open scuttle and shaded his eyes against the early sunset to look over at a light cruiser which had entered harbour that morning and moored astern of Commodore Stallybrass's *Dumbarton*. She was a Dutch warship named *Ariadne*. How did her people feel, he wondered. Carrying on out here with their own country under the jackboot.

He said, 'I'm taking Kipling, by the way. Show him how the other half lives.'

There was a tap at the door and Calvert stepped into the cabin. Brooke saw it all. Self-conscious, defiant, resentful, the solitary crimson ribbon beneath his pilot's wings like a patch of blood.

The white uniform suited him, Brooke thought, and his beard added just the right touch. He would turn any girl's head.

He almost laughed. *You're a fine one to talk.*

Calvert said tonelessly, 'How do we get there, sir? Rickshaw?'

'Well, we're not walking, that I do know!' He looked round as the third member of the party, Sub-Lieutenant Kipling, peered in and gave them an untroubled grin.

'All set, sir!'

Kerr eyed him gravely. 'Even the commodore would be satisfied with you, Sub!'

A telephone buzzed and then Kingsmill appeared from his pantry.

'Main gate, sir. The car's here for you.'

Calvert sighed. 'Damn. No rickshaw after all.'

Islip's O.O.D. saluted as they trooped across the

118

ship's deck. Brooke had been pleased to hear that her captain, Commander Tufnell, had also been invited to the party. There would be at least one familiar face. Apart, he thought sarcastically, from brother Jeremy.

At the gates a small crowd of sailors and idlers had gathered to stare.

Kipling exclaimed with rare admiration, 'That's no *car*, sir!' With the others he ran his eyes over the long Rolls-Royce that blocked the whole of the entrance.

It was pale green with a shining black top, which, with all the dust in the air, must have been a full-time job to keep so immaculate. The front seats had an open roof and Brooke shook his head as a small Chinese in a dove-grey uniform and black gaiters sprang smartly into the road. He threw up a salute which even a Royal Marine drill-sergeant would find faultless.

'Commander Brooke, sir?' He beamed. 'At your service, sir!'

Calvert said, 'What a car. I'd be terrified to drive it in London, never mind here!'

Kipling said, 'A Phantom II. Beautiful motor. We often had one call at the garage for petrol before the war.'

Brooke noticed that he had not called it *garridge*. That was obviously only for Barrington-Purvis's benefit.

They climbed into the car and were greeted by the smell of leather and fresh flowers in a little silver vase.

The driver was watching them in one of his mirrors. 'We go, Captain-sir?'

Brooke nodded. 'We go.' He found time to wonder how the chauffeur's feet could reach the pedals.

The car glided through the traffic and chattering traders and as it began to climb a zig-zagging road towards the Peak so, correspondingly, did the sun dip down into the sea.

119

Nobody spoke. Higher and higher, the massive head-lights sweeping this way and that, and once, when the road was particularly steep, all that Brooke could see was the car's famous mascot, the *Spirit of Ecstasy* and nothing beyond, as if they were poised on the edge of a cliff.

He glanced down, fascinated, at the glittering harbour, the anchor lights, the tiny boats moving like fireflies, the tramp steamers still loading and unloading, their holds gaping open beneath clusters of cargo lamps. A living place, one that was never still by day or by night.

There would be a few sore heads at the defaulters' table when the libertymen returned to the ship, he thought wryly.

'Almost come, Captain-sir!'

Calvert murmured, 'It's like Hollywood!'

Kipling chuckled. 'I could live with it! Just give me the chance!'

Brooke watched two white-jacketed servants padding out of the house to greet the car's arrival.

He climbed down on to the drive and saw his brother on the front stairs which led up to a pillared entrance. He was looking pointedly at his watch.

Brooke nodded to the little chauffeur, then handed him some money as he had seen Jeremy do. *Squeeze*, they called it. He never even felt the cash leave his hand.

The chauffeur reached into the car for a polishing cloth.

'I wait here for you, Captain-sir!' He showed his teeth in a wide grin. 'More exciting going back downhill!'

The war seemed a very, very long way off.

*

Commander Jeremy Brooke smiled and glanced briefly at Calvert and Kipling.

'A word before you go in, Esmond.' He took his brother's arm and guided him away from the others. 'The commodore's here, thought I should warn you, and quite a few of the top brass.' He gave him a piercing stare. 'Don't talk too much about why you came out here. *Operation Boomerang* is supposed to be secret, although knowing this place I imagine that half the island has heard about it already!'

He turned to the others. 'And I want a word with you too, Kipling, before you vanish for the evening!'

Brooke had the peculiar impression that his brother and the unlikely sub-lieutenant already knew each other.

He tried to shake off the strange sense of foreboding and turned his attention to the huge reception hall. There was an archway at the far end, which from the angle he assumed opened on to a terrace with a view of the harbour. He would go and look at it before he left.

His brother said, 'Come and meet your host, before the pack closes in on him.'

It was easy to pick out Charles Yeung, even without an introduction. Tall for a Chinese, with straight silver hair in marked contrast with his fine-boned, mobile features: the face of a much younger man. At a guess he must be in his late fifties, but he appeared ageless. He turned as they approached and Brooke felt his gaze sweep over him, interested, polite, guarded. He was dressed in a perfectly fitting silk suit, the same colour as his hair. A man you could not imagine losing his temper under any circumstances, Brooke thought. He would regard it as a weakness. He would make a bad enemy. As a friend? That was much harder to tell.

Charles Yeung said, 'My friend's brother. How do you do? You are welcome in my humble house.'

Brooke shook his hand. Hard and dry, like leather.

Humble? Hardly that if the rest of the house and grounds matched this reception hall. Long and pillared, discreetly lit to show a tiled floor with several intricate designs, every alcove held a huge Chinese vase containing so many chrysanthemums and gladioli that every cluster must have cost a small fortune.

Yeung was saying, 'You command the destroyer *Serpent*? I hope your ship carries a good sting!'

Jeremy said, 'Just the sort of ship we need in these coastal waters.' He and Yeung exchanged quick glances. 'And the right sort of captain too.' He seemed glad of the interruption as a servant with a tray of drinks approached and gave a slight bow.

Yeung was watching. 'Champagne, Commander? Anything you like. If there is nothing to your taste I will send for what you wish.' His English was flawless.

Brooke smiled. 'Champagne will be just fine, sir.' He looked around at the throng of guests. Quite a few officers, army and navy, some Chinese civilians with their demure little wives, and the commodore in the midst of it, his face already bright red.

Another servant came up to their host and whispered something. Charles Yeung said apologetically, 'I must leave you, gentlemen. Another guest has arrived. We shall speak further.'

Jeremy remarked, 'Assistant Governor.'

'Do you speak Cantonese?'

'Enough.'

'You're full of surprises, Jeremy.'

Jeremy put down his glass. 'He wants me there with him. I'll be back.'

Brooke saw him start with unusual surprise. 'I shall

leave you in good hands. This is Lian Yeung, our host's daughter.' He looked vaguely ill at ease.

Brooke turned and held out his hand. She made him feel clumsy, and he knew he was staring but he could not help it.

Lian Yeung was not merely striking: she was lovely. Quite tall like her father, her hair shining like jet and piled above her ears. She was dressed from neck to toe in a dark green cheongsam, her feet in small gold sandals just showing beneath the hem.

He heard his brother say, 'I didn't know you were coming this evening, Lian.'

She did not look at him but smiled gently at Brooke. 'You will know me again when we meet, I think.'

Brooke murmured, 'I beg your pardon. I wasn't expecting . . .'

'Obviously.' She glanced past him. '*I* shall take care of your brother, Jeremy.'

Brooke glanced between them. He could sense the tension, and in her case something else, some deep reserve or unhappiness.

She slipped one hand through his arm and gracefully indicated the buffet table which stretched almost the full length of the hall.

'You are familiar with Chinese food, Commander?'

'No. I've never been here before.'

She turned towards him without seeming to move, her eyes very grave as she studied him impassively.

'You have been many places. And you have seen too many bad things.' Her English was easy to listen to, but not so practised as her father's.

Brooke said, 'It's something we have to do.' Even that sounded awkward and trite. 'Have you been to England?'

'Yes. I finished my education there.' She paused.

'Where I met your brother. He was training to be an interpreter.' She shrugged. 'No matter. But I did see something of the war in England until my father insisted I should return home.'

Brooke's mind was still grappling with her unemotional comment. Jeremy must have been seeing her in England after he had married Sarah. Perhaps even out here . . .

She said, 'I will help you to choose. The servants will bring you each dish.' She gestured towards another table with finger-bowls and small towels, each with an orchid resting on it. 'Use your fingers. It avoids the embarrassment of not being able to use chopsticks.' She smiled at him. 'You are staring again.'

'Sorry. All I do is apologise. I've never met anyone like you.'

'Some people never apologise.' Her eyes were so dark that it was impossible to read her thoughts.

Brooke said, 'Why did your father tell you to return here?' He expected a quick rebuff. It was none of his business.

Instead he felt her hand tighten on his arm. 'Because he believes that England will be invaded. He was afraid for me.'

She turned away and raised her free hand. A servant hurried across instantly, avoiding the jostling throng which had by now surrounded the table.

The tempting dishes were another glimpse of this exotic, incomparable world. Suckling pig and crisp seaweed, roast duck both sliced and wrapped in tiny pancakes, and a lobster salad that must have been designed by a genius, with the shell and claws replaced after each serving. The line of lobsters seemed endless.

The girl took very little but seemed content to explain each dish to him, as if the other guests did not exist.

'Your ship will be here for some time, Commander?' She smiled gravely and repeated, 'For *some time*?'

'So I understand.' He hesitated. 'We shall at least be based at *Tamar*.'

'I hope you enjoy your stay.' Her eyes flashed. 'I must go. I am expected to mingle with the guests.' She held out her hand. 'It had been good to speak.'

He took her hand in his and knew he was being stupid. Their first meeting and probably the last, and he was behaving like a pink-faced midshipman.

She released her hand from his grip and he almost apologised again. Instead he asked, 'May I call you when my ship comes in?'

'I shall know when that is.' She studied him as if searching for something. 'Perhaps.' She gave a little shrug. 'I am not sure.'

Then she waved to somebody and moved slowly away from him.

'Lian has been taking good care of you?'

Brooke turned and saw Charles Yeung watching him impassively. How long had he been there? Was he protecting her again, and from what?

'None better, sir. You are a lucky man to have such a daughter.'

Yeung's eyes were distant. 'So I believe.'

'Lian. What does it mean?' He saw the eyes snap into focus like a gunsight. 'I'm trying to learn, you see?'

'Yes.' He nodded slowly. 'I do see. Her name means Lotus. It is one of the eight Buddhist precious things, you understand? Purity rising unsullied from the mire. So, too, the woman who bears that name shall be pure and unsullied.'

Brooke watched him. There was no sarcasm, no cheap amusement on his face or in his voice.

'Thank you, sir. This has been quite an evening. I can't remember when I've enjoyed one more.'

Yeung did not smile but said, 'You are welcome here. We have very little time.' He did not explain but walked away as the commodore's massive bulk emerged from the crowd.

Brooke turned towards a long mirror so that the commodore should not see him, and reflected in it he saw his brother speaking intently to the tall slim girl in the green cheongsam. She appeared to say nothing, and when he reached out to touch her wrist she pulled it away.

Brooke stared at his reflection, angry, defensive, and strangely jealous. *What is the matter with me?* Her father was a multi-millionaire who would certainly not welcome or tolerate any unwanted attention towards his daughter, especially from a lowly lieutenant-commander whose only assets lay in the old house his father had made into a country hotel. If he outlived the war, there would be little worth selling after the army had done with it.

Surprisingly, the reflection smiled back at him.

It was like hearing her name.

8

Boarding Party

Lieutenant Richard Kerr leaned under the chart table's hood and switched on the small light. It was all so different after the Atlantic and Western Approaches, where a casual match or uncovered light could bring the hidden periscope swinging in your direction.

He peered at the chart and checked his watch. Five in the morning, the ship plunging and gently rolling in a slow quarter-sea. Kerr had been on watch for an hour.

Serpent had been at sea for three days, patrolling a huge rectangle one hundred miles long and fifty wide. A place without danger, or what they considered danger, and the work was boring and monotonous after the first thrill of excitement when they had entered Hong Kong. Back and forth, up and down. Showing the flag, warning off pirates and smugglers; part of Britain's naval presence here, as it had been since the 1840s.

Like some of the others, Kerr had been shocked by the run-down in naval strength at Hong Kong. A few old destroyers, some equally ancient gunboats and a flotilla of M.T.B.s. Submarines, the aircraft carrier, even the crack Fifth Cruiser Squadron had been sent elsewhere, or sunk in the fiercely contested waters of the Mediterranean.

He heard Kipling chatting with the duty signalman.

He seemed to feel more at ease with the ratings in the bridge team.

Kerr had ticked him off for expounding his own views on the situation in the Far East.

'Like everywhere else! Old duffers who are still fighting Jutland – don't have a clue about real war!'

The fact that he was probably right made it worse.

He stooped over the chart again and adjusted the dividers against the pencilled calculations of the morning watch so far.

Time to alter course again very soon. His thoughts drifted to the captain, in his hutch beneath the upper bridge. Brooke had been like someone else since they had made their landfall. The telling strain was gone, and he looked years younger. The shift of responsibilities, maybe. And Kipling had blurted out some fantastic story about a smashing Chinese girl who had been seen talking to Brooke at the buffet reception on the Peak. Perhaps she had something to do with it.

Kerr jotted down some notes and glanced at the place-name to the north of Hong Kong: Taya Wan, and in brackets beside it, *Bias Bay*. Out there somewhere beyond the black arrowhead of *Serpent*'s bows, with the endless mass of China sprawling beyond that. As a boy Kerr had enjoyed reading about the pirates of Bias Bay. He had never expected to be toiling up and down an invisible rectangle some thirty miles away from it.

It was hard to measure or visualise the internal war between the Chinese Nationalist Army and the invading Japanese. He had expected to find the people of Hong Kong nervous or apprehensive about it, but he had discovered nothing of the sort. The social round went on, and the only war that intruded was *our* war, somewhere else where men were dying for their country and ships went down with guns blazing in the tradition of Nelson.

He thought of Kipling again and smiled. Brooke had told him it was likely that Kipling would get his second stripe shortly, advanced with even more alacrity than usual by the Admiralty. He wondered why. Barrington-Purvis would not be pleased.

'Char, sir?'

He took the hot mug and sipped it. He had hated the Atlantic. Was it possible to miss it now, in these untroubled seas?

He walked back and forth along the wooden gratings, which would soon be getting their morning scrub, and listened to the endless creaks and groans of the ship beneath him as she rolled along at her most economical rate of twelve knots. At speed she was something else, one of the Grand Fleet's greyhounds, the envy of every would-be skipper. He smiled to himself. *Like me.* A quarter of a century of service. As the Chief had remarked with his usual defensive pride, 'She's just getting older, like the rest of us!'

Kipling's pale shape moved out of the darkness.

Time to make peace again, Kerr decided. A sharp telling-off was one thing, but he never allowed grudges to build up.

'Be dawn soon,' he said. 'Best time of the day.'

Kipling turned to look at him, and then his eyes seemed to light up like lamps.

'What the *hell*!' Kerr swung round and saw the light die in the black water, like blowing out a candle. Seconds later the thud, and it was little more than that, bounced off the hull like a hammer.

Kerr snatched up the handset, but before he could speak he heard Brooke snap, 'I'm coming up!'

'Anyone get a bearing?'

A boatswain's mate called, 'Fine on the starboard bow, sir!'

Brooke strode from the gate, his unruly hair blowing in the breeze coming over the screen.

'Starboard bow, sir. One flash and an explosion. Not very big.'

Kipling said flatly, 'About six miles, sir. A grenade.'

Brooke glanced towards him but saw only his pale outline.

'Sound off action stations, Number One. I'm not getting involved in their war.' He gestured towards the invisible mainland. 'I'm not ignoring it either.' He slung his glasses round his neck even as the alarm bells tore through the ship. After weeks of empty ocean, and their safe arrival in Hong Kong, this rude awakening would bring some stark memories to those who heard it. Was it just a fool's paradise after all?

Kipling turned to leave the bridge but Brooke said, 'No. You stay. I might need you.'

The voicepipes were chattering and being acknowledged while the bridge team changed round yet again.

'Cox'n on the wheel, sir!'

The gunner (T)'s rough voice: 'Transmitting station closed up!'

'Main and close-range weapons closed up!' Barrington-Purvis, still very cut-glass despite his obvious irritation.

Kerr said, 'Ship at action stations, sir.'

Lieutenant Calvert was polishing his binoculars and speaking softly to his yeoman by the chart table. He seemed very calm.

Brooke picked up his bridge microphone and pressed down the button.

'This is the captain. Sorry to get you out of your hammocks so early. We are investigating some vessel or

130

vessels.' He glanced towards Kipling and added, 'A grenade was exploded.'

Kipling was so sure, when others less confident would have kept quiet. What kind of a war had he left to join *Serpent*?

He replaced the microphone and picked up the engine room handset.

'Chief?'

'Aye, sir.' It sounded as though he had been waiting.

'Bring her up to one-one-zero revs, but be ready to give all you've got. We have plenty of depth hereabouts . . .'

He saw the salt-smeared glass of the screen light up with a brief flash, then felt the explosion.

The Chief said sharply, 'Ready when you are!'

Brooke thought of the men he commanded. They had seen and done it all. Depth-charge attacks, dive-bombers, sinking merchantmen, sailors screaming in the water as they had cut through them to detect a lurking U-boat. Crying for help when there was none, waiting for the depth-charges to explode. Ordinary men, gutted like raw fish when the charges found their set depth. They would be thinking of it now.

He raised his glasses as the deck levelled to the increased speed, and saw the creaming bow-wave churning away from the straight stem when earlier they had barely raised a ripple.

The sea was already opening up. It was surprising how quickly the dawn came.

Calvert said, 'I got a fix on that last one, sir!'

'Good. Do it.'

Brooke heard Calvert speaking to the wheelhouse, Pike's muffled reply. Like the ship itself, each man was responding, an extension of his own ability, or lack of it.

'Yeoman!' He stopped himself in time. He had been

about to snap his fingers as the same old tension took charge of his senses. As first lieutenant of *Murray* in a hard-pressed escort group, he had often been forced to the limit. And yet he had never forgotten one small incident when he had nervously snapped his fingers at a seaman on the bridge and turned in time to see the resentment on his young features. Only a single brush-stroke of war. But he had not allowed himself to forget it.

Onslow lowered his glasses. 'Sir?'

'Pass a signal to the W/T office. *To Commander-in-Chief repeated Admiralty. Our position is so-and-so . . .*' From one corner of his eye he saw Calvert scribble it on a signal pad. '*Am investigating surface explosions.*'

Kerr turned and saw Brooke's tanned features split into a grin. 'But tell W/T not to send it until I say so.' He saw Kerr and added, 'Otherwise they might interfere!'

Kerr watched the first milky daylight laying the ship bare and giving depth to the green water. A Chinese junk revealed herself, perched on her shadow, motionless, as if she were about to topple over as they surged past.

But Kerr was thinking of the captain's last remark. Did Brooke know about the rift between himself and the previous captain, and why Greenwood had never put him forward for a command of his own?

The convoy had been a bad one, harried all the way by submarines, and then as they got closer to home the big Focke-Wulf Condors had joined in the uneven battle. *Serpent*'s lower decks, from stokers' mess to wardroom, had been crammed with survivors they had managed to drag from the sea. Burned, blinded, choking on oil; they had been even beyond gratitude. Greenwood had snapped, 'Discontinue the action and rejoin convoy, Number One.'

There had been one last freighter, sinking so slowly that they could see the survivors trying to launch a small raft. All the boats had been destroyed by the fatal torpedo.

'What about them, sir?'

The merchant sailors had been staring at the destroyer. Their only hope.

Greenwood had climbed into his tall chair, the same one Brooke was holding on to now while the ship pushed ahead from the retreating darkness.

Kerr could still hear his answer. 'We've made our gesture. Now do as I say and resume position and course.'

When he had looked again, Kerr had seen the men still standing by the remaining raft. One of them had actually waved as *Serpent*'s wash had rolled over them.

Kerr glanced inboard across the bridge and realized that Brooke was watching him. Crumpled shirt, hatless, and wearing the old plimsolls he usually kept in his hutch. But he could not have looked more like *Serpent*'s captain if he had been in full dress.

His words were almost drowned by the fans and the rattle of loose gear as he said, 'Take it off your back, Number One.' He gave a smile which afterwards Kerr remembered as being incredibly sad. 'We've both been there, haven't we? It's not going to get any better.'

Barrington-Purvis's voice rang sharply over the bridge intercom.

'Control – Forebridge! Two vessels stopped, side by side at Green one-zero! Eight thousand yards!'

Even as he snatched up the red handset they all heard the distant roar of powerful engines, more like an M.T.B. than a coaster.

'There she goes! Off like a bloody rocket!'

Brooke called, 'Full ahead together, Chief!' His mind

133

only barely recorded Cusack's curt acknowledgement and the clang of telegraphs from the wheelhouse.

What was it? Instinct? Probably nothing, or perhaps some modern pirate had pounced on an unsuspecting prey.

Onslow was saying, 'Large fishing vessel.' His voice was devoid of everything but professional interest. 'I can just read her number.' He spoke to his leading signalman, Railton. 'Got it, Harry?' Then he said, 'Local boat, sir. Out of Hong Kong, Aberdeen most likely.'

The P.O. steward, Bert Kingsmill, stepped carefully into the bridge, although his action station was in the sick bay. He was obviously feeling out of place, but he walked stiffly to the forepart and held out Brooke's best cap with the new, gleaming badge.

'They wouldn't let me through to your sea-cabin, sir, so I fetched this for you.'

Calvert and Kerr watched as Brooke tugged the gleaming cap down on his tangled hair.

Another small brushstroke. One that these men who shared his life would all remember.

As the hastily lowered motor-boat hit the water and veered away from the ship's side on the attached line, Kerr had to cling to the cockpit canopy in the heavy motion. The sea, which had looked so calm from the upper bridge, heaved and dipped around their small craft in deep, irregular troughs, and when he looked back at the destroyer he saw her frothing wash already mounting again as she appeared to begin another change of course.

The boat-rope was slipped and instantly the engine roared into full power, Macaskie, the boat's coxswain, riding easily to the motion despite his weight and size.

Kipling was also one of the small boarding-party, although Kerr was not sure why.

The captain had merely said, 'Take him with you. I imagine he's done quite a lot of this sort of thing.' He had found time to touch Kerr's arm as he had scrambled from the bridge. 'No risks, Number One. All right?'

The motor-boat was moving at her best speed, planing over the swell like a Cowes racer.

Kerr squinted through the spray and saw the big fishing boat drawing closer by the minute. Even she seemed much larger from down here.

Kipling released his grip with one hand to turn and stare at *Serpent*'s lean grey shape. She seemed to shine in the first sunlight, her pendant number, H-50, more silver than white in the glare. He saw that her twenty-millimetre Oerlikons were being trained round towards them as if to sniff after their progress.

Kerr shouted above the noise, 'The boat's been damaged! The grenades probably!' He could smell burned wood and paint and see deep scars on her hull.

He had half expected Brooke to give chase after the powerful attacker, but even *Serpent* would not catch the boat in time to do anything. It might even have provoked an incident with the Japanese, if there were any of them nearby. The chart was marked as if the invading Japs had seized just about every piece of the coast near here, and Kerr realized for the first time how close they were to the New Territories and Hong Kong island itself.

Kipling said, 'I suggest we board her from the opposite side.'

Kerr had to clear his thoughts to grapple with the comment.

'What the hell for? We'll lose sight of the ship!'

Kipling poked one of his teeth with a forefinger. He

might even have shrugged, as if the whole thing was a waste of time.

But his words said the opposite. 'Our gun crews won't be able to fire with us in the middle. If they have to, of course.'

Kerr called to the coxswain, 'Take her round, Macaskie!'

'Aye, aye, sir!' He was careful to keep his heavy features impassive. But it would make a good yarn in the mess, how the scruffy subbie told Jimmy the One what to do.

They were so near now they could smell the diesel oil, and the clinging stench of fish.

Kerr cupped his hands. '*Boat ahoy! This is the Royal Navy!*'

The boat's stoker nudged one of the armed seamen. 'Better than a bloody film, eh, Teddy?'

There was no response and the fishing boat continued to drift, unmanned. Perhaps the attacking boat had kidnapped the crew on some pretext.

'Slow ahead.' Kerr readjusted the heavy webbing holster on his hip, and did not see Kipling's wry grin.

'You two stay in the boat!' He felt the fisherman's shadow rise over them. After the sun it was cold. Unnerving.

Macaskie said, 'I think the old girl's sinking, sir.'

'*What?*' Kerr stared at the hull's filthy waterline. It did look lower in the water, or were things getting him down so much he couldn't see straight? He seemed to hear Brooke's voice again. *It's not going to get any better.*

He said harshly, 'Follow me! *Grapnel!*'

The boat's engine died away as the bowman hurled his grapnel up and over the scarred bulwark, and Kerr was on the crowded, unfamiliar deck without any recollection of leaving the motor-boat.

His eyes took in the piles of nets, marker floats and other fishing gear. Nothing moved. There was an open hold and he saw what might have been the marks of a crowbar or jemmy where the covers had been forced off. The hold was empty. No catch this time. Maybe they were carrying something else?

He saw a child's woolly coat hanging up to dry and remembered that Hong Kong fishermen often lived in these boats with all the members of their families.

Kipling peered into the hold. 'She's taking water, right enough. The grenades might have done it.' He did not sound convinced. He glanced at the wheelhouse and the nearby hatch, which led to the crew's or living quarters. 'Shall I go?'

Kerr snapped, 'No.' He hesitated. 'What's the matter, man?'

Kipling did not raise his voice. 'Can't you smell it?' When Kerr remained silent he spat it out. 'Death!'

A glance at the apprehensive boarding party was enough to tell Kerr to take action.

'Uncover your weapons.' He stared across the water but *Serpent*'s outline was almost lost in a bank of drifting sea-mist.

Then, angrily, he dragged open the hatch and hurried down the ladder. The boat had been completely taken apart. Cupboards and boxes ripped open, contents scattered and broken on the deck. Menzies, a tough leading torpedoman who was in charge of the party, sniffed the unmoving air. Like a dog, Kerr thought.

'Over here, sir!'

Kerr strode across the crew-space and swallowed hard as he saw the blood, mingling with water in the leaking hull.

137

'What the hell's been going on here?'

He saw a closed door, and with Menzies close behind him he kicked it open.

There were two oil lamps swinging from the deck-head: a poor light, but more than enough to reveal the horror which had visited this small place.

On a large wooden bunk against the curved hull were the bodies of two women. One was older than the other, probably mother and daughter. Both were naked. There was more blood on the bunk, and Kerr guessed that each of them had been raped many times: their contorted faces and savage bruises said something of their terrible ordeal. A small Chinese child lay dead in a corner.

Menzies was breathing hard and someone else was retching, unable to stop.

Kerr reached out and touched the girl's skin. It was still warm. As he made to cover her he saw that both women had been stabbed between the legs.

He could feel the vomit hard in his throat. Any moment now, and . . .

Menzies exclaimed hoarsely, 'Over there, sir! 'Nother door!'

Kerr nodded. He was bitterly cold: it was like some deathly fever. He could scarcely move. The door probably led right forward, to the toilet arrangements and finally the chain-locker. How could he think so logically after what he had just seen?

He pushed open the door and stared down at another corpse. His wrists had been pinioned, and his body had been the source of all the blood in the cabin. He must have died under torture. But first he had been forced to watch the rape and brutal murder of his wife and family.

Something rolled across the deck, and one of the

seamen gave a startled cry. The fishing boat was settling down.

He spoke between clenched teeth. 'Go on deck and tell Burns to signal the ship . . .'

But Menzies was staring at the dead man's mutilated face, his teeth bared like a snarl of defiance.

'There's another over there, sir.' He tried to make light of it. 'Covered him up to spare our feelings!'

Kerr thought of Brooke waiting and wondering at the delay. He must do something.

As Menzies groped over to uncover the body, the 'corpse' leapt to its feet, so that the seaman fell sprawling in the blood.

Kerr could not move. The man was squat and powerful, perhaps a pirate who had been trapped below when his boat had dashed away as *Serpent* had been sighted. He was staring at Kerr without appearing to blink; then he revealed the heavy-bladed knife, which was still black with blood.

Menzies rolled over and gasped, 'Watch out!'

Two things happened in a second. The glass of a filthy skylight shattered overhead, and the crash of a shot exploded in the confined space like a bomb.

Kerr saw the man's forehead burst open, and the bullet flung him down on to the mutilated corpse.

Feet pounded down the ladder and Kipling pushed through the door, one swift glance taking in the butchered women and the man he had just shot from above.

'All right, Number One?'

'*You killed him.*' Kerr had to prop himself against the door as the hull rolled heavily around him.

Kipling thrust what looked like a heavy German Luger back into his belt, but his eyes remained on the corpse.

'You know what it says in the good book, Number

139

One? Don't draw your gun unless you intend to use it. Well, I did, as it happened.' He brushed past him, but paused to tap Kerr's sealed holster. 'If you see what I mean.'

Menzies was on his feet again, gasping in air like a partly drowned man. 'Jesus, I thought I was done for!'

Kerr watched Kipling as he stooped over the gaping corpse; he had shot him right between the eyes, and the back of his head had been blown out. Nevertheless he saw Kipling kick the blade from his fist before opening his jerkin to look for other weapons, his expression detached, only his thin nostrils dilating slightly to show what it was costing him.

A yell came from overhead, 'Signal, sir! *Recall!*'

Somebody was being sick, and another gasped, 'Thank Christ for that!'

Kerr made himself wait as Kipling slipped a few small items into his pockets.

He wiped his face with his forearm. 'Oddly enough, I was thinking about pirates when I was on watch.' He wanted to laugh, but knew he would not be able to stop.

Kipling straightened up. 'There won't be any charts or log books. We might as well clear out an' let her go under.' He stared at the naked women as if he needed to remember everything here.

Kerr released the door. 'You saved my life just now.'

Kipling answered casually, 'Worthwhile then, wasn't it?' He waited for Menzies to go and muster the boarders.

Then, when they were alone, he said, 'He may look like a pirate, Number One, but he's a Jap soldier. I hope our people know what they're doing.'

They stood side by side on the listing deck and waited for the motor-boat's engine to roar into life.

Kipling was very aware of Kerr's distress. A true gentleman, he thought. Completely out of his depth in this sort of war.

'Sea's the best place for these poor sods.' He pulled out the leather wallet he had taken from the dead man's jacket. Details of his army service, no doubt. The Skipper's brother would be interested in that, if anybody would listen to him.

He opened the wallet in the warm sunshine and saw the photograph of a young girl. Daughter or lover, sister or wife? She was not unlike the girl down in the cabin.

Kerr said, 'I'll tell the captain what you did. I'll never forget it.'

He was thinking of the woman's smooth skin under his fingers. How could anyone do that?

Kipling smiled. *He was learning.*

'I know what I was taught, Number One. The quick and the dead. No third party allowed.'

As the motor-boat pushed off from the listing hull Kerr saw the ship slowing down again, men already lining the iron-deck ready to hoist it up to the davits. The Oerlikon guns were still trained towards the fishing boat. *Serpent* was, at that moment, the most beautiful sight he had ever seen.

Kipling turned and looked back. The fishing boat was already raising her bows to the cloudless sky. Where were the other members of the crew, he wondered. Murdered and thrown overboard? Or were they in league with their attackers?

They might never know. Nobody would want to speak of it.

Kerr said, 'What were they doing there in the first place? They know the risks of going so close to the mainland.'

What would he say if I told him? It might almost be worth it to discover.

Kerr was saying, 'Oh – by the way, you should be getting your second stripe very soon.'

Kipling shaded his eyes and peered at the ship. Barrington-Purvis was climbing down from his control position. He grinned evilly.

'Oh good. Mummy *will* be pleased!'

Kerr felt suddenly weary. Empty.

While the boat's crew busied themselves hooking on to the falls, he stared back at the oily whirlpool where the fisherman had given up the fight.

Menzies said quietly, '*Thanks*, sir.'

Kerr asked, 'For what?'

The leading hand looked at his ship alongside, the searching, anxious faces.

'For gettin' us home. That's what.'

Kipling waited for Menzies to leave and then said, 'I'd very much appreciate it if you forgot about the Luger, Number One.'

Kerr gripped his arm tightly. It had been a close thing.

'What Luger?'

Even as the motor-boat's dripping keel rose from the water alongside, the bridge telephones rang out and the surge of froth beneath the stern showed that the Chief's hands had been itching to open the throttles.

It was as if the ship herself knew what had happened and shared the shame with those who had seen it. She was eager to go.

Kerr looked up at the bridge and saw Brooke silhouetted against the blue sky. Waiting for him.

'When we get back to H.K. I'll buy you the biggest drink you've ever had, Sub!'

But there was no reply. Kipling had melted away.

Just for an instant he recalled his attacker's fixed stare as he had raised the bloodstained blade. He himself had not been able to move. At least he now had the chance to live with the realization.

I was afraid.

9

Monsoon

The Peninsula Hotel, *the Pen* as Jeremy Brooke had called it, was a magnificent building on the Kowloon side. It seemed very modern in appearance when compared with most of the others.

The hotel was only a short walk from the Star Ferry, but Brooke was feeling the noon sun by the time he reached it.

They had returned to the harbour in the early morning, to a strangely peaceful and untroubled atmosphere: so much at odds with the horrific discoveries aboard the sinking fishing boat, details of which had pervaded the whole ship like a fever.

Here, in Kowloon, there was only the detachment and serenity usual on a Sunday; and while the small, beautifully dressed children of rich Chinese played on the grass overseen by watchful amahs, a military band was completing a programme of Gilbert and Sullivan for men and women who sat in deck-chairs and sipped their drinks.

In the harbour it was the same. Smart awnings, church pendants hoisted for morning service and Divisions, a few boats' crews sweating and panting while they practised for the coming naval regatta.

Only the merchant ships were busy; they always

were. Any lighterage company or fresh-water supplier could make a fortune in a matter of months.

The hotel had a circular driveway, not unlike the Savoy in London, Brooke thought, what he had seen of it. Like Kowloon itself, there was an air of opulence and confidence about the place. A mark of the Colony's continued expansion.

He had written a full report for the commodore in charge at *Tamar*, and sent a briefer version to Stallybrass aboard his flagship. He had expected to be called immediately to one or the other. Instead he had received a message from his brother to meet him without delay at *the Pen*.

Kerr had described the mutilated bodies, and told him about Kipling's unhesitating action, which had saved his life and probably those of the small boarding-party as well.

Kipling had been less talkative.

'With all respect, sir, the first lieutenant is a good officer, but he's not used to this sort of caper.'

'And you are?'

'I've made no secret of that, sir. I was with the Special Service in the Med. Your brother – I mean, Commander Brooke was with us a few times. Intelligence always wanted to know what was going on. As for the fishing boat – I was prepared, that's all.'

And what of the wallet Kipling had taken from the man he had shot dead? It proved nothing. The man might have stolen it from some careless Japanese soldier.

Brooke paused on the circular driveway and admired the fountains in the centre. Nothing added up.

After Dunkirk and the Battle of Britain, an enemy invasion had never been ruled out. But at least they had been ready for it, as they still were in England.

He thought of the war he had left behind. The

145

convoys, the endless sacrifice to get food to the tables and weapons to defend them ... He shook off the memory and mounted the steps where smart page-boys were waiting to drag open the doors for him.

The vast gilt and marble lobby was packed with people, sitting or standing about while waiters dashed back and forth with trays of drinks. The Peninsula was obviously a favourite rendezvous for the wealthy traveller and the powerful businessman. There were a few uniforms in the lobby: old China hands for the most part, elderly and white-haired, probably only too pleased to be recalled to some volunteer regiment.

He thought suddenly of the lovely girl in the green cheongsam. Had Jeremy brought her here on his previous visits? The idea angered him and he knew he was being stupid.

'Oh, there you are!'

Brooke turned and saw his brother sitting in a cane chair. He was wearing his Number Fives, with three bright gold stripes adorning the sleeve, and he seemed strangely at odds with the tropical rig worn by everyone around him.

They shook hands and Jeremy removed his cap from the chair opposite, which he had been reserving for him.

He said, 'I've checked out. Leaving today. Too bad, really – another week would have been just right.' He gave his brief smile. 'As you will discover, it's a magical place.'

A waiter hovered nearby and Jeremy said, 'Scotch?' He did not wait for an answer. 'Two, boy. Large ones.' He went on, 'I read your report, or rather, a copy of it. Very interesting.'

Brooke handed him the wallet and watched his brother's eyes skim over it. Blank. He gave nothing away.

146

The drinks arrived and Brooke let his mind drift to the people and the sounds around him. Cheerful conversation as regulars greeted each other, which became louder as they drank their pink gins and stengahs. There was music too, from one of the balconies above the lobby.

He looked round and was startled by his brother's intense expression.

Jeremy said, 'Make you sick, don't they? Here we are in Kowloon, under the British flag but in fact part of the mainland. Think of it like that. And just beyond the New Territories, and the rice paddies and the duck farms, is one of the biggest military build-ups the Far East has ever seen.' He drank quickly, angrily. 'It's as if the bastards don't even want to know about it!'

'Can you be certain? I thought Winston Churchill said that the Japanese would never risk war out here. "It would be foolish for them even to consider it", I think were his words.'

Jeremy looked at his glass. It was empty, and he waved it in the air.

Brooke said, 'Let me get them.'

'Save your money.' These were obviously not his brother's first drinks of the day. 'The Japanese have always wanted total power. But for General Chiang Kai-Shek and the Nationalist army, they would have got it by now. Charles Yeung once said to me that Singapore is the key of the gate, but Hong Kong is the real jewel. He was right. The rest of the world does nothing, and the U.S.A. ignores it. But it's *here*, Esmond – it bloody well won't go away on its own.' He had raised his voice and several people turned to stare.

It disturbed Brooke to see his brother like this. He had always been so cool and calm, so much in control.

'What will you tell your boss when you get back to London?'

'Bloody good question! I can save my future and career by telling everyone that Churchill is right. That Hong Kong *is* a fortress if so required. Or I can say that if the Japanese army decided to march down the New Territories to *this* hotel, there's not a damned thing we could do about it.' He paused to drink and realized that the glass was empty. 'What have we got, for God's sake? Antiquated defences, some outdated ships, and a handful of small aircraft that look like survivors from the Western Front!'

Brooke said, 'It would be a terrible blow if we abandoned the Colony.'

'I know. D'you think I haven't thought about it? But I'm a sailor, not a diplomat. General Chiang Kai-Shek's army is the one hope. The Japanese would never be willing to fight on two fronts at once. The Nationalists need guns and all kinds of weapons. It's never easy. Treachery, corruption, incompetence – they put everything at risk.'

Brooke opened the small canvas bag he had brought from the ship.

'What about this?' He pulled out a metal magazine and laid it on the table between their glasses.

His brother took time to light another cigarette. He did not touch it, but said in a more controlled voice, 'Twenty-round magazine. From a B.A.R. Where did you get it?'

'Sub-Lieutenant Kipling found it and handed it to me without telling anybody else. But I think that fishing boat was smuggling arms – to the Nationalists, perhaps?'

Then his brother did pick it up. 'Browning Automatic

Rifle, a light machine-gun to all intents. Bit dated, but it would tip the balance, for a while anyway. Well, well.'

'You didn't know about it?'

Jeremy said coolly, 'No. Not this time, although we know it goes on, of course.'

'*We?*'

His brother stood up as an army driver walked across the lobby, his boots very loud.

'Must go, old chap. By the way, keep in touch with Charles Yeung. Useful fellow. Very influential too.'

Brooke watched the porters gathering up his brother's luggage.

'How influential?'

'Hong Kong and Shanghai Bank, and he owns the Coutts Steamship Packet Company. He's in everything.'

'What happened to his wife? Someone told me she'd been killed.'

'She was very beautiful apparently.' He waved to the driver. 'Made the mistake of visiting friends in Canton. There was a Japanese bombing attack.' He shrugged. 'She didn't make it.'

They walked towards the glass doors and Brooke asked suddenly, 'His daughter . . .'

'Lian?' Jeremy looked surprised. 'What about her?'

'She was in love with you, right?'

He smiled. 'Look, *I must go.*' He held out his hand. 'We did have a thing going in London, but nothing serious.'

He pressed some notes into the duty manager's hand and walked out into the blazing sunshine.

Brooke found that he was clenching his fists. *Nothing serious.* Not to Jeremy Brooke anyway.

He called after him, 'Give my love to Sarah!'

Jeremy tilted his gleaming oak-leaved cap to shade his eyes while the soldier held the car door for him.

He gave him a searching look, perhaps aware of the sarcasm, and replied, 'Will do. Sarah's having a baby – didn't I tell you?'

'No.' The word dropped like a leaf as the car sped past the fountain. 'Neither did she.'

Three days after *Serpent*'s return to Hong Kong and his brother's departure for England, Brooke had still heard nothing more about his report.

The chief-of-staff had merely touched on it when he had telephoned about certain dockyard work which was to be carried out on Brooke's ship. He had said everything was being investigated by the Hong Kong police, and that it seemed likely that the fishing boat's master and his family had been murdered by pirates. There was also the possibility that, as the boat had been so far from the fishing grounds, the murders had been the result of a clash between rival smugglers.

As his brother had so angrily exclaimed in *the Pen*, 'It's as if they don't want to know about it!'

The flotilla leader *Islip* had put to sea on some mission or other, but her captain had hinted that it was more for the entertainment of a trade commission than for any warlike purpose.

'The bloody mess bills will be enormous for the wardroom, I can tell you that!'

It was strange being alongside the wall without *Islip*'s grey hull to provide a sort of privacy. Here, they were observed by everyone, Chinese dockyard workers, British advisers who came and went by the dozen, although the work only entailed the construction of some new mountings for light machine-guns.

Kipling, scruffier than ever, was in charge of them and kept a watchful eye on everything and everyone.

Brooke had heard him telling some serious-faced Chinese with welding equipment where to mount a guard-rail to prevent the machine-guns swinging round under the hands of an excited seaman, and possibly raking the whole bridge by mistake.

There was quite a lot to Kipling, he thought.

He envied his men their comfortable shorts and white tops, and knew that some of them must wonder why he persisted in dressing in a full white uniform. It might look cool, but in this intense heat and humidity it felt clammy and airless.

His injured leg had been troubling him more than usual as well, and he was barely able to conceal it.

One of the dockyard workers had left two steel plates to be ready for the welders and Brooke had walked right into them. The deck had become so familiar to him, and the sun was so bright that it had been entirely his own fault.

He had to be alone. To think out what was happening, rather than sit back without questioning.

It was halfway through the forenoon when he decided to go ashore. It might help to get away from the din of machinery and welders and the unmoving heat throughout the ship, which even the new fans were unable to dispel.

Most of the hands were ashore anyway. He saw Kerr discussing the work with Cusack, the gnome-like Chief, and said, 'I'm off, Number One. Stretch my legs. We're not on standby.'

Kerr eyed him thoughtfully. 'Is there a number where I can reach you, sir?'

'No, there isn't!' It came out sharply and he touched his arm. 'I apologise for that, Dick. Bit under the weather. Sorry.'

151

They all stiffened and saluted as Brooke went down the side.

Calvert appeared, a signal pad in one hand. 'Was that the Old Man?'

They all grinned. The term seemed absurd. Then Kerr said seriously, 'I think his leg's getting worse. Gave it a bash too, on some gear from the yard.'

Calvert shrugged. 'There's a monsoon report, that's all. I thought he should know.'

'It's all right, Pilot. We and the duty part of the watch can deal with the moorings if it blows up.' He stared across the yard but Brooke's figure had already disappeared.

Calvert touched his beard. 'Spanish Civil War, wasn't it?'

'Yes. We should have guessed what was coming after that.'

Calvert tugged at his open-necked shirt. 'I think you should open the bar, Number One.' He looked away. 'I like him, by the way.'

Kerr thought about it. 'When he took command, I wasn't sure. Then, on that damned patrol, I could see the steel in the man. When I came back aboard I nearly broke down in front of him.' He was surprised that he could speak so freely to someone else about what he considered a weakness. 'Some skippers would have skinned me alive!'

Calvert smiled gravely. 'Some.'

Kerr squinted at the sun. 'Well, it's *almost* over the yardarm, Pilot. A gin it is!'

Unaware of his officers' exchange of views, Brooke walked away from the naval base, putting the harbour and the brooding mainland across the water further and further behind him. He found himself walking against a constant throng of people, all of whom seemed to be pushing in the opposite direction, and he was soon swallowed up in the central district, with its narrow alleys and banner-decked stalls stretching away from the main roads where he was constantly returning salutes from wandering servicemen, some of whom he recognized from his own ship.

He was glad he had come ashore. He was wringing wet under his white tunic, and his leg felt as if he had burned it, but the life and movement all around him held him like a drug.

There was a very old temple somewhere in this district: he had heard Vicary, the torpedo gunner's mate, talking about it. He had served on the China Station before the war.

He saw an ancient Chinese man with a tiny wisp of beard sitting cross-legged beside a makeshift newspaper and magazine stall.

'The temple. Can you direct me, please?'

The black eyes barely moved, and yet they seemed to take in all about him. His rank, his face, and perhaps the pain he saw there.

'Pottinger Street, Captain.' A claw-like hand darted out. 'Big hill. Very tiring. Temple is called Man Mo.'

Brooke nodded. 'Yes, that's it!' He wondered if he should offer the little man some money, but he seemed too dignified.

The man leaned forward confidently. 'If Captain has much pain, I have friend . . .' Then he shrugged as Brooke shook his head.

'It's nothing, but thank you very much.'

It was not much further to the street and Brooke paused, staring along, or rather up it. The Chinese man had been right: it was very narrow and extremely steep.

There were no vehicles except for a few handcarts at the bottom displaying their wares, and a metal handrail ran down the middle of the street, without which many older folk would never have managed. Each side of the street was lined with stalls.

An old woman sat balancing a yoke over her shoulders, with a beautifully arranged basket of fruit at either end. It must weigh a ton, Brooke thought. He gripped the handrail and flinched. It felt like a furnace bar.

He began to climb, fascinated by the sights around him as Hong Kong went about its daily business. There were stalls selling bolts of cloth, and dazzling cards of buttons of every kind, and he passed a man standing nonchalantly with one arm bent while a street tailor measured him for a handmade shirt. Behind the stalls were small dark shops, like caves, and he saw a herbalist's display of strange-looking roots, while next door a merchant was selling flour from huge open tubs, and great mounds of rice in hat-shaped baskets. A small, pretty girl was kneeling on the pavement fashioning beautiful table decorations, and there were orchids everywhere, standing in jars and lying on a cloth beside her. She did not look up when he passed.

When he paused for breath he looked down to where he had started: the ascent seemed even steeper from up here. The occasional stairs across the street and the stones themselves were polished, not by thousands but by millions of feet.

He shaded his eyes to stare up at the rickety buildings that stood starkly against the blazing sky. No wonder it was so hot, so breathless: the houses and the shops that crowded on either side held out the air completely. Balcony above balcony, tiny apartments, but many with masses of flowers in tubs and hanging baskets, and some displaying little bamboo cages of singing birds.

He gripped the rail and carried on. Bookshops, stalls of brass ornaments and religious pendants which he did not understand.

The strange thing was that nobody took much notice of him, although if he smiled at a stallholder he received a ready smile in return. There were other contrasts also. The old women, bent double with age and by the burdens they carried on their backs, most of them wearing identical black pyjamas. Faces so lined and wizened that they were like portraits of old China itself. And right amongst them, the chattering children in light cotton school uniforms, all spotlessly clean, even though some of them must live in the most crowded conditions in the decrepit buildings around him.

He heard the growl of traffic ahead and guessed he was coming to a main road which crossed this almost vertical street at right angles. Civilisation again.

He looked up, startled by the sudden bustle along the lines of stalls. Wares were disappearing, men and women dragging their goods under cover with the practised skill of a ship going to action stations. He glanced up at the sky and understood: the sun was gone and the clouds now sweeping over this bustling place were like dense smoke.

All around him umbrellas popped up like mushrooms and some of the hurrying schoolgirls, laughing and calling to one another as they ran, took off their shoes to protect them from the expected downpour. Brooke had reached the road now and saw people taking cover there as well. A few cars and some very ancient vans crowded one another to mix with rickshaws and bicycles.

A man stood smoking in the door of his shop. The contents looked like dried fish or octopus.

'You better come in, Captain! Big rain, longtime come!'

Brooke saw the rain sweeping down the road like something solid, lashing over the scurrying figures and vehicles like a steel fence.

'Thank you!' He felt the rain hit his shoulders, the force of it numbing his body with its onslaught. 'I should have remembered.' Disturbed now, and somehow unsteady, the din of rain making thought impossible.

But the shopkeeper was gripping his arm as if to drag him into the shop. 'What is *wrong*, Captain?'

They faced each other, both streaming with rain. Like the cars and rickshaws which had come to a halt in the road, unable to move.

Other people gathered round, pointing, touching him shyly as if they wanted to help.

Brooke tried to protest but when he looked down he almost fell. The right leg of his white trousers was scarlet with blood. It was running over his shoes and on to the pavement itself.

He did not know what to do, and felt only shame at what was happening.

Beyond the crowd he saw the familiar khaki figures of two Hong Kong policemen, those small, formidable officers, efficient and ruthless.

'I – want . . .' He was going to pass out. The final humiliation.

He became aware of two things. The pale green bonnet of a Rolls-Royce car, which was regarded with immense respect by the two policemen, and the girl's face at the rear window.

It was the same bespectacled chauffeur, assertive and surprisingly strong as he helped the shopkeeper to get him into the sudden peace of the car. Vaguely Brooke heard the rain roaring on the roof, saw someone handing his cap to the chauffeur although he had not felt it fall.

He muttered, 'Sorry about this. Blood on the carpet. So sorry—'

He watched her hands loosen his collar, her face frowning slightly as she gave instructions to her driver.

'Be quiet, Commander! You do not look after yourself!' She sounded angry.

Somebody else was binding his leg with great care. A little old lady in black, like the ones he had seen in the street.

The girl sat back in the leather seat and regarded him gravely. She was becoming blurred, but he saw that her black hair was hanging straight down her back, and that she wore a white jacket and skirt.

She said, 'I will take you to a doctor.' She held up one finger. 'Please do not argue!'

He heard himself say, 'I was going to the temple, you see?'

Then he fainted.

When Esmond Brooke opened his eyes, his senses were slow to adjust. It was like being suddenly struck blind, and curiously he felt no panic. Total darkness, while his limbs felt light. Floating.

He swallowed slowly. An unpleasant taste, his mouth dry. As understanding continued to return he was aware of two things: that he was in a bed with cool sheets, and that he was naked. He tried to move his injured leg, dull memories drifting back of the shopkeeper peering at the flow of blood, and the girl's face staring down at him from the pale green car.

He gritted his teeth as pain probed through his leg.

Numbed perhaps by drugs or an injection, but lurking there as before, waiting for the unguarded moment.

He listened for several minutes while pictures formed and faded in his mind.

She had brought him somewhere. He imagined he could hear music and a kind of rushing sound. It must be the rain. Had it not stopped at all while he had been here?

He moved again. How long had he been here? Where was *here*? Certainly no hospital.

More thoughts flooded through him. What would Kerr do? Had he reported his captain as missing?

His mind strayed back to when he had been given command of the old *Serpent*. His father had been delighted, but nobody had really understood what it had meant. After the disappointments, the deaf ears turned to all his pleas for re-employment in the only life he understood, the destroyer had been like a recognition. And now this. He let his head fall back on the pillow. They would probably put him in front of some medical board.

Sorry, old chap. Too much of a risk. I'm sure you understand? And for a moment he thought the voices were real.

He felt the air move across his face and knew that a door had been opened.

'Who is it?' Even his voice sounded different. Like a croak.

A pale shadow moved beside the bed, and he heard a man say, 'Close eyes. Put on light.'

It was only a small bedside light, the base resembling a Chinese vase adorned with blue and green peacocks.

The man peering down at him was neither young nor old. He wore a plain black coat, almost like a uniform. A servant, perhaps.

But he spoke with dignity and quiet authority.

'My name Robert Tan.' There was pride too. Like the Chief speaking about his engines. 'Mr Yeung valet.' He faltered and added, 'Friend also.'

Brooke stared around the room. Plain, almost spartan, with a shuttered window where he had heard the downpour.

'How long have I been here?'

Robert Tan shrugged. 'Day time.'

Then he bent down and uncovered a jug of juice. He held a glass to Brooke's lips and watched him swallow slowly.

It was cool, almost like barley-water. It could have been anything.

Robert Tan nodded, satisfied. 'I fetch Missy. She worry.'

One second he was alone and the next she was beside the bed. Like a dream: an appearance from nowhere.

She stood quite still, looking down at him, some of her long hair hanging over one shoulder. He was struck by her total composure, the calm appraisal of her dark eyes.

'Are you feeling better, Commander Brooke?'

He swallowed hard. 'What happened? My uniform?'

She moved a pace closer and he could smell her perfume. Like flowers.

'All is taken care of. Not to worry. Your uniform will be clean and pressed when you need it. Your hat also. It fell in the rain.' She toyed with the carved wooden bed-post by his feet and he saw the dark jade ring on one finger, a necklace of jade and silver which barely showed above the neck of her blouse. 'My father insisted that you were brought here. When I told him what you were doing, how sick you were, and yet you

159

walked in such heat he shook his head. "Mad dogs and Englishmen go out in the midday sun," he said.'

Brooke smiled, and winced as the pain touched his leg once more. She watched him, waiting for him to settle again.

'I called a doctor. It was best.' She seemed to sense his uncertainty. Perhaps even what troubled him. 'It was more private.'

Beneath the sheet he touched his skin. It felt cooler, less feverish.

She said gently, 'Robert and William undressed you. You were in good hands. Shan-Cha took care of everything.'

'The doctor?'

'Yes. My sister – she is called Camille.' She watched his surprise. 'She is a good doctor, married to a surgeon. He is an American.' She put her hands on her hips and mimicked, 'Harry's a great guy!'

'I must tell somebody . . .'

'All done. My father has telephoned the head man, all fixed.'

'He called the commodore?'

'Too much questions!' She frowned. 'Camille will see you when she leaves the hospital.' She dabbed his forehead with a small damp towel.

Brooke stared up at her, and wanted to touch her, and wondered if she knew what he was thinking.

'What did the doctor – er, Camille say?'

She looked into his eyes. 'She say you bloody mess!' Then she threw back her head and laughed. 'But she will fix!'

She was serious again. As she folded the little towel before placing it on a dish, she said, 'Your brother left the island. I went to say good-bye.' She walked suddenly to the window and opened the shutters. Her voice was

160

muffled as she added over her shoulder, 'But he was already gone.'

There were stars visible beyond her head and shoulders. A balmy night, the monsoon rain past, for the moment.

Brooke said, 'I saw him.'

She turned lightly. 'Did he speak of me?' Then she shook her head, so that the black hair swirled around her like a silk cape. 'No, do not speak of it. I know it would be a lie!'

He replied, 'I will never lie to you, Lian.'

She folded her hands, losing her composure, surprised by the tone of his voice.

'I think I believe you.'

More lights came on outside the room and Brooke saw another figure standing by the door. It was the girl's father. They spoke briefly in Cantonese and when she nodded Yeung seemed satisfied.

'You are welcome here, Commander Brooke.' He smiled. 'It is difficult to use the same name for a different person, you understand?'

Brooke saw the quick exchange of glances, and was troubled by it. 'But we shall become accustomed to it.'

'I haven't thanked you, sir. For telling the commodore about my trouble.'

Yeung looked momentarily surprised. 'The commodore? No, it was the Assistant Governor. Never require a mouse to squeak when you can obtain a roar from a tiger!'

There were more voices and the valet entered with a medical bag, followed by a woman who was pulling on her white coat to put an official seal on her visit.

She was like her younger sister in many ways: the eyes, the air of confidence. But when she spoke, first in Cantonese to the others and then to her new patient

161

in English, the difference between them was over-whelming.

She had a curt, forthright manner: down-to-earth, as his father would have described it.

'You've had a bad time, Mr Brooke.' She took his temperature without waiting for him to answer. 'Whoever cut your leg did a lousy job, you know that?' After Lian's gentle, almost caressing voice she sounded abrasive, and her accent was very American.

Brooke watched her peering at the thermometer. 'It was at Malta. When we got back.'

'Hmm. Lucky to get that far, if you ask me!'

She washed her hands in a bowl which Robert Tan had provided. While she dried them, finger by finger as if they were medical instruments, she said, 'Are you staying, little sister?'

Charles Yeung frowned at her. 'Do not provoke, Shan-Cha!' He put his arm around the girl's shoulders and guided her to the door.

The doctor smiled and switched on more lights. 'Your brother has a lot to answer for!' Then she gripped the sheet and dragged it from the bed, leaving him naked under her searching glare.

She held some scissors up to the light and clicked them open and shut.

'Sunstroke, fever, and bad surgery. Strong stuff.' She began to snip at the bandages. 'You'll never lose the limp.' She glanced up at him, and only for a few seconds she was very like her sister. 'But you won't lose your leg either.'

Brooke gasped as the last piece of dressing tore away and he knew the wound was bleeding again, then fresh dressings were bound in place, and Robert Tan washed away the blood and collected the stained bandages. His face was a mask of disapproval. He probably saw it as

162

a breach of all he believed in that a woman, even one posing as a doctor, should see and touch an unknown man's nakedness.

She bent over Brooke and lifted each eyelid. 'I shall see you again.' She gripped his arm, her small hand like steel as she rubbed it with some cotton wool before picking up a hypodermic syringe from the table.

Brooke felt the prick of the needle and instantly his mind seemed to succumb.

He did not feel the needle withdraw, nor the rub of the wool on his skin. But the pain was going, along with his senses.

But not before he heard her voice, which seemed to be coming down a long tunnel.

'Do not hurt my sister. There are ways . . .' The rest was lost. But it stayed in his drowning mind like a threat.

10

Friends

The strident south-westerly monsoons that swept the New Territories and Hong Kong were interspersed with periods of intense heat and humidity. When the torrential rain passed on and the sun broke through again to reveal flooded storm-drains, landsides and choked ditches, the steam rose over every town and village like smoke.

But the July monsoon brought something else: *Serpent*'s ship's company received their first mail from home.

Some of it had reached Hong Kong quickly, but much had been redirected from port to port by an overworked Fleet Mail Office. During stand-easy when even the dockyard workers were silent the letters were devoured by the lucky ones, and watched with envy and disappointment by the others.

There were brave letters from mothers and wives, although many of *Serpent*'s company were too young to be married.

Carefully worded, and full of concern for their men on the other side of the world. Little was said about the daily and nightly air-raids, of streets wiped out, of families torn apart by war. Compared with Hong Kong it was a living hell for those who had to grin and bear it.

There was always news of neighbours and friends who had lost someone at sea or in the air. The latter was happening more frequently now, as for the first time the Royal Air Force was taking the war into occupied Europe and over the enemy bases there. Rations, black-out, shortages, all were briefly mentioned, but in most of the letters there was only love. The yearning, sometimes never expressed in words, to see a particular face again.

A few of the envelopes were sealed with lipstick kisses. Fewer still had precious photographs inside to pass around. There was every sort of bad news too. A death in the family: enemy action or natural causes, it made little difference when half the world separated them.

And then, of course, there were the hated letters from *friends*.

Thought you should know, it seems only right with you out there fighting the war and risking your life. We've seen your wife out with so-and-so. Didn't get home until morning . . .

Or, *I'm not one to interfere, but your girl's having it off with a bloody conchie of all people, he works on the farm . . .* There were always a few anxious faces at the requestmen's table the next day.

Even the wardroom was not immune.

It was quiet with most of the officers ashore, and the captain at the naval hospital to see the P.M.Q. Lieutenant Toby Calvert had the place to himself.

With a glass of fruit juice at his elbow while he thumbed through an ageing copy of *Picture Post*, he was half thinking of the mansion on the Peak where he had taken the signals file for Brooke's approval.

Calvert had dealt with rich people several times and had been hired on occasion to fly their private aircraft to the south of France. The plummy jobs as he called them.

He had been greeted by the same lovely girl he had seen at the buffet party. She had been nice enough, but wary. No, protective: that was the word for it.

Brooke had been out of bed and wearing a silk dressing-gown, and he had looked better than Calvert had ever seen him. There had been a kind of boyishness in his face which he had probably believed would never be his again.

Calvert still didn't know how it was between him and the girl. He had heard about Brooke's brother. Maybe it was a rebound. He had seen it often enough.

Charles Yeung had come to see him out when he had been ready to leave.

'I will have you driven, Mr Calvert.'

Calvert had the impression that he had been waiting for him.

'Your captain is much improved, eh?' He had looked at Calvert with those steady, penetrating eyes. 'I have a favour to ask of you, Mr Calvert.'

'Of course, sir.'

Yeung had smiled wryly. 'So typical. A Chinese would first ask what it was, and then if there was money in it!'

The small chauffeur, whose name was apparently William, had entered at that moment. He, too, had been waiting.

Yeung had led Calvert to the front steps. 'Later we will talk.'

Calvert still could not imagine what favour he could possibly want from a mere lieutenant, when he had most of the top brass in his pocket to all accounts.

Petty Officer Bert Kingsmill came into the wardroom wearing his familiar white jacket.

He said in his usual mournful tone, 'Thought you might be here, sir. The dockyard men are aboard to make a last adjustment to the machine-gun mountings.'

'Well, I'm not the O.O.D.' Calvert put down the magazine. 'Where's Barrington-Purvis?'

Kingsmill gave what might have been a smirk. 'Mr Barrington-Purvis is ashore.' He sniffed. 'Playin' tennis.' He made it sound obscene.

'Then tell Mr Kipling. He's on duty.' He smiled. 'I believe he's quite a good hand with guns.'

Kingsmill turned to depart, working out what he was going to say. Then he turned and stopped. 'Almost forgot, sir. Letter for you.'

Calvert took it, thinking it must be a mistake.

It bore his name and rank, complete with V.C., and a whole mixture of blue-pencilled instructions and crossings-out. He did not recognize either the postmark or the handwriting, and he felt himself trembling as he stared at it. Maybe it was from some crew member's relative or girlfriend, trying to track him down ever since it happened, and wanting to know *how it had been*.

He swore and tore open the envelope.

It was a Hampshire address. He turned it over. The last line said, *I hope you will forgive my writing to you like this out of the blue. But you were so kind to me on the train*. It was signed Sue Yorke.

The hammers and drills started up again, and the tannoy droned, 'Out pipes! Hands carry on with your work!' Calvert heard none of it.

He spread the letter on the table and stared at it.

You may not even remember me but I felt I wanted to write to you after what happened. If this letter finds you I shall quite understand if you do not reply. I do not know your circumstances, where you are or what you are doing.

You will know about the terrible tragedy with my husband's ship. She had omitted the ship's name, probably for fear of the censor. *Bob did not survive. I think I knew before it happened. My parents were a great help and it was when I mentioned you to Dad that he got all excited. He keeps a book of cuttings about the war. There were two about you.* The handwriting was slightly smudged. Tears? *You never said a word about it to me, what you did, and the Victoria Cross.*

I decided to write to you because I knew you would understand. Nobody else does. Sympathy is not always enough. It's like an ache, a void. Like a part of you taken away.

I hope you are keeping well. You are not to worry about those little scars on your face. They will go away, Dad says. They are honourable scars, and you must never forget it.

There was a different ink, as if she had changed pens while trying to make up her mind whether to finish or destroy the letter.

Calvert found he was touching his beard. Was it so obvious?

If you write to me, my dad will forward it to me. I am using my unmarried name and hope to be going back into uniform. It might help.

He studied her signature. Round and neat, like a schoolgirl's. He tried to remember her. In that murky first-class compartment it hadn't been easy to see her. Small, pretty, and he thought probably dark, although the hat had covered her hair. A wedding ring and a naval brooch. It was little enough.

He stood up and walked to an open scuttle. Kowloon

was fast disappearing again under a fresh onslaught of rain.

He would not answer her letter. What was the point? Another rebound perhaps, except that this girl had nothing left.

She must feel bitter. Cheated. There would be many more like her before this war ended, either way.

He returned to the table and looked at the address again. Winchester. Not all that far from where he had learned to fly.

Strange how an unknown girl had allowed that memory to return.

Back into uniform. The Wrens? He frowned. No, she had not known very much about ships, even the *Hood*.

He patted his pocket but remembered that his tobacco pouch was empty: he had taken all his stock to the house on the Peak for the skipper. He smiled. *The Old Man.* They were the same age.

He would ask Kingsmill to get some.

But instead he found himself at the wardroom desk, pulling open the drawer and taking out some writing paper with the ship's fierce crest at the top. *Hostibus Nocens, Innocens Amicus.*

He sat down and took the cap off his pen.

When Kingsmill bustled in, tutting to himself, to close the scuttle as the rain splashed unheeded over the curtains, Lieutenant Toby Calvert, Victoria Cross, was still writing.

Kingsmill departed, glaring.

Bloody officers, never thought of anyone but themselves!

The big Rolls-Royce moved smoothly along a narrow

street, untroubled by the uneven surface and the crowds of Chinese and occasional soldier or sailor.

Esmond Brooke was very conscious of the girl's nearness in the other rear seat, of her perfume, and one hand which lay on a cushion close to his.

She touched his sleeve. 'There it is. Where we found you.'

Brooke stared at the untidy corner shop with its array of dried fish, the owner still standing in the doorway smoking a cigarette as if he had not moved. He was astonished to realize he could barely remember anything about it. Almost guiltily he glanced down at the car's carpet, but, like his freshly pressed uniform, there was no trace of blood.

'More comfortable than walking, yes?'

He turned and looked at her: all in white again, with a pale green blouse showing beneath her jacket. Her hair was piled on her head as when he had first seen her and she wore long, ornate jade earrings, which he found himself wanting to touch.

'You are staring again, Commander Brooke!'

He smiled. 'It is a pleasure for me – ' he hesitated over her name, 'Lian.'

'We are coming to the temple that you wished to see.'

Brooke looked between the chauffeur, William, and the tiny black-clad figure of Lian's companion: she had once been amah to Lian and her sister and had stayed on with the family. Her name was Nina Poon, a very grim-faced little woman whose features were covered with lines and wrinkles.

When they had got into the car Lian had remarked, 'We take Nina. Otherwise it is not proper for well brought-up Chinese girl to be seen alone with male person.'

Brooke never knew if she was being serious or whether she was making a private joke.

William opened the sliding glass panel that separated him from his passengers.

'Man Mo Temple, Captain!'

Brooke peered at heavy railings and gates as the car glided to a halt. He pulled himself to the edge of the deep seat and knew she was watching him.

She asked, 'Still hurt?'

He shook his head. 'Much better. Your sister knows her profession.'

She shrugged. 'My father thinks differently. He does not approve. She should be married into a proper life with her husband, have children.'

'Is that what he wants of you?'

The door was opened for them and the car's cool interior admitted the furnace heat of the street. She did not answer him, or perhaps she had not heard.

A chattering crocodile of small Chinese schoolgirls parted to let them through. The old amah followed at a discreet distance.

William saluted and said for Brooke's benefit, 'Be here when you want, Missy. No hurry.'

Through the entrance and Brooke had to pause to allow his eyes to accustom themselves to the near darkness of the temple. Then he gazed around, aware for the first time that there were several people already here. A woman with a shopping basket knelt before one of the gods, bowing several times with her eyes closed, while the pair of joss-sticks she held up to the god made trails of smoke and incense. Overhead hung faded red silk lanterns, decorated with long black tassels, and cone-shaped coils of incense which Brooke thought must burn for days. It all seemed very casual. A couple of attendants in singlets and shorts were burning prayer papers in a great iron censer, while they smoked their cigarettes and chatted to one another. A thin cat slept, curled up on one of the rosewood chairs arranged along the two outer walls; and an old man in a black skull cap was making notes in a newspaper.

She whispered, 'Picking horses for Happy Valley!'

The woman had finished her prayers and left the smouldering joss-sticks in a brazier on the altar before the god.

Lian asked, 'What do you think?'

Brooke hesitated, then whispered, 'I think it's wonderful. I've never seen anything like it.'

She watched his profile against the lights and the gifts waiting for the gods' attention. Fruit, little cakes, even cigarettes. No pomp. No attempt to impress or awe. It was all the more inspiring, he thought.

She said quietly, 'There are many gods here. But the temple was built for two of them, nobody really knows how long ago. Some say there has always been a temple here. The King-Emperor Man, and the holy King-Emperor Kwan. Many people come here for help and guidance.' She watched the old man frowning over his newspaper. 'And for matters of joy and entertainment.'

A chair scraped and Brooke saw the old amah sitting down.

But her bright eyes, which shone in the lanterns like red stones, never left him.

'May we sit down a moment, please?' He did not know why he had said it.

She took his arm and guided him up the steps, closer to the statues. A dog dozed by one of the altars, glad to be out of the heat.

'Here.' They sat side by side, and then she said, 'What did your navy doctor have to say?'

'He was very impressed. I will still have trouble with

172

it. There are some metal fragments left there. Very small.'

She said, 'I saw the wounds.'

He stared at her. 'You *what*?'

She did not turn. 'Do not be angry. The gods will not like it.' Then she said, 'I wanted to help. I know how important your ship is to you. My father told me some of it . . . I think I saw the rest in your eyes. When your officer came to the house I could understand how he felt about you. It is something men share sometimes, women only rarely.'

More people entered the smoky and dusty temple and they watched them kneel and worship as the others had done.

She looked at him in her very direct way. 'When you fell that day,' she grappled with it for several seconds, 'you dropped a wallet. It was all wet when William picked it up.'

She reached out and grasped his wrist, her fingers surprisingly cold. 'There was a picture. I tried to dry it for you. Of a girl. You love her?'

Brooke laid his hand on hers, holding her fingers between them.

'I thought I did.'

'But you do not . . .?'

He knew it was suddenly important. 'She married my brother.'

'I see.' She was pulling her hand away. 'I did not know about her until afterwards.'

He saw her staring around the temple as if she did not know where she was. *Afterwards?* It might mean anything.

She continued in the same low voice, 'It seems we were both mistaken, Commander Brooke.'

She stood up quickly and for a moment he imagined she was going to leave him.

Instead, she walked to one of the attendants and took four joss-sticks from him.

'Come.' She held them over a candle until all four were smoking. 'We pray now.'

He knelt stiffly on one of the well-used cushions and stared up at the images of Man and Mo. They gazed back at him while the incense curled around them from the many smouldering sticks.

She glanced at him, her eyes in shadow; but her jade necklace was moving to reveal the intensity of her emotion.

She said simply, 'Say nothing. They will unroll your thoughts.'

So he thought: of his father, his jokes and his memories of so many places. Hong Kong had been one of them. Had he ever come here?

He thought of Sarah, who was expecting a baby. In other circumstances, it might have been his. Perhaps she had not realized that Jeremy had no use for sentiment. He might display some counterfeit of it if he thought it might help his progress, but it went no deeper. Maybe, after all, she was like him.

And he thought of Lian. Did the gods, who were sharing these thoughts, find nothing strange in this unsettling situation? That this lovely Chinese girl, about whom he knew almost nothing, had helped dress his wounded and, in his eyes, obscene leg? Sarah had been repelled by it.

Did the gods know the future?

He helped her to her feet and together they planted their joss-sticks side by side.

She bowed towards the nearest altar and said, 'We can only hope.'

Then she said in a different voice, 'You will come back to the house for some tea?'

'I have to go to the ship.'

She nodded. 'I will take you to the dockyard.'

He heard the old amah shuffling after them and saw William standing on the pavement, dwarfed by the car he drove with such pride.

She asked directly, 'Will you be sailing for England soon?'

Again, he knew it was important. 'I think it unlikely.' He watched her face but it gave nothing away.

She said, 'I could not rescue the photograph. I am very afraid it had been spoiled.'

They faced one another, and again he was very aware of her, and wanted to tell her so.

'That is *all right*, Lian.'

Then she smiled for the first time since they had come to the temple.

'I hoped it would be,' she said.

They drove back slowly towards the harbour, along Connaught Road and past the piers and busy shipping.

At the gateway to the little naval dockyard a sentry snapped to attention as the car rolled impressively to a halt; but the sailor showed no surprise or curiosity. Charles Yeung was obviously very well known in Victoria.

Brooke got out and looked at her. 'I would like to see you again.'

He heard voices and glanced round in time to see Pike, the coxswain, and his friend Andy Laird the chief stoker, with their arms around the shoulders of Onslow, the yeoman of signals. All disentangled themselves and saluted.

Brooke saw that Onslow wore his new petty officer's peaked cap and shirt with blue badges pinned in place.

He had heard that as soon as Onslow had his proper rate confirmed the chief and petty officers' mess were going to pay for a completely new, made-to-measure fore-and-aft uniform. They had obviously been celebrating.

Pike grinned hugely. 'Takin' Yeo ashore for a spot of sightseein', sir!'

They all chuckled but their eyes were on the girl inside the splendid car.

Brooke smiled. 'Get along with you! And congratulations, Yeo!'

Andy Laird nodded. 'All right for some, eh, Swain?'

But Pike knew exactly how far he could go. 'Beats the Smoke any time, don't it, sir?'

They all tottered away, set on a good time.

He explained quietly, 'My yeoman of signals lost his wife and child just before we came here.'

He turned back to her and saw her watching his mouth as if to read each word.

'They *like* you.' She looked suddenly sad. 'I must be careful, or I might like you also. That would never do, I think.'

He lifted her hand off the lowered window and kissed it. People hurried past and neither stared nor made any obvious comment.

He said, 'I will call you, Lian.'

She held her hand to her cheek, her eyes very bright. 'Good-bye, Es-mond.'

The car moved away and Brooke stared after it, but she did not look back.

Es-mond. He had never cared for his first name. Like everything else, the girl had given it a new value.

11

A Ship of War

Esmond Brooke sat squarely in his bridge chair, an unlit pipe clenched between his teeth. The air was heavy and clammy, but compared with between decks where it was like an oven in spite of the busy fans, and the blazing heat in the confines of an open bridge during the daylight, it was almost exhilarating. He watched the arrowhead of the sharp forecastle rise streaming from the sea, water cascading down either side as far as 'A' gun before ploughing into the next steep roller. Even some of the older hands would be throwing up in this, he thought.

It was pitch black, with no stars to divide the ocean from the sky.

Down again, the spindrift flying over the glass screen like white arrows.

Kerr emerged from beneath the chart table's hood and said, 'Pretty lively, sir.'

'It may get worse.' Strange how easy it was to talk with the first lieutenant now. Perhaps Kerr's admission of his fear aboard the sinking fishing boat was a part of it. Like Calvert, who had even touched very briefly on flying.

Like me. He wiped his face with a wet towel as he recalled his shame over his injured leg. He was not over it, but the girl had helped more than she could ever know.

He had seen her only once more before *Serpent* had been ordered to sea on another patrol. Without effort he could summon her to his mind, even though he had repeatedly told himself he was being ridiculous. Perhaps she was trying to show his brother that she did not care about his behaviour. That she had never been really serious.

Their last meeting had been so formal he had barely spoken to her. Her father had invited some of his own friends to dinner at his fine house on the Peak, dedicated eaters to a man. Charles Yeung had prodded the air with a cigarette, which he was rarely without, and through the smoke had said, 'Lian, sit beside the commander. Teach him the foreign ways of chopsticks!'

She had not looked at him but had watched her hand on his as she had guided his fingers until he had eventually obtained a proper grip on them.

A wet figure lurched across the bridge. Sub-Lieutenant Paul Kipling, at odds with the others in the same old khaki drill uniform in which he had first come aboard.

Brooke twisted round in his chair. 'Number One? What can we do about getting some Chinese dhobi-men on board? Other ships on the China Station have them. They could manage our shirts and other gear in no time, I'm told.'

Kerr's teeth shone through the gloom. 'The old three-badgemen won't thank you for that, sir. They've got their own firm down below, in league with the boiler-room crowd of course, for drying out the clothing!' He considered it. 'I'll lay something on. The wardroom funds can stand it.'

He watched Brooke as he raised himself in the chair

178

to stare into the spray. More like a first-passage midshipman than the commanding officer, he thought.

'You were always in destroyers, sir?'

'Except for a training cruiser, yes. Always wanted to be. I suppose my father had something to do with it.'

Kerr saw him run his hand along the rail below the screen, where canvas dodgers had once been rigged to help protect the bridge team from wind and weather. The dodgers had vanished with many other original fittings.

'I never thought I'd get to drive *Serpent* though.'

'You seem to get along well together!' Kerr staggered as the bows went down again and somebody sprawled headlong by the ladder. The ship was at cruising stations, four hours on and eight off. Welcome under other conditions, but not in this.

Brooke commented, 'My father always said of destroyers, *"Bigger than anything faster, faster than anything bigger"*. Suits 'em, eh?'

Kerr said, 'I hear you've been doing Hong Kong in some style, sir.'

'The car, you mean?' Before, he might have looked for some other reason for the remark. To Kipling he said, 'Phantom II, you said?'

Kipling walked across the rolling bridge like a Liverpool drunk. Against the pale paintwork his shirt looked black. He was soaked.

'Give me a chance to drive it, that's all I ask!'

Brooke wiped his empty pipe on his shirt. So Kerr knew. Then the whole ship would. In destroyers it was like that.

He said, 'Better go round the ship, Number One. Make sure that everything is battened down. I know you've done it, but be certain the hands know what it's all about. After the Atlantic and home waters – well, it might take the edge off them. Sub and I will hold the fort until you get back.' He lowered his voice and added, 'There might be a temptation to open a scuttle or raise a deadlight. It's common enough. But this ship is on active service, although it may not seem like it to some. I want her blacked out, right?'

'Are you still considering the chance of a German commerce raider, sir?'

'No.' He touched his bare arm; it was not only wet but also it was suddenly cold. It was absurd. He reached down and felt the fresh bandages on his leg. It was not that.

'Something wrong, sir?'

'Just me. Forget it. Can't get used to all this, I suppose.'

Kerr peered at him and wished he could see his face. More likely that stunning Chinese girl, he thought. Probably thinking of her right now. The island was about fifty miles astern. It could have been ten times that much.

'D'you think we'll ever be returning to the U.K., sir? I mean, for active duty?'

'It rather depends on . . .'

A bridge messenger called, 'Signal, sir!'

'Tell the W/T office to send it up.' He heard Kerr say, 'Not urgent, anyway.'

The messenger hauled the little brass cylinder up the tube from the W/T office and pulled out a rolled flimsy.

Together Brooke and Kerr crawled under the canvas hood and switched on the chart light.

Brooke read it aloud. 'Broadcast from Hong Kong. Typhoon of unknown intensity situated within fifty miles of Latitude nineteen degrees North, Longitude one hundred and ten degrees East. Moving North-West. Time of origin seventeen hundred.'

'Well, now we know, sir.' He watched as Brooke's brown hands moved the parallel rulers expertly on the soiled chart. Outside their tiny haven the spray hammered the hood like lead pellets, and Brooke could feel the sweat running down his spine as if there was a leak in the canvas.

He said, 'Should veer away before it gets here.'

'Bit early for a typhoon, I'd have thought, sir?'

Brooke tapped the chart with his dividers. 'October is usually the worst, according to the good book. But you can never rely on it apparently. Pass the word when you go round the messdecks, will you? Nothing too dramatic. I'll speak to the lads on the tannoy if it does get bad.'

They ducked out from cover and into the clinging heat. It was not raining, but it might just as well have been, Kerr thought.

'Tell Pilot if you see him. He can log its progress when the watch changes.'

Kerr knew there was something else.

'Have you ever been close to marriage, Number One?'

Kerr gripped a rail as the side went down. 'I know a girl, sir. Known her since I was a cadet. I'm not sure, though . . .'

'About what?'

Kerr looked in his direction. 'In wartime – you know, sir.'

'I suppose so.' He clambered into the tall chair again. 'Carry on.'

'Wheelhouse – bridge?'

Kipling went straight to the voicepipe. He had learned fast.

'Forebridge?'

'Able Seaman Shaw relieving the helm, sir!'

181

'Very well.'

It never stopped. Soon the various messes would start to prepare their evening meals, provided the galley fire was still alight. If the sea really got up they would be sharing the meal with some of that too, Brooke thought.

He recalled her eyes when she had told him about the damage to Sarah's photograph. She must have done it out of anger. She had thought him to be like Jeremy in that too.

A fanny of tea came to the bridge but it tasted salty; it must have had a rough passage from the galley.

Kerr returned and shook his sodden cap on the deck. 'All secure, sir. Told Pilot about it.' He took a mug of tea and grimaced. 'God, I should have brought some from aft!'

A voicepipe squeaked again and Kipling reached out to snap open the cover.

'Busy this evening,' Brooke observed calmly. But his insides were far from calm.

Kipling snapped, 'Send it up, man!'

To Brooke he said, '*Mayday* call, sir.'

Kerr seized the little brass tube again and took the signal flimsy to the chart table.

Brooke said, 'Call the navigating officer to the bridge, someone!'

Kerr called out, 'From Flag, sir. *Distress signal from S. S. Kiang Chen. Has lost rudder and out of command. Requires urgent assistance.*'

Kipling asked quietly, 'Why didn't our W/T pick it up, sir?'

'The conditions, probably. Besides, the transmitters and receivers at the base are giants compared to ours.'

Kerr was still under the cover writing busily on the navigation pad.

He called, 'Signal ends, sir, *Proceed with all despatch.*'

Feet clattered on to the bridge and Calvert swayed like a ghost on the top of the ladder.

'Sir?'

Brooke said, 'S.O.S., Pilot.' Kerr reappeared. 'One hundred and fifty miles south-west-by-west of Hong Kong. Latitude twenty, Longitude one hundred and ten.'

About a hundred miles away. Still time to avoid the storm. Brooke watched the sea explode over the bows again. They could manage half-speed in this if it got no worse.

He said, 'Course to intercept, Pilot. Get the Chief out of his armchair.'

Calvert said eventually, 'Course to steer is two-one-five degrees, sir.'

Brooke rubbed his chin, his mind far beyond the trembling ship. The South China Sea's other face.

Kipling said, 'The Chief's on the phone, sir.' He was smiling. 'He was already down there with his engines!'

Brooke took the red handset. How difficult it must have been in his father's day when the engine room had only a speaking tube. With all that din it was a wonder they got anything right.

'Chief, sir.'

'S.O.S., Chief.' He covered the handset. 'Call W/T, Number One. Ask them if they picked up anything. If not, make a signal to the *Flag* and report our position and acknowledge the order to proceed.' He removed his hand again. 'Can you give me revs for eighteen knots?'

No hesitation. 'Of course, sir.'

He smiled. 'I'll ring down when I'm ready.'

'You are relieved, Number One. Get hold of the chief

183

bosun's mate and put him in the picture. Fenders, line-throwing gun – he knows what to do.'

Kerr hesitated. 'No signals received by W/T, sir.'

'Probably gone under.' That was Kipling.

'Need me, sir?' It was Onslow, still unfamiliar in his peaked cap.

Brooke smiled grimly. 'Mind-reader, Yeo. Check the signal and have a look through the intelligence pack in my hutch. Try and discover what sort of ship we're dealing with. Could be a liner or the Star Ferry for all this tells us!'

Several of them laughed while the ship fell about beneath them. He saw her face, suddenly and as clearly as a photograph, as she had gazed up at him from the car.

They like you.

He looked at Calvert by the chart table. 'Bring her round to two-one-five, Pilot. We should intercept the ship in five to six hours if this gets no worse.' He touched the back of his chair. 'She can make it.'

Then he held up his hand. 'But first things first.' He picked up the tannoy microphone, wet and smooth in his grip. How many hundreds of times must it have been used. While soldiers had floundered in the sea in desperate but patient queues at Dunkirk, or while *Serpent* had circled struggling survivors after a ship had gone down. What she could say if only she could speak . . .

Calvert must be thinking of it too. From Stringbag to destroyer. But the same, bloody war.

He snapped down the button. 'This is the captain. In a moment we are altering course to port. It may be slightly uncomfortable.' The signalman bared his teeth in a grin, and down on the messdeck they would be chuckling or cursing the bridge in equal portions. 'There

184

is a vessel in distress. This is a ship of war, but the other rule is older and as important.'

He hung up the instrument and said, 'Carry on, Pilot.'

Calvert crouched by the gyro-repeater and then spoke into the bell-mouthed voicepipe.

'Port twenty!'

'Coxswain on the wheel, sir! Twenty of port wheel on!'

Brooke gripped the chair as the helm went over. Pike always knew. Like the Chief, and Onslow, and the Buffer, the foxy-faced petty officer who was already gathering rescue gear and the men to handle it.

Kipling muttered, '*Whoops!*'

Calvert felt his shoes slipping on the wet gratings.

'Steady! Meet her! Steer two-one-five!' He wiped the ticking gyro-repeater with his bare arm as he watched the luminous figures come to rest.

Pike reported calmly, 'Course two-one-five, sir!'

Brooke nodded, pleased. The ex-Swordfish pilot had handled her like a veteran.

'One-one-zero revolutions!'

Onslow came in at the bridge gate, but paused to watch the surge of sea and foam against the weather side.

Brooke said, 'Find out anything, Yeo?'

Onslow nodded. Out of breath. He was proud too that the captain had allowed him to go to his hutch and look at his confidential log.

'The *Kiang Chen* is registered at Hong Kong, sir. A coaster, two thousand tons. Built in the Great War.'

Brooke touched his skin again. The same feeling. 'So was this lady, Yeo.'

It must have been something in his tone. Onslow said, 'Nothing much else, sir.'

He asked, 'Who owns her?' He had to repeat the question before the yeoman heard him. He already knew.

'Coutts Steamship Packet Company.'

Brooke could hear his brother's voice again, telling him about Charles Yeung's many interests. This elderly coaster was one of them.

To the bridge at large he said, 'We're on our way.'

But later Calvert thought he had been speaking to his ship.

'Blue Watch closed up at cruising stations, sir!'

Brooke heard Calvert acknowledge the report. Confident, his earlier wariness apparently gone.

He watched the bows rising again, higher this time, before smashing down into a cruising roller like a giant axe. He thought of what Kerr had told him when he had carried out another tour of the lower deck. Some of the messes were in chaos with shattered crockery scattered everywhere and gear coming adrift. Even the fiddles and lashings could not cope with these wild plunges.

In the heads it was far worse as gasping men tried to find a space to vomit, while the confined stench had affected the others. Even Kerr, who was a good sailor, had admitted to being queasy.

The middle watch. Brooke had hoped to find something by now, a flare perhaps, a drifting boat. There was nothing. Worse, they had lost precious time by reducing revolutions to avoid unnecessary strain on the shafts. Before doing so the whole ship had shaken herself like a wet dog when the screws had been lifted almost to the surface.

The vessel in distress had probably gone down. It

happened often enough out here, according to the reports. Old, unseaworthy vessels, sometimes overloaded, or those whose cargoes began to shift when the sea showed its temper.

Beyond the glass screen it was black but for the leaping spectres of ragged waves. Even the cosy red glow below Brooke's side of the bridge had gone: he had ordered all lights out, including the navigation lights. Right or wrong, who was to say? This was not described as a war zone. But the *Serpent* was at war. Whatever happened Brooke was in no doubt of the outcome. If you did right, others would take the credit; make a mistake, and it would end in a court martial. It was a tongue-in-the-cheek joke amongst most commanding officers. Until it happened.

'Bridge, sir?'

Calvert swayed to the voicepipe. 'Officer-of-the-Watch!'

'The interpreter requests permission to come up, sir.'

Brooke turned. 'Affirmative, Pilot!'

The interpreter, Mr John Chau, was the new addition to their company. A serious-faced, eager little man, he was a bank official by profession but also a member of the Hong Kong Royal Naval Volunteer Reserve. During his peacetime training he had acted as a boarding-officer in one of Hong Kong's auxiliary patrol vessels, where his knowledge of both Mandarin and Cantonese had been extremely useful. He would make the chance of a mistake when stopping and searching a suspicious vessel less likely. Graded as an acting warrant-officer, he was permitted to share the wardroom, and he slept on a camp-bed in Calvert's chart-packed cabin. In any night emergency it would be likely that Mr Chau would be trampled to death before he could get up.

It took him an age to reach the forebridge. Groaning

and retching, he was eventually hauled through the gate by one of the signalmen.

'So sorry, sir!' He gripped the compass platform's safety rail and stared despairingly at the sea while the bows lifted once again.

Brooke said, 'Keep your eyes outboard, dead ahead if you can.'

Calvert said, 'Like a roller-coaster, you know.'

Brooke smiled. 'Give him a break, Pilot.'

Under his breath Onslow, the yeoman, who had remained on the bridge since the distress call, muttered, 'Just keep a bloody bucket handy!'

Brooke asked, 'Settled in, Mr Chau?'

'Very much, sir, thank you.'

Brooke thought of Charles Yeung's valet, Robert Tan. Chau spoke like a younger version of the man.

Calvert said, 'Come and look at the chart, John. You might learn something.'

Brooke settled down in his tall chair and smiled to himself. Calvert was making up for his comment in the midst of Chau's seasickness.

Under the cover of the canvas hood Calvert tapped the chart with his pencil. 'The sea shoals to starboard. Although in home waters we'd still think it was deep!'

'What about here, sir?'

'Different matter entirely. A few more miles and we shall have fourteen hundred fathoms under where you're standing.'

Chau was neither impressed nor surprised.

He said softly, 'A place unknown to any man. All-time darkness, fish and creatures so terrible that the gods keep them where they can harm no one.'

Calvert grinned. 'I expect you're right.' Across the interpreter's slight shoulders he called to Brooke, 'Shall I work out a box-search, sir?'

'I think not. Another fifteen minutes. Then I'm turning back.' He was still thinking of the interpreter's seriousness. As she had been, when he had believed she was making fun of him. Chau was not speaking of superstition or fable. To him it was simply fact.

Brooke said to Onslow, 'Have some men uncover the big searchlight. Men who know what they're doing.'

'Aye, sir.' He touched the seaman beside him. 'Get your mate and report when you've cleared away the searchlight, right?'

The young seaman grinned. 'Sure thing, Yeo!'

The old lower-deck magic, Brooke thought. The seaman was the same one that Onslow had sworn at so despairingly when the dead woman and her child had been found under the overturned lifeboat.

They had obviously put it behind them. A solemn handshake, and probably sippers or gulpers from their respective tots of rum, but each man knowing he would react the same way if it happened again.

Kerr reappeared on the bridge. Nobody was sleeping tonight.

Brooke put him in the picture. He added, 'I'm not too hopeful, Number One. How is it below?'

Kerr thought of the sprawled bodies trying to rest, huddled or lying on the tilting deck amidst a confusion of broken plates, scattered food and vomit.

He replied with a grin, 'Just fine, sir.'

'I'll bet.'

'Oh, one thing, sir. I visited the Asdic cabinet. They're having a spot of bother with the set. Leading Seaman Aller is convinced it's something the dockyard did wrong.'

'I'll get on to the yard when we get in. Not that it's much use anyway out here.'

'It wasn't that, sir. The new Asdic chap, Ordinary

189

Seaman Kellock – he only joined a few months back.'
Even in the darkness he knew Brooke was frowning.
'Ginger hair,' he prompted. 'Nice lad to all accounts.'

The round freckled face appeared in his mind as if
on a screen.

'What about him?'

'I *think* he's going to put in a request to see you in
private, sir. The cox'n has had his ear to the ground.'

'Any ideas?'

'He wants to get married, sir.'

Brooke tried to see his expression. 'God, he's only a
child!'

'We all were once.'

'*You* see him, Number One. Welfare. It's out of the
question.'

Kerr had saved the best part for last. 'She's a Chinese
girl from Wanchai.'

Calvert called, 'Better ask Paul Kipling about Wanchai. I think he knows the area!'

Kerr persisted, 'Kellock has the right to see you, sir.'

Brooke grinned. 'Tell me about it!'

'*Flare, sir! Starboard bow!*'

Several pairs of binoculars braved the drifting spray
to find the look-out's flare.

Like a guttering candle, low down, or so it appeared.
Instinct, or had some poor wretch been able to make
out *Serpent*'s great ragged bow-wave as she plunged
through each successive roller?

Brooke said, 'Pass the word to the Buffer.' He wiped
his face with his forearm. 'Stand by with the searchlight.
Give them a rough guide to sweep from the bow to
abeam!'

He leaned forward in his chair, and realized that his
ribs were sore where its arms had been scraping into
him every time the ship rolled.

Kerr said, 'I'll get down there, sir.'

Brooke turned towards him. 'Ordinary Seaman Kellock indeed!'

The youth in question was hunched over beside the Asdic set trying to keep out of everyone's way. The small cabinet was crowded. Leading Seaman Aller was on his knees passing wire to a torpedoman who was stretched out on his back beneath the steel mounting. The sides of the place were streaming with condensation, and more dropped from the deckhead like tropical rain.

The torpedoman, Usher, nicknamed Pop because of his premature baldness, croaked, 'Nearly done, me old mate – just a tick longer.'

Nobody questioned him. He was known as a crack wireman.

Ginger Kellock tried again. 'Look, Hookey, it can't do any harm if I just *see* the Skipper, now can it?'

Aller glared at him. 'Just stow it, will you! I've had just about a jugful of you an' your Chinese bird! She's probably a bloody tom for all you know, after your money-belt!'

Pop Usher grinned up at them, sweat mingling with grease on his tanned face.

'All set, gents! Here we bloody well go!'

It purred into life and Aller thought of all those other times in the Western Ocean.

'Tell the bridge, Ginger. We've got our white stick again!'

They all suddenly froze and stared at one another with shock and disbelief.

Aller moved swiftly. 'Shift your arse, Ginger!' The others watched as he took the controls very carefully until the tell-tale echo pinged back into the receivers.

His voice was quite calm as he spoke into the voice-pipe to the bridge.

'Strong echo, sir, bearing one-one-zero. Stationary!'

Pop Usher muttered, 'That'll stop them farting in church!'

At that moment, the alarm bells began to ring.

'Ship at action stations, sir!'

Brooke acknowledged. If only there was light.

Calvert asked, 'Could it be a wreck, sir?'

Brooke recalled his earlier remarks about the depth hereabouts, and Chau's thoughtful reply.

'Who's on the Asdic?' He already knew. He was merely fighting for time. Had he known earlier that this might happen? He seemed to feel the hair rise on his neck in spite of the damp heat. Suppose this was the Atlantic? They would be sitting ducks.

Kerr said, 'Aller, sir. A moaner, but he's a good operator.'

Brooke moved to the voicepipe. 'Asdic, this is the captain. What do you make of it, Aller?'

'Strong echo, sir. No change.'

Brooke returned to his chair and used it as a crutch while the ship lifted and dipped beneath him.

Suppose it *was* a wreck? It was a common enough mistake in the Atlantic. But not here, surely?

'Another flare, sir! Fine on the starboard bow! Damn – it's gone out!'

'Slow ahead both engines!' It would make the motion worse, but there would be less risk of a collision.

'Scrambling nets ready. In case we can't get alongside.' He felt the chill on his spine and could sense the presence out there in the darkness. Like a hunter. An assassin.

He made up his mind. 'Searchlight!'

Like a long bar of ice the big searchlight hissed out across the water, somehow magnifying the troughs and the breakers into moving glass valleys.

The beam settled on the vessel and held it. The light must be blinding to them, Brooke thought.

A familiar sight. He found he could study it through his glasses, his mind detached, even callous. The coaster was drifting without power or lights; he could see her rust-dappled bilge, the extent of her crippling list. Shifting cargo? It didn't much matter now.

He said, 'We must take off her crew, Number One. A tow is out of the question in this sea. I don't want to risk our chaps' lives.' He had seen the small huddle of crouching figures below the solitary, spindly funnel.

The interpreter had forgotten his seasickness completely. 'Know ship, sir! I have seen her many times!'

'Switch on all navigation lights!'

He recalled his own words to *Serpent*'s company. *A ship of war.*

'Asdic – bridge! Contact on same bearing but moving left!' Even Aller sounded shocked.

Brooke snapped, 'Make a signal to C-in-C. *Am in contact with submarine, position so-and-so . . .*'

'*Bridge!* Torpedo running to starboard!'

The explosion when it came was so loud and violent that the stokers and artificers down in their world of noise and steam must have thought for a split second that they were the target. Fragments of metal splashed down between the bows and the place where the crippled coaster had been; some scraped across the forecastle deck like bomb splinters.

Brooke said, '*Am attacking!* Now send it off!'

He gripped a rail. 'Starboard twenty! Steady! Steer one-one-zero!'

'Asdic – Bridge.' Aller sounded subdued. 'Ship breaking up.'

Brooke imagined the blasted and broken hull dropping so slowly into that great yawning valley of perpetual darkness.

'Stand by depth charges!'

'Asdic – Bridge. Lost contact.'

'Keep on with the sweep.' He heard the hardness in his voice. The Atlantic had not released its grip after all.

There was no further contact. A signal was received from the C-in-C. *Discontinue action. Return to Sector Charlie Zebra immediately.*

Kerr watched as Brooke listened to the curt signal.

'What are you going to do, sir?'

Brooke slumped in his chair and realized that the motion and the violence of the sea were easing. They had missed the worst of it.

He shrugged. 'I'm going back to find out if anyone survived. There's always a chance.' He sounded drained.

Calvert said, 'It might have hit *us*, the bastards!'

Brooke looked towards his head, framed against the sky.

'It was meant to.' How easily it came out. Then he said, 'Fall out action stations but remain at defence stations.'

Through the mouth of an open voicepipe he could hear the regular ping of the Asdic. He knew the attacker had gone. Somehow, he simply felt it.

It had probably been the sudden and unexpected blinding glare of the big searchlight. The eyes at the hidden periscope had been momentarily shocked, blacked-out.

He glanced around the pale figures of the watchkeepers. Unsteady on their feet as if they were too stunned to adjust to the ship's movements. They did not even know what they had interrupted merely by responding to the S.O.S. They only knew that they had nearly died.

At first light they discovered some small charred fragments of flotsam spread over a large area, like spent matches in a pond. They also found an elderly survivor, clinging half-dead to a hold-cover which must have been hurled clear from the coaster by the explosion.

The man was so badly burned that when he was hauled aboard and carried carefully to the sickbay he looked more dead than alive. The petty officer S.B.A., Twiss, did what he could with the ointment which was issued for extreme burns; he had used it many other times when a merchantman had been torpedoed.

Brooke handed over the bridge to Kerr and went down to the sickbay. 'Sister' Twiss's expression was like stone as he worked with each piece of dressing. It was doing more harm than good.

John Chau was bent over the old man's body, his face so close to him that some burned skin was sticking to his immaculate white tunic.

The dying survivor was in fact the vessel's master. He probably did not even know what had happened. It was usual under such circumstances.

Twiss said quietly, 'He's gone, sir.'

Brooke took the burned and sodden identity card from the interpreter. 'You did well, Mr Chau.'

He saw the deep hint of pleasure in his dark eyes.

'Have him sewn up. We shall bury him in the forenoon.' He glanced at the interpreter. 'Perhaps you would help me by reading something for him?'

'Of course, sir. An honour.'

He climbed the ladders to the swaying bridge, each step an effort.

As he walked to his chair he looked around, then aft to the gaff where the ensign made a bright display against the heavy clouds.

It was suddenly a clean and decent place.

12

Destiny

After the overwhelming heat of Hong Kong harbour as *Serpent*'s motor-boat had dashed towards the moored flagship, the atmosphere between the cruiser's decks seemed cool and peaceful.

Serpent had entered harbour the previous afternoon and had managed to get alongside the dockyard wall before dark. Brooke had received a brief message to report on board *Dumbarton* as soon as was convenient: that was an improvement on the last time. He had nevertheless been kept waiting for some ten minutes after being piped aboard.

The commodore's secretary, a nervous-looking pay-master lieutenant-commander, had ushered him below, where he had been given a seat. *Dumbarton* was certainly an experience, he thought wryly. The gleaming passageway with white paint so glossy he could almost have shaved in it; framed photographs of the ship in other livery, white hull and buff funnels, or steaming along what looked like the coast of Africa. Portraits of previous captains: grinning boats' crews after a victory at some regatta. Crossing the Line, a ship's boy dressed in captain's uniform, doing Rounds on Christmas Day. The story of the ship herself.

Brooke had noticed that the anchor cable, which was

shackled to the mooring-buoy, had been painted white, and he wondered when the old *Dumbarton* had last put to sea. He had also observed that the ship's anti-aircraft armament consisted of outdated four-inch guns and no automatic weapons at all. He recalled the screaming Stuka dive-bombers: they would have this ship on the seabed in minutes.

Most of her class, the *Danaës*, had already been converted into anti-aircraft light cruisers, invaluable for convoy work. How had *Dumbarton* slipped through the net? And would *Serpent* escape conversion like her remaining sisters? He could not contemplate her as a minelayer.

He had spoken briefly to *Islip*'s captain, who had had steam up when *Serpent* had been waiting to go alongside. *Islip* was off to Singapore to keep an eye on a naval stores vessel.

There would be no warships in Hong Kong at all at this rate. All they had were *Dumbarton* and the Dutch cruiser *Ariadne*, a cut-down destroyer similar to *Serpent* but missing her third funnel, a few M.T.B.s and the local gunboats.

The secretary was back. 'If you will come this way.'

The big door at the end of the passage and at the sternmost section of the ship was decorated with a painted commodore's broad-pendant. It had a red ball in the upper canton of its cross to show that the officer who flew it was 'of the second class'.

The door was opened by a P.O. steward. Brooke tried not to stare. The man was wearing white gloves.

Commodore Cedric Stallybrass was on his feet, his little button-eyes sunk in crinkles of flesh as he held out one hand in welcome.

The other man was a full captain, whom he vaguely recognized.

The commodore said, 'This is our chief-of-staff, Captain Albert Granville.'

The captain was very tall, with wavy gun-metal hair and a strong high-bridged nose. Brooke thought he looked very like an actor, playing the part he was presenting now.

They all sat down while the steward and a Chinese messman arranged drinks on a brass-topped table. Another souvenir from along the way.

Granville said, 'Found your latest report very interesting. Disquieting, too.'

The commodore waved one finger. 'Easy, Bertie! Give the fellow time to draw breath!'

Brooke had the peculiar feeling that even that chiding remark had been rehearsed beforehand.

Granville picked up his glass and examined it gravely. Brooke could almost hear the line, '*Alas, poor Yorick* . . .' Instead he said, 'If your ship had not been on a mercy mission you would not, of course, have become involved at all. The torpedo? That is something else entirely. I can only assume that it was meant for the coaster. It was foul weather so the submarine commander might have been mistaken, though perhaps it was another vessel altogether.'

Brooke found that he could relax. This was not going to be like the sinking fishing boat and its murdered crew. Too many people had seen the torpedo, and you could not prevent Jack from yarning about it.

He said, 'A torpedo has no conscience, sir. It is impartial.'

Granville's eyebrows rose. 'I know something of your service, Brooke. You have seen war at close hand. Maybe too close. We have an important but thankless task here. We have to uphold the peace as best we can and not provoke a confrontation.'

'The Japanese commander did not know of our presence until the last moment, sir. Lights were off, and the Asdic set was temporarily out of use. The South China Sea is not like the Atlantic or the North Sea. You'd never see a torpedo in those waters until it was too late. My men witnessed the one torpedo passing down the starboard side, the phosphorescence was so bright.'

The commodore smiled. 'We do not *know* it was a Japanese boat, Brooke. That is what I mean. We can never jump to conclusions which we cannot hope to prove. Perhaps it *was* Japanese, and maybe the coaster was sunk mistakenly. But to fire deliberately at a British man-of-war would be unthinkable.' He sounded outraged. Granville nodded in agreement. 'Which is why we must not become *involved*. His Majesty's Government has quite enough on its plate without that.'

They looked to one another like conspirators. Granville said, 'I think I am at liberty to tell you, Brooke, that the Admiralty, at the bidding of the First Sea Lord and with the authority of Winston Churchill himself, intends to reinforce the China Squadron with newer ships, and of capital importance. That suit?'

The commodore signalled to his steward. 'Long ship, this one, Billings!'

They were trying to make it easy for him, advising him to forget it. It was not his responsibility, or anyone else's for that matter.

Granville asked casually, 'You were in the Med during the Spanish Civil War?' But it was a statement. He already knew.

Brooke replied, 'For a while, sir.'

'Got knocked about too. Bad show. But now you've got a ship of your own despite all the set-backs you've had. Not new, but a good command for someone in your position. A lot of officers have been given advanced promotion – far beyond their ability, some of them, in my opinion. But you, Brooke – you're in the race again. The others will be dipped down to their proper seniority when the war's over. Do your best, as I'm sure you always will, and there's no telling where you'll end up.'

The commodore nodded ponderously. 'No more than you deserve.'

Brooke glanced at the empty glass in his hand and was surprised it was so steady, and that someone had refilled it.

A *good command for someone in your position.* If they had threatened him physically, it could not have been clearer. He was to make no ripples, cause no friction. Just show the flag. If not, he would lose *Serpent* and be sent home on some pretext or other. Kerr would get the ship and a half-stripe to go with her.

He thought the glass might shatter in his fingers. They could do it, too. A confidential report to Their Lordships. *Under too much pressure. Combat-fatigue.* Anything. He had seen it happen to others.

He tried to think clearly. But all that remained in his mind was the pride in his father's voice when he had given him the photograph.

The commodore glanced at his watch. 'And don't bother about the Asdic. I shall get the maintenance commander on to it right away.'

Captain Granville said, 'There's a new brigadier or something out from England to join our chief-of-staffs' committee. Another Whitehall johnnie who's yet to get his knees brown, eh?'

He groped around as if seeking a prompt for his next line. Instead he asked abruptly, 'Did the coaster's Chinese skipper say anything before he died? You have an interpreter now, I understand.'

'He said that the S.S. *Kiang Chen* was carrying

building-stone, sir.' In his mind he saw the little interpreter facing him over the corpse draped in the White Ensign. A few words in his low sing-song voice, a bow, and the waiting seamen tipping up the grating for the lonely journey to the bottom.

All-time darkness . . .

'No wonder the cargo shifted, eh, Bertie? Charles Yeung took it very well, I thought.'

Granville said to Brooke, 'You know him, I believe?'

'A little, sir.'

'Best to keep it like that, what?'

Brooke stood up carefully, almost fearfully, but his leg did not fail him.

Yes, keep it like that. Take his favours, eat and drink his generosity. But friendship? *Not the done thing, old chap.*

They walked to the quarterdeck together, the beautifully laid planking so clean he could have eaten from it.

Granville saluted and stepped on to the accommodation ladder. The commodore looked down at the immaculate launch waiting below, the crew with raised boat-hooks and a chief petty officer in charge.

Beyond it, *Serpent*'s small and functional 'skimming-dish' with the lump-like Macaskie at the tiller made a stark contrast. Like everything here, Brooke thought.

The commodore touched his cap. 'See you at the Repulse Bay Hotel on Tuesday, Bertie. Should be a good evening!'

The powerful launch roared into life before speeding amongst the lighters and junks towards the Kowloon side.

Stallybrass was peering across the littered water towards the sleek destroyer alongside the wall.

'Fine little ship. Wouldn't want to lose her. Or you.'

They saluted one another before Brooke went down the long, varnished ladder.

Between his teeth he said angrily, '*Nor will you!*'

Lieutenant Richard Kerr glanced up from the wardroom table where he was leafing through the latest Admiralty Fleet Orders, a coffee cup in one hand.

He stared with surprise, and then apologized. 'Sorry, Pilot! I didn't recognize you for a minute!'

Calvert walked to a mirror by an open scuttle and rubbed his smooth chin doubtfully.

'It got so prickly in the heat,' he said. He studied the cluster of small scars down one side of his face. Maybe he should have waited. Against his tanned skin they seemed pale, more noticeable.

Kerr sensed his uncertainty and said kindly, 'You look fine, Pilot.' When Calvert turned to gauge his sincerity he added, 'Really you do. They'll heal much better and faster, too. You look almost human at last.'

Calvert forced a smile. 'It's stupid, I know. A reminder, I suppose.' He glanced around. 'Skipper aboard?'

Kerr shook his head. 'Gone for a walk. He saw the commodore and chief-of-staff apparently.'

'What did *they* say, or shouldn't I ask?'

'I'm not sure.' He thought of Brooke's tawny eyes, his restlessness. 'I think he was pretty cheesed off with it, whatever they said.'

Calvert stared at his reflection again. A new face. Someone else.

Kerr said, 'If you want to shove off ashore, then do it. I'm duty boy, and I've got to see another joker from the dockyard.' He glanced at the pantry hatch, which was tightly sealed. The gossip-gate to the messdecks.

'Did hear a rumour we might be getting radar. Keep it to yourself. But you know what that would mean.'

'Back to the Atlantic. The real war.'

'Yes.' Kerr looked at the litter of paper. 'You know, I could get to like this place quite a lot. Your predecessor in *Serpent* . . .' He paused, hardly able to believe it. So short a time ago, and he had momentarily forgotten the other navigator's name. The navy's way. Faces came and left: a few months and you were forgotten. Only those around you and the ship that held you all were real.

'What about him?'

'I forgot what I was going to say.'

'You must have it bad!' He did not see Kerr's surprise at his casual remark. He said, 'I think I *will* go ashore. Everybody else is.'

They chorused, '*Except the Chief!*'

Calvert picked up his cap. 'I'll probably get as far as the first bar. That'll do me!'

He walked to the companion ladder and up to the quartermaster's lobby, and saw the bright rectangle of blue sky through the screen door. The heat haze was making the waterfront buildings shiver like a *Fantasia* ballet.

The duty quartermaster called out, 'Shore telephone call, sir.'

'Who for, Monk?'

'Well, she *wants* the commanding officer, sir, but he's ashore.'

'I'll take it.'

It was as if she was right here beside him, her soft voice exactly how he remembered it.

'I'm sorry, Miss Yeung, but he's in Victoria somewhere.'

A pause. 'I wanted to speak with him. I knew the ship was returned. Is he all right, please?'

Calvert thought of Kerr's remark. 'I think he needs cheering up, miss.'

A longer pause. 'Cheering up? I do not understand.'

He could picture her frowning. 'In his work there's always something to worry about.'

How could he tell her that they had been narrowly missed by a torpedo, when one of her father's ships had been destroyed and her crew killed for no apparent reason?

'Will you leave a message? Lieutenant Kerr will make sure he gets it when he returns.'

'No.' She must have thought it was too abrupt. 'That is Lieutenant Calvert, yes? I thought I knew your voice.'

He imagined her in that great house, the harbour laid out below the windows like a tapestry.

She said, 'I will find him.' The line went dead.

The quartermaster said cheerfully, 'I'm afraid you've missed the dockyard bus, sir.'

Calvert shrugged. 'Should have given the phone call to Number One!'

The quartermaster walked out into the sunshine and stood at the salute beside the sentry as Calvert walked down the brow. He waved several ancient-looking rickshaws aside and kept carefully within the shadows of the buildings. At least there were no clouds and no waterfall of rain in the offing.

Was it the girl who was getting the Skipper down, or the thought of having to leave her? Not that there would be anything between them. He stared at a shop window, at the reflection of an unknown flier who, in turn, was acting another role.

And why not? When Calvert had been flying day trips and instructing young men and women with too much money for their own good, he had had his chances. He had explored a few of them, too. But nothing had lasted. Brooke was different. Anyone should be able to see that.

Horns hooted, and someone shouted, 'What side of the bloody road do you think you're on?'

Calvert walked on. A drink, one of those gin slings, and a pipe of tobacco. After that . . .

'Lieutenant Calvert! *Please*, not so fast!'

He swung round, startled by the use of his name. It was a young girl, all in white, with the single blue stripe of a junior Wren officer on her shoulder. She too had come to a halt, her body heaving with exertion and dismay.

Beyond her, a khaki car with some sort of badge painted on it was half on the pavement, one door still hanging open and watched with a mixture of rage and amusement by the other drivers.

'I thought, I – thought . . .' Then she recovered herself. '*It is you.* But the beard – you see . . .'

He said quietly, 'I missed the bus just now. But for that, I wouldn't have seen you.' He reached out and took both of her hands in his. It was impossible. It was sheer lunacy. 'It must be fate.'

She searched his face. 'I – I wrote to you. I had no idea where you were. It was a terrible cheek . . .'

He could not take his eyes from hers. 'I wrote to you, too. You may be able to read it one day.' He smiled for the first time. 'That was a terrible cheek, too.'

She said, 'Only arrived here two days ago. Even then I never dreamed . . .'

The car moved slightly and a tall uniformed figure stepped out into the sunshine. Calvert could tell he was pretty senior, but not a soldier. He was a Royal Marine.

The man said patiently, 'When you're ready, Sue, I have work to do.' He smiled at Calvert's astonishment.

'Otherwise, old chap, I'd let her go with you.' He got back into the car.

Calvert said quickly, 'I must see you, Sue.'

'You remembered my name . . .'

The girl on the train. Her husband Bob had gone down in the *Hood* . . . He touched his face and was still surprised that the beard was gone.

She said, 'That was Brigadier Sexton. I'm his secretary.' She shook her head. 'I can't *believe* this is happening!'

She pulled a piece of paper from her pocket. 'You can call me here.' She was retreating slowly towards the car, her eyes misty as she called, 'It can't be happening!'

There was a big khaki lorry pushing slowly through the crowds.

A red-faced soldier leaned from the car and said loudly, 'Very nice, too, miss, but can you move the car so I can pass?'

Calvert followed her to the car and held the door for her. Two Chinese clapped their hands, and someone gave a weary cheer.

Calvert heard none of it. 'Sorry, sir.'

The brigadier touched his neat moustache with one knuckle.

'I *do* understand, Lieutenant. I'm not that bloody old!'

Calvert watched the car jolt from the pavement and carry on towards the harbour. He saw her look back at him; she might have waved.

Would he ever have recognized her, and why had she seen through his disguise? A dark, dingy train. Rain slashing the windows.

She was younger than he had remembered. Very young. She must have been newly commissioned as a third officer in the W.R.N.S. when she had been married. Her hair was dark and curly, but shorter than he had believed. Her eyes? He was still not certain.

He walked almost unseeingly up a narrow passageway to where some old men were looking at one another's caged birds and listening to their song.

And now she was here. He leaned suddenly against the wall and rubbed his eyes with his hand. They were stinging, and he was unable to stop it.

A woman emerged from a dark doorway and touched his sleeve. She could have been almost any age, and still had an almost mask-like beauty.

'Come into my shop, sir.'

He realized that some passing soldiers were staring at him, probably imagining he was drunk.

It was cool in the little shop, with the fragrance of camphor and incense. As his eyes grew accustomed to the interior he realized that it was full of jewellery.

She said quietly, 'I saw the lovely English lady. You buy a nice present for her, yes?' She guided him to a chair. 'But first we take tea.' She busied herself behind the counter and added, 'No shame in tears. No man is too strong for them.' She handed him a cup of tea with great care.

Calvert cleared his throat. 'What would you suggest?'

'Jade, of course. Jade right for pretty lady. Bring good luck all time.'

He wanted to thank her, but did not know how.

Instead, all he could think of was one word. *Fate*.

Esmond Brooke stopped and looked up at the old temple's imposing entrance. He still did not really know why he had come, nor did he recall much of his journey from the harbour. He had been careful not to overdo it, because when he had left the dockyard he had been reminded of the last time, the breathtaking humidity of the monsoon and the heat across his shoulders in each airless street.

Dusk had fallen early as usual, and although the cooler breeze from Victoria Harbour brought some relief he was taking no chances. And now he was here. He tested his injured leg on the first step. It was still sore, but the girl's sister had given him more ease than he could remember since the explosion.

He removed his cap and stepped through the great doors. Apart from some dusty lanterns and a few small coloured electric bulbs near the gilded statues, the interior was almost dark. But it all came back immediately: her hand on his arm in case he stumbled and injured his leg, the scent of her perfume mingling with the stranger smells of burning prayer-papers, joss-sticks and the overhead coils of incense.

Shadows moved around the statues, and joss-sticks glowed like red fireflies as the worshippers waved them back and forth while they knelt at the feet of the gods.

A thin attendant in singlet and shorts, smoking a cigarette while he plaited some ribbons with delicate skill, merely glanced at him and offered a casual nod. He watched with momentary interest as Brooke took several sticks and dropped some coins in the collecting-box, and then carried on with his work. If he was at all curious at Brooke's presence he did not show it.

Brooke was crossing to the opposite side when he almost collided with a tiny woman who was about to kneel. In the flickering light she looked ancient, like some historic carving.

He smiled an apology and on impulse offered his arm as support while she lowered herself on to the cushion. Her hand on his white cuff was like a claw, but it had a grip of steel.

209

She muttered something and peered up at him impassively.

'Good. Good.'

Brooke sat on one of the old chairs and watched the smoke from his joss-sticks drifting up towards the lanterns. He could imagine her at his side, her dark eyes teasing him, or becoming so suddenly grave.

He thought of his visit to the flagship. It had haunted him along every street and through each narrow market. His brother had once said that to survive you must keep your yardarm clear and your mouth shut. That was *then*. A far cry from the ambitious officer he had become.

If he came back to Hong Kong, would she want him again? Or had it all been in his mind alone?

There were rumours that *Serpent* would be ordered home, so short was the fleet of convoy escorts with the toll in the Atlantic mounting daily.

To think of not seeing her again made him desperate. It was madness, but that only made it worse. She was beautiful, and her father was obviously very rich as well as powerful. *What do I have to offer, even if she considered it?* In any case, her father would want a son-in-law with prospects, someone known and respected here.

After *Serpent*, what then? His mind turned away from the possibility of losing the old destroyer, despite what the urbane Captain Granville had suggested about his future. After the war? It was like thinking of another world.

Like hundreds, thousands in that other war to end all wars, he would most likely be thrown out again. On the beach. Nothing changed. Even in Nelson's time they had gone through it. *God and the Navy we adore, When danger threatens but not before*. Perhaps when it was finally over he might not want to remain in the service: an idea he would once have never even considered. He lit the last joss-stick from a nearby candle and gave a rueful smile. He was behaving like a schoolboy.

Suppose the worst did happen? That, because of provocation or some military misunderstanding, the Japanese decided to invade the New Territories, and eventually Hong Kong island? He recalled what Jeremy had said, his scornful dismissal of the defence forces. The Japanese were battle-hardened troops and had been fighting the Chinese Nationalists continuously for four years. Brooke had seen quite a lot of the British and Commonwealth soldiers they had helped to escort in *Operation Boomerang*. Most of them were as green as grass, untried in anything but basic training and square-bashing.

He thrust out his leg as if he expected to see the blood on it. There were plenty of rumours and half-truths about what had happened on the mainland. It was still going on. Close on the heels of their advancing troops had come a regime of terror. Rape, torture, mass executions by firing squad and beheading: the invaders intended to break the Chinese once and for all. If they did invade . . .

It was not the warfare he understood. At sea you survived or you died. *Bought it*, as the new slang described it. He was aware of the new optimism in the newspapers here. The fact that another island, Malta, had survived constant air attacks from bases just a few miles away, and had taken all that the Italians and the Luftwaffe could throw at it, seemed to have given people heart.

Jeremy had spoken of the handful of planes which were kept at Kai Tak aerodrome on the Kowloon side.

211

At least at Malta they had the support of the Mediterranean Fleet, hard-pressed though it was.

He shook his head. There was no comparison.

Most of the warships were moving to Singapore, the real fortress to all accounts. If the Japanese, on whatever pretext, attacked Hong Kong there seemed little chance of holding out.

He got up and walked to one of the great sand-filled pots and carefully planted his two remaining sticks, his mind suddenly empty.

'*Just so*. I knew this was where you would be.'

He swung round, half believing that he had imagined it.

She was dressed in pale green although in the dim light it could have been almost any colour. Her hair was loose, as it had been the day she had held him in the car, her eyes catching the glow from the lanterns by the gods Man and Mo.

She held out her hand. 'You should have called me. *Told* me.'

He grasped her hand and held it. 'I had no right.'

She did not reply directly but seemed to be studying her hand in his. 'You make trouble for yourself, yes? The sub-mar-ine, all the danger you were in? You have every right.'

Brooke smiled. 'So much for secrecy, Lian.'

He felt her fingers relax, perhaps because he had used her name. 'One of your father's ships, too.'

She turned partly away from him and then slipped her hand through his arm.

'News runs fast here, Es-mond. I am afraid that you get hurt again.'

He squeezed her hand inside his arm. 'Oh, I'm all right. One hand for the King, the other for yourself – that's what I was taught!'

She looked directly at him but did not respond. 'It is not a joke. Always men make joke when I know it is serious!'

'I'm very sorry, Lian. And I *do* care what you think, how you feel.'

She said quietly, 'You believe I play cat-mouse with you because of your brother, that is true, yes?'

He had never seen her so concerned, so emotional, and he wanted to put his arms round her. The watchful amah Nina Poon was probably lurking nearby, waiting for him to do just that.

He replied, 'I would not blame you.'

She said, 'I will not let anybody hurt you again!'

She calmed herself slowly and allowed him to take her to the entrance.

To herself she murmured, 'I knew you would come here.' Then she looked at him searchingly. '*Our* place now, yes?'

He nodded. There were no words.

She said firmly, 'I have only one rival now.'

'Rival?'

She smiled at him, the happiness breaking through like a young child.

'Your ship!'

Headlights dipped across the road and the great car murmured discreetly towards them.

She said, 'I take you to rival now, Es-mond!'

Brooke saw the faithful old amah peering past the chauffeur, as if to seek out some injury or insult.

Once in the car the girl lowered the armrest between them but kept one hand close to his.

'There is important reception on Tuesday at Repulse Bay Hotel.'

'I know about that.'

She turned sharply. 'Who asked you to go?'

'Ask *me*?' He grinned and took her hand without realising what he was doing. 'That'll be the day!'

'You joke again!' She turned her hand over and slipped her fingers through his.

Then she said, 'My father has arranged to have you as guest. Some of your officers too, I think. It will appear more . . .'

'Natural?'

She laughed. 'My father wants to ask a favour.' She squeezed his hand very gently. 'Just a little one.'

Then all at once, or so it seemed, they were at the dockyard gates.

She turned in her seat and after a slight hesitation lifted the armrest and pushed it away.

'Now you not sad any more, Es-mond.' She glanced round as William stepped from the car and walked round to the rear door.

She said quickly, '*Kiss*. One kiss.'

He put his arm around her and kissed her cheek, his mind dazed by her nearness and the perfume of her body.

She pushed him away. 'Quite enough!' But she was smiling, suddenly shy, her poise gone.

The door swung open and he stepped down, his cap still in his hand. The door closed but she lowered a window.

'Take this.' She handed him a small flat package. She dropped her eyes and said, 'New picture for you.' Then she turned aside and called, 'Drive on, William!'

How long he stood there he did not know. He would unwrap the picture when he was alone in his quarters. He did not wish to share any of it. Just her. To go over each moment. How long had she been watching him in the temple before she had spoken? What had brought her to the place unless . . .

He tried to laugh at even such a possibility. But it was suddenly all too real for that.

It had been decided. Maybe right there in the temple.

13

Favours

Repulse Bay, which was situated on the south side of the island and named originally after a British man-of-war, was said to have the most attractive of all the beaches.

Although it was dark when the taxi reached the place, Brooke could well imagine what it would be like in daylight: a long curving beach, backed up by trees and green hills. There were twinkling lights everywhere. They passed several large houses, and Kerr remarked that rich Chinese and British residents owned most of them.

Calvert had gone to the hotel separately, and had said something about visiting a tailor.

Barrington-Purvis was sharing the taxi, a strangely quiet version of his former self, who had never been slow to criticise or complain. The reason was obvious. Paul Kipling's advanced promotion to acting-temporary lieutenant R.N.V.R. had been verified. They had left Kipling in charge of the ship, ably backed up by the Chief and the gunner (T).

Perhaps Barrington-Purvis's father had recommended that his son remain as the ship's junior executive officer for a while longer. For his own good.

The sub-lieutenant looked like a man who had found a shilling and lost twenty pounds.

They swung on to a driveway, and framed against the stars Brooke saw the Repulse Bay Hotel. A place to take tea, and to admire the breathtaking view of the sea and its scattered islands.

The reception was for a new brigadier from England, a Royal Marine apparently. Brooke wondered whether this Brigadier Sexton had seen his brother or had any report from Jeremy after his last visit to Hong Kong; and angrily he remembered the girl snatching her arm away when Jeremy had tried to placate her, or whatever he had been attempting to do.

There were cars of all shapes and sizes parked below the hotel. Brooke felt his heart quicken as he saw the familiar bonnet of the pale green Rolls-Royce, and William, arms casually folded, standing beside it. Very aware that his car was the best there.

Kerr glanced at him. 'Charles Yeung is here too then, sir?'

'Yes.' Was Kerr probing? Was he that easy to read?

It was a very prestigious reception. Uniforms of the services, a few women in light dresses, and a large mixture of Chinese, businessmen or officials it was hard to tell. There were tables full of food, waiters hurrying about with drinks, and flowers galore.

Brooke smiled to himself. At her father's buffet party on the Peak he had remarked that he had expected to see orchids everywhere.

Lian had smiled gently. '*Anyone* can have orchids, Commander.'

Had she been laughing at him again; or at the host, her father's need to gain face, to impress?

They were all here. The commodore from *Tamar*, the chief-of-staff looking over everyone's heads as if preparing to play a new role. Commodore Stallybrass, his face redder than ever, officers from H.Q., from the flagship, but not many junior ones, he noticed. Stallybrass liked to play the field on his own.

Charles Yeung suddenly appeared from the throng. His silk suit was without a crease, and his hair looked as if it was trimmed every day.

He smiled as he took out his cigarette case. 'I am glad to see you.' He shook hands with Kerr and Barrington-Purvis. 'You are here as *my* guests.'

He took Brooke's arm and led him to a side table. 'Champagne.'

Brooke said quietly, 'I am sorry about your ship, sir. Had we been closer, we might have been able to save the crew at least.'

Yeung's dark eyes flickered. 'An act of war. But nobody will admit to it.' He tossed his mood aside. 'But what of you? Are you to remain in Hong Kong?'

'I hope so, sir.'

Yeung studied him thoughtfully. Touched, perhaps, by the sincerity in his voice.

'So do I. There are not so many British warships now. They are gone to Singapore. The *key*, remember?'

'The favour you wish of me, sir?'

He did not seem to hear. 'You see, my friend, if the British decide to pull out of Hong Kong there will be left a vacuum. An invitation to the Japanese army on the mainland, or one to be filled by General Chiang Kai-Shek. We have little choice in the matter. We can only offer aid, wherever we can get it.' He touched Brooke's sleeve. 'The favour can wait. It concerns your Lieutenant Calvert. An interesting man, I think. But I will not spoil his evening.'

Brooke glanced past him and saw Calvert standing by the wall, a drink in one hand while he spoke to the small Wren officer beside him. Even as he watched he saw Calvert's hand move out from his side, and hers close around it. Something private. Something highly charged. He could feel it even across the room.

Yeung smiled and lit another cigarette. 'The visiting brigadier's aide, I believe. Arrived a few days ago. An unexpected rendezvous, it would appear!'

Brooke drank his champagne slowly to give himself time. Kerr with his admission of a secret love for a girl he had known since childhood. Now Calvert, who had never mentioned any attachment, nor even the opportunity of finding one. He looked at Yeung's intelligent profile. *What would he say if he could read my thoughts?*

Yeung said, 'Your Lieutenant Calvert was a good pilot. He must have been. I have taken some pains to discover about him. What he did before the war. I wish to use his knowledge. I have a seaplane here in Hong Kong. I employed a pilot.' He shrugged as if it was of little importance. 'He died.'

'If you are asking Calvert to check over your seaplane I must warn you . . .'

'I know.' He patted his shoulder. 'I understand. But people can change.' He glanced across at the two figures by the wall. Hemmed in by a noisy crowd of people, and yet somehow completely isolated from them. 'Everyone has a price. It is the way of things.'

'Would you like me to mention it, sir?'

Another little pat on the shoulder. 'My friends call me Charles, you know.' He reached out suddenly and gripped Brooke's arm, his eyes compelling. 'There will come a time when I will need more than your friendship.' He let his arm drop, the fire gone from him as swiftly as it had risen. 'Yes, mention it to him. One never can tell.'

Doors were slamming, and feet clicked in the doorway.

Yeung said softly, 'He is coming. To tell us that Hong Kong is an impregnable fortress. That Winston Churchill has promised never to break faith with us.'

'You know what the brigadier's going to say?'

Yeung gave a tired smile. 'I could have written it for him.'

There was a wave of hand-clapping, more uniforms and the red tabs of staff officers.

Yeung said, 'There is a terrace here. On the other side. Take care of her until we leave.'

Brooke said, 'You can trust me.'

'I never doubted it. She has been hurt enough. I would not wish it to happen again.' He turned away and walked towards the small dais which had been erected for the newcomer's speech.

Brooke watched the Royal Marine brigadier's face as he climbed on to the little platform.

Small, neat moustache, thinning fair hair and piercing blue eyes. A military face. Little different from those at the Somme and Passchendaele, perhaps even Waterloo. No sign of doubt. Even less of imagination. Why did they begin wars with senior officers who had learned little from the one before?

But he was also thinking of Yeung's parting remark. It had sounded like a threat.

He pushed through some curtains where a few waiters were grouped to watch and listen, perhaps to discover their own future. The terrace was deserted so that the girl stood out like a statue. Until he drew closer.

She was standing by a balustrade, her hair shining in a solitary light while the sea, shimmering like diamonds, made the perfect backdrop.

She wore a cheongsam again, but of a different

colour, and in the single light it seemed to shine, king-fisher blue. It was sleeveless, and the side was slit almost to her hip. All the while he was watching her she was fastening some yellow flower in her hair, but her eyes never left his face.

She lowered her arms so that they hung at her sides and said, 'You can see, no amah this time.'

He reached down for her hands. 'You are enchanting, Lian.'

'Do I enchant you?' Her voice was low, unemotional. 'Is that what you are saying?' She removed one hand from his and placed it on his chest. 'No closer. I am being a fool.' She shook her head when he began to interrupt her. 'No! Soon you will go away. You and my rival.' She looked at him but the smile would not come. 'I know it happens when men fight wars. It always will. My father says there must always be wars and brave men like you to be sacrificed because of pride and greed . . .'

He put his arm around her waist and turned her towards the glittering horizon. The feel of her supple body, the way she made no protest, filled him with desire for her, and despair at what she had said.

'I have seen it in your country, Es-mond. The bravery of ordinary people with their lives and hopes in ruins because of war. But at least they are *there*. If you leave we will never meet again.'

They looked at one another with dismay. It was as if somebody else had spoken.

'What could I offer you, Lian? Your life is far above mine, war or no war.'

She studied him, feature by feature, her expression very solemn.

'You could give me love, and show me how to return it.'

His hands were on her waist, and he wanted to hold her until neither of them could stand it.

'Your father spoke of your being hurt . . .'

She looked at him directly. 'I was attracted to your brother. I think it was gratitude. He may have seen it as something else. It was hard to understand his thoughts.'

Brooke waited. He could feel her uncertainty and doubt like something physical. He knew too that she needed to explain.

'I was in London. I had been helping some diplomatic people and naval officers to learn the languages. It was where I met Jeremy.'

It was the first time he had heard her use his name. It was like reopening an old wound.

'I was too young, too sheltered by my upbringing to understand.' She faced him again, her eyes pleading. 'There was a lot of drinking. Two of the men took me to a garden and tried to make me do things.' Her eyes flickered as she forced herself to relive the nightmare. 'I was angry, and they forced me down.' Brooke watched one of her hands moving about her throat and between her breasts as if it belonged to an attacker. 'They tore at my clothes and held me down so that . . .'

'Don't say any more.' He put his arms around her very carefully, as if he might break her.

'Your brother came. I was safe. But I have never forgotten it.' She was shaking, as though with sudden fever. 'My father once said England would be invaded, lost. But I have been there.' She looked into his face; it was like defiance. 'And I have met you.' She glanced over the balustrade into the black shadows of the garden below. Like that other one, perhaps? 'I think, Es-mond, they will come here. And sometimes I am very afraid. Do you think that is the mind of a child?'

He touched her hair with its flowers and waited for her to become calmer.

'I think it is the mind of a brave, beautiful girl.' He thought of the speech going on in another part of the hotel. It seemed like a thousand miles away. 'I do love you, Lian. I want you so much I think I am driving myself mad.'

She nestled herself against him, her face hidden. 'It is what I want.' She lifted her chin as he had seen her do before.

'The Chinese always talk of thousands of years, millions sometimes. For us we must take what we can get, and receive what is offered.'

There was a burst of cheering, and the sound of clapping and feet stamping on the floor. All it needed was *Land of Hope and Glory*. But it no longer mattered. Nothing did, but what he held in his arms.

Then she asked, 'Did you like the photograph?'

He nodded. 'I loved it.' He looked at her for several seconds. 'I love you.'

She stroked the skin near his eyes, her fingers so light that he could barely feel them.

'Your eyes. Like a tiger.' She nodded, suddenly sure. '*My* tiger.'

Someone was whistling softly below the balustrade.

She pulled away. 'William. His signal. We will be leaving now.' Then she changed her mind and put her arms around his neck so that he could feel her body against his. Like a touch of fire.

'Kiss,' she said.

Then she slipped from his arms and walked swiftly to the passageway.

One of the yellow flowers had fallen from her hair, and with great care he put it inside his handkerchief.

He thought of his father. What would he have said?

Brooke touched his face where she had caressed it, and smiled. He knew exactly what his father would have said.

The overworked and dust-smeared Ford rattled to a halt outside some tall gates.

Brooke released his grip on a strap and gave a sigh of relief. 'Not exactly like the Rolls, eh?' He glanced at Calvert, who had remained almost silent since the car had picked them up at the dockyard; deep in thought, perhaps, like their inscrutable Chinese driver.

They passed through Repulse Bay, a different scene again in the bright sunshine, the lush trees and shrubs glistening from a sudden overnight downpour.

Brooke said quietly, 'Look, Toby, you don't have to do this just because I passed on Charles Yeung's message.'

Calvert smiled. 'Maybe I'm curious, that's all.'

'About the seaplane?'

He replied, 'No, about me. How I shall react.'

Brooke had been tied up on board *Serpent* for three days after the reception for the visiting brigadier, studying new patrol areas and various instructions from the far-off Admiralty. There was a rumour, too, that *Serpent* might be going home to be fitted with radar. Active duty again.

When the car had lurched past the Repulse Bay Hotel he had remembered it all with a kind of pain and despair, mingled with intense happiness. The feel of her body against his. The impossibility of it.

They got out of the car. Perhaps Charles Yeung had chosen to use it because it was less noticeable than the big Phantom. Or were the mysteries only in his mind? Perhaps Hong Kong changed you like that.

He looked at the gates, daubed with Chinese characters and an uncompromising notice that said: KEEP OUT. NO ENTRANCE WITHOUT PERMISSION.

Above the gates on a sun-flaked sign it said, *Property of Coutts Steamship Packet Company*.

The driver had curled up in his seat and was reading a newspaper. Brooke said, 'We'd better announce ourselves.'

But it was unnecessary. A small wicket-gate opened silently and a bowing figure in a rough leather jerkin beamed at them.

The place was larger than Brooke had expected. Rather like part of a naval dockyard, with rusting cable, pieces of old engines, packing-crates and every kind of gash scattered around in piles. His heart gave a leap as he saw the green Rolls-Royce standing near a jetty, a symbol of success set against decay.

He said, 'Charles Yeung is already here.'

But Calvert was staring at a broad, corrugated-iron building like a hangar, which seemed to perch above the water itself. Brooke thought of the pretty girl he had seen with him at the reception. When he had mentioned her Calvert had been reluctant to speak of her, evasive even. *Third Officer Yorke*. It had sounded so formal, unlike the man himself.

Charles Yeung appeared from a small shack-like office, cigarette smoke trailing behind him.

He shook hands. 'Good of you to come.' He glanced at Brooke, his eyes shrewd. 'Both of you.'

He had some keys in his hand. 'Are you ready?' Briefly, he sounded uncertain. Impatient.

'May I come too?'

They turned as Lian came out of the office. All in white, one hand over her eyes in the glare reflected from the water.

It was perfect timing. Especially for Calvert.

He forced a smile. 'It's all right by me, Miss Yeung.'

They waited while various keys were used before a side door squeaked inwards.

Brooke offered his hand as she stepped lightly over a rusty coaming and felt her squeeze it very gently. As they bowed through the small door she whispered, 'I have missed you. I worried about it.'

Charles Yeung closed the door and said sharply, 'The lights are not working.'

Brooke felt her move against him and sensed the tension like something alive.

After the sunshine it was like a black cave, but more than that it had a dead coldness, with a smell of wet metal and fuel. As the seconds passed he saw a vertical line of blurred gold, like a hanging thread, where two doors blocked off the hangar's entrance.

Calvert was standing a little apart from them, his mouth quite dry whilst he braced himself, facing up to something fearful. But familiar.

He had to clear his throat before he could speak. 'Ready.'

Charles Yeung was talking on a telephone, and then first one and then the other big door began to swing open. Nobody spoke or moved while the doors continued to sweep aside, the sunlight spilling across the oily water and then on to the plane itself. Like a great bird of prey, swaying slightly on the current as if awakening, disturbed by a possible enemy.

Calvert stood quite upright, his knuckles pressing into the seams of his trousers until the pain helped to steady him. More and more light, the seaplane appearing to grow, to rise towards the roof.

He forced his mind to take each moment at a time. A big, powerful, twin-engined aircraft, its twin floats moored and padded to wooden stages to prevent any risk of damage. He wanted to shut it out, close his eyes and hide from it. To explain for Brooke's sake, to plead with the men who had died on that June day so long ago. *Yesterday.*

Instead he heard himself say, 'I used to fly a Fairey Seafox when I was in training. Smaller, single-engined, not like this brute.' A casual, professional remark. No emotion in his tone. Nothing.

Charles Yeung said, 'Have a closer look. I am sorry about the lighting.'

Brooke felt the girl's fingers gripping his arm but doubted if she knew what she was doing. She too was watching Calvert's pale figure, the sudden disturbance beneath one of the floats as he stepped on to it and reached for a handhold.

Calvert could feel his heart pounding so loudly he was surprised the others could not hear it. He touched the cowl behind one of the triple-bladed props. An elegant, stylish plane in its day. It still was. He recalled his father describing the famous Schneider Trophy Race after the Great War. Seaplanes all. The sport and luxury of the few set against the unemployment and the unemployable, whose minds had been shattered in the mud and butchery of Flanders.

He touched the metal, smooth and surprisingly cool. Docile. At a guess it could carry four people and a small cargo.

His voice echoed around the hangar. 'Italian, Mr Yeung. Seven-hundred-and-fifty horsepower Alfa Romeo radials.'

Charles Yeung nodded. 'That is so.'

Brooke tensed as Calvert's hand stilled in mid-air near the perspex-covered cockpit. Did he expect something evil? A reminder, perhaps, of his own experiences?

Charles Yeung sounded preoccupied. 'I have had men looking after it, you understand? But a pilot's knowledge is what I need now.'

Brooke looked beyond the crouching aircraft and watched the sparkling water, a few tiny junks and sampans. It was like being perched on the edge of a continent instead of a small corner of the same island.

'It looks beautiful from here.' He barely knew he had spoken until she gripped his arm again and answered, 'The *feng shui* man chose it well. The sea-dragons can reach their palaces directly from this place.'

He glanced at her and saw that she was quite serious, and yet somehow pleased by his remark.

There was a click and when they turned back to the seaplane again they saw Calvert's vague outline inside the cockpit, groping around while he closed the cover behind him.

Charles Yeung said, 'Good, good.' He did not conceal his relief.

Within the damp silence of the covered cockpit Calvert eased himself into the pilot's seat. A ray of misty sunlight played across the instruments and controls and a bright silver plate with the maker's name engraved on it. *Cantieri Ruinti dell'Adriatico*. He guessed someone had polished it quite recently. Maybe just for his visit.

He reached down to find the log compartment and gasped with shock. How could he possibly have known where it was? It was nothing like the old Swordfish, and the Seafox he could scarcely remember.

He found he was shaking badly. Like those other times. When he had been released from care. The screaming memories, wide-eyed horror when young men had died without knowing why. He covered his face with his hands, surprised that his skin was so cold, that he was not wearing his old leather flying gloves.

228

The two great battle-cruisers firing salvo after salvo, the shattered carrier ablaze and capsizing, her toy-like aircraft tumbling off the flight-deck into the sea. Then the lithe destroyer swinging round in a great creaming wash which he could almost feel.

His own voice, a stranger's as he had screamed, *'I'll get those bloody bastards! Hold on, Muffin! Here we go, Bob!'*

The last name helped to pull him out of his terror. Her husband's name. The one who had bought it in the *Hood*. He felt the seaplane move slightly and knew somebody had stepped on to a float.

He slid from his seat and opened the curved hatch below the cockpit cover.

Brooke looked up at him. 'You OK, Toby?' His voice was so calm.

Calvert took a deep breath. His fingers tingled as if he had been flying, weaving in and out of the bursting flak.

He found he could smile. The Skipper was concerned, genuinely so. A really nice bloke. Not like some.

He said, 'Right as ninepence, sir!'

They studied each other for several more seconds. Two young men who had already seen and done too much, and would be expected to go on doing it at the gates of hell.

Brooke turned and saw the girl watching him, her hands clasped.

He said, 'I think a large drink is indicated.'

Charles Yeung watched the secret embrace as Brooke greeted his daughter by the landing-stage, but ignored it and asked, *'Can* you help me, Lieutenant Calvert?'

Calvert grinned and wondered where the hidden madness had gone. Gone, until the next time.

'You'll have to find a pilot, sir.' He nodded, stunned

by his sudden confidence. 'But, sure, I'll put her to rights!'

Charles Yeung touched his arm. 'You are a brave man. Do not think I do not know!'

Calvert looked back only once as the men began to close the doors again.

Like a big, black bird. No accident. It had been waiting for him.

The small, two-storeyed block of apartments had been built originally for those passing through Kowloon on their way to other parts of Empire. Officers' wives, naval and military officials; simply a bed and somewhere to break the journey.

The occupants of the six apartments now were mostly permanent residents: some senior nurses from the military sick quarters, and on the ground floor, an army chaplain. One apartment was still reserved for its original purpose. Like the others, it had a tiny balcony that looked out across the glittering water of Victoria Harbour, with its unending movement and countless moored ships, towards the notorious district of Wanchai.

The girl named Sue Yorke lay on her side, the shoulder straps of her swimsuit dropped from her shoulders, and watched the busy scene through the veranda rails. She was lying on what looked like a much-used sun-bed, her hair sticking to her forehead while her legs and shoulders burned.

She levered herself on to one elbow and shaded her eyes to stare at the naval dockyard and anchorage, which seemed to lie directly opposite her apartment. Grey ships and spartan buildings, White Ensigns lifting and curling only occasionally in the hot breeze. Which one was his ship, the *Serpent*, she wondered. Perhaps she could borrow some binoculars. It would be lovely to go over there to Hong Kong again, to meet him, perhaps to fight the feelings which would not be resisted.

What she was doing seemed pointless. The brigadier was always busy, seeing people, making statements, but mostly playing golf.

It was so unfair. '*Just hold the fort, Sue. Shan't be long.*' It was wasting time, when otherwise she might . . .

She lay back again and stared at the awning overhead. *She might what?*

Sometimes she awoke in the night and wondered what had happened; how it *could* have happened. Bob carrying his sword and smiling outside the old cathedral at Winchester, brother officers making an arch of blades, the photographs and the hotel for the reception. A few weeks later Bob had gone, as if he had never been. She had tried to remember their intimacy, their brief love, and she had felt shame when she could think only of the man on the train who had written to her. A letter to England which she had never received.

She rolled over on to her stomach again, her eyes smarting from perspiration, like tears.

It might not last, even if they let it happen. *Serpent* could be returned to convoy duty; Toby had told her as much. She smiled and dabbed her mouth. Such a friendly name. Intimate.

On the other hand the brigadier might pack his bags, a fine job done, whatever it was, and she would be sent back to some naval base or barracks.

Toby had called her two days ago but had been unable to meet her. Or was he trying to make it easier for her?

231

He had mentioned but barely touched on the favour he had carried out for some Chinese businessman, the one with the daughter. She had pressed him further but he had replied, 'When I see you. I'd like to tell you. Explain. It would help.'

She stared hard across the water until her eyes blurred. He was over there. Was he thinking of her? Was there any point in it?

It was strange. Most of the girls she knew in the Wrens seemed so worldly, able to deal with everything. And yet she had been married, and still felt like the novice.

There was a knock at the door and someone strode into the adjoining room without waiting for an answer.

Ruth Shelley was a senior sister at the military hospital. She had a brusque, offhand manner, but had gone out of her way to make the young Wren comfortable.

'God, look at you! The life of Riley, you naval people seem to have!'

She came out into the sunshine and regarded the harbour grimly. Tall and dark, with a strong sort of beauty which even a severe uniform could not disguise.

'Another few months and it's back to Blighty for me, my girl.'

'Don't you like it here? I think it's heaven!'

'There are better things to do. You'll soon find out if you stay here. Horny majors, just glad to get away from their dull wives so that they can have a bit on the side, and pink-faced subalterns looking for a mummy-substitute or a favourite spaniel!' She looked at her directly. 'God, girl, I've shocked you!'

Sue Yorke could feel her cheeks stinging and was angry that she was so easy to unsettle and embarrass.

'I suppose I'm not used to . . .'

The tall sister reached over for a towel. 'Not used to

the heat either. I thought you might be here, trying to get a tan before you go home. Believe me, you'll get more than you bargain for if you don't take care of yourself.' She produced a yellow bottle and shook it vigorously. 'Lie down again. I'll do it.'

Sue lay face down and waited for her blushes to leave her in peace. She felt the towel drying her shoulders and spine, the firmness of it somehow soothing.

'Raise up.' She probably spoke to her patients like that.

Sue obediently raised her stomach and felt the swim-suit dragged down her back and beneath her.

Cool drops of ointment, and then a slow, steady massage.

'Still wearing his ring, then?'

The girl had kept the wedding ring on a thin chain around her neck. A reminder? Or was it a protection from something else?

When she remained silent, the sister named Ruth said, 'I was nearly married once, y'know. Wouldn't think it, I suppose.' She chuckled and rubbed the oint-ment into her shoulders. It was a sad sound.

Sue said, 'What was he like?'

'*Like?*' The question seemed to take her aback. 'A lieutenant in the H.L.I. You know what they say about the light infantry, carry their brains between their legs, eh?'

Sue pressed her face into the towel. Was she embar-rassed again? She was surprised that she was not even shocked. If anything she was suddenly sorry for this hard-talking nursing sister.

'It didn't work anyway.'

'I'm sorry.'

'Why should you be? You'll forget what I said once you're through that door.'

She was working on her legs now and Sue was secretly pleased that she had shaved them that day.

'And what about you? Seeing some jolly jack, I hear?'

She half rolled over and exclaimed hotly, 'He's not! I – I mean, it's not like that!'

She stared down at her bare breasts and tried to find the towel. Ruth Shelley rolled her on to her back as easily as she would a weak child.

'I've seen tits before, my girl.'

Mesmerised, Sue watched while she applied more ointment, strong, powerful and yet for once quite gentle.

'Lie still, let your breathing calm down – close your eyes if you like. I'll go away right now if that's what you want?'

Sue pressed her eyes shut. It was suddenly important that she should stay.

She allowed the rhythm to flow over her, muscle by muscle, until there was something else, but again she was not shocked. She said in a small voice, 'I want him so much. We seem right for each other – I don't really understand why. He's a hero, a V.C. I'm, well, just a secretary, no matter what the uniform says!'

Just for an instant the hands stopped moving. One rested on her stomach, the other just touching her left breast.

Then she felt the hands moving her on her side, facing the sea again.

Over her bare shoulder Ruth said, 'Nobody can see you like this.' Again the forced chuckle. 'Except maybe some of the pilots flying out of Kai Tak Airport!'

Sue heard her drying her hands. Then she said, 'If that's how it is, my girl, don't fight it. You've a lot to offer him!'

Then she bent over her and kissed her cheek as if it was something precious. Sue imagined she could feel her unsteady breathing as she whispered, 'Now you know what went wrong with *my* marriage.'

For a long time after Ruth Shelley had gone Sue sat on the sunbed and let the sun explore where those hands had moved. Then she touched herself and tried to understand what had changed.

Aloud she said, 'Third Officer Yorke, you're growing up at last.' She smiled shakily. '*My girl!*'

14

Unlikely Event

It was October when Commander Jeremy Brooke, Royal Navy, returned to Hong Kong. As he walked unhurriedly to Kai Tak's reception area to await the arrival of his luggage he glanced around, not surprised but depressed by the apparent lack of security.

He saw two of the Royal Air Force fighter planes revving up noisily, watched as usual through the wire fence by a cluster of local children. He thought of the dog-fights in the clear skies above Dover and the Channel. Aircraft like these would not last ten minutes in England.

There was a staff car outside the baggage area and he automatically smoothed the creases from his uniform. England, Australia and New Zealand, by sea and in hedge-hopping planes little bigger than the two on the runway. He made a point of never showing tiredness, just as he rarely hurried. It might be mistaken for urgency or strain.

Now he was back in Hong Kong. The humid air, the smells he had come to know so well on other visits, the perpetual movement of people, were like a welcome.

His admiral had briefed him on what he had to do. Like the grim posters in England. *If the Invader comes.*

Jeremy's mouth turned down. He was not going to be popular, not with the top brass anyway.

He crossed to a window and stood directly beneath a revolving fan. Perhaps *Serpent* was in harbour? He examined his feelings about meeting his brother again as he might skim through a despatch or signal. It annoyed him to realize that there was only envy, where by rights there should be none. It was even more irritating to realize that Esmond did not feel the same way about *him*. Even before he had been given the old *Serpent* he had been just the same. Not content; he was always too driven for that luxury.

He saw a porter carrying his bags and said, 'Staff car. Outside.' He clenched his fists and waited for his temper to settle.

Even Sarah was different since the arrival of their son: a tiny, wrinkled thing which either slept or cried the house down. Sarah was an intelligent, charming girl, with looks to turn any man's head, but since the child she had gone through a complete change, cooing and gloating at every sound and function her child performed. The other officers' wives were much the same, although Jeremy had never believed it could happen to her.

'Commander Brooke, sir?'

He swung round, knocked off-balance by the girl's voice.

'Er, yes.' He stared at the small Wren third officer. 'You were expecting me?'

She smiled. 'A signal, sir.' But her eyes suggested *of course we were*.

He waited for her to climb into the car. She was pretty. A nice figure too, what he could see of it through her shirt. She tapped on the seat and the driver let in the clutch.

237

She could almost feel his eyes exploring her. She asked lightly, 'How was Sydney?'

'Getting hotter.' He looked across the anchorage. Still many ships here, but not many grey hulls.

He said, 'Didn't know there were any Wrens in H.K.' It came out like an accusation.

She smiled. 'There aren't. Just me. Here on sufferance. I'm with Brigadier Sexton.'

'Oh. Of course.'

She glanced at his profile. Not all that much like Toby's commanding officer in looks, and not at all in manner.

He asked abruptly, 'Is *Serpent* alongside?'

It was her turn to be startled, but he was too engrossed in his thoughts to notice.

'Er – no, sir. She's been on escort duty.' She remembered her dismay when Toby had telephoned her.

She had exclaimed, 'I might not be here when you come in again!'

He had been silent on the other end of the line. Her outburst had revealed her feelings better than any private letter.

Then he had said quietly, 'I need to see you again.' Such a small voice, she had afterwards thought. A man with the Victoria Cross, whose exploits her father had pasted in his war book. If only she had been with him after it happened. She would have held him, given him comfort . . .

The next morning she had been up at dawn, some borrowed binoculars close to hand, but she had not needed them to see that the old destroyer's berth was empty.

Jeremy said, 'I'd like to see the brigadier as soon as I've changed.'

'I can fix a meeting for this afternoon, sir.'

Jeremy relaxed slightly. *An obstacle*. It always made him feel better. He could recall a line in a play they had performed at Dartmouth Royal Naval College. He had been a Cavalier, in long boots and a plumed hat.

When challenged by a smaller walk-on part he had swirled his hat in the air and proclaimed, 'It will *not* wait. I am on the King's business!'

He said calmly, 'It will have to be sooner than that, I'm afraid. What's your name, by the way?'

She was just beginning to wonder where the brigadier might be, or whether he had yet set off for the golf course.

The commander's attitude was beginning to annoy her. 'Third Officer Yorke, sir.'

He smiled. Another challenge.

'Am I booked into the Pen?'

'Yes, sir. I can ring up H.Q. from there while you're . . .'

He said, 'No. Take the car yourself.' He looked at her directly. 'This is top secret, *Third Officer* Yorke. Even a whisper would go right across the New Territories and Victoria in minutes. I know – I used to spread news I wanted people to hear in that very bar!'

She faced him and asked simply, 'Is it very bad, sir?'

He felt a new excitement. She was worried about something. *Somebody* more likely, with her looks.

'Don't worry. Whatever happens it won't affect you.'

She stared out of the opposite window. When Toby got back she might not be here to comfort him. To help him break the curse that was destroying him.

It won't affect you. Patronising and arrogant. She had seen him looking at her legs, and at the way her damp shirt was clinging to her breasts. *Well, let him look, damn him!* She recalled the new confidence which Sister Ruth Shelley's massage had given her. No blushing or confusion. When she had been in training she had been appalled by the way some of her classmates had strolled about their quarters quite nude without any sort of embarrassment. Sure of themselves? Or had it really been some kind of defiance?

Jeremy asked casually, 'Have you met Charles Yeung while you've been here?'

'Yes. I was at the reception given for my boss at Repulse Bay.' She glanced at him. Toby had mentioned that this man had married his C.O.'s fiancée, and there was some rumour about him and that Chinese girl as well.

She thought of Ruth Shelley's comment, which had shocked her. *A bit on the side*. Was that what Commander Brooke was after? Handsome, mysterious, conceited. Used to having his own way.

She said, 'Here we are, sir. *The Pen*.'

It was not lost on him. 'I'll see you in an hour, right?'

She leaned back and waited for the porters to remove his luggage.

She smiled. '*Right!*'

Commodore Cedric Stallybrass glanced around his flagship's wardroom and said heavily, 'I think we are ready to begin.' He looked questioningly at his secretary. 'Yes?'

The secretary responded hastily, 'All personnel cleared from aft, sir. Sentries mounted.'

Stallybrass grunted. 'A bit over the top maybe, but . . .'

He turned towards Commander Jeremy Brooke, who was tapping a cigarette on a slim gold case while he waited for permission to smoke.

It was hot and oppressive in the wardroom, the only

240

place large enough to accommodate this gathering. Members of the dockyard's senior staff, the commanding officers of the remaining ships in harbour, including the flotilla leader *Islip*'s bearded captain, Ralph Tufnell, the S.N.O. of the motor torpedo boats, and some old China hands who skippered the elderly force of Yangtze and East River gunboats.

The door opened silently and the chief-of-staff, Captain Albert Granville, made a quietly apologetic entrance.

The commodore beamed at him. 'Now we are all here, eh, Bertie?'

Several of them laughed, but most were watching the elegant commander from the Department of Naval Intelligence.

Jeremy did not stand up. 'I am not going to make a speech, gentlemen.' He smiled briefly at Stallybrass. 'We have heard or read more than enough of those lately. I am not even going to offer any opinions.'

Someone said, 'Good show!'

Jeremy's glance passed over the offender as if he were a stain on the carpet.

'The fact is that, whatever the outcome of what lies immediately ahead of us, Hong Kong, and Kowloon to a lesser extent, will be a fortress, closed to all comers. There are, however, precautions to be taken, and without delay. In the unlikely event of an attack on Hong Kong by an enemy, who for the purpose of this review must remain nameless, all unmilitary personnel will be evacuated. Measures are in hand as I sit here . . .'

Stallybrass exclaimed, 'I say, Bertie, did you know about this?'

The chief-of-staff shook his actor's mane of hair and replied, 'Up to a point. But as the possibility of such an action coming to pass is, as Commander Brooke has been quick to point out, *unlikely*, I think we should take it one step at a time.'

Jeremy contained a smile. Bertie's reply was meaningless.

He cleared his throat. 'As I was saying, gentlemen, *evacuated*. Wives and families, dependants, will be escorted by sea to Australia.' He had their full attention now. 'Heavy casualties would otherwise be inevitable. My admiral has stated that the Prime Minister intends the Colony to stand firm and to await reinforcements. Major units of the fleet are already being sent to Singapore, where they will be better placed for our mutual defence and for any future offensive.' He was aware of their intent expressions. '*Top Secret*, gentlemen!'

Stallybrass snapped, 'They do not have to be told!'

He fell silent as Jeremy turned cold eyes upon him. 'There will be a bloodbath if there is any *hint* of retreat!'

It was easy to deflate Stallybrass. He recalled his admiral looking down from his window in Whitehall. Air-raid shelters, policemen in steel helmets, sandbags outside the Admiralty. At least they were *doing* something, or trying to. There had been flowers in the park, too.

His admiral had said, 'Stallybrass will go down with his flag flying if so ordered. You will have to tread carefully. He is a very stupid man.'

Jeremy said, 'Most of our troops here were envied when they were sent to Hong Kong. Some have, apart from basic training, performed only guard duty. If we are attacked they will not be envied for long.' He looked sharply at Commander Tufnell. 'Yes?'

Tufnell did not flinch. 'Why should this "enemy" attack us? We've taken pains to keep out of *their* war.'

'Why, indeed? If we knew all the answers ...' He became business-like again. 'The fact is, we must prepare. Be ready.' He judged the right moment. You could have heard a pin drop. 'There is another possibility. That the defences could not hold out.'

There were gasps of astonishment and anger, as he knew there would be.

He continued unhurriedly, 'In which case, all vessels that could be used by an enemy must be destroyed or rendered useless. Dockyard facilities, stores, ammunition. It would be a final act before . . .'

Tufnell stood up, his eyes blazing. '*Surrender?* Is that what you're preparing for? If so . . .'

Jeremy turned to the commodore. 'I said at the start, it is not a suggestion. But decisions have to be made. It is, I appreciate, a great responsibility for you, sir.'

Stallybrass puffed out his cheeks. 'I am ready to accept it, and more. It will not come to this, but I must agree that the safety of our people is of paramount importance!'

Jeremy nodded. 'Quite so, sir.' The thought of offending somebody in high places had been enough to change Stallybrass's mind. Jeremy asked casually, 'When is *Serpent* due back?'

'Two days' time.' The commodore was very preoccupied.

'I see.' It would be interesting to gauge his brother's reactions.

He looked around at their grim, hostile faces. Most of them had been in Hong Kong for a long time, at least since the outbreak of war.

And not one of them had noticed anything, or at least, if they had, thought it important enough to pass on. And yet, to the Intelligence people in Whitehall even the tiniest fragment fitted into the overall picture. An increase in Japanese fleet movements in the Pacific, and the biggest build-up of troops on the Chinese mainland just across the border from the New Territories. And much smaller pieces. Japanese residents of Hong Kong were suddenly leaving the Colony, the hairdressing salons and massage parlours, the bars which were regularly used by British officers were being left abandoned. Nobody, it seemed, had thought it unusual. If only one Japanese in twenty was a spy, they would have enough information to open the gates from within.

Jeremy glanced at *Islip*'s angry captain.

If something wasn't done soon, they would not even have time to surrender.

Lieutenant-Commander Esmond Brooke stood as high as possible on the starboard side of the bridge to watch the dwindling strip of choppy water between *Serpent* and *Islip* as the final wires were passed across and made fast. Then there was no water at all, and the two steel hulls squeaked against the rope fenders like old friends.

Brooke wiped his forehead with his wrist. It was very hot and there was a chance of heavy rain according to the Met reports.

It felt like months since they had been ordered once again to Singapore to act as additional escort for a fast convoy bound for Australia. They had been forced to refuel at sea, at other times good experience in teamwork and seamanship, but Brooke was well aware of the unsettled atmosphere that pervaded his ship.

Everything they did seemed to lack purpose; even escort work could have been carried out by the Australians themselves. It was as if someone simply wanted to keep *Serpent* employed in case there was a real emergency.

How long this time, he wondered. The Chief had been complaining about a bearing running hot in the starboard shaft gland. Once in the hands of the dock-yard again, it might take ages to repair. There was no queue of damaged and battle-scarred ships here, each desperately needing a dock or basin, as there was in Britain, but in Hong Kong the dockyard seemed to begin work when Colours were sounded, and stop when they were lowered.

'All secure fore and aft, sir!'

'Very well. Ring off main engines.'

The ship shuddered while the duty part of the watch hurried to make the upper deck presentable for any important visitors. Lieutenant Calvert was fastening down the cover on the chart table. Even he had been unsettled lately.

Brooke picked up his pipe and tobacco pouch. *We are all on edge because of uncertainty, and feelings we dare not reveal.*

He shaded his eyes to stare up at the Peak. Was she watching the harbour to see them come alongside?

What of Calvert? Had he recovered from his moment of terror in Charles Yeung's seaplane?

Brock, the petty officer telegraphist, lingered on the top of the bridge ladder.

Kerr, who had come up from the forecastle, his station for entering and leaving harbour, looked at him warily. 'Well?'

Brock glanced towards the captain. 'Restricted, sir.'

Kerr took it. *Oh God. Another one. Who is it this time?*

He saw Brooke's tawny eyes flicker just once as he read the signal, then he said quietly, 'The cox'n, Number One, and a seaman named Robert Dalton.'

Kerr watched him, his face like stone. 'Quarterdeck division, sir. From Liverpool.'

'That's where it happened. His home was wiped out

245

in an air raid. Big family. Only his father survived, apparently.' But neither of them was really thinking of the young sailor. It was something that happened, to others usually.

But not to the coxswain, the core in any small warship. Friend, policeman, adviser, he filled all those roles and many more.

Brooke glanced up and saw Onslow, the yeoman of signals, watching him. He immediately looked away. He had already guessed, most likely. It had happened to him.

Brooke said, 'I'll see them now in my quarters.'

Pike might know, too: they often did. It would soon run through the ship. This was no great carrier or battleship. This was *family*.

He went down the ladder and walked aft towards the quarterdeck, feeling the oily metal under his shoes where the wire springs and breast-ropes had been laid out only an hour ago.

His day cabin greeted him like a stranger. After the incident with the submarine he had been unable to leave his hutch when they were at sea. It had been a hard habit to break even before that.

Petty Officer Kingsmill was opening scuttles but did not look at him.

'Will you need drinks, sir?' He turned then, his face genuinely sad. 'Just 'eard, sir.'

How could they know already? But there was no point in questioning it.

'Yes.' Brooke sat down, suddenly weary. Then with great care he removed the silver frame from the waterproof bag and stood it on the desk. As he had thought of her on the long night watches. How he always remembered her. Her eyes sparkling in the lights, her head partly turned to look across one bare shoulder. What would her father have thought of that?

Lian, help me . . .

There was a tap at the door. 'Able Seaman Dalton, sir.'

'Sit down, Dalton.' He watched the youth stare round the cabin, where he had never been before. An ordinary English face you would not even notice in some dockyard or seaport.

Dalton's eyes settled suddenly on the photograph, but when they moved on again they were filled with tears.

'It's me mum, ain't it, sir?'

The same Liverpool twang you got so used to in Western Approaches. That battered city, which had given its heart to the escort vessels and their men.

Brooke said, 'The signal says that apart from your father . . .' He got no further. The young seaman was staring past him, his wet eyes filled with despair.

'Why them? They never done nuthin' to hurt anyone, sir!'

'I know.' What was the point? There was no explanation to take away Dalton's grief. 'Would you like a drink?' He watched emotions churning through the sailor's mind, then the fixed realisation that his family had gone. Love them, like them, or hate them, there was nothing left to look forward to.

'Ta, thanks, sir.' He wiped his face with a surprisingly clean handkerchief. It was not easy to dhobi clothing in the crowded messdecks. But they managed.

Brooke said, 'I *can* send you home. Get a replacement from the base here, I shouldn't wonder.' *Home* – where was that? In some barracks or hostel until he got another ship. Certainly not the pile of debris that was probably all that remained.

Dalton shook his head. Like Onslow, in some respects anyway. 'No, sir. I was never close to me dad.' He stared at the glass that Kingsmill had placed by his hand. 'I'll stay with me mates.'

Brooke poured himself a full glass and could feel the boy's eyes watching every movement.

'I'm glad you said that. I think I'm going to need every good hand shortly.' He coughed: the Scotch was neat, and he guessed that Dalton had probably never had it in his young life. He added, 'I shall write to your dad in any case.'

Dalton peered at him as if he had misheard. '*You*, sir?'

'I'm your commanding officer. You are my responsibility, you and all the people in this ship who don't know what it's all about . . .'

Words, only words. Someone like Dalton could not possibly know about all those other letters, to friends who had lost someone, to mothers who wanted to know *how it had happened*. Just as well they did not know. Better to leave it to the films and all the comforting lies.

And what am I to these same men? Do they really trust me? Am I merely the authority across the defaulters' table, or the unconcerned captain who refused their request for promotion or transfer?

He thought of her words. *They like you*. Had that ever been enough?

'If you need any help, Dalton, please ask the first lieutenant. We're all on the same side.'

Kingsmill refilled the seaman's glass, then gently took his elbow.

'This way, my son. In the pantry. Nobody'll bother you there.' Over his shoulder he added, 'Cox'n's here, sir.'

The young seaman stared at them. 'Not 'im too?'

The pantry door swung shut.

Not him too. It hung in the cabin like an epitaph.

Pike took the vacated chair and looked at a point above Brooke's left shoulder.

'Bad news, Swain.'

'I see.' Pike turned his cap through his fingers, as if he was at the wheel again. After a moment he said, 'I knew I made a mistake about shiftin' from London to the coast. Southsea, was it?'

Brooke felt drained. 'Big raid. Lot of casualties. It says it was instantaneous.' Did they always say that?

Pike stood up, his boots creaking on the carpet. 'I won't 'ave a drink just now, sir. I've some watch bills to check on.'

'I see.' The Iron Man, but with every good reason.

'Later, if you asks me, that'll be different.'

Brooke had never noticed how blue the coxwain's eyes were, like the ocean they had just left astern.

'I *will* ask you, Swain. You can tell me some more about my father.'

The coxswain left the cabin and could soon be heard tearing a strip off a defaulter who was swabbing out the officers' heads.

If any ship had a living backbone, he was it.

Kerr was in the wardroom looking at the empty letter rack when a messman told him the captain was outside.

'Sir?' But he knew what was wrong. The strain, the same tension was back again.

Kerr had seen the red-eyed sailor leave the pantry, while the ramrod coxswain had marched past him without a word.

Brooke asked, 'Can you take the weight, Dick? If there's no word from the base to the contrary you can send all but the duty part of the watch ashore . . .'

He saw the concern in Kerr's eyes. 'I'll be all right. I've left a number in case you need me. Won't be long.'

Kerr could smell the neat Scotch, but knew it was not that.

Brooke said, 'It's just that I'm sick of *taking* it, not being able to hit back, and having to tell good men that their wives and lovers are gone. Killed. And for what? *I keep asking myself!*'

Kerr said, 'I think you know the answer, sir.' He turned angrily as the quartermaster's legs appeared on the companion ladder. '*What?*'

The man peered at him resentfully. 'Car at the dockyard gates, sir.' He looked at Brooke. 'For you, sir.'

They followed Brooke on deck and into the noon sunlight. Kerr saw *Islip*'s O.O.D. and quartermaster salute him as he crossed the big destroyer's deck, their eyes following while he walked down the brow to the wall.

Brooke knew they were staring at him. Kerr probably thought him round the bend.

He was still in his faded sea-going jacket and the white capcover had a smear of paint on it. He had been wearing the same shirt for twenty-four hours, and the Scotch was making his brain throb without mercy.

All he knew was that she was waiting for him. Had known he was back in Hong Kong.

He recalled the words of a famous admiral when questioned about his ability to perform some great deed.

The impossible we do at once. Miracles take a little longer.

As he saw the great car waiting beyond the dockyard sentry he suddenly broke into a run. He was no longer the captain, the Old Man: all that he had left behind, if only for a while. It was surely a miracle.

The army stores van threw up a wave of muddy water and jerked to a halt outside the little apartment block.

Two white-clad figures jumped into the teeming rain and were drenched to the skin even before they reached the gate. Calvert waved to the young soldier who had taken pity on them when they had left the restaurant and the heavens had opened.

'We'd have drowned without you! Thanks a lot!'

The soldier was a Canadian, one of the replacements in *Operation Boomerang*. This was his first proper posting: it must all be a great adventure for him.

Holding the girl's wet hand in his Calvert ran up the short path to the front door where they huddled together, laughing despite, or because of, the mess they were in.

A security man unlocked the door and sat down again at his desk. What residents and 'passers-through' got up to was none of his concern.

She turned on the stairs, her shirt and skirt black with rain.

'That was a *wonderful* meal, Toby! I can't remember when I've enjoyed myself so much!'

He watched her; like a happy child, he thought. As she must have been.

It had been a nice restaurant, small and very Chinese, just off Nathan Road. A street of lanterns and garish shops, of eating-houses and dark cafés, with hardly a serviceman to be seen: like Aladdin's Cave and treasure trove rolled into one, with street hawkers and a few hopeful rickshaws hovering.

Calvert had bought her a silk kimono at one of the stalls. The women who had taken his money had corrected him politely but firmly. 'Happy Coat. Not kimono, Captain!'

At the restaurant, which *Islip*'s gunnery officer had told him about, there had been no surprise or curiosity when they had walked in. It had even been funny to

251

discover that few people in the restaurant spoke English, a far cry from the island.

They had managed. Beautiful duck, rice and noodles and a dozen other dishes which they enjoyed without knowing what they were. The proprietor even produced some beer which Calvert fortified with a measure of brandy from his flask.

The time had gone so fast. Watching each other across the small table, discovering, understanding.

He had given her a little jade-inlaid box, which he had bought in the shop the day he had felt close to tears. When they had met in the street. *How long ago was that?*

Also some jade earrings. He had apologised when she had told him that she would get her ears pierced as soon as possible, and had brushed aside his offer to change them.

She had been looking down at the little box, her eyes hidden by her lashes.

'I shall treasure them. Always.'

He had moved some empty dishes and reached across the table to hold her hand. With one another, they were alone, although they sat in a crowded restaurant.

She had been admiring the little box again when he had said, 'I'll have to check up on the Star Ferry. They probably stop running at night.'

Then she looked up at him. Very directly, her expression strangely determined if a little frightened.

'If you don't have to get back to the ship, Toby . . .' He had felt her fingers tighten around his as she had finished, 'You can stay with me. If you like.'

They had gone out of the restaurant, saying nothing, but with so much to say.

Now, outside her apartment, Calvert hesitated. 'I don't want you to think . . .'

She turned and had to rise on tip-toe to kiss his cheek. 'I don't.'

She switched on the lights and wondered if Ruth Shelley was next door, listening.

The room was barely furnished, a place without a personality of its own. There was a framed print of a tall pagoda on one wall, and another of English Shire horses ploughing a field. A room which had had no time to glean anything from the steady stream of occupants. But, as in the restaurant, she saw only the man who had come to it with her, someone she had met on a train.

'I – I got some whisky, Toby.'

'*Did* you?'

'I think it might have come off the brigadier's mess bill.' She covered her mouth and giggled. 'I'm soaked. I'll have a rub down and then I'll put on my Happy Coat.' She smiled fondly. 'That woman made me feel like a tourist!'

He made to hold her but she stepped away. He said, 'You know that I love you, Sue.'

She reached for the door. 'That's a lovely thing to say. You've never said it before.'

He tried to laugh it off. 'I did, you know. You can read it in my letter when you get home.'

She was still staring at him as she backed into the other room, her eyes filling her face.

He heard her singing softly in the bathroom, and after a brief exploration he opened a low sideboard where a bottle of Johnny Walker stood in solitary splendour. It was unobtainable in England. For lowly lieutenants, anyway.

He called, 'There's only one glass in the place, Sue!'

'I've got another one in here.'

The door opened and she stood there in the silk robe

he had bought for her in Nathan Road. Short and black, with scarlet flowers on the pockets.

She saluted smartly. 'Excuse my rig, sir!' Then she turned and displayed the gold dragon etched down her spine. 'Dragons are lucky, the Chinese say.'

She held up a fresh towel. 'Take off your shirt, Toby.'

He held the chair while she dried his back, her face hidden from view.

She did not resist when he held her in his arms, her damp hair pressing against his chest. Calvert noticed that she had removed the wedding ring and its chain, which he had seen through her wet shirt.

He said quietly, 'I should have taken you to a hotel.'

She shook her head. 'You know what people would say.'

'Do you care?' He felt the desire for her like something beyond his control, a real need for this young girl he barely knew. The touch of her face, the pressure of their bodies had aroused something which neither of them could contain.

She jerked round in his arms and gasped as fireworks and rockets exploded above the black water of the harbour. It was like cleaning an old painting. Shapes appeared in bright and colourful flashes, tall junks, motionless or moving it was impossible to say, huddles of smaller craft, and dark, resting lighters waiting for a new day.

'What is it?' She turned and gripped the veranda rail, her eyes lighting up in the display.

He reached around to hold the same rail, enfolding her, very aware of her nearness, her touch against his body.

He replied, 'Aftermath of a wedding, or a funeral maybe. I can never tell the difference.'

Her voice was low and husky. 'Hold me.'

He pulled at the sash around the Happy Coat and felt her body go rigid as he opened the front of it.

She said nothing.

Calvert slipped his hands inside the coat and realized she was quite naked. He cupped each breast in turn, imprisoning it firmly until the nipples were hard under his grip. She retained her hold on the rail until he dropped the coat around her shoulders and kissed her on the neck. Then she came round into his arms, the robe falling to the floor so that he saw her body like a perfect statue against the dark water and the fireworks.

He laid her on the bed with great care, feeling her eyes on him as he explored her body, her throat, her breasts and further still until his fingers were caressing her hair, so that she cried out as if to match his own pain of desire.

'If you hurt me . . .'

'I won't.' He knelt over her, feeling the warm harbour breeze across his nakedness.

'Just love me. *Love me.*'

She grasped him with both arms, and he knew she was tensed, ready for the pain, for the ultimate.

But there was none. So very slowly. Down and down, and the exquisite embrace as he entered her until they were linked together, their bodies as one.

She whispered, 'Now. Make it *now.*'

Afterwards, the moonlight flooded the room and touched the bed where they lay entangled.

Tossed aside on the floor their two wet uniforms seemed to mime their embrace. The moment of destiny.

15

No Turning Back

Ian Cusack, *Serpent*'s Chief, watched his commanding officer at his desk while he read through the engine room report.

He said, 'I'm still not happy about the shaft, sir. These dockyard maties are not to my taste.' He looked unusually stubborn and angry.

Brooke reread part of the Chief's highly technical findings. Cusack was not a man to complain without reason.

He said, 'If this was Chatham Dockyard you'd probably say that.'

The cabin was strangely bright without *Islip* alongside to block out the scuttles. She was at sea on another patrol, her departure and return no doubt seen and noted by Japanese agents, if they were still interested.

He glanced at Lian's photograph. At first he had put it in a drawer whenever he was meeting one of his officers here. Now he did not. Defiance? Or was it because he had hardly seen her since he had rushed ashore in his old sea-going gear? Even then they had driven around in the big car, saying little, but holding hands: a bond, but to Brooke it had been a lifeline. Then to sea to test the shafts and the steering. It was not like *Serpent* to play up. He could not imagine how many thousands of miles she must have steamed since his father had first taken command.

Commodore Stallybrass had complained about their time in port, although what strategic use could have been made of *Serpent*'s time was anyone's guess.

Brooke had spoken only briefly to his brother on the shore telephone line. Their exchange had been curt, and Brooke knew that something else was bothering him.

He said, 'As soon as we get clearance I intend to go alongside the oiler. I've already had my request granted. Full bunkers, Chief – three hundred tons, more if you can squeeze it in.'

'May I ask why, sir?'

He smiled. 'Frankly, Chief, I don't know. A feeling, that's all. Better to be prepared.'

He thought of Calvert and how he had changed since their return to Hong Kong. More alive and relaxed than he could remember. As navigator he had the least to do in harbour, apart from sharing the O.O.D. duties with the others. The rest of the time he was usually to be found at Charles Yeung's little shipyard working on the seaplane. He now had another volunteer in the person of Lieutenant Paul Kipling, who had proved to be a wizard with the skill he had gained in his time at the *garridge*.

Jeremy should be on his way home now. Brooke had asked him about his new son to ease the tension between them, but even that had been wrong. Jeremy had snapped on the telephone, 'He's been christened Marcus, for God's sake, after Sarah's father! What sort of stupid name is that?'

Whatever he had come to Hong Kong to discuss with the various chiefs-of-staff it appeared to have had little effect. It would be November in a matter of days, and all local interest seemed to be centred on social events

257

as they moved up to Christmas. A fancy dress ball for the war effort at home, Saturday racing at Happy Valley: people would be jockeying for position and trying to arrange their diaries to accommodate all the invitations to a whole armada of celebrations and extravagances.

There was a knock at the door and Kerr pulled the curtain to one side.

'Sorry to interrupt you, sir.'

Cusack picked up his stained cap. 'I was just going.' He looked at Brooke. 'I just want her at her best at all times, sir, as she's always been.'

The curtain fell back and Kerr raised his eyebrows. 'What's eating him?'

'He thinks they're taking too long with his repairs. I must say I agree. What do you want, by the way?'

Kerr smiled. 'There's a Third Officer Yorke come aboard, sir.'

Brooke glanced at the clock. 'Damn, I let Pilot go ashore. She'll be here to say goodbye. I understand from the signals that the brigadier is off today.' He smiled ruefully. 'It'll give the other golfers a break, I suppose.' He wondered how far they had gone together. Could it last across the miles of ocean, the months or years ahead? He looked at the framed photograph. *I know I could.*

His expression was not lost on the first lieutenant.

'I'll show her aft, sir.'

Brooke walked to an open scuttle and thought of the girl up on the Peak. He must see her. They might get sailing orders soon. He allowed the thought to explore his mind like a scalpel.

It would be impossible to leave her without knowing.

The small Wren officer stepped over the coaming and smiled at him.

'I thought I'd come over myself, sir.' She held out some envelopes. 'From Commodore *Tamar*.'

Brooke pulled out a chair for her. Like Calvert, she had changed in some inexplicable way. She was not the shy-looking girl he had seen at the reception, like somebody in a school play.

She met his glance without flinching: she even smiled. 'I collected your brother when he arrived, sir.'

Brooke grinned. 'Did he stare at you, too?'

'Differently, sir.'

'That was very diplomatic!' He walked to the scuttle again as one of the motor torpedo vessels growled abeam, making a big wash for such a small vessel.

He said, 'I'm afraid Lieutenant Calvert is ashore.' He faced her, surprised that she was apparently unmoved. It was something else. Pride, perhaps.

'I know.' She looked past the commodore's letters to the girl in the photograph. 'I'm staying. I got Brigadier Sexton to fix it. I'm attached to *Tamar* for the present.'

He looked at her gravely. As the brigadier's secretary she would know about the risks of being here if anything went wrong, and Jeremy would have added his own gloom-and-doom bit if she had asked him.

A very pretty girl, probably only twenty, even less. So what was the point of spoiling it for her, for *them*? Young men her age fought and died every hour of the day. In the skies, under water, everywhere they were so ordered, just as they had in Flanders in his father's war.

She must have stunned them in the base. It was unlikely they had ever seen a girl in uniform out here.

He said, 'You've done a lot for Toby Calvert. I know what he went through.'

'So do I, sir. *Now*.' She put her head on one side so that her brown curls bounced over her collar. 'But you're asking me if I'm serious about him?'

'Am I?' He shrugged. 'I suppose I am.'

She looked at him steadily. 'I love him. I know he loves me. I'd never let him down.'

'He's very lucky. I hope it goes well for both of you. May I call you Sue?'

'Thank you, sir. I'd like that.'

They both stared at the telephone as it rattled in its case.

Brooke said, 'Sorry about this.' He picked up the handset. 'Captain speaking.'

There were scrapes and clicks and for a moment he thought he had been cut off.

'Can you come to the house on the Peak?'

Brooke said, 'I thought you'd left the island, Jeremy.' He covered the mouthpiece and looked at the girl. 'Seems today is full of surprises!'

Jeremy sounded unusually on edge. More to the point, he was unable to hide it.

'Have you got somebody there?' When he remained silent, Jeremy said, 'Charles Yeung. He's not well. I think you should be here. You know what I mean.'

Brooke said, 'I'll take a taxi . . .' But the line had gone dead.

The Wren was on her feet. 'I can get a car, sir. I'll drive, if you can stand it.'

But he was looking at the photograph. She must have asked that he be told.

He said, 'You'll have to, Sue. I've never learned.'

They met Kerr on the quarterdeck talking with the Buffer and Podger Barlow, the gunner (T). They were discussing the day's work for the duty watch.

'I'm going up to Charles Yeung's house, Dick. Take over for me.'

Kerr stared at the girl. 'I thought you were going home!'

She smiled, but was very aware of Brooke's sudden anxiety.

'So everyone says, Number One.'

Brooke cut in abruptly. 'Now where's that car?'

The side-party had hurried into position by the brow, and Kerr waited to see them over the side.

The girl hesitated until Eggy Bacon, the chief quartermaster, whispered, 'You goes *first*, miss. The cap'n always goes last!'

The calls shrilled and Brooke saluted as he followed the Wren down to the wall.

Kerr breathed out slowly. 'A nice little thing and no mistake!'

The gunner (T) kept a straight face. 'So everyone says, *Number One*!'

Petty Officer Alec Fox, the Buffer, tugged his cap over his eyes and groaned. ''Ere comes the base engineer officer, sir.'

'Tell the Chief, will you? Maybe they can get things sorted out this time.'

But his thoughts were still on the small Wren officer and Toby Calvert. This evening he would write another letter to the girl in England.

It was a fast but hair-raising drive to the Peak and the house where he had first met Lian.

Brooke had forcibly restrained himself from seizing the girl's wrist when there had been nothing ahead of the bonnet but clear sky as she had swung around one of the many zig-zagging bends above the harbour.

Once she had squeaked aloud when they had appeared to be on the edge of a sheer drop to some houses below.

'Never driven up here before!' She had given a breathless laugh. 'I'll bet you'd never have guessed, sir!'

They entered the familiar driveway and Brooke saw several other cars there, including the pale green Phantom.

Robert Tan, the valet, strode down the steps to greet him.

'You very quick, Captain!' He glanced covertly at the Wren, mystified perhaps as to why the captain of one of the King's ships should be driven by a mere woman.

'How is he?'

Robert Tan shrugged. 'Better, I think. Doctor Camille is here.'

Brooke seemed to feel the sting of his old leg injuries return at the mention of Yeung's other daughter. She was not the sort to take any nonsense, even from her formidable father.

Sue Yorke said quietly, 'Shall I come, sir?'

Robert Tan eyed her impassively. 'I fetch Missy a drink.' He added, 'Cool, with fruit in it.'

She murmured, 'After that drive I could do with something stronger!'

Brooke opened a door and saw Lian there, as if she had been waiting for him. For this moment.

The Wren said, 'I'll be all right alone, sir.' She smiled at Lian, then she was gone.

Lian came towards him and slowly put her arms around his neck. She studied him feature by feature, and said, 'You are looking better. More rested.' She seemed satisfied. 'I asked that you be told about my father.'

Her perfume was like a drug, and he wanted to hold her, touch her, in case she slipped away.

She said, 'He has worked too hard and too much.

262

He thinks he is a young man again. My sister and her husband Harry are here.' Her eyes lit up momentarily as if she were remembering how she had mimicked Camille's American accent, but the humour would not come.

She paused, and then said, 'Your brother is here also.'

'Yes. He telephoned me.' He persisted, 'But your father – he is in no danger, Lian?'

'Not this time, I think. He gives so much. You will see.'

There were voices in the adjoining room, the sounds of tea being prepared.

She whispered, 'Your ship is not going yet, Es-mond?'

'No.' He squeezed her hand and imagined what it would be like to be with her. To love her.

'When you look at me like that, Es-mond, I see myself very differently. A person of wind and dust, and not the sheltered daughter of a great man.'

Brooke smiled at her concern. He knew enough to understand the term she had used. A prostitute. 'I think not!'

She was not convinced. 'When you are close to me, even when I think of you, when we are not together, I cannot but want you to hold me, and not leave me untouched, not to have felt the waves of the wind like other girls.'

A small servant opened the door and ushered them through. Charles Yeung was sitting in an armchair and was rolling down the sleeve of his shirt. He looked strained, but what Brooke noticed most was his hair, usually so perfectly groomed. It was tousled, probably from when he had been lying down to have his heart tested.

'You are welcome, Esmond!' He frowned. 'All this

fuss for nothing!' He reached for a cigarette box on the nearest table.

'Too many of those!' That was Camille. She was folding up her bag of instruments with quick angry movements. 'You must take more care. You can afford it!'

A very large man in a creased, lightweight suit and brightly flowered tie introduced himself. 'Hello, Commander Brooke. I'm Harry, Camille's old man!'

Big and outwardly amiable, but he was no doubt wondering how he was supposed to react.

Jeremy came in from the terrace, and summoned a smile. 'Like the bad penny, Esmond. But I'll be leaving quite soon now.' He took out his own cigarette case and added, 'I saw you arrive with that little Miss Know-it-all.'

Lian watched them both from beside her father's chair. Then very softly, she asked, 'Did she turn you down, Jeremy?'

Doctor Harry Quayle of Nashville, Tennessee held up his big beefy hands in protest.

'It's like this.' He looked at Brooke wearily. 'We had this notice about quitting Hong Kong if the need arises. I don't want to become involved. As an American citizen I'd put my wife first, naturally. But the fact remains . . .'

Camille's eyes flashed. 'I'm not leaving, I tell you that now! I am *needed* here, and if the worst happened, the need would be all the greater!'

It was strange to hear her slightly American accent, Brooke thought, after the soft voices of the others.

Jeremy said sharply, 'It was my duty to tell them. There would be no difficulty in getting them a passage to Australia, as a first step anyway.'

He turned on Lian, still smarting from her cutting remark about the Wren officer.

'And *you* wouldn't leave either, I suppose?'

She touched her father's shoulder. 'You are right. This time.'

Charles Yeung stroked his daughter's hand and asked, 'What do *you* think, Esmond? You are a friend now. I have already said what I believe. If a passage to a safer place is offered I think my daughters should take it. They of course refused, for various reasons.'

Brooke looked at her for several seconds. It was like something physical, unbreakable. He saw her put her other hand to her breast and then nod very slowly.

'I would do all I could if such a thing did happen. You must know that.'

Charles Yeung clicked his lighter, like a gunshot in this quiet room above the sea.

'I do know. I have watched you. But wars do not respect the people who are made to fight them. You may have to leave here. I cannot see that you will be allowed to choose.'

Brooke turned to his brother. Relaxed now, a comfortable spectator again.

'What have you been saying to these people?'

Jeremy gave an elegant shrug. 'I thought they should be told. We owe it to them. In any case, the possibility might not arise.'

You bastard, he thought. So he did know more than he was saying.

'And your yardarm is clear, is that it?'

Jeremy glanced at his watch. 'Something like that.'

Lian said softly, 'I will stay in Hong Kong as long as I am needed here.' She faced her father. 'With you.' Then she turned towards Brooke and the others. 'And with the man I love.'

Charles Yeung leaned back in his chair. Was he displeased? He certainly showed no surprise.

'Have Jeremy driven to the ferry.' He held out his hand. 'Now you owe us nothing, Commander.'

Jeremy paused, and said lightly to Brooke, 'See you in England some time, old son.' But there was no emotion there. Perhaps there never had been.

'I want you to come with me to the yard.' Yeung's authority seemed to exclude the two doctors. 'But first, we will eat.' He smiled gently as Camille began to protest. '*Shh!* I am a man again. I will not be told!' Then he got to his feet and looked around as if he had not expected to recover his strength.

Brooke asked quietly, 'Why did my brother speak of owing something?'

Yeung shrugged. 'My people can always discover things which no intelligence officer would even hear about. In exchange, your brother could be helpful to me.' He shook his head and smiled. 'Not, I assure you, a court-martial offence!' It seemed to amuse him.

Lian said, 'You should have been a pirate!'

He touched her hair, his eyes seeking something. 'Some of my ancestors were, I believe. Too hard a life for me!'

The doctors had gone out on to the terrace, and Yeung asked abruptly, 'Do you love my daughter, Esmond? Above all else? Is that what she is telling me?'

Brooke found it was easy to answer. 'I want her. I have never known real love until I saw her. You may regard my prospects as poor. But for the war I would have been outside the navy because of my leg.'

Charles Yeung raised his hand. 'Suppose you took her back to England—'

She interrupted, 'I have *been* to England, Father!'

'It is not what I meant and please do not interfere!'

Brooke smiled. 'Of a different race and culture, do you mean?'

Charles looked into the distance. 'Not exactly. Lian's grandmother was French, you know . . . and her mother was so beautiful.'

Lian shook her head. 'Do not distress yourself, Father.'

He turned towards her and smiled. 'I am happy with her memory, my child.'

Brooke said, 'I would take good care of her, Charles. And if—' He glanced at her, hesitating until he saw the encouragement in her eyes. It was as if she could read each word before he uttered it. 'If there were children, you would be their only grandfather.'

'Yes. In war, who can tell?' He seemed to shake off the thoughts. 'So let us eat now. Tell your girl officer Miss *Knowitall*, was that her name?'

Lian exclaimed, 'Oh, Father – this is only insulting nickname!' She brushed the hair from her eyes. 'I will find her.'

Alone in the big room Charles Yeung said, 'I could have gone against it, fought you, Esmond. I might even have used my influence to have you transferred. But you are a man of honour, I have never doubted that. And on occasions, when I consider it necessary, so am I.' He reached out and took Brooke's arm and said, 'You have her heart. Do not break it.'

They turned to greet Lian as she entered with the little Wren at her side. They both looked very happy, and somehow shy.

Brooke watched them. So different, so far apart except for one thing.

They had made their decisions. Now there was no turning back.

Lieutenant Toby Calvert stood on the slipway and

mopped his face with a grubby towel. Even with the doors wide open the sun on the corrugated iron roof made it like an oven.

'Well, what d'you think, Paul? Will the brute ever get airborne, or is it all a waste of bloody time?'

Kipling was stripped to his shorts and his bronzed shoulders were daubed with grease and oil beneath the seaplane's twin floats.

He grinned. 'Like a bird, Toby. Boy, I envy you – I nearly had a go at the Fleet Air Arm but I've got no head for heights!'

Calvert took a glass of juice from one of the Chinese mechanics who had been working with them.

He could still scarcely believe it, or what he had done. That first time, in the light of early dawn, he had risen from the bed, choking back a scream as the nightmare had returned more vividly than ever.

But it had not been the same. She had been with him, had held him, pressing his head against her bare breasts, murmuring and stroking him until the horror had receded into the shadows.

It had happened again with her, and each time they had fought it together.

He had discovered that while she had held him he had been able to speak of it. Tell her, as he had always needed to tell somebody who would understand. He had built up pictures of his crew, Bob Piper the observer and the telegraphist air gunner, 'Muffin' McDowall, a kid just out of training when he had been allotted to Calvert's Swordfish. Always together, except when divided by wardroom and messdeck: runs ashore, spirits high even in the face of danger.

Sue had told him once that she felt she had been there in the cockpit, that she could have recognized his friends, so real and clear had he made them.

Even the old Swordfish, the Stringbag. He had described her with true affection.

She had stroked his hair when he had come to the worst part, the realisation that the carrier, *his* carrier, was turning turtle, the heavy shells from the two battle-cruisers still dropping, destroying any hope of rescue for the struggling survivors.

'Then she was gone. There was nowhere for us to go. Nowhere to fly, nowhere to land.' There had been a long silence and he had heard her heart beating against his cheek. 'So I went for the enemy. It was hopeless, I always knew that. They put a destroyer between us and the big ships. There was flak everywhere. Poor Bob got it first. He just hung in his harness, trying to speak, blood pouring out of him. I just watched that destroyer in my sights and kept on going. Then Muffin was hit – even above the explosions and the din I heard him screaming. They didn't want to die, you know. I killed them.'

She had hugged him. 'Tell me about it.'

He had continued without emotion. It was like being asleep. Continuing a dream. 'Then the engine was hit, I could feel the old Pegasus coughing and spitting. There was no more time. I just flew straight in until that bloody destroyer filled the sea, the world. Then I dropped the torpedo. I don't remember much else except that we just made it over the funnels. I thought we were going to smash into them. Next thing I was in the sea and I saw the old Swordfish dipping under. Then there was an explosion. I felt it like a boot in my guts. I was floating in my Mae West and I saw the destroyer for just a few seconds. She must have been going so fast and turning to try to get away that when it hit her the blast tore off half of the fo'c'sle.' He had given a tremendous sigh. 'After that I had the sea to myself.'

'Oh, Toby, I do love you so!' He had felt her tears on his arm and had tried to comfort her.

'A trawler picked me up. God knows what she was doing there.'

'Thank God she was!'

Calvert had realized then that he was no longer shivering. No longer afraid.

He had said, 'So I met the King. Nice bloke, I thought. He said something about being a hero. I don't remember exactly. I was all choked up because of Muffin and Bob.'

'You didn't ask to be a hero. But you *are*!'

Lieutenant Kipling was watching him. 'Penny for them, Toby?'

'Just thinking about my girl. I'm going to marry her if I can.'

Kipling's teeth were very white through his tan and oil stains.

'You funny old bugger! I thought you were bothered about this plane again.'

Calvert touched the warm metal. 'Not really. Mr Yeung's going to get some Dutch pilot from Java to fly it.' He patted it, surprised at himself. 'I shall miss the thing when we leave.'

'Have you heard something?'

Calvert shook his head. 'There was talk of *Serpent* being withdrawn to be converted into a long-range escort. But I gather the Skipper won't discuss it. Not even with Number One. He loves that old lady, you know.'

Kipling sighed. 'I'm damn glad we've got *him* in command.'

Calvert looked at him, aware of his sudden apprehension.

But the mood changed as Kipling threw his rag in the water and exclaimed, '*Shit!*'

'What?'

When he twisted round Calvert saw the reason for his concern. A little procession was entering the hangar from the other end: Charles Yeung with his daughter on his arm while the commanding officer, accompanied by the urbane chief-of-staff, followed behind with the Wren called Sue.

Kipling wiped his dripping chest. 'Look at us, for Christ's sake!'

Calvert smiled. How close they had all become in the little destroyer *Serpent*. And how much they depended on one another. Because of the ship or because of her captain? They certainly belonged. Like one.

The chief-of-staff, Bertie, sniffed the air suspiciously.

'Well, I've explained to *Tamar* and of course the harbour-master, but the responsibility must rest elsewhere.'

Charles Yeung carefully put out his cigarette and smiled.

'I understand that the Assistant Governor is willing to shoulder that!'

The shot went home.

Kipling shouted to the mechanics, 'Jump about! Chop-chop! Let's warp the kite to the end of the slipway!'

Sue Yorke moved nearer to Calvert and whispered, 'Is he *really* an officer?'

Calvert grinned as sunshine flooded over the sea-plane's cockpit. Where he had been so terrified, and yet more afraid of showing it.

Charles Yeung folded his arms. 'Just the engines, Lieutenant Calvert.' He was thinking hard. 'Then you may, er, become clean, gentlemen, and join me at my house.'

Calvert nodded, his eyes on the cockpit. 'Very good of you, sir!'

She said, 'I'd love to fly in it. With you.'

He was amazed that he could treat it so lightly. 'Not in this plane, Sue. It's got no parachutes.'

At the prospect of a party, Bertie Granville brightened up considerably.

'We'll make it an occasion, what?'

Calvert was climbing into the cockpit while the mechanics were perched on either float ready for the start-up.

Charles Yeung said, 'It *is* an occasion, Captain Granville. I am going to offer my daughter's hand in marriage to Lieutenant-Commander Esmond Brooke.'

The hangar erupted in one combined roar of power until the very slipway seemed to shake.

It was as if every friendly dragon in the harbour was showing its approval.

16

Prelude

'Course to steer is zero-four-three, sir.' Calvert's voice was quite steady even though he was fully aware of the tension around him in the dark upper bridge.

Brooke crouched by the gyro-repeater, his eyes glowing faintly in the compass light.

'Starboard ten. Midships. Steady. Steer zero-four-three.'

Calvert could barely hear the coxswain's response from the wheelhouse.

Serpent was returning to Hong Kong after two escort passages to Singapore. Days and weeks of watchkeeping just so that some big troopships and supply vessels could reach harbour unmolested. Not that there was much chance of that.

Calvert raised his head from the chart table and stared at the final approach to the harbour. He could feel a lump in his throat and was surprised at his own emotion. The blaze of dancing lights, the great sheen of various colours thrown across the dark waters of the harbour: it was like a home-coming.

'Dead slow, both engines.'

Calvert thought he could detect the same need in the captain, despite his level tones. It was so unlike him to enter harbour at night, and Calvert guessed it was because he could not wait until dawn.

He thought of Singapore, the great wave of excitement and optimism that had welcomed the arrival of the promised reinforcements. The new battleship *Prince of Wales* and the veteran battle-cruiser *Repulse* had dwarfed everything else in the anchorage. Symbols of true naval power and superiority, a boost to servicemen and civilians alike.

For Singapore, and indirectly the Crown Colony of Hong Kong, the great capital ships could not have arrived at a better moment. At home in Britain, where most of *Serpent*'s people had left their hearts, the news would barely raise any comment at this stage of the war.

For the losses they knew and understood had been real and terrible. The aircraft carrier, *Ark Royal*, the public's darling, not only because of her exploits against the enemy but also because of her ability to survive after being 'sunk' so many times by the German propaganda machine and morale-hitting broadcasts, had at last run out of luck. Near Gibraltar she had been torpedoed, and after two days of trying to save her, she had been abandoned to her fate.

The hateful German radio question, 'Where is your *Ark Royal* now?' was another bitter memory.

It was not over. In this, the closing stage of November, while people shivered in unheated shelters or sorted out belongings from yet another raid, came another blow at sea. The battleship *Barham* had blown up after being torpedoed in the Eastern Mediterranean with a terrible loss of life. The great ships like *Royal Oak* and *Courageous*, *Hood* and *Glorious*, explored by parents and children alike at the peacetime Navy Weeks and Reviews, had been joined by two more legends. It was a wonder that Singapore had been allowed the protection of two valuable warships of such importance when losses in contested waters were so bad.

'Pilot boat, sir.'

Brooke's voice was sharp. 'Where, man? I'm not a mind-reader!'

'Sorry, sir.' It was Leading Signalman Railton, Onslow's trusted assistant. 'At Green four-five, sir.'

Brooke said, 'No. *I'm* sorry. Rank has privileges, but that wasn't one of them.'

'Signal from *Tamar*, sir. *Secure to buoy as indicated.*'

'Acknowledge.' Brooke rubbed his eyes. The slow approach, through moored vessels and avoiding moving ones, was strain enough. Now this, picking up a buoy in the dark. But Kerr would be ready as soon as he got the message. The motor-boat would be lowered to dash ahead of the ship and offload a luckless rating on to the buoy. A buoy-jumper, as he was known. He would cling there watching *Serpent*'s knife-like bows looming over him across the stars and hope to catch the picking-up wire before the ship ran right over him. It would not be the first time.

Even as the thought crossed his mind Brooke heard the pipe.

'Away motor-boat's crew! Buoy-jumpers to muster!'

Kerr was down there now with the fo'c'sle party and their leading seaman, Bill Doggett. He could see their faces as if he were with them. In only a matter of months he had come to know a lot about most of them, and a little about all of them.

At least this approach would keep Kerr busy, might take his mind off the news of his young cousin, who had gone down in *Barham*.

'Signal the pilot, Yeoman. We'll follow him in.'

He thought of the escort duties they had just

performed. Compared to the Atlantic or the Med it was like yachting.

He touched his old jacket and felt the silver frame in the inside pocket in its waterproof bag.

'Signal from *Tamar*, sir. *You can return alongside after Islip has sailed at oh-seven-hundred. Report on fuel and general supplies when convenient.*'

Calvert said, 'Damn nice of them.'

Brooke ran his fingers along the top edge of the glass screen. The caked salt there felt like baked sand.

He said quietly, 'She did well.'

Calvert watched him. Would they ever meet again when it was all over? He would never forget the Skipper and men like Onslow and the Chief, and the formidable coxswain with his grief bottled up inside him like hoarded rum.

'Watch it now!' Brooke was staring across the port bow as a shaft of torchlight flashed out from the drifting motor-boat. The buoy-jumper and his companion were like cut-out figures in the beam, eyes wide as they peered at the slow-moving ship. The second man was to hold his mate in position if the ship accidentally rammed into them.

'Stop both!'

An arm moved in the wavering beam and a heaving-line splashed into the water.

A voice snarled, 'Another line! You want to leave them girls alone, Tom! You must be goin' blind!'

'A touch ahead starboard.' Brooke watched the buoy pivot closer to the port anchor. 'Stop engine!'

The next line was seized and hauled to the buoy, the picking-up wire following it, bobbing above the water like a magician's snake.

There was a metallic thud and Kerr yelled through his cupped hands, 'All fast forrard, sir!'

Brooke waved to him as a heavy cable was prepared for the buoy until first light.

Brooke stared across to the Kowloon side and then exclaimed, 'The *Dumbarton*! She's getting steam up!'

He thought of the jokes they had made about the old cruiser. Her anchor cables painted to hide the rust, the framed pictures lining the cabin flats, all of which would have to be moved. Stallybrass must be furious.

Calvert said, 'They'll miss the big party at the Peninsula, sir.'

Brooke clapped his shoulder. 'Too bad.' But he felt a certain uneasiness. Where bound? An exercise to impress people? Or was *Dumbarton* going to join all the others at Singapore?

'Cable secure, sir.'

'Very well. Ring down finished with engines. I'll try and find out what's going on.'

Calvert looked up as a huge pattern of fireworks exploded over Kowloon. Sue might be watching them, like that first time when he had held her on the balcony, had felt her rise to match his need of her, to give herself again and again. They could get a special licence and be married here, perhaps at the cathedral. The Skipper would put in a word, and a naval wedding would be quite a change after all the grim news. But she would probably want to wait and get married in England. For their parents' sake. He smiled. *We are married now.*

The pilot boat passed down the side and a voice called, 'Welcome back, *Serpent*! Try and stay for Christmas!'

Onslow chuckled, 'That'll be the day, mate!'

Calvert heard Kipling clipping up the chart table and remembered how they had cheered and danced together like two filthy urchins when the seaplane's big engines had fallen silent again. No, they were not the sort of people you would ever forget. Nor the two girls. Prepared to risk happiness, everything that war could tear down in seconds.

He craned his neck as another burst of lights, great feathered plumes, burst across the night sky followed by crackling explosions like machine-gun fire.

Kerr clattered on to the bridge and said, 'I've posted an anchor sentry, sir. Don't want some bumboat merchant slipping alongside to pinch our life-buoys!'

'Good. Call up *Islip* for me while I change, there's a good chap, Dick. If convenient I'll go across and see her skipper before they shove off.'

Kerr kept a straight face. *Always calls me Dick when he's anxious or worried about something. He's really going over to use the shore telephone line.*

So would I if I had a girl like that.

Brooke was hesitating on the top of the bridge ladder. 'We should have a party, Number One.' He did not see Kerr's secret smile. 'I think we deserve it. I'll leave it to you.'

Calvert grinned. 'I know a girl who'd like to come, Number One!'

Kerr smiled, holding the depression at bay. At least his cousin's parents and sister would be spared the ponderous ceremonial of a naval funeral, with a firing party and all the trimmings.

His cousin Tim was still with his old ship, with his friends all around him.

He looked at the stars. Who could ask for better?

Captain Albert Granville, the chief-of-staff, lit a cigarette and regarded Brooke with thoughtful gravity.

'Nobody's certain, of course, but Japanese naval activity is on the increase. Thank God Admiral Tom

Phillips and his Force Z are at Singapore to discourage any hot-headed moves, what?'

'And *Dumbarton*, sir?'

Granville looked at him as if he had already forgotten Stallybrass and his old cruiser.

'Singapore, then eventually England. Major refit, I understand.'

They looked at one another without saying anything, each thinking of Stallybrass who would lose his appointment as commodore. He would probably end up in command of some training establishment, one of those peacetime windswept holiday camps on the east coast. A White Ensign and a lick of paint could work wonders.

Brooke waited, knowing this was not the reason for his summons to *Tamar*, the Ark.

Granville said, '*Islip* will stay with her until . . .' He seemed to become irritated. 'Look, we're not children. I'll spell it out. As your brother told us, we have to be prepared. We have a ship ready to evacuate non-essential personnel although nobody seems very keen to leave before Christmas! Your friend Charles Yeung does not wish to go at all!' He saw Brooke's surprise and added, 'The Japanese would love to get their hands on him.'

'May I ask why?'

Granville smiled, reassured that others did not know as much as he did.

'He has been the prime force for obtaining arms and military supplies for Chiang Kai-Shek's Nationalists. We could not become *involved*, officially anyway, but in my view the Japs would have broken down all resistance by now but for those supplies and would probably have left us alone.' He lit another cigarette. 'I'll be glad when Mr Yeung gets his Dutch pilot for that damned seaplane of his – perhaps he'll buzz off out of our lives, eh?'

Brooke felt for his pipe but found he had left it

aboard *Serpent*. Perhaps he had known all the time. The horrific attack on one vessel and the torpedoing of another had been swept under the carpet. Not *involved*, as Granville had just explained.

'He carries a lot of weight in the Colony, sir.'

Granville stubbed out the new cigarette with angry, quick stabs. 'I know, I know. That's all I hear!'

He relented slightly. 'And you are really going to marry his daughter? I wish you luck, when you get to England, I mean.'

A telephone rang noisily and Granville swivelled round in his chair as if to exclude his visitor.

'Of course, old chap, *naturally* we'll be there! The biggest event of the season – nothing would keep us away!' He replaced the telephone and said, 'With *Islip* at sea, your ship is pretty well the most important one here. What a joke, eh? I'll be damned glad when she returns.'

Brooke saw him glance at the clock. *Here it comes.*

'I must ask you to limit local leave for your chaps. Just until *Islip* gets back.' He waited, watching him impassively. 'Carry on as if everything's normal.'

Brooke stood up. *While you go to the biggest event of the season.*

He said quietly, 'That should be easy, sir, as I don't know what the hell is going on!'

Surprisingly, Granville smiled. 'You destroyer people – you never let up, do you?'

An hour later all *Serpent*'s officers and the whole of the Chief and petty officers' Mess were packed into the wardroom.

Brooke laid his cap on the shelf by the pantry hatch and looked at their faces.

'This ship will be stored and fuelled as if we were going to sea at two hours' notice.' He saw the Chief scribbling on his pad, Kerr frowning as he considered another list which must forget nothing.

'We shall remain at the buoy, and the local liberty boats will be used for any runs ashore.' He glanced at the gunner (T). 'You, Mr Barlow, will issue sidearms to all those present. Sentries will be doubled and a senior rate placed on each watch. All this is confidential, although it cannot stay a secret for long.' He looked at Calvert and saw him touching the fading scars where his beard had been.

'Keep your department up to date, Pilot. Check with *Tamar* that we know everything there is to know.' He looked slowly around at their intent, familiar faces.

Kingsmill, the mournful petty officer steward. He moaned a lot but ran his wardroom as if it were Claridge's. Pike the coxswain, deeply thoughtful, but his eyes very alert and bright. It would be good to know he was in the wheelhouse if things went against them. Andy Laird, the chief stoker and Pike's drinking companion, Onslow, yeoman of signals, Vicary the torpedo gunner's mate, and of course Fox the Buffer. Of the officers Kipling seemed the most unaffected; if you did not know him you might even think him indifferent. Barrington-Purvis, stern and proud, the image of his father and previous senior officers in the family, no doubt. Cusack, ready to go to his engine and boiler rooms, a new garden catalogue unopened on his lap. Calvert, thinking about his girl. *As I am.* Lastly Kerr, remembering perhaps his own fear when he had boarded the sinking fishing boat with its cargo of murder. Only Kipling's inner ruthlessness and experience of survival had saved him. Kerr might even be thinking that if anything went wrong up there on the unprotected bridge *he* would be called to command. He would know that all his training, ambition and hope might come to nothing if that happened.

Brooke said, 'You are all experienced men, a team that held together in that other war which we left behind when we came out here. Make no mistake: this war could be twice as deadly.' He patted his pocket and saw Kingsmill pull out a tobacco pouch. 'Thanks.' Some of them watched his steady fingers as he tamped the tobacco into his pipe. They had to see him as the man they could trust: if the balloon went up there would be more than enough panic to go round if past experiences were anything to go by.

'Questions?'

Barlow, the gunner (T), crossed his legs and folded his arms. It was like a quiet show of defiance.

He asked, 'Would they *dare* to attack, sir?'

'I think they might, Mr Barlow.' He removed his pipe and watched the smoke swirling into the air-duct. Like the old Man Mo temple, he thought.

He said, 'There is one thing you should know. No matter what the circumstances, or what stupid instructions come from on high, this ship, *our* ship . . .' his glance locked with Pike's and he recalled their meeting on the day he had come aboard at Scapa, ' . . . will not be shamed into surrender.'

Kerr asked, 'Shall I delay the party, sir?'

Some of them laughed, and Fox was heard to say, 'Good old Jimmy th' One! Some bloody party!'

Brooke felt the tension running out of his limbs like sand from a glass.

'*Postpone*, shall we say.'

He picked up his cap. 'Carry on, gentlemen.' He looked at Calvert. 'A moment, Pilot.'

He led him down to his own quarters and closed the curtain.

'You are going to marry Third Officer Yorke.' He smiled briefly. 'Sue.'

'We thought we could do it here, sir, but . . .'

Brooke watched the clear sky through a scuttle. He had telephoned Lian when he had gone over to *Islip*. How deserted it seemed now without the *Dumbarton* at her moorings, or the flotilla leader alongside. The Dutch cruiser *Ariadne* had left while they were at sea.

She had sensed his pain at their separation. When he had asked about her father she had said quietly, 'He tells me nothing.'

It was clear now why he wanted to get his daughters out of the Colony. Maybe that was the only reason he had given his permission for their marriage.

Brooke said, 'Captain Granville is sending her out of here in the next ship.' He saw the sudden anxiety in Calvert's eyes. Almost harshly he added, 'I agree with him for once. Shall I explain to her? It might be easier coming from me.'

Calvert smiled at him. Brooke could not remember ever seeing such warmth in his eyes.

'No, sir. I'll do it. You were right. I want her *safe*. The time will soon pass.'

Brooke said, 'Thank you for that.'

Calvert was saying, 'I never believed I'd ever find a girl like Sue.' He looked at the holstered revolver in his hand, which he had just signed for. 'Or that I'd ever get into a bloody plane again!'

Brooke said, 'Take the boat over to *Tamar* now. She'll likely be there. I can spare you tonight . . .' Their eyes met again.

Calvert said quietly, 'Will she be going tomorrow, sir?'

'I think so. We shall know by noon.' He looked away. 'Good luck.'

Later, Kerr came aft and reported that all work was going smoothly. 'I think we're glad to be doing something at last!'

Brooke pushed a sealed letter towards him. 'I want you to take this to Charles Yeung's house. I shall get a car for you. The senior officer will not . . .'

Kerr smiled broadly. 'With respect, sir, now that *Islip's* gone I think you're the senior officer here!'

Brooke touched the letter. 'I want you to explain to Miss Yeung,' he looked up from the desk, 'my *fiancée*, that I need her to come down to the base tomorrow. I have to see her and explain what she must do.'

Kerr watched him as he got up and strode to an open scuttle. Brooke did not turn but said quietly, 'Don't alarm her. I cannot leave the ship, you see.'

Kerr asked quietly, 'You *know*, don't you, sir?'

The tawny eyes settled on him. 'I hope to God I'm wrong.'

Calvert propped himself on one elbow and looked at the sky through the open window. It was surely brightening already. Then he looked down with love at the girl's face on the pillow, her eyes wide while she stared at him.

'I don't want to go, Toby. Not now that I've just found you again.'

He touched her cheek, which was wet with tears. 'It'll be a lot safer for you, and I'll be happier too, knowing that we'll meet in England. Then we'll marry in style . . .'

She held him tightly against her body: that too was hot, feverish.

'I *love* you, Toby. It's been wonderful – so beautiful!'

Calvert thought of the noise which had lasted for

most of the night. It had come mostly from the Peninsula Hotel, the big ball everyone had been going on about.

He said, 'They may change the order by tomorrow.' *Oh God. It was today.*

They had made love, but more with sadness than passion. Longing, the despair of parting, it was all and none of it. It was like a door being slammed. Oblivion.

How quiet the little apartment block seemed. When he had asked her about her neighbour the nursing sister, she had made a little grimace. 'Ruth Shelley? She's gone north for a while. Some new army hospital, I believe. She'll be back.' Then she had cried, unable to stop. *'And I shall be gone!'*

'We'll go down to *Tamar* together, Sue. Find out the latest.'

They fell asleep in each other's arms, unable to fight it any longer.

How long was it? An hour, or minutes?

Calvert felt her naked body stiffen in his arms, her voice frightened as she exclaimed, 'What is that *noise*?'

Calvert tried to clear his mind. It was probably another mob of revellers staggering home.

His limbs seemed to freeze as he recognized the distant banshee hoot of a destroyer's siren.

'God, it's *Serpent*!'

They stared at one another until she said very calmly, 'Then it's happened, Toby. We will be staying together.'

The ship's siren cut out, but the sound seemed to hang in the air like a dying scream.

Calvert dragged on his clothes and buckled the unfamiliar holster around his waist.

He watched her pale shape ducking and opening drawers while she followed his example.

'What shall we do?'

Calvert looked for his cap and said, 'We'll go down to the ferry and get over to Victoria as soon as possible.' He touched her shoulder. 'It'll be safe there. Leave it to the experts.' He examined his feelings. It was strange, but he felt no fear. He took her hand. 'Ready, Sue?'

She nodded. 'Aye, ready!'

'All present?' Brooke stepped over the coaming into the wardroom and looked around at the same assembly of officers and petty officers who had been gathered here before. Faces creased with sleep, eyes questioning, apprehensive.

Kerr said, 'Except for Pilot, sir.'

'I sent him ashore.' Brooke gave himself a few more seconds to arrange his thoughts. He had to appear patient, prepared. For some reason he thought of his brother.

He had peered at his luminous watch without knowing what had awakened him when Barrington-Purvis, who was the O.O.D., had burst into his cabin.

Looking at him now, Brooke was relieved to see he had recovered his aloof superiority.

Brooke said, 'Just before five-thirty this morning I was informed that the Japanese army had crossed the frontier on the Kowloon side and breached the first line of defence. The infantry are said to be supported by tanks and cavalry. I am assured that our troops are ready and able to hold the line on the mainland. If they cannot, this harbour could come under artillery fire in a matter of days.'

Some nodded gravely, other glanced towards their special friends, men with whom they had already seen and done too much.

Brooke continued in his unhurried tone, 'This ship

is consequently at State One readiness.' He turned to Kerr. 'How is it?'

'Slip-wire rigged to the buoy, sir. All short-range weapons closed up, duty part of the watch mustered on the fo'c'sle.'

The deck gave a slight tremble and the Chief said, 'That's *my* department at State One, sir.'

Kerr asked, 'What's the next step, sir?'

'Go around your departments, talk with the men.' He looked across at the petty officer cook's round red face. 'And you, Chef, can rustle up breakfast for everybody!'

They broke up and hurried away. Brooke watched them leave, like the spokes of a wheel, reaching throughout the ship. From him. Their captain.

A telegraphist hovered outside the wardroom until he caught his eye.

'For you, sir. Priority.'

Brooke read the neat pencilled writing of the P.O. telegraphist, Alan Brock. It must have come in even as he had left the wardroom.

He could feel Kerr watching him, sense the man's sudden uneasiness.

'Force Z and escorts have sailed from Singapore, Number One. The Japs are landing in Malaya. Attacking in strength.'

Kerr sounded dazed. '*Malaya?* I thought . . .'

'So did everyone else, apparently. Any attack was supposed to be against Singapore island. Rather like here, don't you think? With all the guns pointing the wrong way!'

How could he be standing here speaking of this disaster so lightly? His whole being was screaming out, consuming him in silence. How could he have been so right, and the *experts* so blind?

On the foreshore opposite the base there were still large groups of people milling about near the Peninsula Hotel. Some were dazed by the rumours: others, still in ball-gowns and dinner-jackets, were too far gone to understand anything. And when some thirty aircraft burst out of the clear sky a few of the overnight revellers began to wave and cheer. *The long-promised reinforcements had arrived!*

But the planes carried the Rising Sun, and as the bombs began to fall the five obsolete aircraft, Hong Kong's sole air defence, were wiped out in minutes.

The speculation was over.

17

Victims

'Is this the place?' Acting-Temporary Lieutenant Paul Kipling jammed his foot on the brake and brought the small fifteen hundredweight army truck to a sudden halt.

The Wren officer in the passenger seat stared past him at the apartment block which in such a short time had come to mean so much to her. Exactly as she remembered it, and yet so completely changed.

She nodded, unable to explain. 'It was good of you to bring me.'

Kipling said coolly, 'Toby Calvert would have killed me otherwise.' He switched off the engine and as the vehicle shuddered into silence he saw her start, the quick frightened thrust of her breasts through her shirt.

She said in a whisper, '*Gunfire!*'

He said, 'Up north somewhere.' He stared at the other houses. They looked deserted, but you could never be certain. He wished he was in his well-worn khaki outfit. You were less of a target.

He said abruptly, 'Better go in. Don't want to be too long.'

'Is it dangerous?'

Kipling shrugged. 'There'll be all the usual fifth-columnists trying to keep well in with the Japs when they get here.' He saw her anxiety. She was a child when it came to this sort of caper, he thought. 'At the most the Japs are only twenty miles away. I'll feel a lot safer when I get this truck across to Hong Kong.'

She replied, 'You haven't got much faith, have you?'

'No.'

She looked at the path to the front door and remembered how they had laughed when they were drenched in the sudden downpour, and they had gone to her small apartment and made love again and again.

It was only yesterday that they had been awakened by the *Serpent*'s siren, and they had dashed from here to the ferry. There had been all those people in evening clothes, running about and staring at the sky when the planes had screamed low over the harbour and the bombs had plummeted down on Kai Tak airport. The enormity of what had happened had stunned everyone. Not only had the Japanese bombed Hong Kong, they had done the same in Singapore, and troop landings had been made on the Malayan coast.

Then, as people had gathered their wits to prepare for a siege, the real bombshell had exploded. The new enemy had also sent its carrier fleet to attack the great American base in Pearl Harbor. Without warning the Japanese had disabled many ships, and sunk others at their moorings.

Only yesterday. She said, 'The place is empty. Evacuated.'

She handed Kipling the key and watched as he pushed open the door, noticing that he unclipped his unusual-looking holster in the same movement.

'I'll go first.' He walked into the hall and she followed close on his heels. The residents had left in a hurry. Even the army chaplain was gone.

She listened to the far-off gunfire. The army was

there. They would stop the Japanese invasion. The staff must have foreseen all this. Even her brigadier had insisted that they would never let the Colony fall to attack.

'Seems okay.'

She followed him up the stairs. There was broken glass halfway up: a window had fallen out during the bombing. The place felt deserted and there was a smell of smoke, perhaps from an air attack.

Kipling waited for her to open the apartment door with her key, and saw her hand go to her throat as she walked through to the bedroom, the sheets still on the floor after they had tried to get dressed.

She looked at the open windows, the flapping blind above the veranda rail. *Oh God, Toby, I love you so.*

Sue glanced at the untidy lieutenant and did not know if she had spoken aloud.

'I'll get my things. There's not much.' She looked at him again, the way he stared at her. Not hostile, perhaps not even curious. 'Will there be an air raid, do you think?'

He took out some cigarettes marked *Duty Free – HM Ships Only.* 'Christ, I hope not!' He grinned. 'Sorry. No manners, they tell me!'

'*They* are right!'

His grin broadened. 'That's the ticket. Chin up, eh?' He became serious again. 'If there is a raid, we get downstairs and round the back against those other buildings. This chicken-coop would collapse like a pack of cards if a bomb dropped too near!'

She dragged out some shirts and her uniform jacket with its solitary blue stripe. She was angry with him, but it helped her not to cry.

'I was happy here, can you understand that?'

Kipling looked at her legs as she bent over a chest of

drawers. *I'll bet*, he thought. But he was glad it had been Toby Calvert. It was not difficult to picture them here, in this bed.

He said casually, 'I suppose so.'

She gestured to the other room. 'There's some Scotch in there.'

'Hell, why didn't you say so first?'

She jammed her few pieces of clothing into a blue grip and stared around the empty room. The picture of the shire horses was crooked, and she straightened it.

Just a room, Lieutenant Kipling might think. Sex and nothing more.

She touched the bed. 'I love you, darling!' This time she did say it aloud.

When she turned she saw Kipling watching her, a full glass in each hand.

'Here. Do you good.'

She thought of saying something clever and refusing the offer. But she took a glass and swallowed some of the contents as he said, 'Don't worry. They'll get you out. I heard mention of a ship. Certain people, you know?' He drank slowly. 'Bloody good stuff. Not had anything like that since . . .' He tensed as a car backfired and said, 'Getting past it!'

'What about *Serpent*?'

He shrugged, as if it did not concern him. 'The Skipper'll fix something, I expect. A good bloke.' He half smiled. 'For a regular.'

The whisky burned her throat, but it was working.

He held up the bottle and shook it. 'We'll finish this an' shove off, right?' As he refilled the glasses he added, 'I hope it all works out, Sue. Toby and the Skipper are the two best blokes I've met after . . .'

'After you lost your friend?'

He studied her. 'He told you, did he, the old bugger!'

292

'He likes you too.' She wiped her eyes with her fingers. 'So do I, in spite . . .'

'I know.' He picked up her grip and downed the rest of the whisky. 'Let's go.' He watched her swallow the last of it, her eyes smarting. But not from the drink, he guessed.

She said, 'I thought there'd be soldiers everywhere. Putting up defences like the navy're doing in the dockyard.'

'The good old stable-door mentality!' Probably all in the Peninsula getting pissed, he thought.

She put on her hat and stared back at the open bedroom. Then she turned and followed him outside on to the landing.

Kipling was saying, 'There are some boats waiting at a pier to offload my stuff from the truck . . .' He whirled round, his hand on his holster. '*Christ!*'

They both stared at the landing telephone, the bell of which seemed deafening.

Kipling relaxed, fibre by fibre. 'Leave it. We're going.'

She was still staring at the telephone. 'It might be for me.'

'Make it snappy, then.'

She picked it up, the sudden silence even louder. 'Hello?'

Sue recognized the voice immediately. 'Where are you, Ruth?' She covered the mouthpiece and whispered, 'It's the army sister from next door!' She saw him frown impatiently.

She turned her back. 'What's happening?'

Ruth Shelley's voice was clear enough, as if she were standing in the room. Like that day she had been sunbathing. But it was different. Flat. Unemotional.

She said, 'They're here. At the dressing station. I just

293

wanted to speak with somebody.' There was a catch in her voice. 'And you answered, dear Sue.'

She felt Kipling was right beside her although she had not heard or seen him move.

Sue held the telephone between them and watched his face as the voice continued, 'They have no idea.'

'What, Ruth? *Tell me!*'

'We had a lot of wounded brought in. The Japanese burst into the place. They bayoneted all the men in the beds, and there was shooting outside.'

There was silence and it was as if the line had been cut. Then she tried again. 'They took my nurses. All of them, and raped them again and again. An orderly tried to help but they . . . they cut off his head.'

Sue felt Kipling's arm around her shoulders as she asked, 'Can you get away?'

'They locked me in here. Didn't know about the telephone.'

There were bangs and shouts, muffled screams too, like something out of hell.

Ruth Shelley said in a whisper, 'They're coming for me now . . .'

The noise exploded on the telephone, sounds, blows and wild, inhuman shouting.

Then Ruth Shelley began to scream, piercing and terrible even as she was dragged away from the phone.

Kipling took it carefully and replaced it on its hook. Then he held the girl's arm, his fingers surprisingly gentle.

'You okay?'

She stared at him, her face like chalk. 'She never married. Never really liked men, you see?'

They both looked at the silent telephone. The stairway still seemed to echo to those terrified screams.

They emerged into smoky sunlight and found two armed soldiers standing beside the truck.

'This yours?'

Kipling eyed him calmly. '*Sir.*'

'There's an air-raid warning, er ... sir.' The word seemed to stick in his throat. 'So all vehicles off the streets, right?'

Kipling could hear the distant drone of aircraft. He guessed they would not come here. After what he had just heard and witnessed, he knew the main target would continue to be the island, the so-called fortress.

He said, 'In that truck is enough high-explosive to knock down seven streets. Are you going to stand here guarding it in the middle of a raid?'

The soldiers looked at one another. 'Well, I suppose ...'

Kipling held out his hand to help the girl into her seat.

He said shortly, 'Just be a sec.' He walked out of earshot and faced the soldiers again. 'I see that both of you are carrying slung rifles. Safety catches on and nothing up the spout, *right*?'

One of them exclaimed, 'Orders!' The other one asked angrily, 'What's it to you anyway?'

They both gaped at the heavy Luger which had appeared in Kipling's fist.

Kipling said, 'Both of you would be dead if I was an impostor. You will be anyway, if you try to stop us again!'

They were still staring after the truck as it rounded the corner, spewing out dust and smoke.

She asked hoarsely, 'Is that really what's in the back?'

He grinned. 'Sure is. Not dangerous though.' He glanced at her grimly. 'Like women. If you treat 'em all right!'

At the pier where some naval boats were already gathered, Kipling leaned against the steering wheel and stared over at the *Serpent*'s pale shape framed against the dockyard. Almost to himself he said, 'Laughed at us when we came here. Another relic, they said. Threatened the Skipper, if he didn't toe the line. Well, it's bloody different now, isn't it?' The bitterness and anger was flooding out of him and he didn't try to stop it. 'The bloke you love, and I must say I've never envied a man so much before, is trying to fix up a bloody seaplane because *they* say it must be done. I'm getting ready to blow up a few things simply because it's all *they* can think of!'

He glanced over at the deserted streets, which were usually full of jostling people.

'My guess is that the Japs will be where we're standing in a couple of days, probably sooner.' He gripped her wrist. 'Go to that P.O. on the pier. He'll take you over to the yard. Keep your head down, eh?'

She stood beside the dusty fifteen-hundredweight, her bag in one hand.

He eyed her steadily, picturing the room, hearing the screams.

'Remember what they say in this regiment?'

He saw her chin lift. Defiance, guts, pride. It was all there. She even managed a smile. 'I know, Paul. You shouldn't have joined if you can't take a joke!'

Esmond Brooke entered the makeshift office in the dockyard and found Captain Albert Granville seated at a littered desk, hemmed in by both regular and field telephones in their webbing cases. The yard itself was a hive of activity, and with all but the smallest ships moved or gone from the harbour there were plenty of sailors to dig defences and build up barriers of sandbags.

Tamar had been moved out to a spare mooring and Granville, with most of his staff, had transferred here to limited accommodation in offices and work-rooms.

Granville looked terrible. With so many others he had been invited to the great ball on the night before the attack. He was still wearing his white mess-jacket and the decorations he had brought out of temporary retirement for the occasion. There were stains on the sleeves, and his normally perfectly groomed hair was all over the place.

He pointed at a chair with a pencil, at the same time talking on a telephone.

But the chair was full of files, and in any case Brooke did not feel like sitting down.

He thought about Barrington-Purvis bursting into his cabin to break the news of the attack, the banshee siren and the roar of bombs from the little airport.

Then the news of Pearl Harbor.

He had heard the Buffer say, 'Well, that's brought the Yanks off the bloody fence for a change, eh, Swain?'

And Pike's savage retort, 'But too soddin' late for *us*, isn't it?'

Granville dropped the telephone. 'No sooner you're off the line and everything changes!'

He got up and walked to a big map of Hong Kong and the New Territories which his staff had already managed to mark with coloured pins and little sticky labels.

The chief-of-staff snapped, 'The Japs are coming right through! If they meet any stiff resistance from the army they simply bypass it and mop up later at their leisure!'

Brooke recalled the few moments when he had held

Lian in his arms while he had explained what was happening, and what might happen in the near future.

'What about the evacuation, sir?'

Granville stared at him. '*Boomerang* was a mistake, a failure.' He waved his hand over sections of the map. 'We've got the Winnipeg Grenadiers, and the Royal Rifles of Canada. They came directly from either their own country or Bermuda, untrained for this sort of thing. They don't even know this territory locally. Won't stand a chance. There's the Middlesex and the Royal Scots, but too thin on the ground for a prolonged siege. The Rajputs are up here . . .' He let his hand fall from the map. 'You know what *they're* like.'

Brooke did not know. It was suddenly crystal clear. The whole line was crumbling even as they discussed it.

Granville shuffled through his papers and swore with disgust when he discovered that his cigarette case was empty. Then he seemed to hear Brooke's question.

'We'll do all we can, of course. It's all happening so fast. *Islip* will be coming back.' He found a solitary cigarette and lit it gratefully. 'Eventually.'

Something in his tone warned Brooke, and he found he was almost unmoved when Granville elaborated. 'They ran into trouble. *Dumbarton* was sunk. *Islip* only just made it.'

Brooke heard more bombs falling somewhere, the raiders fired at by a mere handful of badly sited guns.

He pictured Stallybrass and this same captain when he had arrived here. Their secret amusement, contempt, perhaps, for his concern about the plans for defence.

'I see that you've moved *Tamar* to a buoy?' It was more for the sake of something to say than any other reason.

'Er, yes. She'll have to be scuttled if things get worse. All confidential books must be destroyed.'

A seaman messenger looked in. 'Lieutenant Kipling brought the Wren out, sir.'

'Good, that's fine.' The seaman glanced at Brooke and shrugged. He had realized that Granville had not understood a word.

Granville said vaguely, 'I understand that General Maltby, the military commander, would prefer to withdraw completely to the island. It won't do us any good here, though.'

Brooke looked down at his own hands but they were quite relaxed, even though he wanted to shout at him that when that happened the Japanese artillery would be over there in Kowloon, about eight hundred yards from this room.

Granville glared at another telephone as it jangled noisily. 'But still, when Force Z gets amongst the buggers that'll make the enemy landing-craft and their supply ships run like rabbits!' He did not sound very convinced. He snatched up the telephone. '*Yes?*'

Kipling entered the room and waited for Brooke to see him.

'Got all the gear, sir, no bother.' He glanced over at Granville without expression. 'Sue Yorke, our Wren . . .'

Brooke waited. She had indeed become *our Wren*. Like a mascot.

'She got a call from the new dressing station while I was with her. The Japs bayoneted all the wounded and raped the nurses. It was like a slaughter-house from the sound of it.'

'How did Sue take it?'

He grinned. 'Bloody marvellous, sir!'

Brooke said sharply, 'I want her out of this mess.' In his mind he could see Lian's face, desperate, pleading.

'I won't go and leave you here, Es-mond! Something terrible will happen!'

It was happening right now.

He asked, 'Does the army want the truck back just yet?'

Kipling smiled. 'They're like our lot, sir. You just sign for it and it's all yours. I'm bringing it across on a ferry today.' His eyes hardened. 'Might come in handy, I thought.'

'Good thinking.' He touched his arm. 'And thanks, Paul.'

Kipling walked out of the room. It unnerved him when people were nice to him.

He saw Barrington-Purvis mustering a working-party on the pier.

He would soon change all that!

Granville had put down the telephone. 'Any cigarettes, old chap?' He looked worn out.

'Smoke a pipe, sir.'

'So you do.' He rang his bell. 'Just had a signal about *Islip*. Her damage was worse than reported. Had quite a few casualties, but we can replace them from here when she arrives.' He was looking at his map again. 'Those pins will have to be moved. They've come another six miles.'

Brooke asked quietly, 'What about *my* ship, sir?'

The captain shook his empty cigarette case and passed it to a messenger.

'And bring me some drinks, Campbell. You know what I like.'

He looked at Brooke gravely.

'Whatever happens, *Serpent* will be the last to leave. Or will be destroyed to prevent her falling to the enemy.'

Brooke picked up his cap. 'She'll not fall to the enemy. Be certain of it!'

Granville watched him stride out. He said wearily, 'I'm relying on it!'

*

300

John Chau, *Serpent*'s interpreter, paused for breath on the steep, winding road and removed his glasses, which had misted up in the heat. Then he looked around at the rough, craggy hillside. It was almost bare of trees. For once the sea was out of sight and the sounds of battle so muffled and faraway that they seemed unreal.

He had expected to be stopped by the ferry dock when he had crossed over to Kowloon, but nobody had seemed interested. In another hour he would be safe in the village where he had been born, the son of a hard-working carpenter who had been determined that he should have a life with prospects. One in which he would earn the respect of his employers and customers. John Chau had been packed off to college. He was industrious, and would not bring shame on his father's house. His eventual position at one of Hong Kong's most influential banks had been his reward.

He had learned well the complex but rewarding lessons of banking as well as the social side, when he mixed with visiting European bankers. He had even been recommended for service in the Volunteer Reserve.

His mind was sharp and clear when he decided to leave the naval base. He had done it without shame or remorse; it was the sensible thing to do until the fighting was over.

In the village there would be those who would conceal his presence until life returned, if not to normal, then to something in which banking would still be the dominant force. His widowed mother would do the rest.

All the same, he had been loath to rid himself of his smart white uniform and put on these dull working clothes.

As he shaded his face from the sun Chau thought of his short employment aboard the *Serpent* where he had been accepted as an equal.

He wondered what would become of the navigating officer, the one named Calvert who had won the Victoria Cross but never spoke about it.

That, too, had been so easy. He had shared Calvert's cabin. It had taken no time at all to read through the lieutenant's log book, the patrol areas, how long they would be away and how far they extended.

When the SS *Kiang Chen* had been torpedoed by a Japanese submarine he had spoken with her master, the only survivor. Just before he died he had managed to whisper to him that the arms cargo had been delivered to the Nationalists as arranged, like all the other secret shipments.

Only *Serpent*'s unexpected arrival on the scene had prevented the coaster's crew from being seized, the truth tortured out of them, so that no more cargoes would be possible.

Charles Yeung, who lived like a mandarin on the Peak with his lovely daughter, would be quick to reward him for his silence. With all the other money he had managed to put aside he would be ready for the next step up the ladder, no matter whose flag flew over Government House.

He started off along the rough road again, barely out of breath in spite of the miles he had walked. He had always been careful to study sport and take exercise. He had even played tennis with some of the naval officers at *Tamar*.

Even if he was stopped now he carried nothing which might incriminate him. The bank had given him leave because of the bombing. The navy no longer needed his services. Even that made him smile. They would probably not even miss him.

At the top of the ridge he would see the old monastery. He had been frightened by it as a small child. A brooding, secret place. The village lay just beyond it, and he would see the great reaches of Deep Bay on the territory's western coastline, where his father had once helped to build fishing boats when he could get no other work.

He faltered, his nostrils dilating to the smell of burning. A dying column of smoke was being brushed away by the hot hilltop breeze and sudden caution made him crouch beside the low wall of one of the new monsoon drains. It would prevent the road from flooding, or worse, being washed away, for there was no other here.

Then he saw it: an army car on its side, the interior still smouldering, a blackened corpse pinned beneath the roof when it had turned over.

There were a lot of deep scars on the road. Heavy bullets. John Chau considered more calmly. It must have been raked by some Japanese aircraft. The pilots did not have very far to fly.

He spun round as something moved in the thick scrub by the sloping hillside.

A soldier. He felt his heart pumping painfully as the khaki-clad figure dragged itself on to the road.

Very young. An officer with a single pip on his shoulder, his teeth bared as he stared up at him. He had one of those ridiculous little moustaches which some British officers affected. It only made them look younger.

Mesmerized, Chau watched as he raised one hand towards him. It was obvious that the soldier was badly injured, perhaps dying. There was really nothing anyone could do.

The young lietenant managed to croak, 'Help me! *Don't leave me!*'

He had been lying here for hours. Chau began to step forward but shook himself angrily.

It is too late for him. There is nothing I could do.

He said, 'No, I cannot . . .'

The officer's face ground against the stones and his cap fell in the dust. He was very fair. A boy.

'My driver is badly hurt . . .' He was pleading. Afraid of being left, of being alone.

Chau forced himself to glance at the charred thing under the car.

'Too late for him!' He felt a wild urgency to break away. 'I go now!'

'*Oh God!*' The soldier was trying to pull himself back under cover but the agony held him like a steel trap.

Chau broke into a run. *It was the only way.*

Then he stopped dead, unable to move.

There were five Japanese soldiers in the road, watching him in total silence.

One, an officer of some sort, moved his hand curtly as a man might brush away a fly.

Then he pointed at the burned car, his voice low and incisive. Chau tried to smile, then bowed to the officer to show his respect.

A Japanese soldier slung his rifle and fixed bayonet over his shoulder and touched Chau on the shoulder, turning him around towards the monsoon drain.

He stood quite still as the soldier ran his hands over his body and pockets, dropping his wallet and some cigarettes on to the road. The dying officer was being dragged over to the low wall, crying out at every move.

When he was propped against the wall two of the soldiers searched him also. His papers, wrist-watch, and some letters, then lastly they removed his revolver.

The Japanese officer, his unfamiliar helmet festooned with twigs and leaves in a netting cover, walked to the wall. Then he stooped down and spoke to the second lieutenant in hesitant English.

Chau could not hear what he said, but saw his annoyance. Maybe the injured man was too badly hurt to understand what was happening.

Then he snapped an order and Chau felt his stomach contract as the one with the slung rifle went across and lowered the bayonet until it rested above the soldier's webbing belt.

Then he drove the bayonet into him, holding his body erect against the wall with his foot while he dragged out the blade and thrust it into him again.

They all watched as the corpse rolled on to its side, the eyes still bulging with terror.

The Japanese officer said, *'You! Where are you going?'*

Chau swallowed hard, then cried out as a rifle butt smashed into his ribs. There was another agonising blow on the opposite side and he knew his ribs had been fractured. He was bleeding, unable to stand or even speak. His wrists were pinioned behind his back and someone was hitting him about the head and back. He had to speak. To explain, but nothing would come. His mouth seemed to be filled with fluid, scalding him, and he heard his voice cry out as they dragged him on to the monsoon drain wall so that his glasses fell off, and he was peering dazedly into some trapped water in the bottom of the ditch. It was bright blue, as if part of the sky was down there.

He gasped when another blow smashed into his spine, and he felt something dangled against his face. Even through the pain and the fear he realized it was his identity disc. He had forgotten to throw it away.

He was losing consciousness slowly, too slowly. He

stared at the sky's clean reflection. They would kill him. A bayonet like the man who had cried for help.

He tried to keep his eyes from closing; he could taste blood on his lips. He was going.

Another reflection had appeared in the blue water. But all time was gone. There was just one blink of sunlight as the heavy blade came down.

Two soldiers raised his ankles and tipped the headless corpse into the drain.

Then the file of soldiers was gone, and the deserted road left only to the dead.

Brooke stood on the upper bridge and watched several great columns of smoke twisting slowly across the copper sunset. *Serpent* was alongside, taking on more fuel and ammunition and any sort of food supplies which could be stowed away.

There had been several quick air-raids on the island during the day. There had been thousands of leaflets too, calling for an immediate surrender. *STOP USELESS RESISTANCE. Remember, the Japanese forces will guarantee the lives and livings of those who will surrender.*

Kerr came up to the bridge. 'Nearly finished, sir.'

'Very well. We shall move out to the buoy when the last gear is brought aboard.' He looked at the first lieutenant, his features very clear in the copper light. 'Something else?'

'Our interpreter, John Chau. I think he's done a runner.'

'I see. Well, I don't think we'll be needing him anyway.'

Kerr could sense the disappointment nevertheless. Probably blaming himself as usual.

'How do you think Toby Calvert is getting on, sir?'

'I've told him that he's to report back as soon as Charles Yeung's damned pilot gets here.'

What was Lian doing now? She was in a small hotel near the base with Captain Granville's haughty wife and several other women. It did not bear thinking about.

'Officer coming aboard, sir!'

It was the senior operations officer, Commander Ian Gould. He was just about running the dockyard single-handed while the sailors were strengthening the defences and digging shelters.

Brooke glanced across at Kowloon. It was eerie not to see the thousands of glittering lights. When it was really quiet you could sometimes hear the music from all the bars and dives around the docks there. Now it was like a grave, and there was no gunfire at the moment either.

He greeted the operations officer at the bridge gate.

'Sorry about not meeting you at the brow, sir.' He looked over the glass screen, and down to the crouching outlines of the high-angled anti-aircraft guns. 'I need to be here until we're out at the buoy again.'

Commander Gould was a plump and usually jolly man, and had always been helpful after *Serpent*'s arrival.

He said shortly, 'Bad news, Esmond. *Bloody* bad news, I'm afraid. Just heard from Singapore. Admiral Phillips sailed with his Force Z to support the army. He had no air cover – it seems that an airfield was evacuated by accident or something. It was a brave gesture, I suppose . . .'

Brooke asked, 'Did they engage the enemy, sir?'

Gould barely heard. 'Just dive-bombers, no heavy units at all. *Prince of Wales* and *Repulse* were both sunk.' It was as if he still dare not believe it. 'Within the space of an hour! Both gone, all those men, those fine ships!'

Brooke pulled out his pipe. 'D'you mind this, sir?'

So that was it. He filled his pipe, while the others watched him and waited to read their own fate.

In the space of an hour, Gould had said. It went far deeper than that. In the space of *two days*, at Pearl Harbor and off the coast of Malaya, the whole balance of naval power had been turned upside down.

Force Z was gone. There would be no support for Singapore or for them in Hong Kong.

The pipe smoke floated up past the gunnery control position, a tiny moment of peace. Like a flower surviving in Flanders in his father's war.

Brooke asked quietly, 'What does Captain Granville say?'

'He is consulting with the Governor. The Japanese have demanded that we surrender. The B.B.C. has already broadcast that we will do no such thing. *Fight them on the beaches* all over again.'

Brooke looked at the dying light on the water. 'No white cliffs of Dover this time, sir.'

Gould seemed to shake himself. 'Tell your people, Esmond. We shall begin evacuation of Kowloon tomorrow night. After that . . .' He did not finish it.

'After that, this dockyard will be under fire. What then, sir?'

'All in hand, old chap.' Gould turned towards the dark landmass. 'I retired out here. They recalled me when the balloon went up.' Only Brooke could see the tears in his eyes in the strange, hot glow. 'Love the old place. Can't believe it's happening.'

They watched him leave, then Kerr said harshly, 'Well, he'd better start believing it and bloody soon!'

Brooke reached for the handset which would connect

him to all of his men throughout the ship. Working the loading tackles, stripping the guns again in case they were attacked at first light. In the crowded, stuffy messdecks with their naked pin-ups and letters home. In the boiler and engine rooms and the W/T office. *His men*. Kerr's sudden outburst had spoken for all of them. When their time came they must not be snared by all the folly and incompetence which had allowed this disaster to happen. Men had died for much less, but they had given so much already.

He snapped down the button. 'This is the captain speaking . . .'

It was all he could do.

18

Sunset

Esmond Brooke walked slowly along the *Serpent*'s darkened irondeck, seeing the three funnels and upperworks lit up by the bright flashes of gunfire from across the harbour.

Beneath his shoes he could feel the nervous tremble of machinery, as if the ship could sense the danger like an animal catching the scent of blood.

There was little noise from the harbour itself although Brooke knew there were hundreds of small craft going back and forth, picking their way through the cemetery of wrecks, any one of which could tear out a boat's keel and spew its human cargo into the fast-moving water.

But his seamen could still joke about it, even in the face of disaster.

You couldn't drown in this harbour, you'd die of poisoning first! he had heard one wag say.

The evacuation of the last mainland troops was under way. Separated from their units, some without supervision or proper leadership, they had flooded down to the Kowloon docks in fear and in desperation.

Brooke had heard how some of the soldiers had lurched from bar to bar, beyond caring for discipline or purpose. Dunkirk had been an orderly disaster. This was a rout.

'We goin' to be all right, sir?'

Brooke paused and looked at some men by the motor-boat's davits. They would not need the skimming-dish now – *Serpent* was linked to the buoy, the land, only by her slip-wire. *Raring to go*, as the Chief had said.

'We'll do our best, lads.' He had explained it to them as well as he could. Why they must leave the harbour and head around to the south-west, to the other dock-yard at Aberdeen. In all this confusion it was hard to know if it sank in.

The finality of it had been marked by the old wooden depot-ship H.M.S. *Tamar*. Lying at her buoy, she had been stripped of her equipment and confidential files and prepared for scuttling. The Ark, so familiar to servicemen and civilians alike. It would seem like part of a betrayal.

Before dusk he had been to see Captain Granville again, this time in a damp, airless cellar that stank of the harbour just yards beyond the walls. Occasionally the building had quaked to bombs in the city, and dust and plaster had filtered over Granville's maps and signals.

He had told Brooke that the destroyer *Islip* would be arriving at Aberdeen in a day or so. She was using her radar to make a more secretive approach and avoid enemy patrols. All those who were to be evacuated would be put aboard her. Eventually they would leave in the dark, again using the incredible eyes of *Islip*'s radar.

Lian was already at Aberdeen with several officers' wives. Brooke would make certain she left with the others. It was her only chance.

311

When he had seen her at the hotel her determination to be brave in front of the other women had moved him deeply. Now, as he climbed to the bridge, he paused to touch the little gold dragon medallion which she had put around his neck. *'It is mine, my dearest love. I will take it off you when we are together again. It will keep you safe.'*

He glanced into the darkened wheelhouse where Pike and his telegraphsmen and a boatswain's mate were standing together, waiting for the order to move.

'All right, Swain?'

Pike nodded his massive head. 'Good as gold, sir.'

His eyes flashed in a burst of firing from across the water. The boats were still going back and forth, feeling their way. Exhausted soldiers, and many wounded – what would become of them?

Pike looked at him. 'Don't worry, sir.' He touched the motionless wheel. 'She won't let us down!'

Up and on to the open bridge. After the cellar and between decks, it felt surprisingly clean and cool.

Kerr was careful to stay in the forepart of the bridge, away from Kipling and Barrington-Purvis. The latter was in white shirt and shorts whilst Kipling had changed into his shabby khaki. A mixed pair. Brooke had hated having to ask them. But there was nobody else.

'I can't order you two to stay behind.' He looked at their faces as they lit up in the distant gunfire. 'You will rejoin the ship at Aberdeen when you have finished here, right?'

Kipling said, 'Won't take long, sir. I knew those bastards would be here sooner than we were told.'

There was no need to contradic. him. They had been assured that the army would be able to hold a line of sorts for a week, maybe two. The Japanese would be

312

over there tomorrow, three days after invading the New Territories. It was incredible.

Barrington-Purvis said, 'I'm to take charge of the base party who will assist us, sir?' Like a new pupil repeating a lesson. Very calm, perhaps dangerously so, but equally determined.

Kipling must have been smiling under the sudden curtain of darkness.

'Tell you one thing, sir, old *Tamar* won't sink. The demolition boys haven't taken those extra deck-houses into account. They'll keep her afloat like buoyancy bags!' He held up his luminous watch. 'Never mind. I've got a bit of gear that'll do the trick.'

Surprisingly, he held out his hand. 'In case we don't make it, sir. Been nice knowing you.'

Barrington-Purvis said quietly, 'I'm *glad* I stayed in the ship, sir.'

Voices murmured after them as they went to the side where a pilot boat was waiting to carry them ashore. Another pilot was floating nearby, ready to lead them out.

Calvert remarked, 'In some funny way they're good for each other.'

Brooke glanced at him. Calvert would be doing just the opposite. He would be leaving the ship at Aberdeen. If possible he was to make certain that the seaplane was ready to fly as soon as the pilot arrived, and take Charles Yeung out of it. Or so Captain Granville had said.

Brooke had asked angrily, 'Have you told Lieutenant Calvert?'

'That is your job!'

It had been then, and only then, that Brooke had realized that the urbane captain was losing his nerve, and he wondered if Commander Gould realized it too.

Now, as he climbed on to the gratings beside his tall

313

chair, it felt like every other time. It had to be. Gladstone Dock in Liverpool, St John's in Newfoundland, or Malta in the middle of an air attack.

'Ring down stand-by.'

Kerr joined him. 'Good luck, sir.' He had his big torch in one hand so that he could watch the slip-wire once it was fixed to whip back through the buoy-ring.

'Skill will come in handy too!'

Always the joke. Smile, damn you! But it was never a game. If you thought it was, you were dead.

Calvert was bending over his chart, hidden by the table's hood. Thinking of his girl. Worried about her safety, *as I am for Lian's*.

He heard the telegraph jangle faintly below his feet, and imagined the lounging figures he had seen and spoken with at their stations, probably glad to be doing something.

If they did not leave, *Serpent* would become a sitting target.

Kerr had reached the forecastle and was standing in the eyes of the ship and although he could not see him, he knew that Bill Doggett, the leading hand, and the rest of his party were ready to run aft with the wire as it snaked dangerously inboard.

'Standing by, sir.' That was Podger Barlow the gunner (T), doing his bit on the bridge now that two officers were missing.

'Pilot boat's on port bow, sir!' Onslow, the yeoman of signals, a man who had accepted his loss. For the moment.

Lian would know they were leaving. She always did. Thank God she was getting out of it. Their beautiful house would not avoid bombardment much longer. Her sister was still in her hospital as she had firmly declared she would be. Brooke didn't know about her husband

314

Harry. With America in the war, like it or not, he might have wanted to be back in his own country rather than in *a British colony*, as he had called it.

'Midnight, sir.'

'Very well.' He touched the medallion beneath his shirt. Part of her. *Midnight*. Thirteen days to Christmas. It was better not to think about it.

He stared at the shaded blue light on the pilot boat's stern. 'Slow ahead together!' He pictured the Chief with his throttles. They had discussed this many times. Each trusting the other.

He shouted, '*Slip!*'

He heard Kerr repeat the order and the metallic click of a slip being released. Then men running, the wire rattling over the deck and past A-gun.

'*All clear forrard, sir!*'

'Wheelhouse!' Brooke leaned over the voicepipe's bell mouth.

'Cox'n, sir.'

'Can you see the pilot's light?'

'Yes sir. I've got younger eyes than mine keeping a look out, too!'

They were moving, the dark water hissing down either flank, while the knife-like stem remained lined up on the blue light.

Occasionally wreckage jagged into the side. It would move up and down with the current for weeks. Bitter reminders.

Brooke thought of the shabby dignity of the Man Mo temple. How she had found him there, knowing it was where he would be.

He heard Kerr come to the bridge, his brief exchange with Calvert.

Hong Kong. *Magical city*, as she had called it. Would they ever come back? Together?

315

Calvert said, 'No course to steer until we drop the pilot boat, sir.'

'Thank you, Pilot.' But he was staring at the island, in total darkness but for some flickering fires which still had not been extinguished from the last raid. After tomorrow it would be pointless to sound air-raid warnings any more. The Japs would be using Kai Tak, which was only three and a half miles from the dockyard.

When he looked again, the little naval base had been swallowed up.

He wondered if Kipling and Barrington-Purvis were still there. Watching them leave. In the same breath, he knew that they were.

Sub-Lieutenant Nigel Barrington-Purvis watched wearily while his companion busied himself with a knife and some fresh bread. Kipling's hands were none too clean but the sight of the bread and the thick slices of corned beef with enough butter for a whole loaf made him realize how hungry he was.

It was five days since they had stood together and yet apart, each with his own thoughts, and watched the destroyer's pale shape working clear of the buoy, hearing the sudden turbulence of her screws, those so familiar sounds of fans and telegraphs until, it had seemed in seconds, she had gone.

Since then, they had been working to a plan given them by Commander Gould.

Even Barrington-Purvis had been impressed by the nimble way in which Kipling, with the aid of some seamen from the base, had wired up certain machinery, pumps and stores, heedless of the occasional random shots from Kowloon.

The first full day the dockyard had come under heavy

shelling, with some air attacks for good measure, the noise had been devastating but casualties were surprisingly minor.

Another Japanese delegation had crossed the harbour in a boat flying a large white flag. They had come from their commander, Lieutenant-General Takashi Sakai, with his demand for surrender. It was refused, and the bombardment started up again.

Barrington-Purvis had almost expected Kipling to detonate some massive explosion right under the Jap delegation. He had never seen him or anyone else so coldly angry.

'Look at the bastards, will you? All so proper and correct, so sure that we'll not fire on a white flag while *they* go round killing and raping innocent people! I'd give 'em bloody *flag of truce*!'

It was not even safe to move about in the open. The enemy took shots across the eight hundred yards of water on the off chance that they might hit somebody. But the real danger was right here on the island, from snipers in abandoned buildings. Kipling had pitched a grenade through a shattered window and after the sharp explosion they had heard a few short-lived screams.

Kipling looked up, as if he guessed what he was thinking.

'Cop hold of this. Something *like* a sandwich!'

Barrington-Purvis took a careful bite. He had never tasted better. Even the mustard was perfect. He could not begin to guess where Kipling managed to obtain his various finds. There was beer too. Kipling had found two mugs, explaining, 'I've been cooling the beer in the harbour, so you can't be too careful!'

They finished their food and Barrington-Purvis searched for a cigarette.

Kipling opened a tin. 'Home-rolled, old son. But good Ticklers tobacco!'

They smoked slowly, only half listening to the distant explosions.

'Er – what do you think *Serpent*'s doing, Paul?'

Kiping picked a crumb off his chin. 'Getting ready to leave, I expect. As soon as *Islip*'s ready to make a dash for it.' He grimaced. 'I know I bloody well would!'

Barrington-Purvis looked away. A prisoner of war. It could always happen. But not to this ruthless enemy.

Kipling watched him. 'The island's been told to hold out, right? *Ordered* to do so. Now, you're the traditional naval officer. What do you think?'

Barrington-Purvis glanced at him, searching for sarcasm or amusement. There was neither.

He got to his feet but sat down again as Kipling dragged at his sleeve and said, 'Stay here, old son. You're too young to die just yet!'

Barrington-Purvis dropped his eyes. 'I want to go, Paul. The ship is different.' He looked quickly, afraid he had made a mistake by blurting it out.

Kipling nodded, satisfied. 'Good enough for me.' He was suddenly serious. 'I think they'll be coming at us very soon.' He glanced at the White Ensign above one of the buildings. It was riddled with holes, but strangely brave and defiant. 'They've made three demands for surrender. Not like the Japs, that isn't. I think they weren't quite ready.' He ground out the cigarette with his shoe. 'Now they are.'

'I see.'

Kipling said quietly, 'We've done all we can here. Bloody waste of time anyway.' He blinked as a shell whined over the dockyard and exploded in the nearby houses. 'I've got something to show you.' Like old men they stumbled, half-crouched, to one of the cellars, and

Kipling produced a key for the padlock. Then he opened the door to allow the smoky sunlight to penetrate the interior.

Barrington-Purvis exclaimed, 'A motor-cycle!'

Kipling smiled. He would call it that. He said, 'A Royal Enfield, army job by the look of it. Good bikes. I rode one down the Kingston by-pass not too long ago. Went like a bomb.'

Barrington-Purvis stared at him. 'Where did you get it?'

'Never mind that. You tell me, Nigel, how far is it to this Aberdeen place?'

He frowned and looked somehow vulnerable, lost without the order and purpose of the life he knew.

'About three miles, I think. A bit longer on the coast road.'

'That's the one we'll take, old son.'

'But what about our orders?'

'We've done what we were told to do. Our gallant Captain Granville is in Aberdeen right now.' He winked. 'Can't imagine why. And dear old Commander Gould has enough on his plate. He couldn't care less about us.' He added impatiently, 'Are you game?'

Barrington-Purvis bit his lip. 'Look, I'm sorry about the way I behaved . . .'

Kipling smiled. 'Not much of an angel myself, was I?'

He saw the sub-lieutenant's sudden determination as he said, 'Let's do it then!'

'I'll just look at the petrol situation. I "borrowed" a can this morning. Hope it's all right. But as my old granny used to say, you can't always tell the marmalade by the label on the jar!'

He added in a harder tone, 'I think it will be tonight. If we don't make it for any reason, don't let the bastards take you – alive, that is. Okay?'

He picked up a satchel of grenades, the shabby professional again.

'All primed, four-second fuses. Just in case we meet anyone argumentative.'

'When shall we go?' He had never believed it possible to accept Kipling's word about anything before.

'The main gate's open, what's left of it. I'll have a sniff at the petrol. After that, old son, soon as you like.'

Commander Gould appeared out of the dust. 'You off then? Watch how you go, and thanks for your help.'

They stared after him and Kipling said, 'See what I mean? He couldn't care less!'

Fifteen minutes later Kipling straddled the khaki-painted machine and kick-started it into life. He flicked his wrist up and down until the air was quivering to the din.

Then he shouted, 'All aboard! Don't drop those bloody things, will you?'

Barrington-Purvis climbed on to a rolled gas cape on the back of the motor-bike and clutched Kipling around the waist and held his breath.

Some soldiers guarding a barricade gave them a cheer as they rattled past, and Kipling hoped that none of them had noted the bike's number.

He heard his pillion rider shout, 'What if the ship's already gone?'

Kipling leaned over to take them around a steep bend. He thought of the skipper's face and his voice when he had said good-bye to them.

He shouted back, 'No chance! He'll wait!'

He felt the air stinging his eyes while he opened the throttle even further.

It might very well end in total disaster. He leaned

over again and felt Barrington-Purvis copying his movements. He was learning.

Disaster or not, at least they would all be together.

Lieutenant Toby Calvert wiped his hands on a clean towel and glanced at the gently swaying aircraft. The big doors that opened on to the water allowed the bright sunshine to glint on the fuselage and cockpit cover. He knew the two mechanics who had been helping him were nervous, very aware of the far off gunfire, the muted rattle of automatic weapons. They had done a good job. He grinned. *All we need is a bloody good pilot.*

He heard a door slam and then Charles Yeung's usual outburst of coughing after he had finished another cigarette.

Yeung entered and stared at him, his dark eyes impassive.

'He is not coming. The boat turned back. The master feared for his life. So you see, my friend, you did all this work for nothing. I am sorry, but I thought . . .' He twisted round as a car door slammed in the yard. It was dangerous enough at night, but in broad daylight with Jap aircraft flying at will across the island, driving was extremely dangerous.

A shadow fell across the floor. It was Charles Yeung's valet Robert Tan. He spoke to his master, but was looking at Calvert.

'You have a visitor, Lieutenant, sir.'

Calvert gasped as the small, slim girl with her uniform jacket over her arm stepped from the sunlight into the hangar's cool gloom.

'Sue! What the *hell* are you doing here?'

She ran the last few yards and threw her arms around him.

'*Islip* sailed yesterday at dusk.' She hugged him, her body pressed against his. 'Don't send me away! I want to be with you!'

He held her tightly. 'Mr Yeung's pilot isn't here.'

'I know, I heard that at Aberdeen. It was nobody's fault about *Islip*.' She stared across at the silver-haired Yeung. 'You haven't told him!'

Charles Yeung shrugged. 'I was going to.' He looked calmly at Calvert. 'The enemy landed on the island last night at the place you call North Point and at Taikoo Dockyard. General Chaing Kai-Shek's promised army could not break through to help us. Now they never will. We are not finished, but by tomorrow the Japanese army will be right across the island.' He sliced the air with his hand. 'Cutting us in half!'

He walked across to Calvert and put his arms around him and the girl.

'I will stay here. Someone must lead. I have risked your lives to no purpose.' He squeezed their shoulders and smiled. 'Take the seaplane. Fly this girl who loves you to safety. You could do it. You *must* do it!'

Calvert felt his mind reeling as he stared at the crouching aircraft with sudden fear.

She looked up at his face, reading every emotion. 'If we did fly away, Toby, where would we go?'

Calvert took her arm and together they walked to the edge of the dock.

'*Serpent* will sail soon.' In his mind he was seeing it, as if he had already done it. 'The Japs will be attacking Aberdeen, anywhere that might be used for an escape route.' He paused, hardly aware of what he was saying. 'I could find her. It'll be too late pretty soon. I know which course the Skipper will take. He won't run until he knows *Islip* is clear of pursuit.' His eyes looked bright, feverish. 'I could make some sort of landing near

322

the ship. No matter what happened after that . . .' He hugged her shoulder. 'You crazy little fool, is that why you came? Because you knew I'd never make it without you?'

Charles Yeung said quietly, 'I will wait here with you until you leave. If you cannot do it, I will try to hide you.' He looked at them steadily. 'If they catch you, they will kill you.' He glanced away. 'Eventually.'

The girl whispered, '*Please*, Toby. We've nothing to lose!'

He could feel her shivering. She was probably thinking of those terrible screams on the landing telephone.

He said abruptly, '*Serpent* will sail right away, if I know my skipper.' He made up his mind. 'We'll have a go. *Right now!*'

The doors were hauled open and the sunshine swept over to greet them. It was still early morning: the morning the Dutch pilot should have landed.

He pulled on his best jacket over his stained trousers, the one with the bright wings on the left sleeve and the crimson ribbon on the breast.

He laughed. 'Better to look the part, eh?'

Yeung helped the girl on to one of the floats and up into the cockpit. 'Be safe, my friend!'

Then Calvert was beside the girl, testing the controls. 'No parachutes, remember?' Then he waved his arm out of the sliding window and held his breath as first one and then the other big Alfa Romeo engine roared into life.

There was a harness of sorts, and he made sure the girl was strapped in. Then quite suddenly he kissed her, feeling her respond with eager desperation. He shouted, 'You gave me something I thought I'd lost!'

Then he eased open the throttles and felt the seaplane begin to move across the water, rocking slightly as if to test it. There seemed to be nobody watching but when he peered over his shoulder he saw the green Rolls-Royce standing in the yard, the driver William beside it. In his heart he knew Charles Yeung would destroy it, as he would have destroyed the seaplane, rather than allow the Japs to get hold of them.

Anchored merchant ships flashed past, abandoned or bombed he could not tell. He felt a wildness he could scarcely remember. It was like a drug.

He yelled, 'I'm going for it now, Sue!' He glanced at her as she gripped the harness with both hands.

'*I love you!*'

He saw her nod and then call something to him but the rising roar of the twin engines drowned all of it and made any other thought impossible.

Faster, and faster. Another ship loomed past the starboard engine and he thought Sue had closed her eyes as the wing-tip seemed as though it would collide with the vessel's listing bridge.

Then Calvert saw the edge of the sea. Open water. They were up. *They were flying.*

He saw a large launch far below them, thrusting out a great arrowhead of foam. There were soldiers packed into it like sardines. Even a poor old Swordfish couldn't have missed it. He zig-zagged violently as he saw tracer rising slowly from a solitary gun. But the seaplane's hawk-like shadow was already streaking across the sea, so near to the water now that it left a pair of deep troughs behind it as if some underwater demons were in pursuit.

He blinked in the glare as he eased the controls. A quick glance at the compass. The rest would be so much guesswork. He looked down and was stunned to see several large bullet holes in the side, sunlight blazing through them like stars. She was reaching out to hold

324

his leg, her body lolling towards him while she tried to speak.

Calvert felt the seaplane diving and veering from side to side, and knew he had lost control.

'*Oh my God, Sue!*'

She reached with her free hand but lost the strength to feel her side.

Calvert clung to her. 'I'm here, darling! *Don't leave me!*'

Then she smiled at him, but even as he tried to hope, the smile became fixed and unmoving.

He felt her fall against him and for the first time saw the blood.

How long he flew or on what course he did not know.

He was calling her name. Telling her things, remembering their love.

Then, through a sea-mist, he saw *Serpent*. Moving slowly on a converging course. The sea all round was pale green, shallow, exactly where the skipper would choose to be if he was going to fight.

They would see the plane. The guns would be tracking them, but the skipper would know. He always did.

Calvert began to descend, feeling the wind in his face as he slid open a window. Then he reached over and closed her eyes so that she seemed to be lying against him, asleep.

He tried to speak to her. 'Just got something to do, darling Sue.' He could barely see through the blur of pain and emotion. 'Then I'm taking you home!'

As he flashed over the narrow hull he saw all the faces peering up at him, knew who they were.

He saw, too, the unfamiliar battle ensigns flying from the old destroyer's gaff and yard.

He picked up the girl's hat with its blue badge. There was even blood on that.

'Just so they'll know, Sue. *Nothing can part us!*'

The hat was plucked from his fingers, then he shut the window.

The port engine was coughing badly, but they would make it.

There were more anchored ships and burned-out hulks now, and he dived steeply to weave amongst them as tracer lifted past him, bright green, deadly.

Then he saw the ships, two of them, destroyers, in line ahead as they headed for the open sea. After the kill. But first they would have to deal with the little *Serpent*.

'*And us, you bastards!*'

He clutched her small hand on his leg. It was warm, as if she was still alive.

The first bullets hit the seaplane, and Calvert knew he had been badly wounded although he could feel nothing.

Then there *was* nothing.

'Char, sir.'

Brooke straightened up in his chair and reached out for the mug in the darkness. He felt stiff and cold. Empty.

As his senses returned he glanced around the bridge. The ship had been at Defence Stations since leaving Aberdeen but with all the short-range weapons closed up.

Like Trafalgar, he thought dully, food and clean clothes before the battle.

Serpent had left harbour soon after *Islip*. He had dared not risk remaining at anchor once the reports of possible landings had first been received and later confirmed.

It had been a sad moment when the *Islip* had finally cast off. They had all been shocked to see the damage she had received from enemy bombers when she had stopped to try and pick up survivors from the torpedoed *Dumbarton*. There had been very few. Stallybrass had not been one of them.

One bomb had exploded right alongside the *Islip*; another had hit the forecastle. The explosions and the hail of splinters had put both forward guns out of action and had killed twenty men and wounded others. Her captain, the ebullient Ralph Tufnell, had been killed outright and his first lieutenant had taken over.

But her engine room was undamaged and she still had her radar and anti-aircraft weapons intact.

Brooke had been aboard just once to wish them luck and to give them some charts. Many of theirs had been destroyed in the attack.

He had seen Lian only once more. With other women she had been with sailors who were issuing life-jackets and steel helmets. She had watched him through a clamped scuttle, and had placed her palm flat against the thick glass until he covered it with his own. Then she had been moved away, and a seaman had slammed down the steel deadlight even as orders were given to get under way.

Islip had soon been lost in darkness. Granville had assured him that an escort would be ready to see the ship to safety for the last part of the journey. South, all the way to Batavia in Java, two thousand two hundred miles. *Islip* could do it in three days, and would be with the Australian escorts before that.

But there had been a signal too. Enemy destroyers were reported to be moving from the east. Two in number, the intelligence report had stated. One was said to be a big *Asasio* class, the other one much smaller.

There might as well have been a whole fleet. The *Asasio* class carried six five-inch guns and eight torpedo tubes. If *Serpent* could not delay them, *Islip*'s small lead would prove useless.

He thought of Calvert and wondered what he would do. He had been stunned when he had been told about Sue Yorke refusing to sail with *Islip*. *Our Wren.*

Brooke glanced at the hooded chart table, remembering Calvert and his girl. They were going to be married, he had said.

He had told his men what they might expect. Earlier they had all seen the old destroyer *Thracian*, very similar to their own ship but cut down and less well armed, leave Aberdeen under power. She had been severely damaged when chasing junks packed with Japanese troops who had been attempting an early landing. She had destroyed the junks, but had smashed her hull by striking some rocks. Stripped of her weapons and stores she had sailed out of Aberdeen and had been run aground on a small island and abandoned. It had been a sad sight, and a bitter moment for her company. Her fate seemed to have made *Serpent*'s people even more determined. Perhaps resigned.

The one light moment had been when Kipling and the Sub had appeared on the dockside, filthy but managing to grin and wave before climbing aboard. Within seconds their Royal Enfield motor-bike had vanished, taken by somebody who still nursed some hope of escape.

Before leaving *Serpent* Granville had told Brooke that Sir Mark Young, the governor of Hong Kong, had made another plea for help to London, explaining that they could not hope to continue resistance once the enemy had landed on the island. Churchill's reply had been adamant: resistance would be maintained, *so that the enemy should be compelled to expend the utmost life and equipment.*

With the Japanese on North Point, they could bombard the naval dockyard from the high ground and join the battery at Kowloon in a murderous crossfire.

Kerr came up from the chart table and took a mug of hot tea. He was a good watchkeeping officer, but it seemed wrong not to see Calvert there.

'Be getting light soon, sir.'

'Yes.' Brooke could picture his little ship as if he was a sea bird on the wing. She was steering very slowly to the north-west of Lamma Island. The sea seemed black and vast but in an hour they would sight Hong Kong island again, even Aberdeen, which they had left in the half-light. It was all he could do. It was shallow, not deep enough for a big destroyer to act stupidly. Once within range of the enemy they would attack with torpedoes. They would fire all four of them – the gunner (T)'s big moment, and he had gathered all his crew of torpedomen for a last instruction. The torpedo tubes had no protection. It would have to be fast. The Chief knew. They all knew what to expect.

They had two extra hands for Damage Control if nothing else, Royal Marine bandsmen, one injured in the leg by a bomb splinter. They had been trying to reach *Islip* before she sailed. Exhausted and almost delirious when they had seen the White Ensign above *Serpent*'s deck, they had described the scenes of horror when they had slipped past Jap patrols to reach Aberdeen.

Corpses lay everywhere and much of the city was ablaze. The Japanese were in a frenzy, the corporal had said, shooting, bayoneting and beheading soldiers and civilians alike. Even if *Serpent* was sunk in this coming fight Brooke knew the two marines wanted to be here with faces and voices they trusted.

Kerr said, 'All depth charges were set to safe and jettisoned.' He forced a smile. 'The cox'n says the loss of weight makes the old girl as light as a feather!'

Better to lose the charges than to have the stern blown off by an enemy shell.

Brooke looked at his shadow against the pale paintwork. Was it lighter already? He took his time to think. *Am I afraid of what will happen?*

He felt in his pocket and touched Calvert's Victoria Cross, which Bert Kingsmill had discovered in a drawer when he had been securing the cabins.

'Didn't seem right to leave it there, sir!' He had been very concerned. Brooke found he was relaxing slowly. It would not be much safer here, he thought.

'Number One, you know what to do if anything goes wrong up here?'

He heard Kerr swallow hard. 'Yes, sir. Fight the ship.'

He touched his arm. 'Remember the motto. *Deadly to Foes.*'

He saw a glint of water. The moment before dawn. What would the light reveal?

Kerr held his watch to his face. 'Time, sir.'

'Thanks, Dick.' He felt Kerr staring at him. 'Go round the ship. Action Stations by word of mouth. This is a time for preparation, not panic. Let them see you about.'

Voicepipes began to mutter as the hands went to their proper stations. A few last watertight doors thudded shut, and Brooke heard the squeak of the big rangefinder as Barrington-Purvis prepared himself and his spotters for the inevitable.

We have all changed. From what Kipling had told

him, the haughty sub-lieutenant had changed most of all.

'Cox'n on the wheel, sir. Course zero-two-zero, both engines at seven-zero.'

Brooke stood up and gripped the back of his chair. He could feel the vibrations coursing through it, up his arms, into his body. They were as one.

'Ship at Action Stations, sir.' Kipling sounded calm. Then he said, 'I hope Toby's all right.'

Onslow was speaking softly to his signalmen, and looked over as Brooke said, 'Battle ensigns – what d'you think, Yeo?'

'Hear that, lads. Off you go, chop-chop!' To Brooke he said, 'Make a picture, she will!'

Brooke thought of his father. Now he would never hear about it.

It was much brighter and he could smell smoke drifting on the breeze. Soon they would sight land.

'Ship, sir! Port bow!'

Brooke lowered his powerful glasses. It was a tall, stately junk moving purposefully under its strange bat-like sails. Standing away. Leaving their homes behind. Like *Serpent*'s own company, a ship was life itself. The land was the enemy this time.

There was gunfire again, a merciless bombardment on people who could not hit back. There were fires too, spurts of flame and glowing sparks as shells fell somewhere in the centre of the island. Men fighting house to house, room to room, grenade, rifle and bayonet, until there was nothing left to fight with.

The smoke tasted bitter, foul. An empty hull drifted abeam – abandoned, its crew killed, who could tell?

Here was the sea. He watched it reaching out from the ship as the daylight forced its way through the pall of smoke.

Kerr was back again, his eyes everywhere. 'There's land, sir. Lamma Island, starboard bow. Not long now.' There was neither hope nor dread in his voice.

The sun was coming up at last. Red and orange, like the flames below it. The forecastle and four-inch gun with its crouching crew, like monks in their anti-flash gear, the breech already loaded, a seaman gunner waiting with the next shell in his gloved hands.

Brooke picked up the red telephone and heard the Chief's instant acknowledgement.

'Approaching the channel, Chief. One hand for the King, eh?'

He could picture him smiling at the old naval joke, then repeating it to his stokers and artificers. Lip-reading was all that counted down there.

Brooke opened his shirt and knew Kipling was watching him as he felt the gold medallion between his fingers.

He stared again. Daylight. A curtain going up. He raised his glasses again and studied the littered vessels that lay outside Aberdeen some three miles away. The smoke was terrible in its depth and intensity, covering the heights and rising unhurriedly towards the sky.

'*Aircraft*, sir!'

'Stand by all guns!' That was Barrington-Purvis, clipped and precise.

Brooke listened to the distorted growl of engines. It was there somewhere. Out to starboard, perhaps from Repulse Bay.

Kerr exclaimed, 'That's no fighter, sir!' He looked wildly at the others. 'D'you think it's him? Toby?'

'Aircraft at Green eight-zero, sir!' The look-out sounded dazed. 'No angle of sight. She's almost in the drink!'

Brooke steadied his glasses and felt a lump in his

throat as the dark seaplane darted past an abandoned freighter and then turned towards him.

Kerr shouted, 'Tell the Buffer to prepare a net!' He waved his cap above his head. '*He made it!* I'll bet he's got our Wren with him!'

Brooke snapped, 'Belay that order!' He moved his glasses with great care while the ship lifted and dipped gently beneath him.

It was all suddenly stark and clear. The holes, silver bright, punched along the side and through one wing. There was smoke too from one of the engines.

Men were cheering and waving as the seaplane lifted over the ship where the battle ensigns looked so clean against the sky. Just as quickly the cheers died while men peered at the damage, the fact that only one face showed in the cockpit. Brooke saw Calvert's arm, the light glinting on the unfamiliar sight of his best uniform while he waved to the ship. *To me.*

Something flew from his hand and, once clear of the slipstream, began to float down to the sea.

Her hat. She was with him. Now he had nothing to live for.

The seaplane reeled away again and ten seconds later the gunnery speaker barked, 'Ship! Bearing Green one-three-oh! Range four thousand yards!'

Brooke climbed into his chair. *Serpent*'s three guns, puny compared with the enemy, were already swinging on to the bearing. A-Gun, directly below the bridge, was trained round as far as it would bear.

He said, '*Full ahead!*' He thought of Podger Barlow with his beloved torpedoes. If a shell landed before he could fire them the ship would be torn apart.

He felt the pressure of the chair in his back, the rising bank of surging crests spreading away from either bow.

They will think we're running to take cover from the land. They must.

He saw the blink of gunfire and heard the shriek of a shell overhead.

'Starboard ten – *Steady!* Steer zero-six-zero.' It would be murder for the torpedomen. Until *Serpent* made her turn at speed, they had their backs to the enemy.

Two more shells exploded in the sea, one of them throwing up a tall column like a spear of ice. Splinters cracked into the hull.

Kerr shouted, 'The small destroyer is leading, sir!'

Brooke tried to lick his lips. They were like dust.

A gong rang tinnily and from his control position Barrington-Purvis snapped, '*Open fire!*'

The deck shook to the three sharp explosions, but there was so much smoke in the channel that they could have fallen anywhere.

'*Aircraft*, sir!' It was almost a scream, then the lookout fell silent as the seaplane came round the side of an anchored freighter. It was so low it seemed to be skating on the water. Brooke stared with disbelief, but the understanding hit him like a fist as he yelled, '*Hard a-starboard! Engage with torpedoes!*'

He did not wait to see them fire but staggered up the deck as the wheel went hard over and *Serpent* pirouetted round to drag the leading destroyer across Podger Barlow's sights. Brooke's eyes were fixed on the dark seaplane. He knew it was being hit again and again as it dived, then clawed upwards, then, at the apex of the last climb, he saw smoke streaming from beneath the cockpit and one of the floats spinning away.

He heard himself say brokenly, 'You damned, idiotic, *brave* fool, Toby!'

The destroyer was swinging round, presenting her whole length as the plunging seaplane exploded like a bomb on her open bridge. Flames were bursting from everywhere, tiny figures stampeding from what they probably thought was a loaded bomber.

The leading destroyer was turning as well. Three of Barlow's torpedoes missed, one exploding nearby against some rocks. The remaining torpedo hit the small destroyer on the port side, and a column of water shot from the explosion although there was barely any noise. A pall of steam hung above the stricken ship, and she had already begun to heel over.

The Chief would hear it, feel it. It was the enemy's engine or boiler-room where the torpedo had burst in on them.

Brooke heard Barrington-Purvis calling through his speaker, 'I hope they fry, the bastards!' It sounded as if he was sobbing.

Brooke clung to his chair and stared with surprise at a deep cut on his wrist.

He managed to gasp, 'Report damage and casualties, Dick!' Someone was bandaging his injury: another yelled wildly, 'The big feller's aground!' Men who had expected to die and had accepted it whooped and clasped one another like lunatics.

Even Kipling was staring at him with such emotion that he only got out a brief answer. '*You* are our only casualty, sir!'

They helped Brooke back into the chair. He said, 'Bring her round, Number One.' His voice was flat, formal. 'We're going after *Islip*.'

Kerr wiped his face and eyes with his cuff but could not look away from his captain, as he reached into his pocket and took out the prized medal. *For Valour*.

Then Brooke stood up and clung to the screen as the screws brought the ship charging round on to her new course.

He did not salute, but removed his cap while he watched the writhing pall of smoke pouring from the grounded destroyer.

'Thanks, Pilot. For Valour. They don't know the bloody half of it.'

By sunset they had still not been attacked from the sea or from the air. But *Serpent* kept her ensigns flying. She was old, but she was still a destroyer, and would be ready to fight again, torpedoes or not.

Two days later, watching and waiting while they headed south stripped of Barlow's tin fish and all their depth charges, Brooke called his officers to the bridge. They were tired and unshaven, at their stations day and night. Tea, rum and tinned sausages; but as the miles mounted astern there were no moans from even the biggest grouser.

'All present, sir.' Kerr could not help it, as his eyes moved to the chart table, 'Except one.'

Brooke stared at him. *Not now. Not now, for God's sake! That's all it needs.*

He cleared his throat. 'I've had a signal.' He saw their eyes move from his face to the flimsy in his hand and was grateful. 'H.M.S. *Islip* will enter harbour with her escorts later today. There were no incidents.'

They should be cheering. They had done it. She was safe. But they knew there was more to come.

He looked at their tired, strained faces. After this they might be separated. Sent to other ships as was the navy's way. He knew that they would not want to leave despite all that had been said. There could never be another *Serpent*, as his father had told him.

He cleared his throat. 'I have to tell you that Hong Kong has surrendered. The Admiralty has stated that all transmissions from Hong Kong Radio have ceased.'

He looked away at the wake streaming astern in a white, ruler-straight line.

He knew that the word would be through the whole ship in seconds. It was marked by the silence which hung over the deck like the smoke of a burning island.

He saw the seamen gazing up at the bridge, sharing it, as they had shared all the dangers.

Among them was the Royal Marine corporal.

'Is that man a bugler, Number One?'

Kerr said quietly, 'Yes, sir.'

Brooke turned to the voicepipes. 'Stop engines!' To Onslow he added, 'Strike those ensigns, if you please. She's shown what she can do.' Onslow nodded, understanding.

The marine corporal appeared in the bridge, his bugle hanging at his hip.

'Sir?'

Brooke said, 'Today we lost a lot of good friends.' He thought of the Wren's hat floating on the water. He felt the way going off the ship, the bows butting into the sea like something solid. 'Play the Last Post, will you?'

Then he did salute.

Kerr followed suit, as the familiar call echoed unchecked across the heaving water.

The last Sunset. Just for them.

Epilogue

Commander Esmond Brooke, D.S.O., D.S.C., Royal Navy, paused in the warm sunshine beneath the Cenotaph's tall shadow and looked across the harbour towards Kowloon. It was the strangest of feelings, as if he were invisible, or seeing Hong Kong again through someone else's eyes.

On every side there was bustle, noisy traffic, colour and the clamour he had remembered so clearly. There was rebuilding everywhere, some of the construction much higher than he had expected. He noticed that the Chinese workers still scorned steel scaffolding and preferred their hazardous-looking bamboo poles.

The harbour too was packed with shipping, as it had been six years ago when *Serpent* had first arrived here. Six years: it seemed impossible. Two years had passed since the Japanese had finally surrendered.

The misery and brutality of the Japanese occupation were still evident, but there was determination too, with men of skill and vision to restore the Colony's prosperity and growth.

He glanced at a fussy pilot cutter as it headed for open water, to guide in yet another freighter or tanker. Perhaps it was the same cutter which had led the way through the shoals and amongst the wrecks and scuttled ships when *Serpent* had left for Aberdeen . . .

He turned and shaded his eyes to stare up at the austere Cenotaph, a twin of the one in Whitehall. So many names. There would be many more when the final cost was known. He thought of all the thousands and thousands of servicemen and women who were still being released into civvy street, when all their youth had offered them had been war. It would be a new world for them. He smiled. *For me too.*

He swung round, off guard, as a squad of sailors marched past and a petty officer bawled, 'Eyes, *right*!'

So he was not invisible. He returned the salute and was almost surprised to see his white sleeve after all the months back in the Atlantic again, when he had been given a brand new frigate and had handed over his old *Serpent*.

She, too, had returned to the Atlantic, but he had never seen her again. It was as if she were insisting that it should be that way. All those familiar faces had gone to other ships, except for one, Ian Cusack, the gnome-like Chief who had stayed with her to the end.

A lucky ship: when many others, newer and more powerful, had been destroyed, *Serpent* had survived.

In 1945, within three months of the end of the war in Europe, *Serpent*'s famous luck had run out. Somewhere to the east of St John's, Newfoundland, while despatched from a convoy to search for survivors, she had been torpedoed. There were no survivors.

Just a line on the radio news with the usual, 'Next of kin have been informed.'

So the Chief had been with her even then. He still was.

Kerr had been promoted and given his own corvette, and had managed to come to the formal wedding at

Portsmouth Cathedral. Even Kipling had been there, scruffier than ever, but grinning from ear to ear as, with Lian on his arm, Brooke had walked beneath the upraised swords. Two passers-by had stopped to watch, a young lieutenant and an even younger Wren officer.

Only for a moment Brooke had felt her hand tighten on his arm. *It could have been them*. When he had looked again, they had gone.

Brooke walked to the water's edge and watched the tractors and bulldozers hard at work, reclaiming more land, covering the scars.

He glanced at his watch. She would be up on the Peak with her sister Camille. The great house, or what was left of it, was to be sold, the money used for a new wing for the hospital of which Camille was now the senior doctor and administrator.

Like many others who had lived under the Japanese occupation, Camille was withdrawn, distant even with her sister. Brooke could not imagine what she had endured: he suspected that the hospital had been her anchor. Her husband Harry, being an American, had been interned, put in charge of the sick and emaciated prisoners, doing all that he could without drugs or sustaining food. In the end he had died of beri-beri, one of those diseases of deficiency he had originally come to the Far East to study.

Brooke turned away to avoid further salutes from passing sailors. In six months he would be leaving here. Out of the navy. Once he would have dreaded the prospect: now he could barely wait. But a shore appointment in Hong Kong would make all the difference. Lian would be with him. No more separations. No more brave good-byes.

Then back to England. A friend had said, *England*

will never be the same again, but at least it will be ours. And they would be together.

Another glance at his watch. She was coming. He could feel it.

He walked along the road and eventually stopped beneath the imposing façade of the Hongkong and Shanghai Bank.

He was suddenly unsure. Nervous. Perhaps returning after six years would change her mind?

He heard the taxi pull to a halt and went to meet her. In a white suit, her hair hanging free because she knew he liked it, she stood watching him. Beside her and holding her hand was their daughter Charlotte, a tiny miniature of the lovely girl who was watching the man she loved.

She said quietly, 'You were early. I knew you would be.'

'Was everything all right, Lian?'

She touched his arm and nodded gravely. 'You should not worry, Es-mond. England is my home now.' She glanced at the busy street. '*This* will always be my country.' She smiled, shaking away the mood. 'Come now.' They held hands with the child and together they entered a small leafy garden. There was a plain, simply carved memorial in one corner, with a brass pot of sand for joss-sticks, and there were flowers too, some fresh, others wilted in the sun.

In silence they looked at the square bronze plate. And remembered.

It was written in English and in Chinese characters.

In memory of Charles Yeung, a patriot who died that others might live. Under Japanese occupation he risked everything to help his fellow citizens of Hong Kong. Eventually betrayed, he was captured by the Japanese military police and tortured for six days, after which, mercifully, he died.

May his courage, strength and vision live forever.

Brooke picked up his daughter and held her hand on the inscription while Lian placed sprays of orchids in one of the bowls. She bowed briefly, and he knew that she was praying. Then she stood up beside them and said softly, 'You see, my father. We *did* come back.'

Brooke could imagine he heard him laugh. He would have liked that.

Together they walked out on to the street again, and Hong Kong offered them its welcome.